GIRL IN A BIG B[

Lobbe wants his pai[nting back.] [When]
the Nazis raided Rotterdam. But now [it's]
located, and the German government wants to return it. So
Lobbe sends his assistant Manny deWitt to Munich to fetch it.
The painting is Vermeer's "Apple Girl," Lobbe's prized
possession. The mission seems easy enough. But as deWitt soon
discovers, those who have the misfortune to come in contact
with the elusive Vermeer seem to experience an early and
unpleasant death. The sooner he gets the painting and gets out,
the better. If only it were that simple.

THE SPY WHO WAS 3 FEET TALL

This time Lobbe sends Manny to a recently emerged African
nation called Motana. It's deWitt's job to negotiate the contract
to build a road through the country. As usual, Lobbe doesn't
muddy the waters with too much information for deWitt. But
this time, everyone seems to be up on the project but him. Yum
Lee, the Chinese emissary who also wants the contract, is one
step ahead of him. Inge, Lobbe's delightful niece, is strictly
undercover. And then there's his ubiquitous taxi driver, Baby,
who is much more (or less) than what he seems. Just what the
hell is so important about this road anyway?

CODE NAME GADGET

As gadgets go, it was supposedly a fairly large one, large
enough to fill a medium-sized factory. Manny's mission is to
buy it for his boss Lobbe before the competition beats him to
it. The mission takes him to England under the eccentric
guidance of a pilot named Max Garten, and into the
unexpected arms of Meghan Bushmill. Together, the three of
them form a kind of team as they try to figure out who are the
good guys and who are the bad guys—and if it even makes any
difference anymore. Because whoever has the gadget can
destroy the world, and even Lobbe may not be able to buy his
way out of that one.

PETER RABE BIBLIOGRAPHY

From Here to Maternity (1955; non-fiction)
Stop This Man! (1955)
Benny Muscles In (1955)
A Shroud for Jesso (1955)
A House in Naples (1956)
Kill the Boss Goodbye (1956)
Agreement to Kill (1957)
Journey Into Terror (1957)
Mission for Vengeance (1958)
Blood on the Desert (1958)
Anatomy of a Killer (1960)
My Lovely Executioner (1960)
Murder Me for Nickels (1960)
The Box (1962)
His Neighbor's Wife (1962)
Tobruk (1967)
War of the Dons (1972)
Black Mafia (1974)
The Silent Wall (2011)
The Return of Marvin Palaver (2011)

Daniel Port series:
Dig My Grave Deep (1956)
The Out is Death (1957)
It's My Funeral (1957)
The Cut of the Whip (1958)
Bring Me Another Corpse (1959)
Time Enough to Die (1959)

Manny deWitt series:
Girl in a Big Brass Bed (1965)
The Spy Who Was Three Feet Tall (1966)
Code Name Gadget (1967)

As by Marco Malaponte
New Man in the House (1963)
Her High-School Lover (1963)

As by J. T. MacCargo
Mannix #2: A Fine Day for Dying (1975)
Mannix #4: Round Trip to Nowhere (1975)

Short Stories
"Hard Case Redhead" (*Mystery Tales*, 1959)
"A Matter of Balance" (*Story*, 1961)

GIRL IN A BIG BRASS BED
THE SPY WHO WAS 3 FEET TALL
CODE NAME GADGET

Three Novels by Peter Rabe
Introduction by Rick Ollerman

ROUND LAKE AREA
LIBRARY
906 HART ROAD
ROUND LAKE, IL 60073
(847) 546-7060

Stark House Press • Eureka California

MANNY deWITT OMNIBUS: GIRL IN THE BIG BRASS BED /
THE SPY WHO WAS 3 FEET TALL / CODE NAME GADGET

Published by Stark House Press
1315 H Street
Eureka, CA 95501
griffinskye3@sbcglobal.net
www.starkhousepress.com

GIRL IN THE BIG BRASS BED
Copyright © 1965 by Fawcett Publications, Inc., and
originally published by Gold Medal Books, Greenwich.

THE SPY WHO WAS 3 FEET TALL
Copyright © 1966 by Fawcett Publications, Inc., and
originally published by Gold Medals Books, Greenwich.

CODE NAME GADGET
Copyright © 1967 by Fawcett Publications, Inc., and
originally published by Gold Medal Books, Greenwich.

Reprinted by permission of The Estate of Peter Rabe. All rights reserved
under International and Pan-American Copyright Conventions.

"The Industrial Complex of Peter Rabe and Manny deWitt"
copyright © 2017 by Rick Ollerman

All rights reserved.

ISBN-13: 978-1-944520-30-4

Book design by Mark Shepard, SHEPGRAPHICS.COM

PUBLISHER'S NOTE
This is a work of fiction. Names, characters, places and incidents are either
the products of the author's imagination or used fictionally, and any
resemblance to actual persons, living or dead, events or locales, is entirely
coincidental.
Without limiting the rights under copyright reserved above, no part of this
publication may be reproduced, stored, or introduced into a retrieval system
or transmitted in any form or by any means (electronic, mechanical,
photocopying, recording or otherwise) without the prior written permission
of both the copyright owner and the above publisher of the book.

First Stark House Press Edition: September 2017

FIRST EDITION

7
The Industrial Complex of
Peter Rabe and Manny deWitt
by Rick Ollerman

11
Girl in a Big Brass Bed
by Peter Rabe

139
The Spy Who Was 3 Feet Tall
By Peter Rabe

257
Code Name Gadget
By Peter Rabe

The Industrial Complex of Peter Rabe and Manny deWitt
by Rick Ollerman

Peter Rabe wrote two series in his career. The first was his five book "Daniel Port" saga about a fixer for the local mob machine who always believed he would either take over for his boss, whom he truly felt affection for, or that his boss would let him walk away. Sadly, for Port, neither one of these scenarios turns out to be true and it's up to his own wits and intelligence to be able to gut out a solution that ultimately would allow him to walk away. And remain alive.

Rabe said he hadn't necessarily intended Port to be a series character, but then again he never said he didn't. He'd wanted to write a series and Port presented himself around that time with *Dig My Grave Deep,* one of Rabe's best. (But there are so many you could throw in that bucket, with all sorts of different plots and characters, I'm not sure what that means.)

Opinions, as with most series, differ on which Rabe books are the better ones, with many people liking the second, *The Out is Death,* best, or even the final one, *Time Enough to Die.* Regardless, in total they paint a fascinating picture of a one-time insider not only trying to distance himself from the mob but also trying to capitalize on his reputation to make his own life easier or to do favors for his friends. Neither of these goals work out as easily as Port thinks they will.

Finally, with as much distance as he thinks he can give, with the surrendering of his former identity, Port thinks he can lead the idyllic sort of life he wants. But the chains of the past are not the easiest links to break, and things end very differently for the man. And that, because Peter Rabe was the author he was, is how he wraps up the series.

If he'd continued, Rabe said it would have been with a new turning point for Port, far from his roots. Only Rabe moved on. Eventually he wrote another, far different series, only this time it consisted of just three books. Instead of his protagonist trying to escape the mob, this time his protagonist, Manford deWitt, is a lawyer simply trying to do the best job he can for his boss, an almost incomprehensible multi-national industrialist name Hans Lobbe.

Lobbe is the head of Lobbe Industriel, with offices all over the world. DeWitt is merely one of presumably many lawyers Lobbe has on staff. Another character, Speers, is deWitts drinking buddy and specializes in investments. The only other regular is Miss Moon, Lobbe's executive secretary based out of the New York office.

The relationship between Lobbe and deWitt is at the heart of each of the books. It is complex yet fragile, based on a precision of misunderstandings seemingly carefully choreographed until a third party knocks something off the rails and deWitt's smarts and attention to detail usually puts things to right—mostly.

It is difficult to classify the three books: *Girl in a Big Brass Bed*, *The Spy Who Was 3 Feet Tall*, and *Code Name Gadget*. Crimes abound in all three but the books are not really *about* a crime per se, with the possible exception of *Gadget*. While Rabe said he admired the work of LeCarré and Deighton, who wrote spy thrillers, DeWitt is not a spy. He's just a lawyer, trying to carry out whatever instructions Lobbe has given him. And then trying to carry out the opposite, when and if Lobbe happens to change his mind. The relationship between the two men is not an easy one.

On the other hand, there are spies in all three of the books, working against deWitt, so while Manny is working to accomplish one thing, he is pitted, usually unknowingly, against the forces of a hostile foreign government. The reader must make up their own mind. The spy stuff all happens *to* deWitt, while he merely gets his job done, as you get the sense he would do against any other sort of opponent.

There is also humor in the three books which, for the most part, comes off flat. Not only is it not actually funny, it is inappropriate, such as the dialogue that takes place at the scene of a near fatal accident where deWitt and a police officer fail to understand each other's meaning of the word "blue." Rabe himself describes the humor as arch, and not in a favorable way.

Sometimes it is precisely this arch humor that can take an impatient reader out of the stories. A more careful reader can appreciate what Rabe is doing though, even while possibly questioning his choices in that area. In some ways, throughout the first two books especially, the stories can almost be read as chains of extended "shaggy dog stories," though ultimately they are decidedly not. Instead of ending up with no point, the hallmark of the first two books is that they end up precisely *on* the point.

DeWitt and Lobbe go back and forth, with deWitt trying doggedly to carry out his boss Lobbe's orders to the letter even though he's never been informed of the overall picture, and Lobbe being cryptic to an absurd level, often contradicting himself in light of deWitt's progress on his original orders. There are dashes of Rabe's arch humor here, and we feel deWitt's frustrations as he tries merely to do his job, sometimes in spite of his boss.

But in the end, we come to the hidden meaning of Lobbe's intention, and how without deWitt's freelancing, Lobbe's ends would never have been achieved, even though there was plenty of third party intervention going on and, at least during the course of the stories, deWitt's inability to make logical sense of his boss's plans keeps him—and the reader—from ever knowing one way or the other if deWitt's decisions are actually the right ones.

Consider that Lobbe initially gives deWitt an assignment, believing he has everything set up and arranged so that all Manny has to do is physically go and provide the boot on the ground. Unbeknownst to Lobbe though, a third party has been at work, which initially surprises deWitt, who thinks the best thing he can do is get a hold of his boss for new instructions.

In typical Lobbe fashion, deWitt is belittled, informed that this information is old hat to Lobbe, and if he'd just done what he'd been asked to do already, things would have been satisfactorily concluded. And how dare deWitt call him on a trans-Atlantic line for four dollars a minute with such trivia?

Properly alienated, deWitt squares his jaw and sets off to complete his mission. When things go even more awry, when deWitt can no longer reach Lobbe (because Manny's been kidnapped, been imprisoned, is on the run, etc.), Manny deWitt has to do what only Manny deWitt can do, Lobbe be damned. After all, this is just a job, right? The most Lobbe can do is fire him and all that will mean is that deWitt will simply find a new employer.

So Manny strikes off on his own, adding his own twists to an already twisted story, and in the end, when Lobbe either shows his beak or is handed the solution, deWitt has given him what he's asked for—though not necessarily in the same fashion—even though it may not have been how Lobbe had envisioned it. From deWitt's point of view, if he hadn't acted as he had, Lobbe would have had nothing. As for Lobbe, the animus he expresses toward Manny during the book seems to evaporate, at least until the next book.

From a purely structural standpoint, the reader is presented everything from Manny deWitt's point of view, including his befuddlement of the lack of information when it becomes clear he hasn't been made privy to Lobbe's ultimate goal. We follow deWitt along as he does his best to serve his employer the best way he thinks he knows how, and even though Rabe has us believing in what deWitt is doing, one phone call to or from Lobbe is enough to blast that vision from both the reader and deWitt.

We move with Manny through this chaos, ourselves not knowing what Lobbe is really about, as in the dark as deWitt, until some point very near the end, when the curtains are parted for both ourselves and Lobbe and we realize that at some point in the very near past deWitt had figured things out and left us just far enough behind to surprise us.

This is what gives the deWitt stories a deceivingly delicate structure. Rabe's prose never pulls any punches and the arch humor, the inscrutable Lobbe and his acidic temperament, the hard-hitting nature of the plots when they're ultimately revealed, all demonstrate this. But when you consider what it takes to get from the beginning of each of these books to the end, it is quite likely they will probably be the most underrated works of Rabe's career.

It takes a master plotter to pull something like this off and though Rabe didn't like what he did with the archness of the books, if the reader is patient and tolerant, the payoffs are very rewarding. Clearly in the final book, *Code Name Gadget*, where there is less humor and more of deWitt leading things along, Rabe had given up his attempts to make his original vision work.

At this point it's too late, though. Even after creating an international business support system if you will, and creating a strong and willful protagonist in Manny deWitt, who more than anything reminds us of James Bond (while Hans Lobbe can't help but leave impressions of Gert Fröbe's portrayal of Auric Goldfinger), Rabe abandons the character just when he seems on the verge of shifting his original "experiment" and granting his readers something more conventional.

But, as readers of Peter Rabe will know, as a writer he was anything but conventional. And nowhere more so in this trio of books. If you're new to them, I urge you to read them slowly, to move at the pace of Manny deWitt, the lead character. Explore at the pace that he does, learn when he does, enjoy (or allow him to enjoy) his interactions with the other characters. Get a feel for what Rabe wants him to do and how he wants the story to unfold around him. Slow is the way to deal with the arch humor—indeed, it may be the only way it makes sense. Reading these books too fast is like that old line from your childhood dinner table: "How can you enjoy it if you eat so fast?"

As long as you didn't get ice cream face, you didn't care, but reading a book is different. If you have read the books before, read them again, but slowly. You'll see all the things Rabe did to build a hollow-tube sort of plot structure that ultimately may bend but will not break. And who knows, you may even enjoy the humor this time….

June, 2017
Littleon, NH

GIRL IN A BIG BRASS BED
by Peter Rabe

CHAPTER 1

I had been in Paris thirteen days and by then I knew altogether four people quite intimately, none of whom I'd known when I first came to Paris. They were Evelyn, Kim, Bobby, and Toni. I was with one or the other of them, or with all of them at the same time, practically twenty-four hours a day. My concierge, a little toad of a woman who never seemed to sleep either, used to say, *"Encore, monsieur? Mais vous avez la figure d'un cadavre!"* Which, kindly put, means I was beginning to look a little worn.

Paris! City of Light and of Love, my foot!

Evelyn had a great deal of white hair, including a mustache. He was Sir Evelyn Peyton-Smyth, vice-president for foreign exploitation, the Carbon and Allied Chemicals Company, Ltd. Bobby was fat and bald. His full name was Robert Drummond and he was heading the European division of Drumco Polyesters, Inc. The rest were not beautiful girls either. Kim was a savage-looking Afrikaner and spoke for a Johannesburg group in synthetic rubber. And Toni, Antoine Ledage, was a Belgian in coal. I was by far the youngest of the group though the company for which I spoke was the oldest. Lobbe Industriel was its simple name and it covered a multitude of sins. It was suffixed Inc. in the States, AGmbH in Germany, Ltd. in the British Commonwealth, and SA in France and its remaining possessions.

The merger of interests, the pooling of resources, and the splitting of costs which was at stake here was just one of the many maneuvers in which old Mijnheer Hans Lobbe embroiled himself. In this instance the maneuvering was designed to make I. G. Farben look like a corner drugstore compared to Lobbe Industriel's chemical complex. However, this hadn't happened so far.

I am not a vice-president or director or anything like it in one of the Lobbe companies. I am simply one of Mijnheer's lawyers. There are typist pools. Lobbe also has lawyer pools. I am sometimes one of his favorites and then I am sent off to work twenty-four hours per.

Nothing final was at stake at the Paris meeting (or Hans Lobbe himself would have been there) but it was very much a matter of the proper paper language so that everybody would know what the next meetings were going to be about. Lobbe always worked during these stages. Unfortunately, this stage was not working at all.

Every morning at seven-thirty I was driven down the old Rue de Faubourg St. Honoré, a rather quiet, well-kept street with old trees. Little brass plates on the fronts of big, solid buildings show the names of some of the richest corporations on this globe. One of the buildings was Lobbe's and the plaque by the baronial door said only "Lobbe Industriel, SA."

This morning's ride was the pleasantest part of my Paris stay. The air was cool and moist, the trees breathed freshness. The ride started at the Rue de Jasmin, which is a hell of a distance, but Lobbe kept an apartment there and he thought it economical that I should use his quarters.

"His quarters" is only a manner of speaking. The bedroom was all pink fluff with a permanent atmosphere of Ma Griffe, a rather violent perfume. The bathroom had one wall which was entirely glass and the glass was a mirror. (No, there was no mirror on the bedroom ceiling.) Two additional rooms were in character, which is to say, given to intimacies, to adorations, to frolics of many sorts.

In all fairness to old Mijnheer Hans Lobbe he did not furnish a place like that for himself. But now whoever had lived there had gone (Lobbe had not been in Paris for months) and why waste a beautiful apartment like that? "It is yours, Manny! Make use of it," he had said.

Make use of it. I left there before seven in the morning and came back around midnight. I have mentioned what the concierge thought of all this....

Sir Evelyn's cottony hair made a halo around his head and his hands on the green baize of the table were the color of fish.

"Mister deWitt," he said. Sir Evelyn was the only one who insisted on using my last name. "I am at a loss to understand," he said, and idled pearly fingernails up and down on the baize.

"Look, Ev," said Kim from South Africa. "We know you don't split stock as a matter of principle. You've said so for thirteen days."

"However," said Sir Evelyn, "it does not seem to have penetrated, don't you know."

The furniture was old, ornate, and very heavy. I felt I might easily take the long table and fling it out through the glass door which led to the miniature balcony.

"Gentlemen," I said. "We are by no means at the point where feasibility of stock splitting is a fruitful subject for discussion. We...."

"Then why is it brought up—uh—repeatedly, I might wonder?" and Sir Evelyn looked at the sheen of his fingernails.

"My Lord!" said Bobby Drummond. He thought that was very funny when Sir Evelyn was around. "We've been through all that! Manny here"—and he nodded at me—"has said loud and clear...."

I did not look at Sir Evelyn nor did I answer immediately. I lit a cigarette first. Perhaps this meant to him that I was thinking the whole thing over carefully.

"All topics broached during these present negotiations," I said, "comprise the total of the possible steps available to the companies represented. It is not the topic of this meeting which methods of cooperation shall eventually be employed." I could have said that in my sleep.

The only thing of interest to me was why Sir Evelyn, who was actually quick-witted and shrewd, should insist on stalling around when there was no possible consequence but a loss in time.

"I fail to see...." began Sir Evelyn.

"*Bien sûr,*" said Antoine, and his tone reminded me of Ma Griffe, the velvet perfume with a claw in it.

He was closest to my age, though not a minion in his company but rather the heir apparent. He inclined his head as if apologizing for Sir Evelyn. The insult of imputing the other with stupidity was beautifully executed and the War of the Roses was on again.

I had been worried once or twice before that Sir Evelyn and Ledage might break things up. I didn't let them. The image of Lobbe Industriel was at stake. Lobbe Industriel would do the making or breaking around here. I got up.

"Gentlemen."

I did not raise my voice, I did not affect anger. Instead, I made the message slightly bored. That should worry them.

"This is so inefficient. Our little repartees would be fun over an apéritif at a tiny, round table. But here they do not fit our purpose." I liked that: "our purpose."

I stretched a little and then I picked up two piles of tables and papers. I had secretaries to do that for me but I thought it a nice touch to do it myself at this point.

"I suggest, therefore," I continued, rattling papers, "that we leave things as they are for the moment. No great loss,"— I smiled with a touch of weariness by no means simulated—"since we are practically nowhere as it is." I straightened up now, a farewell gaze pointed at the window and beyond. "Miss Sterling or Mister Lundt will keep in touch with your secretaries," I said. "Perhaps tomorrow, we shall see—uh—will you excuse me—"

I meant this all to be a most severe kind of wrist-slapping and warning of worse to come, but actually I could only think of the rest of the day before me, of the bed in the Rue de Jasmin, of myself sleeping there hour upon hour and to hell with this bickering over millions of dollars.

I walked out of the conference room, closed the big door behind me, and told Miss Sterling to ring down for the chauffeur cum Bentley which Lobbe provided. I had to tell her twice because it was only nine o'clock in the morning.

"Is something wrong?" she said.

"No. Wonderful."

On the way to the apartment my mood changed. All told, I was in effect a tired, thirteen-day failure. I might have mishandled matters so badly on this particular morning that Sir Evelyn would take off in a huff, and Antoine would resent me for reprimanding him for his mere touch of venom. From there I went on to much more disastrous speculations, including my wrecked future with Lobbe.

The Bentley had stopped whispering for some little while, it seemed, because the chauffeur was tapping on the glass partition. I gave a start. I thought he had a brutal face.

"When will I return back?" he asked in his lousy English.

"*Jamais. Alors, va t'en—*" I said, offensive both in tone and in choice of expression. It showed how upset I was.

I hoped he would blame it all on my lousy French, got out of the car very quickly, and went into the apartment house. All I needed now was some comment or other from my toad of a concierge. She was there, of course, framed in the open door to her room, but something worse than cadaverous must have looked at her from my face and she closed her door quickly.

Blessed solitude amongst the cushions of Lobbe's vanished cocotte!

I sat there and could not sleep.

I got up from this particular divan which faced a French window with a film of a curtain across and a birdcage of a balcony on the other side. I kicked off my shoes, pulled down my tie, and decided to find a drink. Where might Lobbe's cocotte have stashed a drink?

None in the bedroom. I skipped the bathroom. I went to the kitchen which was smaller than the sunken tub in that mirrored Versailles of a bathroom and did find three bottles of something. It was crème de this and crème de that and it came in different jeweled colors. One of the liqueurs was blue as a boil and I refuse to this day to recall what the name of it was or to speculate on the source of its flavor. But I took that stuff to the divan with me, sank down there, and belted a jigger. Perhaps it would poison me and then Lobbe would feel very badly and would forgive me for the conference failure.

Lobbe feel badly? Another belt, fast.

That one reached something on the inside, making the breath in my nose feel hot like fire.

Bring on your charges! Charge! I am ready!

The telephone rang.

Boil-blue turned yellow inside me and I dashed for the telephone. It was the kind of stilt-armed, ivoried model which American fairies have successfully made into lamp bases for the American home.

"Hello!" I said, much too loud.

"Monsieur deWitt?"

"Hello, yes!"

"I have a cable call for you from New York. Will you stand by, please, while I make connection after which I will call you back."

"Ohmygod—"

"*Comment?*"

"Sorry."

"*Mais je vous en prie.*"

"Me too," I said stupidly and then I hung up.

By my watch, which I looked at for almost all of the time, I waited a mere fifteen minutes. I had another boil-blue and watched the eternal fifteen minutes go by. Then the phone rang with a sweet, lovely tinkle. By the time I got to it and snatched it up the sound seemed hysterical to me.

"Yes? DeWitt here."

"*Mennekin!*" it bellowed. "This is Lobbe!"

"Charge," I mumbled and sat down by the delicate instrument which I wished had been the base of a lamp.

CHAPTER 2

Mijnheer Hans Lobbe speaks with an accent which it would be difficult to duplicate. I will not attempt it. Lobbe is Dutch. Only the Dutch speak Dutch, which means that anyone in that waterlogged country who wishes to communicate with the rest of the world has to learn additional languages. Lobbe, I think, has learned nine additional languages. This is wonderful and I envy the man, but the trouble is that Lobbe is apt to use all of them at the same time. That too cannot be duplicated. Some of the things he says I cannot spell and others are better left unspelled. A severely edited version of one of his paragraphs might end up simply as "Go to hell."

In addition to nine languages he also has a private vocabulary. "Buy Royal Dutch at half and mit der first flubber dump."

You need to know, of course, what the total quotation is for that day, and what size blocks Lobbe is currently shifting, and for all of this he has experts trained in the market. However, you do not learn the word "flubber" there. When stock flubbers that means it is wobbling in such a way as to make a drop a foregone conclusion. But what is a "first flubber"? Well, I don't buy and sell for Lobbe, thank Heaven, but one of the men who does told me at one time that a first flubber is a different percentage of drop from a second flubber, and so on. Such secrets you must quickly glean or intuit from Lobbe himself, or get fired. He fired me once because I cost him a sixty-million-dollar loss (by his reckoning) and because he didn't need me for the next six months. "Nothing is there as instructive as failure. Good-bye."

He was built low and wide like a river barge and he moved just as slowly. But he had a brain as nimble and as tightly trained as a ballerina. Naturally, he was full of tricks, as shall be seen....

"Manny," he said from New York, "I just happened to call the office and what do I find? You are not there."

"Yes, sir."

"So I thought maybe you are at the Rue de Jasmin and there you are!"

I did not believe for a minute that he just happened to call Paris that morning, and I am not referring to the fact that he happened to make that call at about four o'clock in the morning, New York time. That meant nothing. It is much more likely that his brain had been pirouetting about in wondrous ways all night long and had then reached some grand finale at about four.

"You walked straight out of the meeting this morning," he said.

"Yes, sir, I did."

"You could cost me maybe sixty million in U.S. dollars just for a beginning, *Mennekin*."

I will now, finally, see Paris at leisure, I thought.

"Are you alone there in the boudoir?" he asked me, like a snake.

"Of course."

"Humm," he said. "So that wasn't it. Why did you walk out, if it was not a matter of the boudoir?"

Old Lobbe had that kind of a mind. He would have happily listened like a lecher to any boudoir venture I might care to tell him about, and then fire me.

"I walked out because I decided it was the only way to break a long, useless streak of bickering. The impasse might have come about because of my mishandling the earlier meetings but at this point only an interruption made sense to me."

"Did you mishandle before?"

Sixty million dollars' worth, he must be thinking. And then I decided, to hell with his thinking.

"No, sir," I said. "I don't feel I mishandled. For some reason unknown to me Sir Evelyn has found it necessary to stall negotiations from the beginning. He has managed to make his conduct appear like so many little personal animosities at the conference table—however, in view of Sir Evelyn's caliber, that makes no sense at all. Obviously, he was stalling for time but since I don't know...."

"I know," said Lobbe. "Carbon and Allied has a *groot* flubber coming. Just found out. *Ça va sans dire*, Sir Effy doesn't know yet what to commit, *hein?*"

"Oh," I said.

"So to the *Duivel* with the bickering, I will do something else about this. You are through."

And so, Paris without conference table—and without salary, it goes without saying.

"Have a vacation," said Lobbe. "You broke the talk off at the right time."

"Huh?"

"You like Germany, Manny?"

"I beg your...."

"Not the same, not the same at all anymore, you know that, Manny?"

What sounded like a talk on the new look in German politics had to—absolutely had to—mean something else. I said nothing and waited for him to come out with it.

"First, you see, nothing but *Schweinehunde* taking what they can, and now *die lieben Kinder* want to give it back to me."

I could hear him laugh with satisfaction and then there was a brief silence.

"You don't know what I'm talking about," he told me.

"No, I don't, sir."

"This is going to cost a lot of money explaining on the telephone, so don't interrupt."

I said, "Yes, sir," and nothing else, knowing full well that at over three dollars per minute of his cagey type of trader's talk there had to be a whopping profit in it. Naturally, I was not surprised when he kept playing it foxy.

"Ah, what a beautiful place I had by Rotterdam and in there all the things I loved. The rugs from Arabia, the paneling from India, the good solid beds *met* roof, you know, made for comfort and not for crazy health torture on the Hollywood bed close to the ground. What kind of bed is that!"

When his English got that bad he was either thinking of something else or he was not thinking at all. Perhaps he really was reminiscing about the good days and the good nights when he had still lived in Holland....

"... and a vase from China big like an elephant head, I tell you, and the Delfter tile all over the kitchen—huh—a big kitchen!"

I was sure it had been a very big kitchen.

"And pictures, pictures, and most of all the little *bordelje* by my great Vermeer! How I loved that *bordelje!*"

"The what?"

"What? What it sounds like."

"Uh—it sounds like you had a—I mean, in English the word would be cat house, for example."

"Exactly."

I was not overly surprised. This was Lobbe speaking. Perfectly natural for him to build himself a private cat house decorated with Vermeers.

"The painters, like Hals, Vandyke, and my Vermeer, they used to go to the cat house for the exercise, you know?"

"Right."

"They do the happy little pictures there of all the saftig country girls who work there, the sparkle in the eyes, the round, red cheeks, the round white bosoms, and the big, strong arms they have, they work there with the girls and did perfect their techniques, I tell you Manny, such techniques they have never been surpassed in three hundred years!"

"They must have been something, those techniques."

"Don't interrupt. So, those pictures of the milkmaid, of the goose girl, of the girl with the lute, Manny, since they were painted in the cat house we call them *bordeljes*."

"Ah. How apt, sir."

"And then in '41 the *verdreckte Schweinehunde* march into Holland and straight away to my place and my Vermeer!"

He made it sound as if Hitler's invasion of the Netherlands had been specifically organized to rob Lobbe of his cat-house masterpiece, but the fact of the matter was that the Germans had carted off trainloads of art works wherever they could lay their hands on them. But it was not too much of an exaggeration when Lobbe claimed that they had come "straight away" to his place.

"The Vermeer," Lobbe went on, "was for Reichsmarschall Hermann Goering, they told me, seeing how well-known the *bordelje* was. And rare. Not many Vermeers of that type left anymore. Or maybe he liked the fish and bread and flowers better, *wer weiss*."

Quite abruptly Lobbe's voice changed. If he had been reminiscing before, he wasn't anymore. He became precise and to the point.

"I have here a letter from the war damage restitution and so forth office of the Bonn government, Manny, and they found the Vermeer."

It occurred to me that this was the reason why he had "happened" to call me just at this time. He had already known about Sir Evelyn's plight and had decided to take other steps, which meant that the Paris conference was no longer important to him. To cancel the conference he would have simply left word at the office.

"Manny, I love this Vermeer so much, do me the favor and run right over there and pick it up, eh, Manny?"

"Of course, sir. I'll wind up here...."

"Don't wind up. I wind up. I send Richie over from London and he'll handle everything. You take a vacation, Manny, and get me my Vermeer."

I knew that Lobbe loved good things. I have eaten at his table and I have seen the way he has fitted out his place on Long Island. He has many paintings there, many acquired since he had moved to the States, and I remembered his showing me a Vermeer. Lobbe had said it was a copy, and that it was regrettably bad. The original had been lost in the war. The picture was perhaps fifteen by twenty-five inches, showing a laughing girl carrying a basket full of yellow apples. The apples were too yellow and the laugh on her healthy face seemed brash enough to suggest hysteria. Her bodice was carelessly open and the rise of her young breasts was slightly obscene.

"Am I picking up the original of the copy you have on Long Island?" I asked him.

"Yes, Manny. The original of that piece of *Dreck*. Made from a print. Sentimental reasons. Soon I can throw it away, *hein*, Manny?" and Lobbe laughed happily.

He had never talked of the copy much, or of its original, though he could be voluble about his possessions when he took you around his place on Long Island. Lobbe never talked much about his losses.

"Now have your vacation, Manny." He paused. Perhaps he was looking something up. "And here are the simple instructions."

I had afterthoughts about the instructions. They turned out a little strange. And I had afterthoughts about the vacation. It never materialized.

CHAPTER 3

Lobbe's love for his painting showed what type of a man he was. He was not a collector whose interest was primarily a need for possession. For instance, the gigantic Chinese vase had also been lost in the war but he had never looked for it very much. Its dragon and bird design, he explained, had been very confusing. Without an intrinsic fascination for the object itself the thing meant nothing to him. In contrast, he had waited for his *bordelje* of the laughing girl and her apple basket with hope and with longing for all the years since the war. How much he concerned himself with the painting came out later when he told me a few things.

The first Lobbe on record had been a contemporary of Vermeer's. This was verified by the family records. Hans Lobbe's claims went a little bit further. Not only did Piet Lobbe know Vermeer in person, went the tale, but those two had gone to the same cat house together!

"*God verdomme, Mennekin,*" Lobbe would say, "why do you think the *bordelje* has been a family member for so many years?"

(Acquisition date turned out to be 1771, in payment of a debt owed for one sack of cayenne pepper corns. At that time Vermeer had been long dead.)

"I tell you why!" Lobbe cried, relishing his storytelling. "Because that little *Appel Meisje* is a family member! You think old Piet Lobbe was playing cards with that girl?!"

There were other claims. Once Lobbe had pointed out to me that he and the apple maid had the identical forehead, noble and smooth. I need go no further.

For that matter, the yarn might have been true. Piet Lobbe sounded a lot like the Hans Lobbe I knew and Mijnheer Hans wouldn't have played cards with the girl. Altogether, the Lobbes had not changed much over the centuries.

The first Lobbe, the carousing Piet, had started out as a pirate, plain and simple. Or perhaps he had staged a successful mutiny. The records are a little discreet. But at any rate, this Piet Lobbe turned up in the port of Amsterdam one fine morning, in command of a trading vessel in which he had not left the port. The holds were full of muscat and raw cinnamon, making the docks fragrant for many blocks. From that day on there was no stopping the Lobbes. They remained traders from that time on, changing only their cargoes. Depending on demand they might change from spices to raw silk, then to kautchug, then tea. Somewhere along the line they acquired and lost a shipyard in Rotterdam, a rubber plantation in Borneo, a warehouse in Calcutta perhaps, and a ship or two. But the only real failure of the family had been one Mies Lobbe, a slaver. He became so attached to one of his cargo that he turned back in mid-ocean, disembarked on the Gold Coast instead of New Orleans, and went back—cargo and all—to the village where he had made his purchase. Though the move was strictly bad business Mijnheer Hans Lobbe had only affection for ancestor Mies. The chief of the Congo village in question rewarded old Mies with the gift of ten additional wives and a flock of fat goats. The contemporary Lobbe has on those grounds claimed kinship to various heads of state whenever a new African nation has gained independence.

It seemed there had been no bad business move since the time of Mies Lobbe. With no shred of modesty Hans Lobbe pointed out that he had been by far the busiest. This was true. His trading fleet was not as big as some of the Greeks', but it was much more diversified. His rubber plantations had mostly been nationalized since the loss of Dutch Indonesian possessions, but their raw products were still processed in Lobbe plants here and there on the globe.

It was Hans Lobbe who'd gone beyond the trader tradition. From rubber processing he went into synthetics. He belted into that business as if possessed with a fear that the age of plastics would end promptly at midnight.

But he was never so rapacious that he would end up dead to all other pleasures. He wanted me to bring back his Vermeer.

As I have mentioned, he gave me very detailed instructions. I took the white telephone to a desk, a little kidney-shaped rosewood thing at which a mistress of Louis XV wrote loving notes to her king.

"Go ahead," I said. "I've got paper and pencil."

"Good. I have this idea, Manny, that we can do this thing faster than the good Germans. I mean, they are good Germans but they are also bureaucrats."

"Yes?" I said, and three thousand miles away he caught the inflection in my voice.

"This is not a *Schwindel*, you understand."

"So far, sir, I don't understand yet what I am to understand."

"*Kalbskopf*, listen now. The Vermeer is mine and the German government wants to give it to me. The sweet *bordelje* is not in Bonn but in Munich. The present owner—I use the wrong phrase for that thief—he lives in Munich and still has the picture. From Munich it would then go to Bonn so that a clerk with a box can put it in the box and send it to me."

"I understand."

"*Cretin!* You don't understand. I don't want to wait that long, *capice?*"

"I certainly do understand."

"So. Now you go directly to Munich, *Mennekin* dear, and pick up my picture directly from this Hun by the name of Freiherr von Tilwitz who is the *Krautfresser*...."

"I thought Hermann Goering had been the owner?"

"Hermann is dead, *Ezel*, and this *boche cornu* who is a thief also, of course, he took possession...."

"All right. I understand. Give me the address."

He gave me the address.

"Two more things, sir. What about my identification as your authorized agent and what about notification to the Bonn office about this—uh—quicker way of doing things?"

"I have prepared everything."

"Yes?"

"Yes. Your authorization is now en route via airmail, General Delivery, Munich, your name, arrival tomorrow."

"That's fast."

"Naturally. And the arrangement with Bonn I handle through the office in Solingen. I have channels there."

"Very good. Anything else?"

"Just be careful with my *Liebling*, just be nice to her. Do not leave her in a locker in some airport, do not give her to a baggage man. They *throw* things!"

"I know."

"Keep her on your knee where you sit, on your knee like a darling. Sleep with her, Manny."

I laughed and was about to make a joke of my own on the subject when he fairly cracked me across the face with his voice.

"Do not let her out of your sight. Is that clear?"

"Why—yes. But I think...."

"Not out of your sight, Manford."

When Lobbe is excited he starts talking lousy English. But when Lobbe is angry his English becomes very precise. He said, "If no other consideration impresses your type of mind, then fasten on the fact that this picture is worth a great deal of money."

I was hurt by his tone but also impressed with his anxiety. I just nodded my head, as if he could see me.

"Manny?"

"Yes, sir."

"I apologize for the tone of voice."

There was that about old Lobbe.

"Accepted, of course," I said, and I meant it.

"I don't want you to be unhappy with the job, Manny."

"I'm not. I need sleep, a good meal, and then I'll love going on this vacation." He did not seem to think I was being sarcastic so I went right on. "I don't know Paris at all, as you know, but is it true, sir, that the food is exceptional at something called Le Chien Qui Fume?... Hello, Mister Lobbe?"

"I am here."

"Is it true...."

"You have a ticket on vol numéro 135, BEA, 3:46 p.m. Paris time. The airport is Le Bourget. No mistake, please. It is Le Bourget, not Orly."

Then I blew up.

"I fail to grasp the importance of this damn hurry and I don't like instructions which leave no elbow room on one hand and which leave entirely too much to the imagination on the other. If you follow my meaning."

I have never seen Lobbe take offense when someone expressed himself directly and he didn't now. In fact, he almost ignored the whole thing.

"When the chauffeur comes for you," he said, "he will bring you an envelope given to him by the office. Your ticket is in there. And there are five thousand dollars enclosed, in one-hundred-dollar bills."

Might this turn into a vacation after all?

"You were talking before about instructions which leave you no elbow room. I give you five thousand dollars of elbow room, Manny, to get my Vermeer from that impoverished *Junker Schwein* so that he does not insist on a bureaucratic insanity such as waiting for Bonn to pick up my picture."

"You mean to tell me I should pay five thousand...."

"Not all of it! Use your head, *Ezel!*"

"I understand."

"We understand each other?"

"We understand each other."

"Which is why I picked you." And with that testimonial of confidence he simply hung up.

He had not responded to a single one of my objections and he had never doubted whether I would take the job on or not.

I slammed the phone down, had my moment of indignation and fury alone in the boudoir on Jasmin Street, and then I didn't doubt either that I'd do the job for Lobbe. He wanted that painting in a criminal hurry; he wanted no one to get near it except over my dead body; he wanted to avoid all official channels. And he had spared my lawyer's conscience by not telling me one damn thing which might explain any of this. I took on the job because I am very curious....

My brute of a chauffeur left me at Le Bourget half an hour before plane time. Le Bourget is a dismal place. One hour away from the heart of Paris and the throb does not reach. On one side of the highway is a dinky hotel, a bar, and a row of mean houses. On the other side is the airport which has more compounds for freight than for passenger service. The highway itself seems to lead into potato country, very flat and gray.

I mostly sat on a bench and stared out of a door where I could see some of the cement of the field. Lindbergh had landed there and it must have been something to watch. Now there was nothing to watch. At 3:25 p.m. the PA announced one of the infrequent planes. BEA's Gibraltar plane was due in from London in something like three minutes and would passengers please gather for embarkation. There was not much of a stir of things. Five or six travelers started moving about, which seemed to indicate that Gibraltar does not have much to recommend it. Six minutes later came the last call for the Gibraltar shuttle, but there was no one left who wanted to go.

I had nothing else to do so I waited for the sound of the plane leaving outside on the apron, but nothing happened. I checked my watch and according to the board which showed plane times the BEA outside was already five minutes late. A young man in the BEA uniform walked past and he was looking at his watch too.

"Trouble with your plane?" I asked him.

"'Course not," he said. It was hard to tell whether he sounded offended or whether it was his normal, British accent. "Merely holding the plane for someone. Courtesy matter, you know."

Someone came, rapidly. The youngish man looked vaguely familiar, definitely British, and was in such an all-fired hurry that his regimental tie was flapping. He carried two attaché cases and headed straight for the door which led to the apron.

Someone I had known in London? I had not been in London for two years, on Lobbe business. Lobbe business... was he somebody's secretary?

I didn't have to work the answer out for myself because then came the man to whom the young one was secretary. He worked his black cane rapidly and wisps of longish white hair stuck out by his ears, under his bowler. Sir Evelyn Peyton-Smyth, looking intensely anxious to get to Gibraltar.

He didn't see me and I didn't bother to wave. And then, within minutes, the plane took off for its non-stop run to the southern tip of Europe.

At the time the event had no significance for me, but I wondered just the same what Sir Evelyn might want to be doing in Gibraltar. Carbon and Allied had no offices on The Rock.

CHAPTER 4

I had a seat built for three all to myself. Outside my window the Rolls-Royce turbos had settled down to a whine, sounding as if they might die at any moment, but Le Bourget was gone, Paris was behind us, and the cloudscape below the big plane was turning pink with the setting sun. This cloudscape was so vast that it robbed the flight of any sense of motion. The plane simply hung there, the turbos whined as though mortally wounded, and the featureless pink below us reminded me of nothing familiar at all. The horizon was now turning bloody. It was an unsettling sight. I picked up my London *Times*.

"You read English."

It was a statement and not a question and it came from the other side of the aisle where the seats were twin instead of triple. He looked at me through pince-nez and smiled.

"I read English too."

One would think that this put an end to the conversation. It did not.

"May I sit with you?" he asked and got up.

I was still phrasing the sound "Uh—" when he came over and sat down.

"I am German," he said, "but I read English also."

I wasn't about to pick that discourse up again, nor did he give me a chance.

"The real reason I addressed you," he said, "was to get this opportunity for the seat on this side where I might see the sunset much better."

I moved over. He could have taken the triple in front of me, or several others on my side. The plane was quite empty. But he sat close enough to me now to make lifting the paper an awkward matter, for fear of obstructing his view. I moved away a little and while he watched the sunset I watched him.

He needn't have told me that he was a German. He looked like a German of the Burger variety that was standardized at the time of the Kaiser. There was a wing collar. I had not seen one since Emil Jannings was castigating his class while in love with the Blue Angel. Even if your neck were made of rubber, collapse would be impossible with this white exoskeleton. While the collar was severe, the man's face was not. The cheeks were cherubic. The mouth looked too satisfied to be severe in the slightest, and the well-fed double chin made it clear that the man was not a self-disciplinarian. The gray mustache was not very tidy and the blue little eyes behind the pince-nez seemed very curious. Maybe he had never seen a sunset before? For a German of his class and age—I thought he might be around sixty—he had been unusually forward.

"I wonder," I said, "if I were to read my paper, I wonder if that would interfere with your view?"

"Not at all, not at all," he protested and waved a fat little hand at me.

"But on the other hand," I kept on, "if you were to sit in the seat in front of us, you would not only not have to look past me but you could actually sit right next to the window."

For a moment he looked crestfallen, and I felt just slightly sorry to have said all this to him, but then he recovered very nicely and with admirable spunk.

"It was presumptuous of me," he said, and his little shrug was apologetic, "but if I had sat down there I could not have discussed it with you."

"Discussed it with me?"

"The sunset."

I was going to repeat that verbatim too but would have felt too much like an idiot. At that point he laughed, which made his belly roll up and down, which in turn caused the elkstooth on his watchchain to jump as if with joy.

"I will tell you a joke on me and on all other Germans who can take a joke—there are some, you know." And he shook his finger at me. "Especially in Bavaria. I am from Bavaria," he added seriously. "Ah yes, not like those others, in the North." This caused him to look sternly at the sunset. He had, of course, lost his thread.

"What's the joke?" I asked him.

"Oh. You see, after you pass the Pearly Gates—you see, I am speaking of heaven."

"I thought so."

"After those Gates, you see, you go up a little ways along this road and then you come to a fork in this road."

"I can see it clearly."

"Good. At this fork there is a *Wegweiser, na*, it points here and there—"

"Road sign."

"Of course. And one arm says: To Paradise. And the other arm says: To Lectures About Paradise. You can see this?"

"As if I were there."

"Me too. Well, up from the gate comes a busload of Germans, like tourists, you see, but they are now permanent guests. They stop at the *Wegweiser*, decide which way to go, and then go. You know where?"

"Should I guess?"

"Don't guess. You don't have to guess because they are Germans. They go to the lectures about paradise instead of to the real thing." Then he closed his eyes and went heeheehee, just like that, three times, which was a laugh to make you laugh, it was so funny. I laughed and he opened his eyes.

"Funny?"

"Very."

"Very, no. For that it is too serious. But you see, don't you, here I have been leading up to the discussion of the sunset, to discuss it, and the sun is almost gone. Such a violent Van Gogh, don't you see," and he peered out at the sun which now seemed to roar with hot color, and at the cloud blanket below, which was now full of waves, cracks, and shadows. The shadows were blue and green, and the bright stripes of light went from a lemon-yellow to a deep, fruity cherry-red. I wished he didn't want to discuss it.

For a while he let me look and then, with an abruptness that was shocking, the sun disappeared. Mauve and deep blue were the colors now, and there was a peace which the German was bound to fill with a comment.

"Well now," he said. "That was beautiful."

I picked up my London *Times*. It served no purpose. "Do you know Van Gogh and his violence?"

"Hardly."

The sarcasm escaped him because he commenced to lecture.

"I don't know him either, he is dead, but I know him nevertheless. I am an art expert."

You are a braggart, I thought.

"I am with the Alte Pinakothek, Munich," he said and then he pulled out an enormous billfold which had many compartments and pockets, each of which seemed to be stuffed with innumerable papers. It was a rolltop desk *en poche*, so to speak, and he found what he wanted immediately. "My card," he said, bowed perceptibly, and held out his hand. We shook and I said, "DeWitt, sir. Lobbe Industriel," and he said, "*Sehr angenehm.*"

It seemed he was not a braggart at all. His card said that he was Dr. August Baumeister, *Kunstwissenschaftlicher Assistent der Restorationsabteilung, Alte Pinakothek.*

The card was not very large but they had it all on there. Baumeister was an art appraiser for one of the major European museums.

"You can see, Herr Dewitser...."

"The name, sir, is deWitt."

"Haaa!" he laughed when he understood his mistake. "I am funny!"

I did not correct him. Taken in the most good-natured way his remark really applied, and even though the sunset was over now, August Baumeister stayed. The man loved conversation; in fact, he loved it so much that he did not ask a single personal question. Only in retrospect did it occur to me that he had actually learned a great deal....

"And now that it's over," he said and nodded at the emptiness which was left where the sun had burnt out, "I now have happy news for you."

"How nice," I said. "Give it to me."

"No," he said, looking reverent. "She will give it to you," and he pointed out the window. Then he grinned, without transition, and the grin made his cheeks round and shiny. "She will give you two sunsets, *die liebe Sonne*. This one was *numéro* one, and *numéro* two when we land and she goes down over Munich. Not nice?"

"Very nice," I said and suddenly I liked the old man.

"It is the same in my work, this happy twice," he went on. "I now come from the Louvre, you see, where I had insurance talk about a shipment of pictures from them to the Pinakothek. Loan exhibit. I am there, I look at the pictures—Titians mostly, you know—and to appraise them is a great deal like a love affair. I remember, haha. You must be very intimate or you know nothing. That is *numéro* one. *Numéro* two, I go back to the Pinakothek and, hocus-pocus, there she is again! Again I am intimate."

"Why the expert scrutiny for a little trip from Paris to Munich?"

"To check on the condition at departure and arrival, to be sure that the same picture that left is the one that arrives. I have seen some beautiful fakes, you know. Oh, what beautiful fakes, substituted en route, you know."

His eyes had been going this way and that, looking at me, at the stewardess, at the sky outside, just moving about the way a lively person's might. But at this point they stopped on me and held.

"Sir deWitt," he started.

"No, no, no, Herr Doktor. You misunderstand again. When I said 'sir'

I was addressing you. It is Mister deWitt."

"I am stupid."

"Not really."

"But I observe very well. You were amused with my talk, but then you became suddenly interested."

"Why, of course. I like to hear...."

"Uh, uh, uh," and he waggled his finger. "Not general interest of the alert, not omnivorous interest of the tourist, but specific. When I spoke of transport and fake."

"By God, you're right," I said. "You've got a good eye."

"But you're not in the art business, Mister deWitt. Or else we would have been talking shop long before now."

"That's true. I was interested because I'm picking up a picture, for its owner."

He looked at me, almost with an air of recognition, and then he slapped his thigh and said, "*Ja, natürlich!* The 'Apple Girl.' Such a lovely *bordelje.*"

He looked dreamily at nothing while my mouth hung open. In a while I cleared my throat and said, "May I ask, Herr Doktor...."

"You don't have to. I will tell." He hitched around in his seat, very much enjoying the topic. "You introduced yourself—deWitt, Lobbe Industriel. Well, to you Lobbe means perhaps stocks moving about, or perhaps factory chimneys that belch, or a tank ship on the ocean. Now, to me and my colleagues, Lobbe means only one thing. Lobbe means Vermeer's 'Apple Girl,' and it was lost in the war."

"As a matter of fact, Herr Doktor...."

"I know. The *bordelje* just turned up! *Wunderbar* to know that it was not destroyed, though a little bit sad to think that Lobbe will take it back to America. You understand?"

"I understand."

We both sat musing about this for a while, or at least I pretended to muse. I imitated his beatific expression directed slightly up, where the heavens would be, the heavens where you are intimate with such a *bordelje*.

But I knew this: while Lobbe seemed to have a legitimate claim on the picture he had also shanghaied me into a job of retrieving it by corner-cutting methods.

I no longer could hold the beatific pose. I was cursing Lobbe for the way he was handling this, which was to give me the sternest instructions to guard against the vaguest of threats. Reasonably, therefore, the fewer the people who knew of my errand the safer I would feel, though I did not know from what. And here it turned out that Baumeister's entire profession seemed to be watching with bated breath what would happen to Lobbe's *bordelje*. In brief, I had an audience. I felt haunted.

"Doctor Baumeister," I said in a dead-casual voice, "how in hell do you know all this and who else does?"

"Who else? Hardly anyone, I should think. I know of the reappearance of the *bordelje* because a *Saupreiss* by the name of...."

"What was that word?"

"Uh—forgive me. The expression simply reflects how the Bavarians regard the Prussians. You need know no more."

Indeed I didn't. Good old Baumeister—as much as his satisfied face allowed—looked disgusted.

"You were saying?" I prompted him.

"Never mind what I was saying. What I wanted to say was this. I am an appraiser, an authenticator, and one fine day a friend of mine at the Schack Gallerie called me up, I should recommend an expert of the Dutch Masters—I myself am late Renaissance, you see—an expert like that, who is particularly knowledgeable about Vermeer."

"Because someone wanted to sell the Vermeer and an authentication was needed, is that the reason for the call?"

"Yes. The best man on Vermeers lives in Rotterdam and his name is Kornbluth. Excellent man. Russian immigrant from long ago, trained at the Hermitage in what was then called St. Petersburg. But that is neither here nor there. I did not like the secrecy surrounding the approach and simply said no, I could not help. A few days later my friend called me back and said, it's a good thing I did not get involved, some *Saupr...* excuse me, one Freiherr von Tilwitz, formerly a staff adjutant in Goering's industrial ministerium, wanted to sell the *bordelje*."

"Why would he?"

"He is broke. He has lost his East Prussian estates to the Russians. He has lost a great deal more. There is his stature, his influence, his hereditary importance. Poof. But that's neither here nor there. In the course of finding an appraiser, in the course of revealing the existence of the Vermeer, Bonn hears about this, identifies the 'Apple Girl,' and dispossesses the impoverished Freiherr of his lovely loot."

"I thought he still has it."

"Yes. Until transfer it is in his possession. The Freiherr is cooperative. He receives a small pension from Bonn and if he sells the Vermeer in the interim he goes to jail at the age of seventy-four."

At this point, of course, none of his talk was in the least bit academic for me. I had a job to do for Hans Lobbe and Baumeister was telling me things which would help me complete it. At least, that's why I stuck with the topic.

"Bonn has identified the Vermeer," I said to him. "You told me this. Then why does it have to be identified again before delivery to Mijnheer Lobbe?"

The point was important to me because if Bonn did not have to handle any further delivery and inspection procedures, then all of Lobbe's stringent instructions need no longer bug me.

"But you forget," said Baumeister, "how this talk started."

"You wanted to discuss the sunset."

"I mean later. When I told you how a forgery might be substituted for an original in transit. The same is true with Lobbe's Vermeer. It is identified, von Tilwitz keeps it for a brief time, Bonn holds it for a brief time, and then it is delivered to the owner. Between identification and delivery, *mein lieber Herr* deWitt, so much can happen!"

That's what Lobbe must have thought.

"And what do you think your Mijnheer Lobbe would say, if you delivered his beloved *bordelje* to him and it turned out to be no Vermeer at all but an imitation?"

I did not want to think of what my Mijnheer Lobbe would say. I knew very well what he would say and what he would probably do to me and to my career, and I sat there resentful that there might be so many thieves around to harass me.

"Kornbluth?" I asked Baumeister. "In Rotterdam?"

"That is my opinion. Once you are in Munich, ask around for an expert." He grinned at me. "I gather you do not want to take the wrong picture back to your Lobbe."

I did not grin back at him. The matter was fairly serious for me.

"No," I said. "I most decidedly do not want to take the wrong picture back to my Lobbe."

CHAPTER 5

The meal came, and for this event August Baumeister moved back into his own seat. He wanted room and solitude, I suspect, for the intimate relations he enjoyed with good food. And the food was good. The main dish was crabmeat sauteed in light butter and lemon. This was not served with potatoes but with thick toast. Unfortunately, the toast was English, which means it was cold. But there also was a fine demijohn of Chablis, very cold, and a watercress salad sprinkled with walnuts. Very simple, very good. I had yellow cheese and an apple for dessert and two very good cups of coffee. Paris, to be sure, had never been like this. Then I picked up my *Times* once again, traversed the world via unrest in Mississippi, bloodletting in Vietnam, crop failure in India, palace *putsch* in Kashmir, beheadings and disemboweling somewhere in Africa, arrests in Portugal, and a trunk murder in Nottingham. I looked at the financial section as a matter of routine—Lobbe Industriel steady, Carbon and Allied Chemical up—up 3½ points, which was fairly unusual in view of the company's conservative policies. Perhaps somebody had not heard yet how I had botched that up. A few entries down from Carbon and Allied was Commercial Trust of Tangiers. Holding steady. But this was not the point. I remembered suddenly that Carbon and Allied was owned to the tune of 23 percent by this holding company, and it struck me that Sir Evelyn might not have been on his way to Gibraltar at all but to Tangier, a mere two-hour ferry ride across the Straits of Gibraltar. Commercial Trust of Tangier was a financiers' combine set up for investment and profit distribution by a number of interests from all over the globe. Tangier, being a free port, offered a number of corporate and currency advantages, and whenever a member of the firm was in any trouble, the problem was frequently handled through Commercial Trust. And Sir Evelyn had been in one all-fired hurry to get on that shuttle heading south....

The plane had been descending. I didn't notice it until the view from the window showed nothing but milk, a very even blur of thick cloud which left little droplets on the glass. The drops appeared suddenly, trembled a moment, and then stretched out into a finger of water which raced from one end of the glass to the other and then swam out into nothing. Next, more drops formed, to lance across the glass and then disappear.

"Mister deWitt, sir," said Baumeister from across the aisle. He was determined to get that "sir" in someplace. "When you are settled in Munich," he said, "and if you need any help with your picture, please feel free to call on me at the Pinakothek. You still have my card?"

"Yes, I still have your card, thank you."

"On the other hand, the Bonn office for restitution and return of properties uses the best available people for authentication, you know. There is nothing for you to worry about."

He did not know, of course, what I was worried about, which was precisely that the experts in Bonn would get their hands on the picture.

"What I have not mentioned," Baumeister went on, "is that they might appoint an appraiser in Munich, you know. Not only because the picture happens to be in Munich, but because Munich is full of *Kunstwissenschaftler*."

That too worried me. Anything that made it easier for Bonn to do an expeditious job worried me....

"In fact, I'll tell you what I'll do. I will arrange...."

"You are too kind, Herr Doktor. Really."

"No, no. Not at all. Besides, it would give me a chance to see the picture. I only know it in reproduction. I can arrange with Bonn to have the Vermeer officially appraised at the Alte Pinakothek; we have an excellent...."

"Please, I mean really, Herr Doktor, we don't have to go to any such lengths. I'd just as soon...."

"I would like to insist," said Baumeister. His remark made me very uncomfortable. "Give me the address of von Tilwitz and all will be arranged."

No doubt everything would be arranged and Lobbe would have a fit and I would be out in the cold.

"Doctor Baumeister," I said. "I will call you, I will show you the *bordelje*, I will do all this if you promise not to take any of those unnecessary steps you are suggesting."

"Bonn can be slow," he said.

"Good. I mean, fine with me. It doesn't matter. Really."

We left it up in the air like that. We fastened seat belts at that point, the plane broke out of the clouds and streaked through gray, rain-filled air, and the turbos changed their pitch perceptibly. I looked through the wet porthole, Baumeister looked through his wet porthole, and then he turned to me, shrugged, and said, "You will have to do with only one sunset, I'm afraid."

I remember the remark because he said it with so much charm and with so much genuine regret. We were separated upon landing and I saw him ahead of me when we went through passport and baggage control. And then I got fairly shook up when I saw two policemen approach him, place themselves on either side of him, and walk out into the rain with Dr. Baumeister to where an Opel with the coat of arms of the city of Munich was waiting for them.

The taxi ride from the airport to the city was fairly long. The half-light of early evening came and then it began to drizzle. The trees on both sides of the highway drooped with moisture and the fields became intensely green. I saw these things for a while but was interrupted often by thinking of Baumeister. I do not believe I would really have been upset about the man if I had not turned on the small light to my left where I sat by the window (this shut out the damp evening view) and started to read the London *Times* again. Somehow I seemed to see nothing but notices about thefts.

Thames Tug Disappears from Pier Three.

Soho Gang Robs Pawnshop of Musical Instruments.

Objets de Vertu Stolen from Wren Collection.

Lady Treck Collects Ten Thousand Pounds After Grünewald Tryptich Theft.

Man Loses Wooden Leg.

International Art Forgery Crackdown.

The last article bothered me particularly. It listed two proven forgeries of paintings by Ribera, one of Fra Filippo Lippi, and one overpainted Tulo, an obscure Titian student, palmed off as a Titian. "Evidence indicates," I read, "culpability and connivance of well-placed experts performing legitimate work for certain well-known European collections and museums."

The point of my concern was this: The listed forgeries spanned the Italian Renaissance. And Dr. August Baumeister, by his own statement, was a Renaissance specialist. And, of course, he had just been arrested before my own eyes....

Mijnheer Lobbe would now have been proud of me. I started to worry like hell. I worried myself into an academic corner of understanding full well why the prospective thief of my charge, the "Apple Girl," would talk enough to make me suspicious, would then not offer his own assistance in authenticating the picture (which is precisely what he had avoided doing) but drive me into the expert clutches of some other renowned specialist, also a member of the art trafficking gang, who would tell me that my Vermeer *bordelje* was indeed the genuine article, as he returned a forgery to me.

None of this had happened, but none of it struck me as total nonsense. I took the newspaper, folded it unnecessarily, and threw it down. I thought of Lobbe and his vague instructions, and cursed him with great relish. But the instructions themselves had not been vague, only the context in which they had been given. I stopped cursing Lobbe. I would now ignore the void of information he had left me, I would forget about the plottings of round-cheeked little Baumeisters, and instead do simply what I had been told, but fast.

"*Haben Sae sich entschlossen?*" said my driver.

"Pardon?"

"*Wohin?*"

I understood that. For the third time he wanted to know where I wanted to be taken. But I did not know the German word for General Delivery, which was the place where Lobbe had sent my reservation, the covering letter to the Freiherr, and authorization to transport the picture. Those things I needed first.

"*Postamt,*" I said for the third time and for the third time he launched into a lengthy discourse to the effect that the post offices would all be closed by the time we got to town. I'm almost sure that's what he said.

We were passing through the suburbs now, past four-storey houses looking gray with lack of light, wet, and uninviting. Only where yellow lights began to show behind the windows did all this change and a warm, sheltered aspect appear.

"Stop the car, driver."

"*Was?*"

"Halt. Stop."

"Oh, *stopp*," he said and then he stopped.

I rolled my window down and waved at the policeman who directed evening traffic. I had been told that practically every German has at least a smattering of one or two additional languages. My driver had to be one of those who had no smattering whatsoever. The policeman came to the window, saluted, sucked on his mustache once because it was so wet, and said "*Jawohl?*"

"Excuse me, but do you happen to speak English?"

"*Englisch? Ja, etwas.*"

"Thank God. Now, listen. Where is your General Delivery office here in town?"

"What town?"

"Uh—never mind. General Delivery. *Wo?*"

I made the tourist's mistake of shouting at the native, as if that would make everything clearer.

"Excuse me, but I hear you," he said with patience. "Yes, General Delivery. I understand. What do you deliver? It makes the difference."

"Christ—never mind. Look, you speak French?"

"*Ja.* That too."

I was more cautious about my expectations this time. I had just heard him speak *Ja, Englisch.*

"*Poste Restante,*" I pronounced carefully. "*Où est la poste restante?*"

He said carefully, "*J'expliquerai ça à votre chauffeur.*" He spoke excellent French. He then turned to the driver, said something short with the words *poste restante* in it, and so help me, my one-language driver understood the whole thing, and we were off again. I didn't know then that they used the French expression in German too. Little annoyances like that were getting to me.

We drove to what appeared to be the center of town. The traffic got thicker, the lights brighter, and the women more elegant. There was definite transition from skirts down to the middle of the calf, a thickish calf, to skirts no lower than just above the knee. No Bavarian peasant types, these.

We pulled into a complicated square full of traffic islands. The whole thing spreadeagled out into many streets. At one end of the square was the railroad station. My driver pulled up to the curb and talked to me. I assumed it was German simply because I was in Germany. The building where we had stopped showed in clear letters that it was the *Telegraphen Amt.* That's the telegraph office in any language.

"*Poste Restante,*" I said, feeling suddenly tired. It was the only phrase which he and I had in common and it was the only place where I wanted to go.

More talk which I took to be German.

As it turned out—I was literally shooed into the telegraph office by my driver so that he could make his point—General Delivery was handled by the telegraph office. I mention the incident in order to point up my condition. I was feeling pushed around, harassed, and impatient of misunderstandings. I was running through my curse list rapidly—Baumeister, Lobbe, the driver—when the telegraph clerk came back to the counter with a thick envelope, franked in France, return address Lobbe Industriel, Paris.

At this point I was much too impatient to read or even look at anything that was in the envelope except the covering letter.

My hotel reservation was at the Vier Jahreszeiten. I should have known. Lobbe was a show-off. This hotel, as far as I was concerned, existed only in movies, paperbacks, and the conversations of liars. It was perhaps the best, and certainly the most renowned, in Munich. Even my driver was duly impressed and drove me without further Bavarian arguments to this aging palace.

Once in my room I didn't bother to unpack. I figured that, with luck, I might leave town again that night, walk in on Lobbe maybe twenty hours later, and earn a real vacation. I called the desk and asked for two reservations to New York. It was after seven at the time, and the first available plane would be three hours later, TWA to London and from there to New York. The next available was SAS to Paris and from there, over the pole, to New York. While this was being discussed and checked I sat on the too-soft bed and started feeling hungry. There was no time for that. I distracted myself by checking out the room, a large, high-ceilinged square, softened along the corners and the frieze with baroque plaster ornaments. The ceiling was a delight. I lay down on the bed and looked at it. This too displayed the baroque curve where plaster leaves and plaster ribbon shapes twined into an oval.

"Mister deWitt?"

"Lovely. Really lovely...."

"I beg your pardon, sir?"

The clerk's accent was intriguing—the result, most likely, of speaking half a dozen languages.

"Uh—nothing."

"Both reservations have been accepted. If you would care to deposit the money with us two hours prior to departure...."

"Yes, of course. Now, would you connect me with a local number?"

He would not but he gave me the switchboard. It was now eight p.m., a decent time to call a private residence. I called the Freiherr von Tilwitz. A woman answered.

"My name," I said in English, "is Mr. deWitt. I represent the Lobbe interest...." I hesitated, to find out if I had been understood.

"DeWitt?" said the woman, and then, in well-learned, proper English, "What did you say is your interest?"

"May I speak to Freiherr von Tilwitz, please."

"I'm sorry, he is out. I am Fraulein von Tilwitz. You may address yourself to me."

The daughter, I thought, or some old Tilwitz sister. The Germans are big for family. The slight metallic ring in the voice made it difficult to guess her age.

"I represent," I said again, "the Lobbe interest, ma'am." A very neat way of being correct and cagey, was my thought, but there was further silence at the other end. "I am here in regard to the Vermeer painting, Miss von Tilwitz. I have been authorized...."

"I am quite certain, sir," she said, "that you have the wrong von Tilwitz. We know nothing of a Vermeer painting." And then she hung up.

CHAPTER 6

I stared at the ceiling a moment longer, just long enough to realize that no message was coming from there. I felt like an idiot and sat up. I still had the phone in my hand and the whole thing properly placed to my ear.

"Your party has hung up, sir," said the operator.

"Thank you," I said and hung up.

I dislike feeling like an idiot. I am no international operative, I am not a seasoned detective, and I was not even being a very effective agent for Mijnheer Hans Lobbe. But an idiot I am not. I jumped off the bed, grabbed my raincoat, and left the hotel fast. It was now past nine o'clock in the evening, but the von Tilwitz clan was going to get a most unseemly visit.

The field marshal commanding the hotel entrance flashed his gloved hand into the air and a cab flashed up. From under its hood came a dangerous clacking and rattling. Any lover of well-run machinery would have blanched, not knowing that some of these Mercedes have diesels under the hood. At eighty cents for a gallon of gas this makes sense. I was placed into the rear by the field marshal and when he saluted I almost saluted back.

"Let's get out of here," I told the driver.

"*Wohin?*"

"Schraudolf Strasse," I said, and gave him the number.

By American standards these cars have no pickup at all. We crept away from the curb, labored along into the traffic, and all the while the motor sounded as if rods, shafts, and other parts of the metal anatomy were going to fall apart and clatter into the street at any moment. But my anxiety again was unreasonable.

This driver spoke English. I wished he did not. I wished for the surly bastard who had driven me from the airport instead of having to sit there and strain for a meaning which was of no interest to me and to ask for more clarity each time I was addressed.

"America, no?"

"Yes."

"Dat must yet but a interessanting land be, yes?"

"No."

"No? Why no?"

"Never mind."

"You dink so too? Halm! We here often dink so too dat der Americaning human bings have never a mind. Why can dat been, what?"

"I haven't given it much thought. Would you mind going a little bit faster, please."

"Aha! Mein dinking is also exactly so. It goes too faster, den the mind is goink, and den comes no doughts. Right."

I didn't say anything. I thought this was a remarkable conversation. He had taken three words from my two previous sentences and woven them into a skein of almost psychological complexity. Meanwhile, he took my silence for active thought.

"And now den," he said, "what haben we for a conclusion?"

"What was that?" I was sure he couldn't make anything out of this sentence.

"Exactly my dinking also again! As we say in German, *wass gewesen ist soil gelassen werden*. To hell mit what was. *Vorwärts! Aber wohin?*" he said with a weltschmerz droop in his voice.

"Schraudolf Strasse. The number is...."

"I know dat. I mean was, what is the Americaning human bing planning over de national, de trans-human, de metaphysical destinies of de land?"

"If you don't mind—" I hesitated, fearful I had used the wrong word again—"mind"—to a German philosopher.

"Aha!"

"Of course. Yes. You are right."

"Right! Always de mind! De Don't Mind must make rum for de Do Mind."

"It is possible for you to go a little faster, for God's sake?"

"Yes. De time is gecoming. God's word, like always and shtill dotay, I mean, today, is to us gecoming for...."

"Shut up a minute, will you? I want to go to the Schraudolf Strasse and no place else. I want to...."

"Och," he said and jammed on the brakes. He stopped on a pfennig. "I have driven past it from de interesting discussioning. *Augenblick mahl*," and then he hastily made a U-turn which glued me abruptly into the opposite corner of my seat.

He drove back on the same street we had come up—it was Schraudolf Strasse—and when I had loosened myself out of the corner he jammed on the brakes again.

"We are here."

I did not say a word. I was afraid of what he might do with it.

I got money out and he told me how much he wanted. I gave it to him in silence and started to get out of the car.

"You don't live here," he said.

"No."

"I wait for you."

"No, thank you."

"You have to the hotel to go again later, no?"

"No!"

"Aha!" And then he laughed like a comrade. "In de morning perhaps? What time?"

"Go away! Good-bye!" And I left the cab.

"Good luck, *Kamerad!*" he called after me. "But if not, in one hour I come to see, yes?"

"No!" And I went into the apartment building.

It was new, full of glass bricks and exposed structural steel. I had read that it is a sign of honesty to build that way, to leave the bones of the structure exposed. I had also read that this is beautiful. It was not, in this instance. It was only new. I got into an elevator which was almost all glass, clear glass, so that you could see everything that went on and went by. The cage was very small. I let the door hiss shut and had my choice of claustrophobia or vertigo.

On the third floor I got out. The foyer was all concrete which had been left the color of concrete, and there were three doors, painted black. Little white cards in little chrome frames said who lived where. Only the Freiherr's card was not standard size. It was large, which was understandable in view of his name. I read that here aboded Freiherr Dieter Heinz-August von Tilwitz and Schroff. The card frame seemed silver and was ornately crafted in the Chippendale manner. I looked at the name once more and then at the bell. Good luck, *Kamerad*....

What had I expected, a bugle call? A roll of drums? I heard nothing. I waited and heard nothing. This rather angered than discouraged me. I rang again and then several times more.

"*Wer ist da!*" She was angry too. I recognized the metallic voice of the old maid sister—I had now decided it was an old maid sister—and then I heard her say it again. The second time a bugle call would have sounded prettier.

But I was cagey now. I did not say a word but rang the bell again—the soundless button, rather—and counted on outrage and curiosity. The door flew open.

I had been wrong about the old maid sister. She was beautiful in a rather terrifying way, not because she looked so angry, but because she looked like the idealized image of an Aryan, in the Nazi sense. I had the objective thought that she had perhaps been scientifically bred in one of those mating camps the Germans had established. But attractive as she was, you felt she would never need a chastity belt. A flick of the corner of her mouth and the man would shrivel with shame. A look from those stone-still eyes and needles would pierce his heart. She tried to do it to me, though no foul play was intended, and she was a success.

"*Also, was stellen Sie sick denn vor, hier so die Klingel zu leuten? Antworten Sie!*"

I went mostly by the voice. It said, Where in hell do you come off raising hell with the bell. But what really jabbed me were her last two words: Answer! And it would be my last, useless chance before sentence was pronounced.

"Miss von Tilwitz?" I can be fairly cold too and the question I asked clearly meant that I damn well wasn't going to speak to just anyone. I think my tone surprised her.

"Yes...." One of her eyebrows went up.

"I called you earlier in regard to Mister Lobbe's Vermeer."

But now she had her accustomed manner back.

"And I told you at that time, Mister deWitt...."

"I know what you told me. That's why I'm here."

"It is after ten o'clock in the evening, Mister deWitt." She kept using my name as if it were a dirty word.

"And, may I point out," I said with a studied court-room manner, "that I have thus far come alone, without official assistance, so to speak."

She responded to that. She responded to that just fine. There is an old adage you hear in army circles which goes: "Those who are to be worthy of command must first learn to obey." To the extent that this makes a fetish of commanding and obeying it's sheer crap to me. But it's really worse than that. It also exonerates those who obey from fear and therefore command out of vengeance. And now I had my Fräulein pegged because she looked respectful, with just that mere touch of fear.

"Yes?" she said and at this point it sounded like: "Command me and I shall follow."

"Thank you," I said and walked through the door.

She was sufficiently unnerved for the time being to simply step aside and then close the door behind me. There was just dim light coming from the frosted glass in the black front door and she did not turn on any other light. It was a thrifty habit. She went past me, down a very dark corridor, and she opened a door farther on. There was light now. I followed her into the room.

It was not small, but it was so full of furniture that I felt deprived of air. The decor had nothing in common with the steel and glass affectations of the building. Here was old wealth, old care and craft which had been preserved from some other time. But it did not fit and it had no room. Six high-backed chairs with large, protective armrests stood almost shoulder to shoulder around a dwarfed table which was not part of the set. There was a chaise longue whose headrest curved around a mahogany ornament like a gigantic ram's horn. There were as many as three desks—a Duncan Phyfe, an Empire, and a very old hand-painted job with little doors and many faint angels and saints everywhere. I could not grasp much more than that. All this had been in a much larger place, uncrowded, without the mixing of periods, and rich. They had brought only what they could, in great haste, perhaps the best or the most cherished pieces. But now there were only pieces, like a broken crock, and perhaps the pieces should best have been thrown away.

I heard her close the door behind me and then nothing. In the silence she might have sensed some of my feelings.

"This is temporary," she said. She was hostess now, and somewhat defensive. "When we had to leave the Tilwitz *Gut* there was not much time."

"I don't know what *Gut* means."

"Estate, I think. Our family has—I mean, had been there a very long time."

I made a guess. "East Prussia?"

"Yes. Near Schroff. We left when the Russians were only ten kilometers away. They came fast." She looked at one of the windows which gave her nothing but a black reflection. "I understand they shot all the horses," she said absently. "And ate them...."

She had suddenly become a human being. I sat down carefully on a petit-point chair which also did not belong anywhere in this room.

"But excuse me," she said abruptly. "May I offer you something? A glass of wine?"

"I would be delighted."

I felt rather courtly. The beautiful woman with the improbably perfect face stood by an oaken closet with carved Gothic lines and behind her, on the wall, hung two aged portraits, dim except for highlights on a helmet, a nose, and two golden epaulettes. It was this kind of tableau which gave her meaning. Not at the door of a modern apartment, not by a glass window which looked out on a severely straight street, but as the young chatelaine in some ancestral palace with a view of deep woods, with cool stone walls made warm with tapestries. She was Sigismunde waiting alone and the Crusade was almost over....

She brought out a slim bottle and a glass with a very long stem. I was not certain, but I thought the shape meant I would get a white wine. I hoped it would not be sweet.

"A simple Moselle," she said. "But my father says that it has a lovely bouquet."

"I drink alone?"

"I don't drink; please don't hesitate."

"Miss von Tilwitz," I said after she had sat down in one of the big chairs at the small table. "You remarked on the phone...."

"It was my way of avoiding any discussion of the matter with someone I do not know," she said.

It was time for credentials, of course, but I thought it would be much more proper if her father were there. I pulled out my envelope and took papers out.

"I will identify myself, Miss von Tilwitz, but would it be possible for your father to be present?"

I had been too familiar. I was a boor. She did the small flick with the mouth, a dart of disdain, and said, while she folded her hands, "General von Tilwitz cannot be present. You gave no advance notice, if you recall."

"Of course. I realize it is very late...."

"He is not asleep. He is at a meeting."

Of course. They go to meetings. They go to putsch halls or beer cellars or whatever you call them and have meetings. I had peevish visions of the old Junker as figurehead of some rowdy new clique, their brutal speeches all larded with mysticism. I became fairly businesslike.

"Well then, if you will look these authorizations over, please, you might then show me the painting."

She did not answer. She took the letters of identification and authorization and specification or what have you and read every damn one of them without a word. I sipped wine and looked around the packed room. There were paintings, I don't know by whom, but there was nothing that would pass for a *bordelje* of a cheerful girl with a basket of green apples. There were white chargers and black chargers rearing, with martial men on them who could not possibly fall off. There were glowering family heads, fit to inspire old ghost stories. There were fairy-tale landscapes. I put my glass down and watched her read for a moment. If she knew I was watching her, she gave no sign.

"You have the painting...." I let it hang in the silence.

"Yes and no," she said, and kept reading.

"*What did you say?*"

Of course, she had to look up now. I had not shouted but I had flung the words right across the table at her.

"The painting is not here, Mister deWitt. We keep it in a safe place."

It was a most reasonable thing to say and to have done. I felt somewhat foolish and wished I were not so unpredictably jumpy on this simple job. But for my speculations, it was still a simple job.

"We kept the Vermeer here, of course, until quite recently," she said.

"I see."

"Until two days ago, actually."

She put the papers down either because she was finished identifying me and checking me out, or because there was reason to interrupt.

"I thought you knew," she said, and looked at me. "But apparently you do not."

"Do not what?" and I swallowed the "godammit" which wanted out next.

"There was an attempted theft."

I sat very still.

"We were then advised to move the painting."

"Where did you take it?"

"The Pinakothek." She folded the papers and stacked them together.

"Miss von Tilwitz."

"Yes?"

"Which Pinakothek?"

"The Alte Pinakothek, of course."

"Of course," I said. "The Alte."

Which is how my job came to look sticky for real.

CHAPTER 7

There was really no point in staying. It was eleven p.m. and her father, she said, rarely came back from his meeting before one o'clock. And the Vermeer was safe—she said.

"Ah yes. Those political meetings." I don't know what possessed me, aside from a new access of peevishness.

"It is a chess club," she said.

We walked out into the dark hall and to the dark foyer. "Of course. Chess club," I said. "Not a meeting at all. Wrong English usage."

"Not really." She opened the door which led out of the apartment. "They do not necessarily play chess. They have lectures on chess."

On that variation of Baumeister's joke, I was dismissed. I did not like being reminded of Baumeister.

My philosophical taxi driver was waiting for me. I will not speak of the ride, and I will most emphatically not report the conversation. Of course, there was conversation. He also drove past the Vier Jahreszeiten on account of the conversation. This time the hub of his metaphysic was not Mind (I had naturally resolved not to mention the word in any context whatsoever) but Love, in deference to the blasted hopes of my assignation on Schraudolf Strasse. Why else, according to my driver, was I back after one hour instead of having roiled there in bed all night? The man was maddening, but as I said, I won't go into it.

I slept a reasonably sleeplike sleep until seven o'clock in the morning after lying in bed until one a.m., when I'd phoned down for my first nightcap. I'd had three more before falling asleep.

I had arranged with Fraulein von Tilwitz to meet her father at eight-thirty that morning. She had told me that the Herr General always began his day at eight.

My driver was the philosopher of the previous night.

He discussed the Love of Mind and the Mind of Love. He did not, however, overshoot the address on Schraudolf Strasse. This may well have been due to the fact that I did not utter one single word during the trip.

I pressed the soundless bell button under the Chippendale frame of the Freiherr's name; the Freiherr's daughter answered, looking exactly as she had looked the night before, and had always looked, I imagined. And then there was no point in going in.

"I must apologize for my father," she said, "but he went riding."

Her distress was not apparent so much in the tone of her apology, as in the fact that she had referred to him as her father. She was distressed enough to forget that she was talking to the lout for whom, eternally, her father must be the General Freiherr von Tilwitz. I, in contrast, became immediately formal.

"May I ask, Miss von Tilwitz, why a formal appointment of some moment, and I mean this both in the official sense and as a matter of personal promise, has been broken for the sake of a horse?"

She was not equipped to handle this kind of address, which combined formal severity and informal lunacy. It made her frank.

"He—I apologize—he forgets. The distress is mine—what I mean is...."

"Please do not feel responsible," I said. "Where is he?"

She was glad to change the subject. She told me that he was riding in the Englischer Garten, a park with a lake and trails and a brook, and with a coffeehouse as well as the Haus der Kunst. The latter was a museum. This only made me more anxious.

"If there is any regularity to his—uh—schedule, could you tell me where I might find him in the park?"

She told me and sent me on my way with specific instructions which included a description of the Freiherr on his horse and of his retainer—attendant, now that the estate was gone—jogging along on foot.

"Englischer Garten. Boat house. *Schnell.*"

The snap of the last word, "hurry up," uttered in German, catapulted my driver on his way. Several times I could hear him mumble my instructions, which gave me concern. He was turning the thing over and over in his head to find a cue to discourse. But he had been outfoxed. There was nothing he could make anything out of. He devoted himself to driving. From the utility of new streets we passed to the charm of old ones which looked lived in and loved in and not very efficient. We crossed a part of Schwabing, Munich's Greenwich Village. And then we drove into the park.

I got out near the boat house, leaving my driver to chew on two words: "Wait. Good-bye."

The woods were lovely. There was a lake, liquid green under the trees, and slow rowboats moving, and ducks. Green is a cool color and all the green seemed to make the air cool too. Even the morning sun made coolness. I walked down a path with old leaves crackling underfoot and came to the first sign. It asked one in a gentle, most engaging way not to molest the ducks, lest they leave the lake and deprive us of an idyllic pleasure. I thought this was lovely.

I walked round the rim of the lake till I came to a bridge. It was a small wooden bridge with dark-looking foliage beyond it, and if Little Red Riding Hood had passed me now I would not have been surprised. Ducks drifted out from under the bridge and made hardly a ripple in the green water.

I found the bridle path, a dark alley under the trees, smelling loamy. One moment it was empty, the next I was almost killed by a cavalry charge of three. It was led by a man in his fifties who wore lederhosen and had big, chunky legs. They were heavy enough to squeeze the breath out of his horse. He was followed by what might have been his children, also lederhosened, towheaded and happy. All three were singing.

After this thunder came silence, and then I saw my Freiherr.

There is an old steel print of fine detail which shows, appearing over the rise of a barren landscape, with the sun behind, Don Quixote astride the tall bones of a horse and fat Sancho Panza on a donkey so low that he seems to be walking on foot.

What I saw now reminded me of it, though some of the proportions were different. Panza was really walking and did not have a donkey and he was less fat than muscular. He had a bull neck and a face like a carved potato. My general's horse was not a scaffolding of bones, but a long-legged Arabian, white, faintly dappled. The general himself looked rather small on top. He gave an impression of frailty. His servant had one hand on the side of the horse and he might have been holding the general up. I don't know. As they came closer, at a dreamy walk, the hand dropped and the general sat up there without help.

I stepped into the middle of the bridle path, my feet feeling heavy with the loam on my shoes, and like an Indian emerging suddenly out of the wilderness, raised my hand.

"*Verzeihung.*" I felt a little awkward, what with this mixture of Indian sign and polite German.

I noticed that it was the retainer who bridled the horse by the snaffle, close under the horse's chin.

I walked up and had a good look at General Freiherr Dieter Heinz-August von Tilwitz und Schroff. He was frail. His riding habit was immaculate. It existed all by itself and did not seem to belong to him. He looked as if wasted by a disease. His skin had a dry papery quality which suggested an arrested aging, a preserved condition. He wore a silly mountaineer's hat with an *Auerhahn* feather and a monocle which was very much part of his thin, severe face. A short bristle mustache emphasized his long upper lip and the wide, slitlike mouth. The eyes were like his daughter's, blue, steady, but with a quality of deep dreaminess.

"Freiherr von Tilwitz?" I said.

"*Jawohl. Wer sind Sie?*"

His voice was as impersonal as the color gray, and I was a prisoner at the front, brought in for questioning from across the line. I set out to correct that situation immediately.

"My name is Mister deWitt," I continued in English, "representing Mister Lobbe of Lobbe Industriel, SA. I had an appointment with you, arranged for half an hour ago this morning."

"By whose authority?" he said, without changing his voice.

"Miss von Tilwitz."

Von Tilwitz touched his hat, the tip of his nose, the bristle on his upper lip. The gestures were tense and the face was severe.

"Ah, Ingeborg...." he said with a voice as soft as velvet.

Then he was silent. He was looking at something else, I don't know what, and I did not know what to do or think.

"Stefan," said the general without transition, "*le grand cours, s'il vous plâit.*"

I doubt whether Stefan, the servant with the face like a potato, understood French. Instead, there seemed to be a set of riding trips that could be performed in this park, and each had a signal and this one happened to be in French. They set out on *le grand cours*. Stefan held the snaffle; the general held the curb. The horse started nodding and hoofed delicately through the mud of the path.

"Herr von Tilwitz," I said (the omission of "General" intended), and ran after the long-legged horse. "You are forgetting that you and I have an appointment. Your daughter distinctly arranged—"

I stopped talking when he stopped the horse. He turned in the saddle and for a moment I thought he would say "Ingeborg" again, but he didn't.

"Thank you for reminding me, Mister deWitt. My memory is not at its best since the wound. Stefan? *Runter lassen.*"

Stefan stepped to the side of the horse, folded his hands one into the other, and held his palms like a cradle. Von Tilwitz took his left foot out of the stirrup and stepped into the cradle. Then he swung his right leg smartly over the horse and descended straight-legged to the ground as Stefan bent low.

It was the first time I had seen von Tilwitz stand at full height. He was a doll, a small replica of a full-sized man, delicately boned but straight and self-possessed.

"*Meine Blume*, Stefan." He held out his hand.

Stefan reached into a large pocket and very delicately pulled out a flower wrapped in thin paper. He peeled the paper off and there was a white rose.

"*Danke*," said von Tilwitz and held the rose in front of him with two fingers, stem straight up and down, blossom an inch or so under the nose. "Marvelous for my headaches," he said in English. "Let us sit on that bench."

We went to the bench and sat down. I went right to the business for which I had come.

"The Vermeer," I said, "is at present at the Alte Pinakothek, Herr General. I have credentials here which cover the immediate transfer of the painting from you to me, directly. However, since the painting is not in your physical possession at the moment, your presence will be required to effect transfer of the object from the Pinakothek to me. I would therefore request...."

"Can't do that," he said, looking straight ahead.

"May I point out, Herr von Tilwitz, that the ownership of the painting has been officially established and that...."

"The matter goes through Bonn, as I understand it. Am I correct?"

Now Lobbe's boy had to go to work. No more preliminaries such as flying there, making phone calls and setting the scene with a small stack of documents. All that was done and now came the work.

"You have been cooperative, Herr von Tilwitz. You have undoubtedly undergone hardships both of sentiment and of a practical nature in regard to the loss of the Vermeer. If we—Herr Lobbe and myself—can in any way compensate...."

"Yes," he said to the green distance under the trees, "the loss has been hard. But I will have to bear it alone, Ingeborg."

"I beg your pardon?"

He turned his head and let me see his rather incredible eyes, the softness and the youngness in them, which didn't match the rest of his face.

"*Verzeihung*, Herr deWitt. My head. However, I have heard everything you have said."

He took off his Alpine hat and put it next to him on the bench. Under the thin hair, which was surprisingly long and quite white, ran an ear-to-ear scar over the top of his head. It was so deeply indented, so sharply defined, that I had to wonder whether more than skin held the two halves of the skull together. He inhaled his rose.

"It is not a very honorable scar," he said into the flower. "Have you been in the war, Herr deWitt?"

"Yes. Herr von Tilwitz, may I return to the object...."

"I am about to tell you about the object. The picture was Goering's, you may know."

"I have been under the firm impression that the picture was and is Herr Lobbe's."

"What do we ever own?" he shrugged. "Let us say, Herr deWitt, that Goering felt he owned the Vermeer, though even he, who possessed more than any of us, did not really—do I digress?"

"Yes, sir."

"You must remind me. Well, by some idiotic happenstance, the crated picture went to the Eastern front with a consignment of staff material for von Bok. He is now a defector, but he was always a cultured man. He sent the picture back and Goering sent me to pick it up. We were close. Remarkable man."

"You digress, Herr von Tilwitz. As a matter of fact, it is much more to the point now for us to discuss...."

"But the canvas is still in Russia, Ingeborg. Listen. Will you listen?"

"Of course." I was afraid to say anything else.

"I picked it up at an estate on the East Polish border, an estate which was used for a prisoner depot. Not camp. Depot. The sound of small-arms fire was almost continuous."

"Herr General—"

"You don't understand? I'll explain this to you. To feed thousands and thousands of Russians was, of course, out of the question. We shot them in honorable fashion, *coup de grace* through the back of the neck. My second morning—I was waiting for transportation—no rifle fire, nothing. We could no longer afford the ammunition. That morning I received my scar."

"I understand." It was the wrong thing to say. It drove him into further detail.

"While taking my constitutional at six o'clock on that silent morning, I heard a buzzing. I followed the sound idly, from garden through orchard to the farming and service sheds. There, in the yard, was a buzz saw running. On one side of it lay a pile of heads; on the other lay the headless bodies. It took only two men to guide the prisoner through the saw. Of course, there were more guards to contain the line of those who were waiting."

"Why are you telling me this revolting story, may I ask? I must insist, Herr von Tilwitz, that we return to the business at hand."

"But this will explain how I came into possession of the Vermeer. This will show you, Herr deWitt, how I really paid for it. I really paid for it, and you seem to ignore that in your cold-blooded way, sir."

"I was not aware...."

"Listen, Ingeborg. I stepped closer with no design to taunt or arouse the unfortunates. Their fate was decided and sealed, and as a soldier you accept that, you respect the prisoner, you do not taunt him. They misunderstood me. I simply stood there to see how the thing worked. Perhaps my uniform made them excited. I was—in your order of rank—a brigadier general at the time. Well, they broke. Riot. Screams. Shots, of course, and then I was hoisted into the air, manhandled, and next, the wind of the spinning blade blew into my face." He paused, but there was nothing for me to say. He wanted to finish his story. "I was rescued."

"I see that."

"Remarkable thing to me, Mr. deWitt, I was conscious throughout. No providence spared me the details. I really paid."

"What?"

"When discharged from the hospital, the Vermeer was among my effects. The war was over by then and Goering was dead. You understand now, I'm sure, why I have loved the Vermeer ever since."

I understood nothing of the sort. I understood only that this maimed old man would not be easy to handle.

CHAPTER 8

Von Tilwitz had talked himself out. He seemed to be under the strange impression that we had settled something in regard to the Vermeer. Alluding to the briskness of his ride and the freshness of the morning, he now said that he must go home and eat.

Let him go home, I thought, watching him get up. I'll go home with him, and perhaps make some headway with the help of his daughter.

My taxi easily caught up with the black, very upright vehicle, a vintage Daimler, which was the general's conveyance. Stefan was driving slowly and von Tilwitz looked like practically nothing in the big rear seat. My own driver was, curiously, silent.

At the elevator, we took turns, since it would not hold three of us. The general went first (two of him might have fit), then Stefan, then I went up.

When I reached the landing, the door to von Tilwitz's apartment stood open. Stefan was waiting for me.

"While Fraulein von Tilwitz attends the general," he told me in German, "you are most courteously asked to wait in the salon."

That's normally polite German. I nodded and Stefan led the way to the room in which I had been once before. Daylight did not alter the impression of last night. In fact, the dense clutter of furniture and ornaments kept me from seeing the other man right away. Stefan had closed the door; I wound my way to the window in order to look down to the street, and then I heard the conventional, polite cough.

I turned, eyeballs swiveling, and then someone rose from a Biedermeier love seat I did not remember having seen before, and bowed.

He was youngish, bland, with mouse-brown hair that hung straight. I could not have described his clothes nor his face five minutes afterward, and his voice was colorless too.

"*Verzeihung.*"

"*Angenehm.*"

He bowed and I heard a faint click. New generation, old school. We both meandered past things which were in the way and reached the safety of the little round table with the big, carved chairs. We sat down sort of facing each other, and then there was silence.

He took out a cigarette. I looked at the papers which Lobbe had sent me. I had nothing to do for the moment and thought of Sir Evelyn in Tangier....

The man had knocked the first half-centimeter of ashes into a little delft dish which was not an ashtray when Miss von Tilwitz came into the room. Her uncluttered perfection was as fascinating as ever. And as forbidding.

She immediately introduced us. "Mister deWitt is a representative from

Lobbe Industriel, Paris." She made no reference to my business in Munich. "And Mister Spinn represents the Office of War Damages and Restitutions, Fremdamt, West German Republic, Bonn."

Spinn and I did not shake hands; we just bowed. He clicked again and pulled a big brown leather folder out from under his jacket.

"My credentials," he said. His credentials told, first, who he was, then what his particular bureaucratic calling in the governmental labyrinth was. Next, who had sent him to Munich, why he had been sent to Munich, how he was to conduct himself in Munich, and when all of this was to take place. I will not describe all of his papers. There were many more, but they all added up to one thing. He was in Munich to take the Vermeer away from me and to make life miserable for me in every official way.

"If you are finished," said Spinn while he watched me put his big folder down, "we can discuss the exact steps of the authentication and transfer procedure which will restore the Vermeer to its owner." He coughed, the sound dry and meaningless. "That is, Herr deWitt, after I have seen your credentials, please."

"Of course."

I got out my envelope and selected the documents fit for his eyes. It was out of the question, naturally, to let him see Lobbe's letter which authorized von Tilwitz to transfer the painting directly to me. While I was rummaging, I asked, "How did you happen to know, Mister Spinn, that I would be here?"

"I didn't, Mister deWitt. I came for the picture in my official capacity, and was then introduced to you as representing the Lobbe interest."

Quick thinking for a bureaucrat. I took note and decided to watch my man closely. He took the documents I handed him and flipped through them once as if counting them. The first glance told him that they did not compare in any way whatsoever to his own mighty credentials.

I said, "Before we discuss the transfer of the painting, Mister Spinn, it will be necessary for me to discuss this entire Vermeer situation with Freiherr von Tilwitz. I say this so that you will not feel you have to rush ahead with your job."

He looked up from the papers, examined my face as if for a blemish, and said, "Why?"

"There are details of the recovery which are important to my employer. I need to search out the Freiherr's memory in that regard." Which was as fine a bit of shyster talk as I had ever achieved. To Spinn it was to mean that I wanted details on how von Tilwtiz had got hold of the picture. To me it meant that I had to discuss how in the name of heaven von Tilwitz was going to help me recover the painting before Spinn got his hands on it. That was the form my instructions had taken now. I had no idea why

Lobbe wanted to avoid a Bonn inspection, but want to avoid it he did—explicitly.

Miss von Tilwitz had been sitting quietly in the Biedermeier love seat. She got up now, and so did Spinn and I.

"Please continue," she said. "I will see when the Freiherr might be free."

After Miss von Tilwitz had shut the door behind her, Spinn looked at me with his bland stare.

"Where is it?"

"Pardon?"

"Excuse me. We were discussing the picture."

"Of course. The picture isn't here."

"I know that, Mister deWitt."

"There was an attempted theft and...."

"I know that too, Mister deWitt."

"You do?"

"Miss von Tilwitz told me just before you and the Freiherr returned."

"Tell me about it. I don't know the details."

"It seems someone broke into the adjoining apartment, which bears no name over the bell, but just a blank card. There were three pictures on the walls there, two of which were mutilated in one corner as a result of an alcohol application. This was presumably done in an attempt to ascertain if the Vermeer had been disguised by overpaint. Both pictures were the approximate size of the 'Apple Girl.' The third picture was not."

The deduction was very much to the point. There seemed hardly any doubt that someone had been after the Vermeer.

"Nothing was taken?" I asked.

"Nothing. There was some damage due to hasty searching, but that is all."

"You found out an awful lot in a very short period of time, Mister Spinn."

He did not take it as a compliment. "That is my business, Mister deWitt."

I thought of von Tilwitz chomping his way through an East Prussian breakfast in another room. I tried to think of some topic to distract Spinn further from his purpose. But he was already back on the track.

"I don't think you answered me, Mister deWitt. My question was, where is the painting?"

"I'm sure that the insurance company involved can give you that information."

"They are not here."

"Didn't Miss von Tilwitz tell you? I only suggest Miss von Tilwitz because I, myself, am not sure where the painting is."

"She didn't mention a place in the course of our rather brief discussion. She only mentioned a name."

"Name?"

"A curator's name, the official charged with the safekeeping of the painting, since the attempt."

"Mention his name, Mister Spinn."

"Kasper Kraut, Mister deWitt."

"Not familiar. I just got here myself, you know."

"I know, Mister deWitt."

"Only curator I know is called Baumeister," I said.

And then I sat very still. Hagridden as I was with suspicion, it was time to let the hag ride again. Baumeister was still a potential art thief to me, and now I tried to include Spinn too. I had no doubt that Baumeister was a legitimate art appraiser and I had no doubt that Spinn was an official from Bonn. But my coincidental reading about the theft and forgery ring spoke of members who were highly placed. And why overlook a wrinkle? An attempt to steal the Vermeer had already been made, and apparently by men who knew their business. All this had happened in Munich just a matter of days ago, and both Spinn and Baumeister had shown up in the town about that same time. Besides, what had cued me was the surprising amount of information Spinn had of the attempt, all gathered, so he had implied, in the briefest span of time, after meeting Miss von Tilwitz. Yet he had not learned from her where the Vermeer was at the moment, which, from an official view, would be a much more relevant point of inquiry.

I watched him with a look I had learned in law school. It is designed to shake up the hapless witness. But I have no courtroom experience and Spinn was not hapless. For a while he said nothing, then he stared back at me.

"Yes, Mister deWitt. I know of Dr. Baumeister."

"You do?" I did not know what else to say.

"In my line of work I know of several highly placed appraisers."

And that would hold true if his line of work was what his credentials said it was or if it was thievery.

"Do you know where Dr. Baumeister is now? I ask because I met him recently in Paris and then lost touch with him."

"I assume he is here in Munich, Mister deWitt."

"I know he is in Munich, Mister Spinn. But where?"

"I assume he is at his place of work, Mister deWitt."

"Impossible."

"*Wie bitte?*"

"Impossible. He has just been arrested."

If Spinn already knew of the arrest, then it was almost certain that both men belonged to the same gang. If Spinn did not know of the arrest, then it would be very much more plausible that he was simply a bona fide official who had just arrived from Bonn.

His reaction was interesting. He showed no concern about my announcement and I don't think he was acting. He said the most natural thing for someone discussing a matter of slight importance.

"I would not have thought it of Dr. Baumeister. What was he arrested for?"

"I don't know."

"It does not sound plausible, Mister deWitt. Perhaps you are mistaken."

"Not mistaken. I witnessed the arrest myself."

"Indeed," said Spinn and shook his head slightly.

If he was acting, the performance was superb, because with Baumeister as an arrested gang member Spinn's own safety in Munich was seriously at stake.

He glanced at my papers which he was still holding in his hand and then he shook his bead again.

"I don't know Dr. Baumeister personally, but only by reputation, and that reputation, Mister deWitt, does not fit any cause for arrest whatsoever." Then he began to read my credentials in all seriousness.

It was time to shake him up. It was time to speculate less and to do more. There was a telephone on top of a Gothic-looking chest, a telephone of the type made into lamp bases like the one in Lobbe's Paris apartment. But this phone was wired. I picked up the receiver and asked Spinn how to dial information. When a man's voice came on, I asked how to reach the Alte Pinakothek. I dialed the six-digit number fast before I forgot it. An elderly voice answered almost immediately and said that this was the Alte Pinakothek.

"Please connect me with the office of Dr. Baumeister," I said.

"*Danke. Sofort.*"

I waited while things hummed and clicked. I wanted to get the kind of confirmation which might really shake up the mysterious Spinn, once I got my connection and once I put Spinn himself on the phone.

"*Ja bitte?*" said the man's voice.

"I would like to speak to Dr. Baumeister, please."

"Ach! Even in your bad German I recognize your voice, Mister deWittser, I mean, deWitt, sir! How nice of you to call me!"

"Ak—" I said, or something idiotic like that.

"I did not know where to reach you," said Baumeister. The voice, speaking English for my benefit, was unmistakably his. "I left the airport rather—uh—officially, you know, and had not time or thought to exchange addresses with you."

I recovered—it is easier on the phone than face to face—and took him up on the last point.

"I know," I said. "I was worried about you, seeing your—what shall I call it—arrest?"

"Arrest?"

"The policemen and so forth."

"That was no arrest, my dear friend," and he laughed his sudden, high laugh. "I was carrying a precious little *objet de vertu*, a tiny porcelain statue on a golden base, made by an unknown for Madame de Pompadour. It had been on loan, you know, for a Paris exhibit. The police were for protection. I will show you the little treasure. Ah, such a little delight! But anyway, Mister deWitt, it was sweet of you to worry."

I wanted to ask him something else, something to impose on our friendship and to get me out of Munich, but Spinn was in the room. I was anxious to hang up. I did not think that my worry had been sweet at all and I did not enjoy my discovery of Baumeister's innocence as much as I might have. There was too much personal idiocy to be acknowledged in all this, which spoiled the relief I felt. But I did feel a measure of relief because Baumeister was now apparently innocent of any plots and connivings in regard to Lobbe's Vermeer. And with that same flush of relief I concluded that Spinn, too, was legitimate. Which still left me with the problem of getting rid of him.

CHAPTER 9

"He was there," said Spinn.

It was not a question and it required no answer. I put the phone down, feeling a dislike for Spinn. He sighed, stubbed out his most recent cigarette, and held my papers out to me.

"I am satisfied," he said and handed them to me. "We will now discuss, if you please—" He stopped when he heard the door open behind him.

"Freiherr von Tilwitz," said the Freiherr's daughter from the door, "is ready to see you."

Spinn got up immediately and turned to leave the room.

"Just a minute, please."

Spinn stopped out of sheer surprise at the tone of my voice. I had meant to stop him.

"My appointment is before yours, I believe," I said, and I went to stand by the door, perfectly willing to stuff Spinn back into the love seat by main force, if need be.

"Mister deWitt," said Spinn, "in my official capacity...."

"You can wait," I finished for him. "I'm first."

He turned to Miss von Tilwitz, who looked her most withering. Spinn ignored it. I do not know how.

"Miss von Tilwitz, your guest, Mister deWitt, being a foreigner"—and he got fairly icy himself at this point—"does not seem familiar with the customary demeanor when official steps are involved. I would therefore ask you...."

"The general asked to see Mister deWitt," she said, and the way she said it settled the matter.

I saw Spinn's face. The blandness slipped for one instant and I saw something swift and cruel. Then it was gone. And then Spinn did a peculiar thing. He said, without any transition, "Where is the Vermeer, Miss von Tilwitz?"

"At the Alte Pinakothek."

"Thank you," said Spinn, and he sat down on the love seat. I had the unreasonable impression that he was waiting for me to leave the room.

As I followed my hostess into the next room I had some fast, nervous thoughts about what to do next. There was some juggling to be done, which included getting Spinn out of the room with the phone, now that he knew where the "Apple Girl" actually was.

Again, there was too much furniture. It was heavy and dark and too busy with carving. I found the Freiherr. He seemed prostrate, which, in view of his breakfast session, was no surprise. He had changed from riding habit to tweeds, the very hairy and lumpy kind which need to be hung on a six-foot, two-hundred-pound frame. Lost in his suit, white face and veined hands visible, he sat, staring blankly, on a sofa covered in a wine red velour which the light from the window made hideous.

"Freiherr von Tilwitz?"

"Yes, yes. I am here, Ingeborg."

"No, sir. The name is deWitt."

"Of course."

He closed his eyes and I started to worry. A man with a drifting memory and with no interest in the present was about the worst partner I could find for any cooperative conniving.

"Mister von Tilwitz," I said, and the strain made my voice sharper than necessary, "it is imperative that I make a phone call immediately, but in the absence of Mister Spinn."

"I don't like him, deWitt. I don't like him at all."

That was fine with me. As a matter of fact, that was a break. He and I would now join in dislike for the man from Bonn.

"The point of the matter, Mister von Tilwitz, is that your phone is in the next room, and Mister Spinn is in that same next room."

"I recognize his accent, don't you see. I'm sure he speaks Polish."

"Uh—Freiherr von Tilwitz—"

"He is from the lake region, around Pisz. Even before we lost Ost Preussen they spoke Polish there, besides German."

"My point...."

"You have made it, Mister deWitt. I have made mine. Therefore, go into the next room, ask the man from Pisz to leave, and use the phone to your heart's content, Mister deWitt,"

"Most helpful of you, sir."

He had been no help at all, but I went to the next room in order to fetch his daughter. I could not throw Spinn out, but she could, once her father had told her so.

She was in the next room. Spinn was not.

"You came for Mister Spinn?" she said. She put a magazine down and looked at me as if she knew everything.

"Yes, in a manner of speaking."

"He left."

"He left, did you say?"

"On official business which could no longer wait."

"Did he explain, Miss von Tilwitz?"

"Those were his words. And that he will be in touch."

I did a dim-witted thing but it was the only concrete step that occurred to me under the rush of my fears. I went to the window, opened one side, and leaned out to look down at my taxi. I wished I had bothered to find out the name of my cabby—it was suddenly very important to be able to call him by name—but even namelessly I had to call him but fast. Feeling conspicuously like a fool, I simply yelled down, "Hey, you there with the taxi!" I yelled that three times before a kid who was rolling a hoop down the street stopped, heard me, and then without being asked, went up to the taxi and leaned into the window.

My cabby scrambled out of his car and looked up.

"I was asleep!" he yelled up.

And I yelled down, "Ask the man that comes out where he would like to go! Understand?"

"Yes!"

"And then don't take him! Understand?"

"No!"

"Do it anyway!"

"Yes!"

Spoken like a soldier, but then he showed that he was alert. He shook his head at me and looked away, down the street. Next, I saw Spinn come out.

It was a likely assumption that he was in a hurry, that as a visiting minor official he would not have his own car, that, therefore, he would walk up to the first cab that presented itself. Which he did. While he talked to my cabby and while my cabby was talking to him, I pulled back from the window and waited.

"Why did you ask the taxi not to take Mister Spinn?" Miss von Tilwitz wanted to know.

I gave her half of the answer. "Because I will need it myself."

I leaned out the window again and saw Spinn wave his arms with animation. It was not typical of him but he did it just the same. I imagined his stress. Then I heard my cabby's voice, loud and angry.

"*Saupreiss!*"

This was all he said, and Spinn stopped windmilling. He stood stock still, then turned and walked away.

"Did you hear that loud word, Miss von Tilwitz?"

"Yes. Unfortunately." She did not look up from her magazine.

"I wonder what it means."

I now learned that this unbearable woman was also a true lady because she answered me without losing face.

"The word *Preiss* is simple vulgar Bavarian for the word *Preusse*, or Prussian, in your language. The use of the word *Sau*, which actually means a female pig, becomes a most vulgar addition in this form of address and, you must now have gathered, the whole thing is insulting in the extreme."

"I'm sorry I asked."

"Bavarians are jealous people," she said as if that explained anything.

"My taxi driver said it to Spinn."

"Bavarians are stupid also. Spinn is not even a Prussian."

"Oh?"

"If you knew—if the driver knew our language better, he could have told by Mister Spinn's intonation. Mister Spinn seems to be from East Prussia but the language at his home was undoubtedly, at least part of the time, Polish."

My Freiherr, it seemed, did know some of the time what he was talking about.

I leaned out of the window to check how far Spinn had gone down the street. I saw him turn the corner. My cabby was watching too. When Spinn had disappeared, the cabby looked up.

"Where to?" I yelled down.

"Die Alte Pinakothek!"

And that, as expected, was that.

I closed the window and felt suddenly very fast and efficient. It was time.

"Miss von Tilwitz, may I use your phone?"

She nodded, got up, and left the room. She had manners.

I went through the routine with information again, got the museum number and asked for Baumeister, urgent. Someone on his office extension came on almost immediately and said something which I did not understand.

"My name is deWitt," I said. "I must speak to Dr. Baumeister immediately, please."

Again the voice, as if from Outer Mongolia, and the connection was faulty. I was going out of my mind.

"DeWitt to speak to Dr. Baumeister, *aber sofort!*" I yelled.

"Yes, my friend, yes! I hear you very good. This is Baumeister."

"Dr. Baumeister, I'm so glad you're on. Before you came on...."

"That was me."

"What?"

"I was eating."

"You were eating," I repeated.

"The phone from the desk called and said it was you and I had a Weisswurst in my mouth, you understand."

No, I didn't. Not a thing.

"Anyway, it is swallowed. You sound—what is the word—*ängstlich*—"

"Whatever it is, yes. Dr. Baumeister, I need an immediate and most important favor. I'm calling for help, plain and simple."

"Ask."

I have had a friend in my life now and then, but I don't remember the relief and the sense of safety, ever, which Baumeister gave me with that simple word. And on top of that, I had to lie to him. I worked up to it slowly.

"You remember the 'Apple Girl,' Dr. Baumeister. We talked about that Vermeer on the plane."

"My friend deWitt, I have seen her! She is here, you know!"

"I know. Which is why I am calling you."

"Ask," he said again.

"There is a matter of theft here, Dr. Baumeister. A fairly serious matter of an attempt to steal the Vermeer."

"I know. I have been told of the attempt since I have come in this morning. Very wise to have the canvas put here. *Der Saupreiss* is not so stupid."

"Uh—yes. Dr. Baumeister."

"You sound so serious."

"It is. And I am. There is a man coming over to the Pinakothek—he is on his way now, Dr. Baumeister—and he presents himself as the Bonn official who is to handle the release of the Vermeer."

"Yes?"

"The man is an impostor."

"A what? I don't know the word."

"He *pretends* to be an official, Dr. Baumeister."

"A thief! Again!"

"I'm afraid so. The reason I am calling...."

"I will call the police instantly!"

"No!" I fairly yelled into the phone and the silence at the other end of the line seemed to mean that I had startled the old man. I talked very fast now, but tried to sound reasonable.

"Dr. Baumeister?"

"You don't want me to call the police," he said.

"Yes. Please don't. I will try and explain everything later, but at this point, Dr. Baumeister, would you simply do me a tremendous favor and bring the picture to me, here, at the apartment of Freiherr von Tilwitz—"

I stopped and there was silence at the other end. I was sweating blood.

"I have release papers and authorization to receive the picture. I have them right here with me, Dr. Baumeister. If the question of legality...."

"I will bring it," he said simply. "Give me the address."

I gave him the address and then we hung up.

CHAPTER 10

The problem was now to get von Tilwitz sufficiently organized to cooperate when the picture arrived. In absence of a written statement from Bonn, saying the "Apple Girl" has been duly restored to Hans Lobbe via his agent deWitt, it would be neat to get a similar statement from von Tilwitz. I might never need it, but then I hated to be without it in case any procedural question arose, as at the border. When I went back to the other room, von Tilwitz was asleep. I addressed him by rank and title but he kept on sleeping. I coughed. Then he coughed, but still went on sleeping. Then his daughter came in.

"The general is asleep," she said and gave me a fairly stern look.

"I am aware of that. I wish he would wake up."

"I'm sorry," she said, "but the general always sleeps at this time."

"Miss von Tilwitz," I said and took a long, patient breath. "I have made arrangements with the Pinakothek to have the Vermeer brought here to your house. One of the curators himself will bring it." I paused for effect. I, myself, thought that all this sounded rather good. "But as a matter of formality, Miss von Tilwitz, I require a statement of release from the general. For that reason, I would like him to wake up."

"I'd rather not," she said. "I'm sure the matter can wait."

The matter could decidedly not wait though I couldn't explain that to her.

"And besides," she went on, "Mister Spinn would have to be present."

"Mister Spinn has already been present. And he is also present at the Pinakothek at this very moment."

"He is?"

"He went there from here, I just learned. Will you therefore...."

"I would not advise the general to give you a release except in the presence of Mister Spinn."

"My dear young woman," I started to say when the general released a shuddering snore, smacked his lips, and said, "Ingeborg...." And continued sleeping.

She looked at her father with concern. I had only seen two expressions on her face before, the haughty one and the severe one. They had not enhanced her beauty. But quite suddenly now she looked soft and lovely. She looked as lovely as she would always look, if she were happier.

"Who is Ingeborg?"

Her face snapped back into a blankness that killed everything that had been there before.

"I ask," I said, "because he has addressed me by that name." A little bit of a personal assault, so to speak, might help at this point, was my notion.

"It was the name of my mother," she said. "Would you please leave the room now?"

"Was she as beautiful as you?"

"No. Much more so." She looked away. "With lights in her eyes...."

"He lost her?"

"Oh yes." She went to the door which led into the other room. "Would you mind...." She left it there and finished the sense of the sentence by opening the door. I nodded and went through. A little concession at this juncture might work miracles....

"It must have been tragic, to have shaken him to this day," I said when she had followed me.

"You needn't stand," she said, "while you wait for the curator."

My personal touch had improved nothing between us. I sat down at the too small table with the too large chairs and decided to wait no more than five minutes before waking von Tilwitz from his loving dream of his wife.

"I will tell you this."

I had not expected her to speak again and looked up at her where she stood by the table.

"I tell you this," she said, "so that you will not misunderstand my father, so that you will go away with respect for him, and perhaps with understanding. Also, it might explain to you, Mister deWitt, why I will not permit any undue demands to be placed upon him, or any pressures which require decisions."

"I'm listening, Miss von Tilwitz."

"When my father came back from the hospital—do you know about his head injury?"

"He told me that he had been injured in a prisoner-of-war riot in Poland."

"Yes. We lost track of him in those last days of the war and he did not come back to us until after the war was over. We had left East Prussia. We were living here. My mother and I." She looked around the room as if wondering where her mother might be. "You see how we lived, because we live the same way today. Cramped with old things which we no longer need...."

"Yes."

"And then he came back. Like any invalid."

"Do you mean that?"

"I don't know of a German family which does not have someone dead or crippled because of that war."

"And he came back, you said."

"Yes. Wanting his wife and his child, Mister deWitt. He came back for just that, just like any other man hurt in the war, and we were happy."

"You don't sound happy, Miss von Tilwitz."

"No. Not now."

She sat down at the table at this point and rested her elbows and folded her hands. She somehow looked like an executive at a meeting which dealt with some advertising campaign. She had to make a point whether she felt it or not.

"He came back," she said, "with a cardboard suitcase of clothes—hospital nightgowns—five, I remember—a robe, and a flat leather box which contained decorations."

"I would imagine."

"And under one arm he carried the Vermeer, wrapped in brown paper."

She looked at her hands on the table, two hands folded in an orderly fashion, except that they held on to each other with unusual stillness.

"He came into the room, this room, and sat down at the table. This table. He was still wearing his hat. He put his things down and then he took off his hat and showed us his scar and then told us how he got it, how he had watched the prisoners and had meant no harm. You said he told you about it?"

"Yes. He did."

"And when he was finished telling the story, my mother stood up very slowly. She was tall and beautiful. I mentioned that."

"Yes."

"She stood up and said, 'Dieter, you are a swine for watching them while their heads were sawed off. I am sorry they did not kill you.'" Miss von Tilwitz took a deep breath and refolded her hands. "And then my mother walked out."

"You mean she left?"

"Yes."

"A tragic story, I'm sure." I felt a little awkward, especially since there seemed no point to this very personal tale.

"Since then, Mister deWitt, he has often spoken to 'Ingeborg.'"

"I see."

"But the point of the story is this, Mister deWitt. On each anniversary of their wedding, for five years in a row, my father would send the Vermeer to my mother, for a present. It was the one beautiful thing, he would say, he had brought back from Poland. Each time my mother sent it back without comment."

"Is she still alive?"

"She is dead now. Once a year, however, my father still sends her the Vermeer."

There is a kind of tragedy, I believe, which gives no cause for compassion. The quality is sick, drab, and quite hopeless. The von Tilwitz story was like that. I looked at my watch and wished Baumeister would show up soon.

"I am almost finished, Mister deWitt." She sounded as if she did not like the story either. "I told you this so you would understand why I want the painting out of the house. I want it out of his life. Perhaps it will make him better...." She looked at me and I felt that she wished I would agree with her. I made a slight nod. I hoped it would mean anything to her that she might wish.

"It is the first painting I have heard of," I said, "which seems to have something of a curse on it."

"I want it out of the house," she repeated, as if she had not heard me. "It was I who informed Bonn of the painting's existence. It was I who attempted to sell it once. And I want Spinn present so that there is no chance, once the painting is gone, that it is given back to us."

"No chance," I said. "Rest assured."

"I am not assured."

She stopped, looking at me, but it was not the kind of silence which meant she was done and now it was my turn to answer. She simply held back for a moment, the way you might rein in a horse, to get its attention, before giving it a sharp press of the spurs.

"What assurance do I have, Mister deWitt, that the painting will not be returned to us, once you are caught?"

"What?"

"Yes, Mister deWitt. I do not think you are altogether legitimate." She watched me react and waved a hand at me, the way you might ward off a fly. "You may well work for Lobbe Industriel. I do not dispute it. And Hans Lobbe may well want this painting very badly, and may obtain it in the end."

"Listen, Miss von Tilwitz. He damn well...."

"Let me finish."

"Of course."

"You have avoided the official attentions of Mister Spinn. This has been obvious to me. You have attempted to bribe my father into releasing the painting to you, without Bonn's intervention. He has told me about it at breakfast. You have come to us rather than to the proper bureau which is in charge of releasing the painting to your—shall we say—employer. Does all this fit?"

She looked at me and was very serious. There was no banter, there was no trap. I felt she was being very open with me. I was open in turn.

"It fits, Miss von Tilwitz."

"Thank you," she said.

It was not immediately clear to me how to proceed, but what with honesty abounding, I took a stab at a course as novel as honesty.

"Miss von Tilwitz, you want this thing, this picture, out of the way, and you want assurance that you'll never be saddled with it again, legally or otherwise."

"Yes. Very much so."

"If I give you a paper...."

"Spoken like a lawyer," she said to my surprise.

"I am not speaking as a lawyer, Miss von Tilwitz. I am, if you'll pardon the phrase, speaking as one crook to another."

I will say she bridled, but she took it.

"You will give me what," she said after a moment, "in return for my releasing the picture? Which is what you want."

"Which is what I want. I want something that will pass border inspection, something which says in your father's handwriting that he renounces all claim to the Vermeer, that I am the duly authorized transporting agent of the Vermeer to Hans Lobbe, and in return—you will pardon me once more—I will pay you...."

At which point, the bell rang at the front door.

"Yes?" said Miss von Tilwitz and looked straight at me.

But then the bell rang again; the spell of money was broken, and she got up, hostess and chatelaine, to answer the goddam bell.

I expected Baumeister, and that was good, but I would have liked to finish this money business first.

It was at this point that her father came in. He did not look like a man who had just woken up. He looked busy and acted as if there had been no lapse of any sort since he and I had talked in the park that morning.

"Mister deWitt," he said, ignoring his daughter, and stepped up to the table. He had a white rose in one hand, wrinkled, bent, and maltreated. He sniffed the rose exactly the way he had done in the morning. Then he dropped it on the table and slapped the side of his leg.

"Yes?" I said.

"I resent your attempt to bribe me. My wife says that she does not wish me to sell or dispose of her painting in any way whatsoever. Anniversary present, you understand."

I understood. I understood something other than his imaginings, but the curse of the Vermeer was still there. The bell rang a third time. At this point, his daughter, my salvation, left the room.

I did not feel suspended or anxious anymore. This was not because I had settled anything. I had not. But there is just so much back and forth I can take and follow, and after that, it is like allowing the events to take over, to follow the cues as they come. Besides—and this was why indifference came easy—a lot was being solved for me by others: the general by refusing to deal with me any further, his daughter by agreeing to deal, and Baumeister by coming with the object of all this conniving.

Freiherr von Tilwitz had gone to the window and I no longer existed for him. In a sense, he no longer existed for me. He stood at the window, opened the right half of it, and took a dark slice of bread out of his pocket. After his ride, and his breakfasts, and his nap, after all those morning activities, it seemed he fed birds. He crumbled the dark slab of dry bread on the windowsill and in a moment, one, three, eight pigeons alighted there. Also, a number of sparrows.

"It is best to feed them bread regularly," said von Tilwitz without turning around. "Or else they begin to eat flesh."

I did not answer him. The sparrows were battlefield crows and the pigeons were vultures. This was the substance of the general's forenoon, and I did not care to disturb it. He no longer disturbed me. His daughter was willing to sign over the picture and the picture was here because Baumeister had brought it.

I sat and waited with that thought. No one came to the room. The door remained closed. The silence on the other side was polite and reassuring. Then I heard the thump.

At that moment, the birds took off with a hysterical clatter of wings. The General Freiherr von Tilwitz und Schroff stood stiff as a daguerreotype, black against the light from the window. This was my last sight of him, and my last thought of him was that he had perhaps thrown some piece of raw meat, some dead horse flank even, out on the windowsill to the beasts who had ogled him there, tired of stale Bavarian bread. I got up and fairly lunged for the door.

As always, it was dark out there because the only light in the hall and in the foyer came from the frosted square of glass in the black door of the stairwell. This, perhaps, is why the tableau by the door took so long to register.

Miss von Tilwitz stood erect and still, as always. The thing that had thumped lay on the floor near the open front door. It was Stefan, the general's servant, and his shaven skull had an unnatural blotch of too red blood on top. The red had run two ways down from the crown of the skull, somehow in the shape of his master's scar. Stefan lay still. There was no expression on his potato face.

And the man by the door (I discovered the second one only now) held a gun. The gun looked odd and ugly, because of its shape, though guns can sometimes look most elegant, exciting and right. As it turned out, it was a Smith and Wesson .38, Banker's Special, which is the most snub-nose, bulldoggish gun ever made, and it had a silencer on it. Benjamin Spinn, bland, lank-haired, was holding the gun, looking mean. There is nothing uglier.

"Mister deWitt?"

"Obviously," I said as if I were on a stage.

"You will come with me."

"Obviously."

I stepped to the door, which is when I discovered the second man, a runt of a thing, with leathered face and bent body like a very old peasant; and then I saw Spinn lash out with the silencer end of his gun and cut the immobile Miss von Tilwitz, the forever waiting chatelaine, across the side of one white temple, very hard and with purpose, so that she instantly folded down to the floor, out cold. I think she was maimed forever. I never saw her again.

CHAPTER 11

Three of us went down in the glass-type elevator together, all at one time, and I thought there was a special groan to the cables, a special swiftness to the descent. Spinn's totally threatening face was held two inches from mine; the peasant behind me held my right arm in some kind of unnecessary, muscle-twisting grip, and the Smith and Wesson Banker's Special with silencer was screwed into my solar plexus, also unnecessarily.

Nothing was said until we got to the lobby. There Spinn's problem began.

"Stop here, Mister deWitt."

I stopped. I could see through the glass of the front door. My taxi was still there. I did not think that Spinn knew about my cabby waiting.

"We are now going out to the street," said Spinn. He took the silencer off his gun and put it into his left pocket. The gun he put into his right pocket. "Just to the right," he went on, "stands a closed truck. We are all going into that truck."

"I'm not."

"Then I will shoot you, Mister deWitt."

"Is that the official Bonn policy?"

"It is the policy under which you and I will operate."

"Just exactly what do you want, Mister Spinn?"

"You are alive and you are well, Mister deWitt. You may wish to remain so. Ready now?"

"No. But I'll go, if you insist."

My little witticisms did not impress him one way or the other. He nodded at the peasant, who went to the door, and then he stood very close to me so that I could feel the gun in his pocket.

"The way they do this in the movies, Mister Spinn, the best way...."

"Quiet. March."

I was quiet and we marched. As soon as we got out to the street my cabby jumped out of his car with an expectant grin on his face. I looked right through him. From Spinn's point of view, the cabby's face must have looked like a study in disappointment. It was my guess that my cabby was simply dumbfounded.

"Thank you, no," I said to him. "I prefer a truck."

Spinn could not see my face. Just before turning right, I winked at the cabby and made a small motion with my head. I was hoping to heaven that all this would convey a great deal: don't call the police, follow discreetly, come in swinging at the strategic moment, save my life—but not yet, and other thoughts of that nature. I don't know what he saw in my face. Perhaps all he thought was that I was a little bit nuts and also had a facial tic. I passed, feeling tense and edgy.

There was the truck. It was a small delivery van, metal body, with a door in the back but no window in it. That, I thought, was a lousy situation, since I wouldn't be able to see if the taxi was following us.

The peasant took the driver's seat. Spinn motioned me to sit in the middle, and he sat on my right. It was like the elevator situation again, with no room to move and with nothing to do. There was an outside mirror on the driver's side, but at an angle which didn't do me any good. We started off.

"What is this, Spinn?"

"We will discuss it later. Turn left here," he said to the peasant.

"Discuss what?"

"Later."

"If this is any example of our future conversations, Spinn, then neither you nor I will get anything out of it."

"There are also other methods," he said without any inflection. It shook me up.

In the left turn, I looked past the driver's face, down the street from which we had just come. There stood the taxi, as before, and there stood my cabby, as before. I was beginning to feel shaky on the inside and did not know what to do about it. In a while, I knew, I might get angry.

It was not a long ride. We went through traffic, we stopped at a light once, and then Spinn told the driver to swing through the square and pull up next to the board fence.

Parts of Munich have been laid out with sweep and a good eye for architectural beauty. A series of Bavarian kings did a generous job of it. I have forgotten the name of the square, but I remember the size of it and a kind of emptiness which made me think of a street on Sunday. There were a few cars and a few people. All movement seemed very leisurely. The sun shone and a dog barked somewhere. A weird kind of normalcy existed while I sat there with Spinn and his gun in my side. And then we pulled into a side street where a wooden fence ran the length of the entire block. Behind the fence stood the tremendous shell of the bombed opera house. Perhaps it was left there like the similar monument in Hiroshima. It was big, wrong, and ugly. Chipped plaster giants supported arches which were no longer there. The tremendous curve of the ruined roof seemed to hang in the sky like a broken, black egg. No more weird sense of normalcy now. This felt ominous.

"We will get out of the car," said Spinn, "and walk through that broken gate in the fence."

"Into that?"

"For privacy, Mister deWitt."

"Of course. I already guessed nobody is home."

"But you are mistaken."

I didn't answer him, nor did his remark really register. As I stopped by the board fence, I looked the length of the street, toward the square, and saw a taxi. It came nudging into the turn rather slowly and then it stopped. But I had heard the unmistakable rattle of the diesel engine. Then Spinn pushed me through the broken gate.

I have said that the sun was shining, and since there was hardly any roof left on the opera house, there was sunshine in the interior too. But even so, the sight was gloomy. Blocks of cracked stone nibbled the floor. Empty loges hung on one wall. A black girder, twisted, hung out of another like a dead limb. A breeze seemed to be blowing, because the girder swayed slightly.

"Follow me," said Spinn.

"Into that?"

"We are almost there."

"But it is hardly there any more."

"Mister deWitt, I am not here to joke."

"And you're a messy housekeeper. I'm not going in there. Something might drop on my head."

"It has already dropped. And the city inspects the place."

I looked at him because I thought, lo and behold, dour Spinn has made a joke, but there was only the same unemotional face; the remark had been serious.

"Listen, Spinn, the last time this place was inspected was through a bombsight. And with that inspection, the place was declared uninhabitable. So don't stand there like an idiot trying to soothe me with lies. Why am I here?"

"For privacy. I have matters to discuss with you. Come."

But I just stood there. Then Spinn surprised me. He very quietly walked up to me and, as quick as a snake, lashed out with his fist. I thought my head had come off. I landed on the ground, hearing mighty sounds. I saw Spinn's feet in front of me, six feet altogether.

"Enough jokes now," said Spinn from on high.

Enough jokes now. He was right. I sat there just long enough to take three deep, ragged breaths of air. I felt very dizzy, but tried to get up. The peasant was behind me to give me a hand with that grip of his. I got up very quickly, for fear of having my arm torn from the socket. Then I followed, as directed. But by and by there was going to be a change. By and by Manford deWittnitt would have to come through or else I would never be able to speak to myself again.

Over the rubble, under the girders, and then we came to dark stairs which took us into the basement. There were the catacombs. These were moist passages for rats and for leftover phantoms.

"I will tell you who it is, Mister deWitt."

We had stopped at the end of the passage and there was a brick niche. The light was not very good, but I saw the man there, his face black with blood, his arms stretched by his weight because rope held his wrists tight and high to a hook and his feet were off the ground. He had a fat, distorting gag in his mouth.

"This is Dr. Baumeister," said Spinn. "He has so far refused to tell me what he has done with the Vermeer."

I wasn't dizzy anymore. I wasn't hot with anger or cold with fear, but I suddenly felt as if I had turned solid with hate—solid, hard hate.

"Take him off."

Spinn looked at me with surprise. I hadn't known he was capable of the emotion, but then he hadn't seemed to know that I was capable of more than funny jokes and confused chitchat.

"Just stay where you are, Mister deWitt." He took his gun out again, and for a moment he seemed actually nervous.

"Once more, Spinn, take him down from there."

"Or else, Mister deWitt?"

"Or else nothing." And I made a very sudden grab for the peasant who stood right next to me.

I was fast and knew what I wanted, so before anything else, I got the peasant in front of me. I snaked an arm over his Adam's apple, bent him back a little, and got my knee in his spine. I gave him enough air to scream once.

"That was very quick," said Spinn. "I did not know you were capable of it."

"Get Baumeister off the wall or I'll break this one's spine. Slowly."

"Go ahead, Mister deWitt."

"It's a matter of sound, not of pain, Mister Spinn. He'll scream and scream."

Spinn shrugged and started to sidle around. I thought he wanted a shot at me. I turned the peasant his way.

"If I wanted to shoot you, Mister deWitt, I would have done so already. Right through my companion."

I believed him. It made things a little more complicated for me and I had no idea for the moment what my next move would be. The peasant took the problem out of my hands.

The throat lock cum knee press is undoubtedly one of the most enervating experiences a victim can have. He is possessed with the simultaneous panic of getting choked to death and of having his back broken. Both events are almost instantly possible. But the grip is not an efficient killer hold. I have read there are better ones. But this iron maiden of a grip is a very good pacifier. You have all the advantages of balance and of inaccessibility to the victim while he is only concerned with saving his life by holding very still. The danger occurs only when you don't hold on tightly enough—and the peasant suddenly noticed that. He made the mistake of tensing in an effort to bunch up his strength for some kind of vengeful maneuver, but there is never enough time for that. There is always enough time, however, to clamp down in time to pacify. And I did it too hard. A brief moment of wild tensing, and then the peasant slumped.

I let go immediately, and the peasant slid down. I went down with him, to lower him, and to see what the damage was.

"Let him lie," said Spinn. "We have business."

"Hold it just one goddamn minute, Spinn. This might be bad."

The peasant was semi-conscious, his throat swelling, his breathing a struggle for life. A fraction more force applied to the voice box when I had clamped down on him and this could have been a case of black death, the almost instant death from shock and suffocation when the cartilages are broken.

But the peasant was going to live. And he was going to save my life, so help me, in case Spinn changed his mind later on and decided I should be better left dead than alive.

I had felt it in his pocket when he had slid down in front of me. Maybe it was a gun, maybe it was a knife. Or it could have been a sap. Whatever it was, it would have to do....

"Mister deWitt, you may simply leave the body where it is."

"One lousy minute, Spinn," I said, and kneeling over the body, I kept my arms engaged with it and grunted.

"The last time I hit you, Mister deWitt, it was with my fist. If you do not get up instantly, I will do it with my foot."

Then I had it in my hand. It was a goddamn fountain pen.

Spinn took two steps and started to pull back one foot. I wasn't going to get killed yet, but this would hurt.

"Wait!" I groaned and leaned a little bit sideways. I did nothing with haste now because the image for Spinn was to be crippling agony. "My back—" and I worked an almost operatic sob into my voice. "Help me—help me up—"

He didn't bother to kick me. He stepped close and leaned down a little.

You know how sometimes a word sticks in your mind, a word in a foreign language, though there will never be any conceivable use for it. The word just sticks forever, for no good reason. My German word of that order was *Hexenschuss*. It refers to that sudden and crippling pain in the back which can come when you lift something as insignificant as a spoon. Literally, the word means a witch's shot.

"*Hexenschuss!*" I yelled.

"I told you not to try and lift him," said Spinn very reasonably.

Then he bent down to lift his crippled enemy to his feet.

I did it with a revulsion almost as strong as my hate for the man. The cap was off the fountain pen and then the metal point of the thing dug deep into the softness under Spinn's chin. I had missed the bone, had made it into the root of the tongue, full of blood vessels and nerves. The shock is paralyzing, though there is not much pain.

My left hand was close to Spinn's hand holding the gun. I did not think he had raised it since stepping up to me, though I couldn't see that, what with my crouched position. I simply slapped out for it. I missed. I pressed up to get on my feet with Spinn suddenly very heavy on me, and then his arms came around me. It was like a cramp. The gun was still in his hand, and it now pressed into my back. But he wasn't aiming it. He held it because it happened to be there in his hand—and then he trembled, and the cramp was gone.

Because of the heaving pressure I was putting on him, he now literally catapulted across the small room and crashed to the stone floor. So did I. But I got up.

I had really no clear idea how badly he was hurt, how much he might be faking, but I had a very clear idea how little I wanted to tangle with him. I got up and kicked him in the head.

Baumeister, though it was more of an act of love, was more difficult. I first got the gag out of his mouth and watched him gasp for a moment. Then came the knots. I am lousy with knots and these were fairly high up. And Baumeister hung heavy. But I got them off in a while and lowered him to the ground. It seemed I was lowering people to the ground all over.

"You all right?" I said, close to him. "Can you—no. Stupid question. Will you just sit—hey, you all right?" I felt very upset; the shakes were coming on, now that it was all over.

He didn't move, but he looked at me. His eyes were not damaged.

"About this," he whispered, "I rather go to the lecture."

CHAPTER 12

My shakes left me a little. I grinned at him and gave his shoulder a soft squeeze. Then I went to work.

The fountain pen was the worst. I got it out and a great deal of blood followed it. Spinn's eyelids fluttered. I turned him on his side. Then I dragged his buddy across the floor and laid him next to Spinn. There was a little bit more resistance with the peasant because he was quite conscious now, though totally preoccupied with his breathing. I put him on his side, too, the two bodies belly to belly. I worked their arms around each other and tied each man's wrists behind the other's back. I did this tight and close, hoping the intimacy would be repugnant to them. Spinn's left ankle I tied to the peasant's right, and the latter's right to the former's left. You get the picture. I'd call it the pretzel waltz, except that you can't move. How do I know about this? I invented it. After this I waited another five or ten minutes because Baumeister couldn't move either. Then his hands came back to life with a roaring pain, and he had to throw up. Eventually I more or less carried him up the basement stairs, into the ugly open air of the opera house, and across all that rubble. At the wooden gate an eye peered at me though the broken part.

"Ach! If you were not comening now, I was comening!"

My cabby and I got Baumeister into the cab, and then from the cab we got him into a hospital. They let me see him after working on him for about half an hour. He sat bundled and swathed in a hospital bed.

"Hi," I said and felt like whimpering. "Can you talk?"

"Always," he said.

I knew this about him, but hadn't thought he would remember at a time like this. He had patches and bandages all over his face and bandages at his wrists. One cheek was blue and one was pink, its natural color. And his eyes were as blue and shiny as ever.

"How do you like my nose?" he said.

I hadn't wanted to mention it. It was a Santa Claus nose, but befitting a Santa Claus perhaps ten feet tall. Also, it glowed.

"It is large," I said. "How does it feel?"

"Like not my own, Mister deWitt. It lies next to me and throbs. It has a heartbeat of its own, you understand. It looks back at me and is a stranger. I am lying in bed with a stranger."

He sighed carefully and closed his eyes. When he opened them again, the humor was gone.

"I will go to sleep soon, Mister deWitt, because of the pills. I will tell you what happened."

"Please."

"You called me that an impostor called Spinn was coming?"

"Yes."

"I immediately mentioned this to my assistant who...."

"I wish you hadn't, Dr. Baumeister."

"I can trust him," he said very simply. "I mentioned it to him because he has had occasion to know some of the Bonn art treasure people."

"What I told you about Spinn...."

"He knew Spinn."

"No! You mean he is for real?"

"Yes. Don't talk, Mister deWitt. I am getting sleepy."

I bit my lip. I had difficulty sitting still.

"I felt time was of the essence—your hasty call, Spinn is coming, what does all this mean—you understand." He yawned. "So for safety I send my assistant away with the Vermeer. Then, from my office, I call Bonn."

He yawned again.

"You called Bonn, Doctor Baumeister. Your last words were...."

"I call Bonn. And soon Benjamin Spinn answers."

"Just a minute."

"He answers on the phone, we talk, and while we talk Benjamin Spinn walks into my office."

"Goddamn it," I said.

"Yes. I should have listened to you and left immediately, then the impostor would not have found me there."

"He wanted the Vermeer, of course."

"Of course. I tell him it is a forgery and he says, 'Fine, I'll take the forgery.'"

"Is it?"

"I told you, I don't know."

"Another question. Do you hear me, Doctor?"

"Oh yes." He yawned.

"Have you ever heard of an art theft which involved such concentrated violence as you have been subjected to?"

I thought he was asleep.

"No," he said after a while. "But many collectors, Mister deWitt, are really insane. And many have all the money to pay for any method necessary to still the craving, to satisfy the obsession."

"Must be damn sure, in that case, that they are after the original. That this Vermeer is *the* Vermeer."

"I don't know. I will tell you a story about that shtoa...."

"Dr. Baumeister. Dr. Baumeister!"

I shook him. He had not told me where the Vermeer was now. Some madman was after it badly enough to maim, perhaps kill, and I felt fairly frantic.

"Is it back at the von Tilwitz house?"

He stirred. Perhaps I had hurt him.

"Kapitän," he said with his eyes closed.

"General. General von Tilwitz."

"No, my Kapitän."

Hallucinating....

"In my Kapitän, Opel."

"A car?"

"Parking lot...."

I left him alone then. He fell asleep and it occurred to me that his sedative dosage must have been massive, and that, therefore, his earlier pain must have been massive too. He looked sunken and small now, and his swollen nose did not look so funny anymore.

It was a shabby way of saying good-bye. He was asleep and I was in a hurry. I hoped I could soon let him know that the "Apple Girl" was safe again and that the rest of the chase had been easier than a lecture. He would enjoy that....

His assistant had walked out of the office with the Vermeer and gone to the parking lot where Baumeister's Opel Kapitän was parked, in order to await the arrival of his chief. All that must have been hours ago. Where was the assistant? To hell with the assistant—where was the "Apple Girl" now?

In all this world there was really just one thing I could rely upon, and that was my cabby waiting. Outside the hospital, there he was, waiting. I got into the taxi and told him to go to the Alte Pinakothek. The trip had already taken five long minutes when I realized he had still not said a word.

"Uh—the old gentleman," I said, "will be all right."

"Ja."

"Uh—by the way, I don't know your name."

"Ja."

"I mean, what is it?"

"What is it? I am afraid of you is what is it."

Under the circumstances, his reaction was reasonable. I'm sure he would have preferred driving me to assignations with the forbiddingly beautiful Miss von Tilwitz and as a matter of fact, under the circumstances, I would have preferred that too. But I was close now, damn close, to getting my hands on Lobbe's "Apple Girl," whose existence I had almost begun to doubt. Except for the Spinn episode. No one gets that violent over nothing....

"Is it much farther?"

"No."

"Very good. Uh—one more thing. You recall the two men with whom I left the Schraudolf Strasse?"

"De two men who never came out of de old opera house anymore. Yes."

"They are still there."

"Dey are still dere."

"Yes. Now, there is something you could do for me."

"No!"

"What's the matter with you?"

"Dey hurt de old gentleman?"

"Yes. On the other hand, I in turn...."

"No! Let dem be de ghosts in de old opera house!"

"Look now, whatever your name is, they are, as a matter of fact, close, very close to that state. All I would like you to do, and I'll tell you when to do it, is to call the police and tell them to come with an ambulance to pick up the two ghosts."

"When?" he asked.

"After you have taken me to the airport."

My compassion for the two was theoretical, but my respect for the danger which they might still constitute was heartfelt and personal. Let them swoon in their pretzel waltz a little while longer until I was about thirty thousand feet up and on my way to Rotterdam. I had decided on Rotterdam for several sufficient reasons. One, it would hardly be out of the way. Two, if any other bland madmen were sent after me, a Rotterdam stopover might well act as a throw-off because it was probably known that my destination was New York. Three, the question of the picture's authenticity remained, and the certainty of Lobbe's reaction to receiving a fake remained too. An insane collector might be content to steal a fake, but no Hans Lobbe would be content with a swindle. That is, with someone else's swindle.

"Alte Pinakothek," my cabby announced.

The parking lot in back of the museum was small and there were not many cars, but I didn't know an Opel from a mole hole, be it a captain or an admiral. The cabby had to show me. He pointed, said nothing, and made no move to get out of the car. Perhaps, as he had said, I had frightened him.

The car was sort of compact and all black. And there was nobody in it or nearby. To be expected. It had been hours, as I have said. But I did walk up close to it and then I saw the man in the back seat. I had another moment of panic. I looked at him and thought, the bastards have gotten to this one too. But he was only asleep.

He came to with a start as I shook him and hit his head against the roof of the car. He was young, bespectacled, and at least as nervous as I. Baumeister must have really read a riot act of severe instructions to him about safeguarding the picture.

Nevertheless, we had our problems. He did not speak a word of English and my German did not impress him either. He had been instructed to check my credentials very closely, another Baumeister precaution, since the assistant did not know me by sight. My credentials—and I should have thought of this sooner—were in German and explained the whole thing to the young man.

The Vermeer, he conveyed, was in the trunk of the car. Now we had to find the key to the trunk of the car.

To make a nervous three minutes short, I will say that the keys had dropped out of his pocket while he had been asleep and we found them in the crack of the seat.

There it was. A flat plywood box which would fit nicely under one arm. The box was hinged and by opening a catch, it would flop open. My first impulse was to grab the box and run, but then I decided not to budge, not to take another breath, if need be, until I had made sure that the "Apple Girl" was actually inside. A few more nervous minutes now, I might add, with the infernal catch....

And there she was. There was the canvas over the stretcher, no frame, and the four corners of the picture had been carefully wrapped to lend cushioning.

She was beautiful. There was the happy and healthy face of the peasant girl, sweet young breasts pushing up over a shawl in disarray, plump arms holding a basket which was full of apples. I felt like biting something. I felt like laughing with her. I had the "Apple Girl."

I accepted a Lufthansa reservation from Munich to Amsterdam after assurances that Rotterdam was just a stone's throw away. One forgets how small some countries are—and one also forgets that they have survived the longest....

The plane did not leave until evening. I did not spend the intervening time at the airport, having now become a most cautious man. I spent the time riding around in the taxi with a cab driver who would not utter a word. I made a few stops for telephone calls, made from major hotels and, once, from the Telegraphen Amt. They were all to Hans Lobbe, in New York. But he could not be located and I never spoke to him. All I found out, finally, was that he had gone to Tangier.

At one hotel, the Königshof, I bought a London *Times*. On the way to the airport, I read that Carbon and Allied had dropped eight incredible points.

CHAPTER 13

The first leg of the trip, Munich to Brussels, was fine. I was out of Munich and I had the Vermeer, which gave me a sense of double success; to have escaped and to have captured. My sense of safety and relief was so great that I fell asleep after the evening meal and did not wake up till Brussels.

There was a ten-minute layover during which time I was allowed to remain in my seat. Twelve passengers disembarked, and about twenty-five entered. Perhaps more. I could not see the first-class compartment. Since I was traveling tourist and sat close to the entrance, in the rear, I also could not see the faces of most of the new passengers. I saw mostly the backs of heads passing me and started to worry again.

There was not much time to worry because the flight from Brussels to

Amsterdam is just a short hop. It was nighttime now, and raining. When I'd arrived in Munich, it had been raining because, so to speak, it had been raining. But it was raining in Amsterdam because this was Holland. From the plane to the airport building I saw nothing but flat blackness, and the low building showed very modern rectangles of light. The airport compound seemed surprisingly small.

Passport and customs procedure was quick and perfunctory, as expected, since the Common Market was coming into its own. With suitcase and plywood box, which I carried like a briefcase under my arm, I stood to one side and watched the passengers leave. I looked at them, some looked at me, but they all left. I did not think that any of them had been interested in me.

I had not thought about transportation. The bus to the city of Amsterdam had left and there was no string of dormant taxis on the other side of the building. There would be no further planes until seven o'clock in the morning, which meant there would also be no further transportation into town until seven o'clock in the morning. Holland can be dismal at night.

I lay down on a bench and laid "Apple Girl" next to me. I slept. Suddenly, she woke me up.

"*Goede morgen!*" she said and when she smiled her cheeks shone like healthy fruit.

I jumped up, feeling disheveled, and made the confused observation that she had covered her bosom most properly, and that she wasn't carrying her basket anymore.

"*Blijft U rustig zitten. Kan ik U helpen?*"

The first thing she had said had conveyed a meaning. She had said good morning to me. Now my "Apple Girl" was dressed like a stewardess and I couldn't understand a word she was saying.

"Excuse me," I said. "What was that?"

"Oh, American," she said in English. She touched the tips of her white collar and said, "I should have known by the buttons you have there."

"Uh—of course." I had an impulse to ask whether it was clean. I felt uncomfortable.

"You look uncomfortable," she said. "Would you like to come to my room?"

I smiled in a fixed way, so that nothing else would show on my face. Here was my *bordelje* talking. Here was my "Apple Girl" in the flesh, though she was dressed like a stewardess. The same happy country face, same cornsilk hair, same ready bosom, though it was covered up in a most cruel manner. And she had just asked me to come to her room. It was the first time that the Vermeer trip was taking a happy turn.

"Yes," I said. "Very kind of you."

"Not at all," she said. "I do this with many customers," and her smile washed all depravity out of the remark.

What she had meant by her room was her office. She was not really a flying stewardess, but a reservation attendant—partly, she explained, because she was afraid of flying, and partly because she spoke only Dutch, English, and German. To fly with her airline, she explained, you need two additional languages.

Her office had three desks, three desk chairs, and one couch. Some flight officer was using one desk to write a report, another one was using the next desk for his feet, and the couch was occupied by another *bordelje*. She was sleeping there.

"I can wake her," said my *bordelje*.

"No, no. I'll sleep on the desk. I've done it before."

She laughed and started to unbutton her jacket.

"I get undressed now," she said. "'You pardon me?"

"Uh—yes, by all means." And I went to my sleeping quarters.

In back of me a locker was opened. There were sounds of rummaging and of clothes being taken off and put on. None of the two officers turned around, so I, like a dolt, did not turn around either. I sat on the swivel chair and put my feet on the desk.

"Ah," she said, "I am ready now."

Preoccupied with my own fantasies about her, I almost jumped to my feet prior to leaping like a goat across the swivel chair in the direction of the locker. But I am civilized. I restrained myself and only turned to look.

She had, indeed, taken her clothes off. She had replaced her uniform with a dress cinched by a belt, with red and yellow flowers printed all over it. The flowers shaped themselves in a most loving manner around her lovely female shape. I could understand the flowers.

"I go home now," she said. "It is six, so you still have an hour to sleep till your plane comes in."

"I'm not waiting for the plane. I'm waiting for transportation to Rotterdam."

"Oh, good," she said. "I live in Rotterdam. You want me?"

"I beg your pardon?"

"You want to come with me?" And she laughed. "My English is so incorrect."

"Not really," I said, feeling gallant. "My understanding is."

"So you come with me?"

"I would love to."

My *bordelje* smiled at me as if this were the happiest moment in her life. I picked up my things. She turned to her locker and picked up hers. She straightened up and with one hand and one cocked hip, she held a round basket full of green apples. I was back in my dream.

"Mijnheer van Mier," she said, "brings them to me. He grows them and everytime he flies through, he brings them to me."

How the ages change. Had Vermeer lived today, he would have done his work in an airport.

She had a Citröen, *deux cheval*, in the parking lot, the little gray car with the high rear end which reminds me of a miniature tank. Gray light was beginning to show in the sky and it was no longer raining. There was now only the permanent, submarine atmosphere which is due to a drizzle, something which the Dutch, I am sure, hardly credit with the name of precipitation. We got just a little bit soaked and then sat down in the car. She drove well.

It is not really hard to drive well in the Dutch countryside. The roads are straight and the land is flat. I don't know what grows on their fields, but the ones I saw were all very green. Black ditches divide the green, and big hulks of windmills stand here and there. I did not see a single one turning. And all the rest is flat. The fields are flat green and the sky is flat gray, the two predominant colors. The road, of course, is a glistening black. Whenever the palette of the old Dutch masters is colorful, it occurred to me, the picture is a still life, artfully arranged indoors, not outdoors. Their outdoor scenes have a different kind of color, the color of rollicking feasts, of maidens getting rolled in the hay. But with the countryside so wet, so flat without interruption, how can anybody in Holland make love outdoors....

"Tell me, Miss—" I paused, and looked at my *bordelje* steering her *deux cheval* with concentration.

"Miss Ruyker," she said.

I did the proper thing and gave her my name too, and then asked her, "Miss Ruyker, when does the sun shine here?"

"Oh, sometimes."

"Hm. Does it ever shine long enough to dry the grass?"

"That's not good for the grass, Mister deWitt."

"Of course. Though I wasn't thinking of the grass."

"Of what, Mister deWitt?"

"Uh—like—if you wanted to walk barefoot in the grass and not catch a cold, you know. Does that ever happen?"

"I love to walk barefoot in the grass, Mister deWitt. Have an apple."

"Thank you." I had an apple.

"I walk barefoot in the grass during vacation," she said.

"In the sunshine."

"Yes. I always go to Sicily for vacation."

That made sense to me.

"They have mountains there even at the sea!" she said.

"How nice. You go there for the mountains at the sea."

"Yes. That, too," she said and then she laughed very loud and slapped me on the knee.

I was a little bit startled. I had one *bordelje* on my lap and one *bordelje* sitting next to me driving a car and I would very much have liked them to change places. She stopped laughing, but then she surprised me again.

"When we get to Rotterdam," she said, "I'm going to bed. What are you going to do?"

"Well, first," I said, "I have to look somebody up."

"Oh. If I weren't going to bed, I'd show you Rotterdam."

"I tell you what, Miss Ruyker."

"What?"

"When do you get up, Miss Ruyker?"

"Just before I go back to work."

"Oh. You spend an awfully long time in bed."

"Yes, I do. In this weather, what else is there?"

"There is Sicily, Miss Ruyker."

She laughed very hard and I thought she was going to slap me on the knee again, but she didn't.

"But if you go to Sicily only once a year," I said, and waited a moment, hunting for the right words. I didn't need them.

"I have a very good boyfriend in Rotterdam," she said earnestly. "He does not know about Sicily, you understand."

"That's why he is very good."

"Very good," she repeated earnestly.

I now had a notion why she spent so much time in bed during the rainy season, and contented myself from then on with holding my two-dimensional *bordelje*. The other was driving into Rotterdam.

The access road was a freeway and the wide streets we passed were modern as tomorrow. There were no leaning gables, no ancient alleys, there was nothing to suggest that this was ancient Rotterdam. Of course, it was not ancient Rotterdam. Ancient Rotterdam had exploded in one of the worst saturation raids the enraged Hitler had ordered, because that morning's porridge had been served too cold. I exaggerate. But the military reasons for the destruction had been negligible, I knew.

I now saw the large granite façades of office buildings. There were expanses of glass, modernistic arcades, abstract bas-reliefs on the buildings, and free-form statues in the squares.

"Where would you like to go?" asked my three-dimensional *bordelje*.

"I only have a name. I have to look up the address."

"I take you there," she said.

I looked at her sideways, but she seemed composed and unperturbed. We drove along a canal with wide bridges, which was the first time the city looked a little Old World. There were also large old trees on the other side of the water. This section of town had not been touched by the bombings. You can revive an old look by building in imitation, but you cannot duplicate a two-hundred-year-old tree.

"I am taking you to the railway station," she said, "and there in front"—she pointed—"is a round building where they know everything."

The round building was an overgrown kiosk where it said "Information."

"Shall I wait for you?" she asked when I got out.

"No, no, Miss Ruyker. I'll catch a taxi. Your big bed is waiting for you."

"Oh, yes, he is," she said, smiled, waved, and drove away from the curb.

CHAPTER 14

I held on to the *bordelje* which should have meant more to me than the one who had just left, put my suitcase down, and asked the girl at the window for a telephone book. She gave it to me and I started looking for Kornbluth. Baumeister had given the spelling to me and the first name too——Ilja Kornbluth—but the man wasn't listed. That was bad. The girl at the window seemed to have noticed my face.

"Not listed?" she asked.

"No. Not listed. I have the name but no address."

"But you asked for the telephone book. You should ask for the address book."

I looked down at the slimmish volume in front of me and discovered that all the names had a telephone number listed, but nothing else. The volume she brought now was five times as thick.

"I will look it up for you. What is the name?"

"Ilja Kornbluth," I said, and spelled it for her.

She flipped very fast, looked, and then she wrote something down.

"Do you know this town, sir?"

"No. I just got here."

"Then you'll need some help. The Van Rijn Straat is in the Old Quarters."

"I thought they were all bombed out."

"No. Just all the good parts were bombed out."

I thought that a strange answer, but then she came up with a colored map for streets; a sepia map simplified for the sightseeing of all the worthwhile places; a green and brown and blue map showing the whole city in relation to the environs, including the Channel coast; and two brochures, written by two different historical societies, both dealing with Rotterdam.

With a black graphite pencil she was now drawing serpents, snails, and gutlike shapes—all continuous—all over the city map. The curlicues were tightest near one section of the deep harbor area.

"Isn't there a shorter way?"

"Of course," she said. "But you won't see the city."

"Later. Draw me the shorter way."

It was not much better and I ended up by having her call a taxi for me. Then, in her own unspeakable language, she told the driver who showed up that he should take me to the Van Rijn Straat No. 3. He grunted—at least, I thought he grunted; perhaps it was Dutch—and we drove off.

Now the streets looked like the Rotterdam I had imagined. The taxi drove slowly because the streets were so narrow, and it bounced because of the cobbles. It had stopped raining, but it still smelled wet. Not rain wet, but dark water wet. I got a view of the houses we passed only when we crossed a bridge over a narrow canal, and at some distance. The crowding of narrow buildings was incredible. The houses were always taller than they were wide; they shouldered each other or leaned into each other, and the very steep gables put me in mind of a tight row of jagged teeth. Under each gable protruded the typical beam with a hook. By this device they hoisted their furniture up, and then into the windows. They couldn't have furnished their narrow houses in any other way.

Van Rijn Straat No. 3 was like that. It was an old building, in good repair. It was built well to begin with and it must have been cared for ever since. The downstairs windows were leaded. I got out of the cab, paid in American money without any difficulty, and then stood there on the wet street with my suitcase, my *bordelje*. It was around seven o'clock in the morning. An old tree nearby dripped on me.

At the next corner, where a street angled away from the canal, hung a sign which said "Broodjeswinkel." I had no idea what that meant, but I went there because yellow light shone out of a large window. It was out of the question to knock on No. 3 at this hour, so I went to the corner.

At first I thought the Broodjeswinkel was a shop. It had a shop-size window (Old Town size, that is) and there were a few plates behind it bearing one thing each: a roll, a sausage, a bun, a fish. Between each plate was a flowerpot with a geranium. The flowers were red. It was the first vivid color I had seen since my *deux cheval bordelje* had left me.

There was light inside, and then I saw the little tables.

Since my arrival in Holland, I now spent my happiest hour. The place was a hundred years old. The proprietress came through a curtain in back, and she was a hundred years old. She spoke an incomprehensible variety of Dutch. But we managed. I went to the counter and simply pointed. The more I pointed the more enthusiastic she got. I am sure it was not the money that lit her up with each additional order, but simply that she loved to see somebody eat.

I ate smoked eel, shrimp in aspic, liverwurst made from the liver of geese, chopped herring mixed with apple and caraway, and in between, crunched my way through three rolls smeared with ripe Camembert cheese. I had a coffee pot on my table and drank coffee with thick cream and coarse sugar. I always drink my coffee black, but I didn't in that place. When I was done, I felt I was done forever. I got a cigar from the old woman. The Broodjeswinkel sold no cigars, but the old woman was smoking one, and when she saw my look, she pulled one out of her apron for me.

At eight o'clock the light had not changed whatsoever. I got up, bowed to the old woman, thanked her in the three languages in which I know a polite form of address, and went out into the drizzle. I got hit by some fat drops when I stopped under the tree, and put my suitcase down in front of No. 3. There was a handle and I pulled, and a bell sounded dim and far in the house. Then I waited. I watched a barge drift by in the black oil of the canal. Two men walked along the narrow catwalks on each side of the barge, leaning into poles which they had rammed into the bed of the canal. Laundry was strung from stem to stern of the barge. It hung limp in the drizzle. Most of the shirts were blue. I rang the bell again. Then I heard rapid steps which sounded as if they were coming down a stairwell. I imagined Kornbluth a wizened old man, scurrying like a mouse. Then the door flew open.

She was a fine-boned young woman with very light, blooming skin. She had long, nervous hands and big eyes like a nighttime animal. Her thick hair made waves of black gloss.

"*Ja, mijnheer. Kan ik U helpen?*"

It sounded polite enough.

"*Ja*," I said, which was my Dutch vocabulary. "May I speak in English?"

"*Ja.*" She looked a little bit puzzled.

"I would like to see Mijnheer Kornbluth."

Now she looked neither polite nor puzzled. Something went out of her eyes and something went down over her face.

"I have a picture here, an original Vermeer...." Her stare embarrassed me, and I interrupted with a smile. "Very famous. I came to ask...."

"Get away from here!" she said. It was an explosion of hate.

She hauled back with one slim arm and grabbed the door, ready to slam it. I know the gesture. I've seen it before. So I did not jump back, but went at her to catch the door before it was too late.

"You wait a minute, young lady. I came on business. I want to see...."

"He is dead," she screamed, "he is dead!"

CHAPTER 15

My first thought was, the bastards got here first—though that didn't make much sense. Kornbluth's connection with the reappearance of the "Apple Girl" was zero and my decision to go to Rotterdam had not been a long-standing one. Besides, killing Kornbluth was not going to get them the Vermeer. *I* had it, under my arm. In my consternation, I had stepped back from the open door and into the drizzle again. The tree nearby reached far enough over to give me another fat drop. It woke me from the shock the girl had given me.

Kornbluth killed? Hell, deWitt, she had said he was dead, that's all....

I took a deep breath and looked around, checking to see who might have observed Manny deWitt act the sensational fool. Two children came weaving down the street on bicycles, intent on not missing a single one of the puddles. The barge on the canal was just passing under a bridge.

I stepped back to the open door, picked up my suitcase, and walked into the narrow hall. I put the suitcase down and closed the door behind me. In this hall there was just enough room for the front door to swing open and then the staircase went up steeply. One wall was blind. It was attached to the next house. The other wall had a door in it, to some downstairs room, but I had seen the girl run up the stairs. I left the suitcase below, but took the "Apple Girl" with me.

She was in a room which faced the street and the canal beyond, a room which, in spite of the dismal, gray light from outside, had all the warmth of good living. There were two paned windows with flowerboxes outside. A delicate watering can sat on a wide windowsill. There was a round table with carved claw feet; chairs whose back was a fine, baroque curve; a chaise longue covered with woven flowers; and a cherrywood desk which had scores of tiny drawers. On one wall hung a small triptych painted with Byzantine figures: Christ on the Cross, the two thieves, Mary kneeling and the Magdalene comforting her. Three soldiers stood with averted faces.

The young woman also stood averted. She was by one window, her back to me, and when I came in I saw her go rigid. I closed the door.

"Excuse me for just walking in," I said. "But I did not want to leave you like this."

"I'm all right. You may leave."

Shades of Miss von Tilwitz, I thought.

"I came because of you, and I came because of me. Perhaps we can help each other."

She had not turned around until then. Her two hands were clasped, and her posture was very erect. There was none of the tower straightness of

Miss von Tilwitz, but rather the poise you might feel after taking a deep breath. But her composure was precarious.

"It was a kind thought," she said, "but really—really unnecessary."

I watched her, the way she stood and held herself in, and I moved a little closer. I put the plywood box down by a chair.

"You are Ilja Kornbluth's daughter," I said.

That did it. I hadn't been trying for any effect, but had just expressed that moment's realization. She stiffened, and then slumped with a sob. Anyone does the next thing automatically, unless one is a beast. I stepped up to her, put her head against my chest, and stroked her hair. She cried hard now, though she bit her teeth into her fist, and with the other hand, she hung onto my lapel so hard that I could feel the pull in my shoulder. The relationship was impersonal. Only her grief mattered. She cried hard and was done very quickly. She straightened up, took the handkerchief which I offered, and blew her nose.

"Thank you, Mister...."

"DeWitt, Miss Kornbluth."

"Please sit down, Mr. deWitt." She patted her eyes and face with the handkerchief a few times, and with each pat she seemed to become more calm. "I have some coffee on the stove, and perhaps I can offer you some rolls...."

I sat down, but I shook my head at her.

"I just had all that at the corner, Miss Kornbluth. If you want to offer me something for the shoulder I gave you, remember that I said from the start that there was something I wanted."

"Oh, yes. I remember." She looked a little bit tired. I don't think she regarded my request as any part of a bargain. She would just listen, while I talked.

"First of all, Miss Kornbluth, I came on business, as I said. I came to have this Vermeer authenticated." And I tapped the box which was leaning against the leg of my chair.

"Reasonable," she said. "But my father is dead."

"I am really sorry," I said. Then I got back to the other business. "May I ask why you wanted to throw me out when you heard why I had come?"

She sighed and let her shoulders drop.

"Nothing," she said. "Nothing reasonable, nothing that makes sense. But just coincidentally, there was—or is—a Vermeer which has bobbed up again and again—what I mean is, I've known of it or heard of it several times, and each time, it seems, something unfortunate's happened. I mean, happened to me. It's just personal. I don't really want to talk about it."

"Your father was a Vermeer expert. Doesn't it stand to reason that you'd hear of Vermeers all the time you were living here together?"

"I didn't say Vermeers, Mister deWitt. A Vermeer."

"Does it have a name?"

"The 'Apple Girl.'"

There was a pause because I didn't say anything. I did not know what to say. If I told her that I had brought the "Apple Girl" just when her father had died, I would be confirming her superstition.

I noticed that she was looking at me, not waiting for me to say anything, not puzzled that I was silent, but looking the way you might in order to confirm what you already knew. Something went back and forth between us, and then she said, "You have the 'Apple Girl.' There in that box."

"Yes, Miss Kornbluth."

She did not burst out crying again, nor did she freeze up. She gave a very brief, tired laugh.

"You see?" she said, and then she laughed again.

Beyond the sadness of the laugh I could not help but notice how pleasant the sound might have been, had the occasion been different. And then she looked actually amused. She came and sat down on the chair next to mine, leaned over, and patted my hand.

"How much you show in your face, Mister deWitt." She smiled a most uncomplicated smile straight at me. "You are so worried that all this might make me superstitious or something like that, and you would so like to save me from such nonsense. No?"

"Yes." I smiled, too. I suddenly liked her very much.

"Don't. There is no cause and effect between disaster and the picture. My father died before you came. I learned of his death three days ago. You came today." Then she wrinkled her forehead. "It's just so annoying, such a repeated annoyance to be reminded of the picture every time something is bad."

"I can understand that."

It was a nothing remark and she was not listening.

"Does it still belong to Hans?"

"To—Hans?" I knew whom she meant, but it was startling to hear anyone call Lobbe by his first name.

"Hans Lobbe."

"Oh, yes. I work for him. I came, you see, to have it checked out for him after it was lost for all these years."

"Dear old *Oom* Hans," she said and looked at the wall without seeing it.

I was getting used to these terms of intimacy, though they fit the Lobbe I knew the way Little Red Riding Hood's grandmother's cap fit the wolf.

"Miss Kornbluth, there are two things I would ask of you."

"Yes?"

"One, do you know anyone here in Rotterdam, or elsewhere, who might reasonably make an appraisal of this Vermeer's authenticity? I must get this thing to the States very quickly, and the sooner...."

"Mies Ruygrok, yes. He was my father's assistant. A pupil, really."

"He lives in Rotterdam?"

"Yes. But you can't see him now."

Here it is again, I thought. Why don't I get used to these buts and these laters.

"His wife," said the young woman, "had a baby last night. I just came from the hospital myself—or else you wouldn't have found me up." She looked at me and smiled down into her lap. Then she looked up again, composed. "His wife and I are friends."

"Reasonable reason for going to see her baby."

"It would be, wouldn't it?" The curious thing happened between us again, for the second time, knowing somehow that each would understand the other—knowing somehow ahead of time what would come. "But it wasn't the reason why I went."

"Go on," I said.

"Three days ago I learned that my father had died." She blinked, as if she didn't know what to say next. Then she shrugged, and looked straight at me. "So I quickly went to see a new baby get born."

I nodded. There was no need to say anything.

"You understand."

"It needs no explaining."

She smiled and then she folded her hands in her lap. "Well, now. I was going to say something else."

"No. You started to say something else. You were telling me why I can't see—I forgot his name. Your father's pupil."

"Mies, yes. What I meant was, you can see him this afternoon. When I left the hospital, he just came in and he said he would not be in his shop until noon."

The delay was minor and I relaxed. I had been thinking in terms of insane Nazi generals, of course, and in terms of unemotional killers. But this was nothing. This was a little delay of a few hours because a man's wife just had a small baby.

"What was the other thing you wanted to ask me, Mister deWitt?"

"Oh, yes. I know you have already told me it's personal, but I would like to ask you just the same. I would like to know what you meant when you said that something or other always seems to happen whenever the 'Apple Girl' appears on the scene."

She thought for a moment, and then she said without much force or emphasis, "My scene, at any rate." She hesitated, and then, "It is personal, yes. I hardly know you, Mister deWitt."

"I know." And regrettable, too, I thought. "But perhaps, if I told you why I ask...."

"*Alstublieft*."

"Huh?"

"I'm sorry." And she laughed. "All I said was, please. I mean, please tell me."

"Well, you probably know that this *bord*—, I mean, that this...."

"*Bordelje*, yes?"

"That this—uh—yes, is very valuable."

"*Do* I know it," she said. "The fuss there used to be."

"When it was found again I was immediately sent to pick it up. Mijnheer Lobbe told me to do this thing fast, without any delay, and without letting the picture out of my sight. He was afraid he might lose it again." I left out a few things about his instructions, but I thought they would only confuse the story. "Now, since the time that I came to pick it up, several attempts have been made to steal the picture. It was in an apartment. The adjoining apartment was ransacked. It was in a museum. The curator was attacked. I have myself been kidnapped and manhandled. I don't know how the would-be thieves knew where the picture was at any one time. I don't know who the would-be thieves are. It is for these reasons, Miss Kornbluth, that I'd be interested in anything pertaining to the—uh—difficulties that have arisen in connection with the picture in the past." I looked at her and saw that her mouth was partly open and that her large eyes held very still on me. "Did you follow me, Miss Kornbluth?"

"Yes. Of course. But that must have been terrible for you!"

Her concern embarrassed me. And that in turn, embarrassed me a little more. I don't often feel awkward.

"Are you safe now?" she said.

The angel! She had not said, is the picture safe now. She had not said, is my house safe with you in it—yet, who knows, perhaps she had language difficulties.

"It's all right now. I managed to elude them."

"Elude?"

I repeated the silly word again and said, "Yes. It means, nobody knows I am here."

"I'm glad." Then she made a rather comical shrug, raised her hands, and dropped them into her lap again. "After such a terrible story," she said, "I really don't have anything to tell you that would help. What I could tell sounds rather silly."

"Tell me just the same. When you first brought it up, there was nothing silly about the way you felt."

"That's true. Are you sure you don't want any coffee?"

"Quite sure."

"Will you excuse me while I get myself a cup?"

In answer I half rose from my chair and sat down again as she started for one of the doors. I watched her walk and forgot about *bordeljes*, the kind that drove Citroëns and the kind that come in two dimensions. I watched her walk and I didn't even think about that. I just felt something undulating up and down my spine. Then she closed the door behind her. It struck me that I didn't even know her first name.

She came back with a cup as big as a barber's shaving mug. It was full of black coffee. She sat down and sipped for a while, eyes down, showing her lashes.

"What's your first name?" It just came out like that. I was not being lawyer, visitor, Lobbe's errand boy, or anything with a name. I just wanted to know. She looked up from her cup and answered the way I had asked.

"Elke." She looked at me a moment, and then she said, "You didn't sound at all as if you were here on—on that business." And she nodded at the box with the picture in it.

"It didn't feel like that business, Elke."

"In America the first name comes very soon, doesn't it?"

"Well, look at it. It comes first."

She smiled and I was glad that she didn't beat me down for a feeble joke, but just ignored it with her smile.

"And yours?" she said.

"Manny."

"Manny," she repeated. "You know, Manny, you don't act very much like somebody who works for that old bear, Lobbe."

"Perhaps not like somebody who works for him very long."

"No. Somebody who works for him."

"Your father did."

"Yes. But not like an employee. Only to lend a hand with his skill when nobody else would do. You understand?"

I nodded. "He was a straight old man, my father." She smiled. "And a little confused, like you. Or at least, it looked that way."

"It doesn't only look that way, Elke."

"I think it does. You were very straight when you asked me my first name."

"Oh, yes. I can be very straight when asking a name, when asking directions, when buying a cup of coffee—"

"You don't flatter me, Manny. You don't flatter me at all." She didn't really laugh now. I can only describe it as a grin. "That was straight of you, too."

"In a way, that is true." I felt unaccountably serious. "Actually, I want much more from you than your first name."

"Oh?" she said.

I was surprised at her facility for banter by doing no more than uttering one word, by slowly cocking her head, and by turning her mouth down—and it still looked like a smile. I also had the distinct impression that she was slanting her eyes at will.

"Manny. It's your turn to say something."

"I—uh—don't know anything straight to say right this minute."

"Say something crooked."

"Stop slanting your eyes at me."

She threw her head back and laughed. I did not think it had been that funny.

"*Oom* Hans used to say that. I was little then, and used to sit on his knee and he'd say, 'Elke, *kind*, stop slanting your eyes at me like a witch. You had enough *gebak*.' That's pastry."

"Oh. And what's *oom*?"

"Uncle. He wasn't my uncle, but we were close and that's why I called him uncle."

"If we were close, Elke, does that mean you would call me *oom*?"

"Certainly not."

"What then?"

"I will tell you if we are ever close. I mean, closer."

I really loved her for that afterthought because it saved me from being crushed by a mere slap on the wrist. But at any rate, I took the cue.

"You were going to tell me about the curse of the 'Apple Girl.'"

It embarrassed her. I did not think so much of the embarrassment she felt as of how lovely she looked with her head inclined downwards so that I could not see her eyes, only the lashes moving, like the flit of a shadow.

"It's not a curse," she said. "I told you that. It's just a personal annoyance."

"Tell me about it."

"All right. I told you how I loved *Oom* Hans, I mean, Mijnheer Lobbe to you. Well, at one time, the first and the only time I remember, he got terribly angry with me. It was early in the war and the Germans were coming and there was a lot of preparing and moving going on. With everyone. But Father and I spent a lot of time at the Lobbe place then. Father did a lot of restoration work for *Oom* Hans just then, and I was along because Mother had been dead a long time."

"Restoring what?"

"Paintings."

"What paintings?"

She thought back for a moment, and then, "I can't think of any of the others, but there were supposed to be several paintings. Actually, I only know about the *Appel Meisje*."

"That's the Vermeer."

"Yes. Father did an awful lot of work on her."

"And what was the bad thing about all that?"

"It was the first time she caused me any trouble. You see, I had only Father and we stayed at the Lobbe place during that time, and any time I wanted to see him—we would eat together, he would put me to bed—I couldn't. He was too busy."

"With the 'Apple Girl.'"

"I guess. Mostly. So one day, I mean, one evening I just went into the room where Father was working on his restorations. I wasn't supposed to go there. Sometimes I watched Father at home, or even when he worked at the Reiksmuseum in Amsterdam, but mostly not. And especially not at the Lobbe place. Anyway, I walked in and *Oom* Lobbe was there, and when he saw me, he came rushing over—big, fat, and very red in the face and—and he hit me!"

"And what was your father doing?"

"He was working on the *Appel Meisje*. Oh, you meant what did he do when Hans hit me?"

"Yes."

"Well, he tried to smooth it over, but the bad thing was done." She had not been looking at me while telling the story, but at one thing in the room and then another. Now she looked at me and made a small smile. "You see, Manny, it's just a little thing, a personal thing. Nothing like what happened to you because of the 'Apple Girl.'"

I thought a moment and wasn't so sure.

"What else happened, Elke? I mean, some of the other things that happened with you and the picture."

"Nothing happened with me and the picture. It's—not that clear a thing, or straight."

"Tell me about it, would you?"

"Almost a year ago I fell in love."

"Not clear, and not straight, you said?"

"Stop it." She was suddenly angry.

"I'm sorry."

"All right. If you want to hear about this, don't interrupt again."

Chastised, I nodded.

"I will make it very short, since you don't seem to like hearing about it." I made no comment. She was obviously dealing with things which had nothing to do with me.

"His name was Swen—he was not from any of the Scandinavian countries, he was from Latvia, an emigré—and he was very big, strong, and sort of silent."

I considered the inventory and noted that I was neither big nor strong, nor particularly silent.

"Too silent, at certain points," she said. "Anyway, I met him just shortly before Father left for Russia."

"I didn't know...."

"You are interrupting."

"I'm sorry."

"All right. Anyway, I became very much attached to him. He was, I was going to say before you interrupted, a great kind of love to me." She paused. "And a few weeks ago he left me."

I did not dare open my mouth. She was watching me intently, waiting for me to interrupt. I inclined my head as if to nod, but said nothing. She started off again with her favorite word.

"All right. All I am going to tell you, Manny deWitt, is that throughout this short-lived affair, he professed, aside from an interest in me, an interest in art."

"I would say, Elke, that the two are by no means so totally unrelated as...."

She simply glared. I stopped in mid-sentence.

"All right. Interest in art was an easy thing to work into the relationship," she said, "because of my father's work. But it was more specific. In a specific way, he talked—no, he asked about the 'Apple Girl' more than once. I don't mean more than once. I mean often. You understand?"

"Yes." I dared go no further.

"All right."

"Elke?"

She put the cup down and looked at me, waiting.

"Where did your father die?"

"On his trip."

"Not here."

"He went to visit where he was born. Always St. Petersburg to him."

"Leningrad."

"Yes. He was old," she said. She looked away and said it again, as if to remove emotion by speaking of him as old instead of saying that he had been someone she loved.

"You saw much of Swen?"

"We saw each other all the time. Also"—she twined her fingers and looked at them—"he was very jealous."

"Some lovers are...."

"He always knew where I was, even when we were not together."

The picture was not very attractive to me. From a number of points of view....

"And that's all I'm going to tell you about Swen. I told you the important part, that I lost him, that he often asked me about the 'Apple Girl,' and that this must look very silly and truly superstitious to you."

I smiled, hoping I looked reassuring, and shrugged, to show that I did not know what to say. In fact, I did not know what to say. But I felt there was more than silliness and superstition here to engage my interest. Though I was not quite sure what it was.

"How did you two part?"

"He just left."

"Just like that?"

"He sent flowers," she said. "I don't want to talk about it."

I did not talk about it. I decided to go on.

"Elke, was there any other time that the 'Apple Girl,' so to speak, got in your way?"

She looked away and shook her head. She looked resigned about the whole topic.

"She never got in my way, don't you see that, Manny? It has just been my way of blaming her for something when I, myself, did not want to look at what really went on. When I did not understand something, when I, myself, was to blame, you see that? *Oom* Hans slaps me; but I was told not to go into the room. Swen leaves me; that is something for which I may be at fault. My father dies; that is something which shocks me and I cannot bear it. So I blame *Appel Meisje*. It is no more than that."

"You know a great deal about yourself, Elke," I said.

I did not say the rest, that there was a great deal, a damn sight too much, which I did not understand about Vermeer's *bordelje*.

CHAPTER 16

While I did not doubt the existence of some demented collector who had sent someone like Spinn after me, I was also confident that no interested party knew of my presence in Rotterdam. To have traced that switch in plans on my part would have required an international organization devoted twenty-four hours a day to nothing but hunting me down. The very thought was preposterous. There were a number of things which disturbed me—nagged me, is the better word—about the affair "Apple Girl," but these were either vague or disconnected and, therefore, did not become a part of my conscious thinking. So between that morning and noontime, when I intended to see Mies Ruygrok, Kornbluth's former pupil, I would do only concrete things which made simple sense.

"Do you need to know more?" said Elke. It sounded like a plea not to ask her any more.

I said, "No, Elke. I don't even know if anything you have told me means anything to you other than a loss and a pain."

She got up from the table and shrugged. As far as I could judge her reaction was much too casual.

"It is not even ten yet," she said. "Is there anything you have to do before I take you to Mies?"

"Yes," I said, and got up, too. "I have to find a hotel. This face needs a shave, this body needs a bath, and Beau Brummel deWitt needs a change of clothes."

"Why don't you do all that here?" she said.

I did all of it there. I took my suitcase into the narrow hallway and left the Vermeer in the front room. I hated myself for the hesitation I felt when I left the box behind. In spite of my hesitation, I didn't touch it. But my Elke knew.

"If someone should come," she said, "I will move the box into another room."

Even to say thank you seemed idiotic, and I went down the hallway to the bathroom, passing a bedroom which was almost completely occupied by an enormous brass bed.

There is something about a bathroom which transforms me instantly into another being, living in another world. I look in the mirror, I grin, and it does not seem foolish. I make steam, I lather, I cannot see a thing, and it all feels wonderful. I also sing. There is no routine in this. The songs I sing have never been sung before. In the end, I come out altogether new. That is how I came out, looking for Elke.

She was standing at the other end of the hallway. Only the light from the bathroom helped me see, but I saw more. Or I felt more than I saw. There was a stiffness about her, as if from great control. There was a stillness about her that was somehow like a hysterical scream.

"Elke—" I was whispering.

Nothing much changed in her attitude, but she moved. She came closer and stopped. For a moment, it looked as if she meant to touch me, but was still again, with the words stuck in her throat.

"Say it, Elke."

"Swen is back. He is in the room."

I turned blank. There is a blankness of thought which is smooth as glass; nothing sticks to it, everything slides, jumbles, and falls off and away. And there is a blankness of thought which is like the vacuum which nature abhors. It sucks in from everywhere in order to fill itself.

What I now knew had nothing to do with close reasoning, nor was it clear until later what my knowledge was based on.

Right or wrong, there was a knowledge now, nevertheless. Swen was back because of the "Apple Girl." Swen might not know that the picture was here, but the Latvian had come back because of the picture.

"What does he want, Elke?"

"He wants—he says he wants to take up again where we broke off. He is sorry, he says."

"Get rid of him."

"He knows you are here."

"*What?*" I pulled her into the bathroom because I did not feel like whispering anymore.

"You were singing so loud, he knew I had a man in the bathroom."

"Does he know my name?"

"No. I didn't tell him your name."

"Where is the picture, Elke?"

She didn't answer. She pulled free from my grip on her arm and went quickly down the hall and into the front room. I don't know if she did it on purpose, but she left the door slightly open.

It was the first time since watching my brother neck with a girlfriend that I stood by the crack of a door and watched. I think I had been eight the other time.

Swen was a hulk of a man with a head like a chopping block. His hair was blond, almost white. I could not see his face. I imagined, with great satisfaction, that his eyes would be blue and his eyelashes white and that, therefore, he must look like a pig. It appalled me to think that Elke should have found him attractive. Of course, I hated the man with a most holy fervor. The "Apple Girl," in her box, was leaning against the leg of the chair as before, and Swen sat in that chair.

They were speaking in French.

"... found out in the end," he was saying, "that I cannot live without you."

"*Ta gueule*," said Elke, which is pretty rough language.

"But my dearest," said Swen, "can't you see that I suffer?"

He was sickening. I enjoyed it very much.

"I can see you are suffering," said Elke, precise and cold. "I enjoy it very much."

"Dearest...." He got up from the chair in an access of who knows what, jogged the chair in the process, and made the box with the "Apple Girl" topple over. Something jumped up into the back of my throat, something from way inside which did not belong in the back of the throat.

Swen interrupted his agonizing to look down at the floor where the box was lying.

"What's that?" he said.

"My lover's paintbox," she said. "Give it to me."

She did not even get up from her chair. She sat there, hands out, and waited for Swen to pick up the box, bring it over, and give it to her. At the sight, I glowed in the dark.

After Swen had delivered the box, he turned in such a way that I could see his face. He had blue eyes, white lashes, and the face of a Greek god. I hated him with pagan fervor.

"Who is this man?" demanded Swen.

"I told you," said Elke. "He is my lover."

"Awk—" said Swen.

"Excuse me," said Elke. She got up with the box under her arm and came my way. I dashed to the bathroom and heard her next remark only because she said it from the opened door of the front room. "And when I come back, Swen, I want you to be gone."

She came to the bathroom and gave me the Vermeer without a word. Then she leaned against the wall and trembled.

"He doesn't want me," she said, in a low voice. "He doesn't want me. I can feel it."

My emotions were at severe cross-purposes now. I was glad that her feeling supported what I thought about Swen; I was crushed by the fact that she was so upset about Swen's not wanting her.

"Stop trembling." It was all I could manage to say.

"I can't help it."

"The hell you can't."

"*Ta gueule!*" she hissed at me, eyes wide and very angry. "To stop trembling I have to go out there and kill him! You want me to kill him and end up in jail?"

It took me a moment, and then I was still surprised by what I said next.

"Elke, I love you!" I smiled so that my ears must have moved to the back of my head. Then I gave her a hug big as anything.

When I let go, she looked at me and I looked at her, and we did not say a word. Suddenly, she said, "Humph," or some such thing—I don't think it was Dutch—and left the bathroom fast.

By the time I got back to my post at the door (she had left it open again) they were in full swing.

"I demand to see him!" Swen was saying.

"Very fortunately for you, he has already left!"

Elke was raising her voice and Swen was raising his voice, and it got louder and louder as they went along.

"He could not have left!" said Swen. "I've been in this room all the time and no one has passed through. Unless he is a mouse, a very tiny mouse!"

"He is not a mouse!"

"There is no back way. Therefore, he must be a mouse."

"There is a back way, and he is not a mouse!"

"Show me!"

"Get out and don't ever come back!"

"I love you, Elke!"

"*Ta gueule!*"

This time he'd had it. I could see him hunch, and his beautiful Grecian face became sodden with a surprising hate.

"Listen, you bitch," he said, not so loud anymore. "You are lousy in bed. Your arms are too thin and your breasts are too big, and only decency prevents me from describing the sluglike action of your truly inferior regions. I thought to take pity on you, to help you get over the shock of losing your father and of losing me."

"Get out," said Elke.

"I will devote my time to making things miserable for you. I will...."

"I will call the police. Right now!"

"You don't have a phone!"

I could not see Elke. I could hear her quick steps, and then the sound of a window being thrown open.

"*Haal de politie! Arresteer deze man!*" she yelled.

You didn't have to know Dutch to know what she was saying. In one instant dash Swen disappeared from my sight. I heard a door bang, and then his footsteps further away, making a quick staccato on the stairs.

When I came into the room, Elke was still at the window. She turned quickly and glared at me, which I thought was a carryover from her anger with Swen. I came to the window fast because I wanted see what Swen would do once he got to the street. I never got to see him—that is, not until later.

"You!" Elke said to me loud and strong. Her voice stopped me as if she had stiff-armed me right in the chest.

"I? What...."

"You were behind the door?"

"Why, yes. You left it open a crack for me, didn't you?"

"You stood there and heard him?"

"Of course."

"You stood there and heard what he said about me? About how I look, how I'm built, how I move?"

"As a matter of fact—"

"As a matter of fact, you stood there behind the door and listened to that pink and blond pig insult me in a horrible way and you stood there and said nothing!"

"Elke, close the window. You are talking very loud."

"*Gott verdomme* the window!" And she raised her voice even more. "You are nice to me and you hold me when I need it, and then you say something to me in the bathroom, something that sounds as if you might mean it, just a little bit, and then you stand there behind the door like a mouse and...."

"Just a minute, Elke."

"Mouse!"

Only then did she close the window.

In a way, she was right. I had stood there, not thinking of Elke at all, but only of the strange possibility that Swen was here in connection with that damn Vermeer.

"Go ahead," I said when she turned around from the window. "Yell some more. It might even do me some good."

"Yes!" And then she did yell some more. Some of it was in Dutch, but even then she came across loud and strong. She was angry and hurt and humiliated, and Elke was not the kind to crawl into a corner like a sick dog. I stood there and listened to her so that she could finish. It was almost as if she did not know I was there. And then she stopped.

"So," she said. It now sounded as if she did not quite know which way to continue. I leaned on the windowsill, looking at her, and just nodded. Elke sighed.

"I'm glad I said some of it in Dutch."

"I'm glad you said it. Any old way."

She shrugged and looked away.

"Now, what," she said, in a low voice. It was not really a question. It was just a thing to say.

"I'll show you," I said.

I stepped up to her and put my arms around her, as I had once before. She did not step away. She hung on for a moment as someone might do who does not know where else to go, and then she hung on because she wanted to be there. In a moment, she stepped back.

"I'm using you, Manny."

"Does it feel good?"

"It did. Yes."

"Then go ahead."

I took her arm, turned her around, and walked her to the couch with the flower print on it. We sat down there, and I kept my hand on her arm.

"Tell me about the bastard," I said.

"May I lean against you? That way I don't have to look at you."

I put my arm around her, and we sat like that, her head on my shoulder.

"It's simple," she said. "I just thought he was the biggest thing that could ever happen to me."

"Like a first love."

She didn't answer for a while, and since I could not see her face, I didn't know whether she meant to drop it or was thinking about it.

"No. I had a first one before," she said.

"And what happened to him?"

"I don't know. We went to England before the real invasion and lived there a while after the war. That's where Mother died." She did not sound upset. It was more as if she were absorbing something. "When she died it was bad, but then it just turned into being alone. Father traveled a lot at the time—Rotterdam, Paris, Florence—and I was alone a lot of the time. That's when I grew up."

"That's how you grow up sometimes."

I could feel her nod. It was very strange. That nod against my shoulder was a most intimate thing.

"I wasn't really a woman yet," Elke went on, "but he was a full-grown man." For some reason, she sat closer and settled herself in a different way. It was a good fit. "He was a student at the conservatory and he gave me piano lessons twice a week. And one afternoon we became lovers."

"Was it good?"

"He must have been a very patient man," she said into my jacket.

She left a pause after that, as if wondering if she should say more about it and deciding not to.

"And then in a while," she went on, "we moved back here. And the next big thing was this *varken* who came along, this Swen pig, and I fell really in love."

"Did you want to?"

"Oh, yes." It sounded eager, not like a reminiscence at all. But not seeing her face, I was not certain about her mood or meaning. "I found my first lover," she said, "when I was alone, when my father was away. And the next one—Swen—I met immediately before my father went to Russia."

"And he left you when?"

"A month ago."

"And came back?"

"When my father died."

"When you got word that he had died?"

She sat up and looked at me.

"You know, Manny, the official note they sent of his death did not say when it happened?"

I had ugly thoughts. I wanted to feel very differently, sitting there with Elke, but instead I had ugly thoughts.

"When did you bury him, Elke?"

"Two days ago. They sent his ashes."

She watched my face.

"Whatever you're thinking, Manny, I don't like the thoughts you are thinking."

"I don't know what I'm thinking. I just don't feel right."

"Come here," she said. "It was better before." And she put her head down as before, and we held each other.

It was like before, and then it changed. We were almost through talking. I could hear the rain outside and I could feel Elke breathe.

"And now he's gone away again," she said quietly.

I thought she was talking about Swen.

"Forever, this time," she said, and then I knew she meant her father.

"Don't talk about it anymore. It's done."

She said the next thing as if she had not been listening, as if she'd been thinking of something else.

"And you came," she said so softly that I could barely hear her.

I understood her now, what she had been thinking and the connections she had made. Perhaps she was a fool, both sentimental and superstitious, though that's neither here nor there. Most decidedly, it was not important then. We spoke very little now, and perhaps we thought even less. She moved again, and I felt her against me the way you might feel a woman whom you have wanted a very long time, whom you have not known before, and yet who seems very familiar. She looked up and I bent down and kissed her. Her answer was immediate. It was not abrupt or in any way frantic; it was simply an answering kiss without hesitation. She stayed with it and let the kiss grow. I no longer heard the rain, but felt her breathing, which was vastly exciting now. She spoke just once more. She kept her mouth on mine so that I could feel her words.

"You remember what you said in the bathroom?"

"Yes, Elke."

"Was it a little bit true?"

"Yes. It was a little bit true. And a little bit truer now."

"That's not much of an answer...."

She was right. We stopped talking then, and went into the other room, the one with the big brass bed. And I answered.

CHAPTER 17

It was still raining when Elke took me to Mies Ruygrok shortly after one. We walked arm in arm and felt very happy. Under my other arm I carried the "Apple Girl."

Once or twice, I looked down the street in back of us, but I was not really concentrating enough to tell what any of it meant. An empty street meant that Swen's shadowing job was very excellent or it meant that he wasn't there. A slow-moving car meant that it did not want to overtake us or it meant that the driver was looking for a house number. I didn't know. I did not care too much. On the way, Elke called Mies' apartment from a booth. She told me, with a nod through the glass of the booth, that Mies was on the phone, and then they talked a while. I couldn't hear much through the booth, and besides it was Dutch, but Elke laughed a few times. She looked very good. Then she hung up and came out. She took my arm and we walked.

"All he can talk about is the baby," she said. "He talks and talks about the baby."

"The baby is fine?" I said for something to say.

"Fine? Manny! That baby is not fine. That baby is the standard of fineness by which all other fine babies are measured. But Mies will tell you. You'll see."

"I don't understand Dutch."

"No matter. He will tell you in Dutch, in English, in French, and in German. And if you still won't understand he will tell you in babytalk. There is the house." She stopped and pointed.

"Aren't you coming up?"

"I'll pick you up in an hour. Mies wants me to go to the hospital and sit with his Anne for a while. And he'd like me to bring her something from the candy store."

I did not want Elke to leave, but that was personal, and my seeing Ruygrok was all business anyway. It was the big step forward in getting that *bordelje* back to Lobbe with a clean bill of health. I kissed Elke good-bye, watched her jump on a streetcar, and went into the apartment house she had indicated.

The building reminded me of the one in which von Tilwitz wed. The recognition was not very pleasant. There was the same functional blandness, the same cold efficiency of design. One could say, of course, that the same thing is true of the bomb which destroyed the house in the Schraudolf Strasse and, identically, of the bomb which had leveled this street here in Rotterdam. These houses were all bomb-created. I hesitated to speculate about Mies Ruygrok, and stepped into the small elevator. I pressed the button for Mies' floor and the doors slid slowly together. But before they had shut they opened right up again.

"*Venez ici*," Swen said, his finger still on the hall button. He looked terribly big.

"If you say it in English, I'll understand you and come out."

He said it in English and I came out.

I must say at the outset that his accent irritated me. Sometimes an accent can have charm. It can be expressive of a person's effort to make himself understood, and an honest difficulty is never offensive. But an accent can convey something else. It can show a speaker's disregard, if not disdain, for the language. It can say very clearly that the speaker leaves all responsibility for understanding with his listener. This is how Swen spoke English.

"Where is she?" he said in a tone of command for which English was never built.

"Screw you," I said in a tone for which both words had most emphatically been built.

"I don't understand the expression," he said. "Are you saying no to me?"

"Emphatically."

"Pardon?"

"*Ta gueule*. It amounts to the same thing."

"Aha!" he said very loud. "You are the one! Nobody speaks that obscenity ever exactly the same as Elke Kornbluth unless one knows her well!"

I nodded, but ignored the remark otherwise. I wanted to bring this meeting to a head.

"Apparently you followed us, correct?"

"Correct. Where is she?"

"Why did you follow us?"

"Because Miss Kornbluth is my fiancée."

"Then how is it that Miss Kornbluth does not know this?"

I was sorry I had said that for two reasons. One, it prolonged an unnecessary discussion. I already knew why he had followed us, namely, he seemed lovesick in the peculiarly snotty way of the very tough. Two, my remark caused Swen to launch into a hard-to-follow explanation of his feelings and of Elke's feelings. I was getting irritated.

"Stop sounding like a psychologist. I am not interested in you, Miss Kornbluth couldn't care less, and from here on in, stay out of my sight."

"Or else?" His overbearing grin made me angry.

"Or I will kick you in your truly inferior regions."

His jaw hung a little while he remembered the phrase, and then he snapped it shut. It now seemed to stay shut while he talked.

"I agree you look very mean," he said. "But you are smaller than I. I will take that paintbox away from you and break it over your little head."

I was glad he had said paintbox. He had said it with such uncomplicated directness that all speculated connections between the Vermeer and Swen went by the board. And if he had been after the painting, he would not have done what he did next.

Swen lunged for me or the box—it was hard to tell because he was as imprecise as an ape—and got hold of the box. He wrenched it out from under my arm with such ease that I might as well have handed it to him. Then he swung it high over his head.

I stepped forward and the precious *bordelje* flew over my head and crashed somewhere—somewhere where my head was meant to be smashed. The sound increased my anger, which might well explain what I did next. My anger frightened me, which gave me pause, which made me fill the pause with thought for what I had learned. I moved back.

This is what lures the bully. The shrinking, sideways stance with the presenting elbow up, both hands curled in front of the face, the supporting leg away from the attack, and the leg closest to the attacker doing nothing at all. It just sort of hangs there while the rest of you shrinks away. This is the trick which kills the bully. You shrink and invite his destruction. I tried this.

When Swen saw my terror, and the patent fact that I could not hit in this coward's position, he came at me as if I were something already dead. I now curled up my forward leg somewhat—the weak move to prevent emasculation—and then, with that bent leg, lashed out very suddenly, very hard and straight to a point under Swen's knee.

Nothing holds that joint but tendons. The bone articulation is quite shallow. With a look of astonishment, and then with a harsh bellow of pain, Swen started to collapse. He clawed at me, and when he fell, I fell on top of him. His throat rattled with pain.

I rolled away from him because I did not want him to clutch into me with all the added inspiration of his pain. His pain, without question, was great. I got up and watched him curl himself into a ball, except for one leg which he kept sort of straight, not really straight because below the knee it angled off unnaturally. His face was wet with sweat. His color turned from pink to red to sodden red, and then to purple. His eyes started to glitter and protrude; they stared straight at me, though I don't know if he saw anything.

No longer worried for the moment that I might get killed or maimed by Swen, I turned my attention to the *bordelje*. I saw the box. In fact, I saw the box all over. It had split open and the Vermeer had skidded across the floor. Protective like a mother hen—no, panicked like a man whose pants are dropping off in public, I dashed for painting, box, box top, and one splintered pane that had come off the side. I gathered all these up as if I couldn't do without a single piece. Swen groaned behind me. I whirled around, dropping a piece of box, but held the painting in front of me in very much the posture of the man sans pants doubling down to pull them up.

Swen saw this. He had rolled over partly and his eyes still glittered, but now they registered what they saw. They were not even looking at me. They held still on the canvas, boring into it, and then they traveled up. He looked me in the face as if he wished to disintegrate me, and then, with a rash exhaling like a death-rattle, he said, "*You*...."

Some directness of recognition passed between us, some instant knowledge, so that no speculation was left, only the necessity for action. I knew I was no longer just somebody who had taken Elke from him, and he knew that I knew that he wanted the "Apple Girl" even if it meant he had to tear me limb from limb. I don't say that this was reasoned. But there it was, all turned into a matter of survival. I dropped the canvas—I couldn't have cared less what happened to it now—and leaped at Swen. I was up and he was down, and I leaped at him and grabbed him by the throat. I don't know the details from his point of view. Perhaps I jostled him, and he could feel the pain leap into him out of that angled leg and slash through him like a lightning bolt. At any rate, his eyes rolled up and the purple of his face turned to a sickening green. I had never seen anybody turn green, but he turned green, relaxed, and then turned gray. I let go of him; he closed his eyes and stayed where he was. I envied him his peace. That's when I heard the sound of the elevator.

I don't remember how or why I decided on what I did next, because my actual recollection is one of great confusion. I thought the elevator was getting louder and louder, descending like doom.

Actually, the elevator was going up. I saw the pebble glass of the sliding doors wiping its light out and then it went up. The hum diminished. The silence was like a breathing spell. And then I moved.

As I have said, out of confusion came action. I don't think I had a clear idea at all about each step that I had to follow because there was no plan, not even an idea of one. There was now just a first act, to be utilized in some way later. I fell on Swen like a scavenger. I went through every pocket; I even felt around inside his clothes. The elevator was coming down again. I stood there with his passport in my hand, and a key which seemed to be from a hotel. His wallet held Dutch money and an American Express card. I kept the card because it had his name on it—Swen Leswik—but put the wallet and the money back. The elevator was quite close now. I stuffed his other things into my pocket, pulled out my passport, and dropped it on the floor. When the elevator doors slid open, the man inside saw me bend over, pick up the painting, and put it inside the most intact part of the box.

"*Ja*—wat is—" he stammered and stood frozen there. He was a little man in an ulster and his pince-nez began to shake.

"*Haul de politie!*" I yelled at him. "*Politie, politie! Haal, haal, haal!*" and I looked at him with desperation.

It worked. I looked endangered to him and, therefore, was no threat. Besides, what's better under any circumstances than to run to the police? He ran out of the elevator as the sliding doors were just about to jaw him in half. Shortly after that, he was out on the street.

So I'd gotten rid of him. But what was I to do with the police?

CHAPTER 18

There was, of course, the ploy with the switched passports and the papers I had taken from Swen Leswik, and a half-conceived design that I had little time to develop. It was patently out of the question to walk away from Swen and leave him to the fates. He was an agent of whatever demented collector was after the Vermeer because he had recognized the picture for what it was and his address to me clearly implied that he had identified me as the man who had gotten away with it that other time in Munich. My difficulties in Munich and my problems here were, therefore, created by the same persistent hunter. In order once more to erase my trail, I needed time while Swen was incapacitated, more incapacitated than a busted leg made him.

I waited for the police with some impatience because I did not want to leave before they came, but also I had to get in touch with Elke before she left the hospital to join me here. Meanwhile, I did a little more stage setting.

On one side of the elevator was a staircase; on the other was a door which, I hoped, went to the basement. This turned out to be correct. I took the "Apple Girl" and all the pieces of the busted box down there. The "Apple Girl" smiled up at me. With more force than was necessary, I stuck her and the box through the lattices of somebody's cellar compartment. Then I went back up to the ground floor lobby. On the way, I rumpled my hair some more, pulled my tie more out of line, shifted jacket and raincoat on my frame so that it looked as if I had been fighting for my life with a dipso who thought I was a bottle. Actually, I did not need much rearranging, but I was nervous about the coming performance. When 1 came up to the lobby door I could already hear the violent jangling of the police bell.

Four of them came charging in, and the little man with the pince-nez was right behind them. They heard his fast tripping and one of the policemen yelled for him to get out, and the little man turned and ran back into the rain. Another policeman stayed at the door and wouldn't let anybody in. The remaining three came my way. They slowed when they saw Swen because he wasn't moving anyway. They slowed some more when they saw me because I was apparently going to collapse.

"*Schuldig?*"

"Huh?"

"*Kan ik U helpen?*"

"I really don't know. If you would get somebody who can speak English or French...."

"*Wilt U langzamer spreken, Mijnheer.*"

That was the end of that for a while. My interrogator, who had a face like a sleeping baby, but with mustache, looked at me for a moment, and then joined his colleagues by the body of Blackout Swen. Their interrogation of him, which involved going through his pockets and marveling at the strangeness of one leg, produced nothing but a billfold with some money and a sudden bellow of pain. Swen had woken up. The baby with the mustache then turned back to me while a companion ran out to the street. He said something to the cop at the door, something including the words Arts and Dokter.

"You speak English," he said and opened his notebook.

"Right."

"Name?"

I told him.

"Passport?"

"I don't have one."

He looked at me as if he were wearing glasses and was peeking over the rims. If you also have a baby face, that can look most peculiar. I reminded myself of my role, kept a straight face, but looked back at him as I imagined a lost dog might look.

"The other one," said my policeman, "the one on the floor there. He doesn't have one either."

"I know."

"What?"

"I mean, that's what I thought."

He looked confused and, to cover, he immediately looked suspicious. He licked his pencil, and then poised it over his book.

"Everything goes down here."

"Right."

"You know the man on the floor?"

"No."

"What?" The sharp look and the confusion again. "A moment, please. You know the man has no passport, and you don't know the man. How is that?"

"I'm glad you're here to straighten that out," I said to him. The general air I affected was one of gratitude. He liked that.

Swen made a noise and we all looked at him. But it had been only a small noise, not repeated, so we went back to business.

"Who hit him?"

"I did."

"Ah." And it went down in the book. "And who hit you?"

"He did."

"Ah." That went down, too. "And why, Mijnheer?"

"Well, I don't know this man and...."

"I have that down here already."

"I'm sorry. I'm walking down the street and he and I get in a conversation. It's raining...."

"Wait, wait. You have a conversation and you don't know this man? How can you have a conversation with...."

"Wait." I paused and he waited. "We are standing in the rain, waiting for the light to change down there"—and I pointed vaguely—"and we just happened to be standing there at the same time when he asked me something."

"What?"

"I don't know. I think it was in Dutch."

"How do you know...."

"Never mind. I mean, when he said something and didn't understand it, I said in English, 'I don't understand.' You understand?"

"I think so," he said. Then he shrugged and looked down at his notebook again. "There is more?"

"Of course. So he said he spoke English too, and was happy to meet somebody besides all these stupid Dutch—"

"*What?*"

"Stupid Dutch."

I think he wrote it down. At any rate, he scribbled with mad intent.

"And he said he was lost in the city—all these crazy streets going in crazy directions—"

"He said crazy streets going in crazy directions?"

"Yes. Anyway, to make a long story short, he didn't know anybody here, he had no money, and"—I leaned closer to make things more confidential—"and I think he is wanted." He scribbled and scribbled.

"Well, to make a long story short, I gave him some money, Dutch money, and wished him good luck with his papers."

"What papers?"

"I mean documents. He said documents. He said he had to get out of the country and needed documents. Now, when I gave him the Dutch money, he saw the passport I had in my billfold."

"What passport? The one you don't have?"

"Yes. American. And then he said, 'If I get money, will you sell me your passport?'"

"And you said?"

"No. Then he pleaded, then we argued, and then he pushed me into this hallway."

"And?"

"I pushed back."

"Hm," said the policeman and looked at Swen. "I can tell you pushed."

"And that's all, sir. Except that he got the passport away from me in the struggle and I don't know what happened to it."

The last part was a fact. I thought for sure the cops with Swen would have seen it right next to him where I had dropped it.

Outside, an ambulance was howling. Swen was shivering with pain and tried to say something in one language after the other. They told him to shut up and save his strength and everything would be taken care of; he should not worry. Two orderlies came dashing in, unfolded their stretcher, and lifted Swen on the thing with such industrious speed that he did not find time or breath to start howling with pain until they were halfway down the hallway.

And that was mostly that. I would have time while they knocked him out in the hospital, sorted out his protestations and traced his identity. He would have to be damn careful what he told them because any direct kind of reference to me and the picture would surely make things hot for him, since his shirt was no cleaner than mine. He could call confederates. But that would take time. He could tell them to call Elke for a safe identification, but I intended to reach her first.

"Well," said my policeman, "I now believe you a little bit more."

Swen was gone, and I looked back at my note-taker. He was leafing through my passport.

"When they lifted the man," he said, "there it was under him."

The power of an American passport is great. It is not as great as it was right after the war, and there was some more note-taking, more questioning, more promises to be good and next time call the police first and kick later. But I was given a clean bill. I told the man I was here for only one day and therefore had no address. I had just wanted to admire the beautiful city. I had landed in Amsterdam to change for an evening plane going to Trondheim; but I would stay longer, of course, find a hotel, and report at the station in the morning for more depositions. If I didn't, I knew I wouldn't get back the money I had given to Swen. I said I was very anxious about that. Then I got my passport and a cute little salute. Everybody left while I leaned by the wall, exhausted. Everything had been a lie except the way I felt now, like a sack of potatoes with all the potatoes gone.

CHAPTER 19

When I rang Mies Ruygrok's apartment on the third floor, I had completely forgotten that I had arranged my appearance so that I would look like a disaster victim. Mies Ruygrok threw open the door shortly after I had rung the bell, and it was plain that he had been expecting me. But the expression on his young face faded almost immediately.

He had a thin, eager face and the kind of shortsighted eyes that keep reaching out for you. And there was happy expectation in the way he kept wanting to smile. He had a big shock of black hair, looking forever rumpled, which made his very blue eyes that much more important.

I caught a glimpse of all this, just a glimpse, before be suddenly turned reluctant and glum.

"You are not the one who Elke said was such a—uh," he stammered, and looked down to where I was holding the Vermeer in the open box. "You mean you *are?*"

"I was, correctly speaking. May I come in?"

"What happened to you?"

"There was a war on, you see, and I had to cross both lines. May I come in, please? It's rather urgent."

"I believe you," he said and became very lively now. "Do come in. Please come in. You see that door?" And he pointed. "The bathroom. I will turn on the hot water and you....."

"Have you got a phone?"

"Phone? Uh—the bathroom is...."

"I need a phone very much more urgently."

"Ah, phone," he mumbled, and dashed off ahead of me.

I went to the phone which he showed me on an untidy desk in a corner. I sat down at the desk while he stood by, looking anxious.

"I have to speak to Elke immediately," I said to him. "'Would you dial the hospital room for me where your wife just had a beautiful baby?"

He became transformed immediately, and I could not help smiling. I held out my hand to congratulate him while Mies grinned from ear to ear. He shook my hand as if I, too, had just had a baby, and there were tears in his eyes. Then I took my hand away, got up, and started to stuff my shirt under my belt properly. I rearranged jacket and overcoat, and straightened my tie. Mies, recognizing that ceremonies were at an end, dialed the hospital while I used my hands on my hair.

Something of my tension must have come across to him because he made no attempt to converse with his wife, but got Elke for me immediately. Then he gave me the phone. I could hear her say, "Manny?", before I got the instrument to my ear.

"Yes, Elke. Darling, listen closely and don't ask about details now."

"Yes, Manny." She did not sound scared.

"Swen followed us. He was after the picture. I managed to get away with the damn canvas and Swen is now being held in confinement. I arranged it so he has no identification...."

"What do you mean you *arranged* it? What happened, Manny? Are you all right?" She practically screamed in my ear and I could imagine how large her eyes had become.

"Don't interrupt. Swen might try to use you for an identification. If that happens, Elke, if the police ask you if you know him, deny it."

"Say no?"

"Yes. Say no. One more thing. When you leave the hospital, take a taxi straight to Mies' apartment and have the cabby bring you upstairs."

"It is serious."

"Sort of. Understood?"

"Yes, Manny."

I hung up. Mies, at a table near the windows, put the Vermeer down and looked at me.

"You 'arranging it,' as you put it—was that what disarranged you?" And he nodded at my clothes.

"Yes. But it's all right now. Mister Ruygrok...."

"You mispronounce the name or you break your tongue. Why don't you call me Mies?"

"Thank you, Mies. The reason I'm here...."

"I know why you are here. Elke told me. I will analyze the picture as fast as I can."

I liked his efficiency when it came to work. He looked rumpled and he moved as if he were just learning all about his joints, but there was nothing stupid or slow about him. "Does it look like a genuine Vermeer, Mies?"

"Oh, yes. It looks like it."

I literally held my breath.

"And, of course," he said, "the better the forgery, the more it looks like the genuine article."

"You mean to tell me, I mean, are you trying...."

"No, no. Without tests, everything is guessing. Right now it looks like the *Appel Meisje*, a genuine Vermeer."

I admired the man. I admired him in the same way I admire the surgeon who says to the terminal case: "Don't worry, chum. We'll know everything after the operation."

"You scratched the panel. But I can fix it."

"What goddamn panel?"

"Oak panel," he said as if talking to a child. But he was friendly about it. "The Vermeer is on oak, with canvas glued over it. A method which coincides with the period."

I was pleased. I was very glad that the method coincided with the goddamn period.

"Now what do we do?"

"We go into my workroom and I put on my glasses."

These things are a matter of taste, but I thought his workroom smelled delicious. There were acetone odors, a touch of ammonia, a slight alcohol sting, and the distinct bouquet of cloves. I am not a smoker. Smells matter to me. All the smells were in bottles, some with sticky drippings on the glass, and the labels were handwritten in Latin. All of them belonged to solvents—solvents with which you remove varnish, make yellowed varnish clear again, or destroy paint.

Mies had found his glasses. I don't know how he had done this because the mess in the room was insane. Canvases, boards on wooden horses, boxes with translucent windows, wires leading to blue bulbs and red ones, paint pots, pencils, cotton balls, scalpels, bricks of hard glue, and a thing like a microscope. But he had put the glasses on, turned on a strong light, and was now going over the canvas with a magnifier.

"Hard to tell about the varnish," he said. "Ilja had cleaned it, of course, and perhaps somebody else since then...."

"I don't know what you're driving at, Mies."

"Age, Mister deWitt. There are more precise ways, but first I look at the varnish."

I waited while he ranged over the canvas with an almost tactual intensity, as if his eyes were touching and prodding....

"It looks new and it looks old, but restored. Hard to tell this way."

"Try another way."

"I will. You will excuse me, but I go step by step, even when I know that the first three steps are useless. But it helps me know the picture, or feel the picture. You understand?"

I thought I did. It seemed like fingering the ball before the pitch even though the twisting and fingering in itself does not make the ball fly at the batter.

"*Ja*," he mumbled. "Maybe Pettenkofer treatment did it. No discoloration, no powdering, no disintegration. We forget about the varnish and look at the paint."

This required no comment from a layman, though I, too, felt strongly that he should look at the goddamn paint already.

"The scratch is very new," he said. "I'm sure it happened just now when you, how did you say it, 'arranged' things with Swen."

"Possible."

"I knew Lobbe's Vermeer. I worked in Mijnheer Kornbluth's shop. No scratch. Even before the last restoration. And this scratch is still powder-white."

I was looking down at the canvas, at the scratch which disfigured the background in the upper left corner, and I must confess that I had no special feelings about it. The *Appel Meisje* was not a work of art to me, but only an object which caused me danger and harm.

"But don't worry about it," said Mies. "It is deep, so I will build it up. Then a little copaiba balsam and the scratch color disappears. Don't worry."

"I'm not worried. I just want to get rid of the thing. Once you've authenticated it, I'm going to jet us to New York, scratch and all. Let Lobbe worry about it. I'm more worried about life and limb."

He took a bottle down from a shelf and held it up to the light. He jiggled it this way and that. The bottle was empty.

"I have not been working here lately," he said, "I will telephone for the alcohol."

He made his phone call and then came back to the workroom. He looked at me, but said nothing.

"Anything wrong?" I asked.

"No." He sat down at the table where the Vermeer lay under the strong light.

"Why do you need the alcohol?"

"Perhaps I don't," he said. "We will see."

He had a habit of humming and muttering while he worked. It sounded as if he were about to say something, but nothing came.

"What are you doing now?"

He had stopped hummimg. He was moving the lamp on its long, jointed arm so that the light shone across the painting from one side. He got up and looked down at the painting from the full distance of his height.

"I will not need the alcohol," he said.

His tension was palpable.

"The jewel-like quality of the color is typical Vermeer," he said without looking up. "And so are the tiny white dots in the highlights. Remarkable...."

The slanting light on the canvas brought out contours of paint which were not visible under ordinary illumination.

"It looks ugly that way," I said.

"Masterful...." He shook his head, but stood otherwise very still. "Exactly where did you get this painting?"

"I actually took it over from safekeeping in the Alte Pinakothek."

"Hm."

"A Doctor Baumeister—"

"Hm. I know him. Good Renaissance man." Then he was silent again. He bent very close to the painting now and used the magnifying glass to inspect the paint.

"What are you looking at?" I asked him.

"The brush strokes."

He put the glass down, sighed, and rubbed the back of his head. He did not look at me until he had sat down on his chair.

"It is a remarkable painting," he said. "A masterful job." I said nothing. I had the feeling he was not quite finished. "I am even certain I know who painted it."

"What's that?"

"This Vermeer is a fake."

"*What?*"

"Ilja Kombluth painted this copy."

CHAPTER 20

I will not pretend that I felt any sort of a shock. I felt nothing. I had heard the words Mies had said, but instead of meaning there had only been sound. The first thing I said was, "I don't believe it."

Mies shrugged. He looked at me and tried to smile. I think he meant to be kind.

"Mies, listen. None of this makes sense. The German government doesn't hand out fakes."

"I told you it is a very good copy. Who authenticated it in Germany?"

"Nobody."

"But why not?"

"It's a long story." I started to pace back and forth in the room, around chairs, books, canvases, and all the rest of the clutter.

"Didn't Lobbe insist that the canvas be checked?"

I knocked into something on the floor, but didn't bother to look at what it was.

"His precise instructions," I said with considerable venom, "were to avoid all official inspections whatsoever."

"That makes no sense."

"Lobbe always makes sense. Sometimes ordinary humans just don't understand him."

"He will be upset."

"That is hardly the word. Is there a chance that you are mistaken, Mies?"

He raised his hands and then dropped them on his knees. "Kornbluth was my teacher," he said very simply.

"But isn't it possible, Mies, that a judgment of this type, something complex like the manner in which a picture is painted—I mean, what are the chances that you might be wrong?"

"It is complex, yes. But the manner in which a man uses the brush is as individual a thing as his handwriting. I think you would have no trouble telling one handwriting from the other, would you?"

"I guess not."

"I can make further tests, chemical tests, if you like."

By now, my numbness had worn off and the rather frightful aspects of the turn in events came clear to me. A great deal of chasing and conniving had gone on, a great deal of illicit plotting had taken place, and over what? A lousy fake.

"Mies, I have to make two phone calls. One to Munich and one to New York. Would you place them for me?"

He got up without a word and went to the telephone in the other room. I gave him Lobbe's business number in New York and I gave him the number of the Alte Pinakothek. While he placed the calls, I paced around in the room and tried to think. My thinking got no further than my pacing. I went back and forth over the same route, getting nowhere. I got a rather second-rate satisfaction out of only one thing: the maniac who had been sending his strong-arm men after me didn't know he was chasing a fake either.

"The Munich call," said Mies, "can be ready in fifteen minutes. New York might take an hour." He watched me pace for a while. "What will you do now?"

"I don't know yet." Then I stopped pacing. "Damn it, Mies, why in hell would Kornbluth make such an elaborate copy?"

"Because Lobbe ordered it, I imagine."

"Did you know of such an order?"

"No. I only knew of the restoring he did before the invasion. He stayed at the Lobbe place at the time."

"That's when he must have made this copy."

"Possible. No one saw him, except Lobbe. I mean, no one went into the room where he worked."

"Is that unusual, as far as his work habits went?"

"It was rather unusual that I was not allowed in. I went out once to speak to him about something, I forget what it was, and I had to wait for Ilja to come out. He came out, locked the door, and then we talked."

"Did the talk have anything to do with the Vermeer?"

Mies didn't answer. He was still sitting at the desk with the telephone and seemed to be looking at nothing.

"Did you hear me, Mies?"

"I was mistaken."

"What?"

"Somebody besides Lobbe did go in. I remember now."

"Anybody you knew?"

"Not personally." Mies blinked and seemed to be thinking. Then he looked at me. "It was a little bit strange. We were sitting in the hall, you see, and then the butler went to answer the bell."

"Nothing strange so far, is there?"

"No. Then a man came in, an elderly man with a goatee. He carried a black attaché case and there were two men with him. I will describe the picture to you. Here is an elderly man, he looks scholarly, and he carries a case. The case seems heavy. With him are two men who do not look scholarly. They do not help to carry the case. They have their hands in their pockets and always stand a little bit away, looking."

"Sounds like a cheap movie."

"It does. But I did have the distinct impression that they were along to watch the man. Then Lobbe came into the hall and told the two men with their hands in their pockets that it was all right, they could go sit down. Then he brought the elderly man over to where I was sitting with Ilja. Lobbe said to Ilja: 'This is Geheimrat Doctor Wende. You can give him the key, Ilja.'"

"And Kornbluth gave this Wende the key?"

"Yes. Then he left with Lobbe."

"Who was this man?"

"I asked Ilja. All he said was that the Doctor was with Lobbe Industriel in Brussels."

"That may be important. Lobbe Industriel, Brussels, does only one thing and never did anything else. Research. Chemical research."

"Oh?" said Mies.

I felt very much the same way as Mies, as if standing in front of a wall without any door. For that matter, it was not really my business to find the door. Lobbe had asked me only to pick up a painting and the way he had handled the matter, it was really not my worry that the object of all this activity had turned out to be a fake, that a chemist with bodyguards had gone into Kornbluth's locked workroom, that I had got manhandled at gunpoint in Munich and attacked in a hallway in Rotterdam. At that point, the phone rang. It was the Alte Pinakothek.

"Doctor Baumeister, bitte."

"*Ein moment*," said the voice. Then another voice came on, but it was not Baumeister. "*Ich bin der Assistent*," he said.

He was the one whom I had met in the parking lot, and I remembered that he didn't speak English. I said, "*Ein moment, bitte*," in turn, and gave the phone to Mies.

"You speak German, don't you?"

"Yes."

"This is Baumeister's assistant. Tell him you're calling for me—he knows my name—and I must speak to Baumeister. I've got to start tracing that Vermeer, every move it made before I picked it up."

Mies turned to the phone and talked in German. From what I gathered, he stopped talking before he had finished his explanation. For a moment, he just sat and listened.

"Oh, *mein Gott*..." he whispered. Then he listened again. "*Und sonst wissen Sie nichts?... Auch nicht die Polizei?*" Then he listened again. In a while, he hung up without having said another word.

"Baumeister," he said, "is dead."

"Christ, I'm sorry to hear that."

"Did you know he was in the hospital?"

"Yes. I know about that."

"Two doctors went to his room late last night, or at least, the nurse who saw the two men thought they were doctors."

My hands were beginning to sweat.

"But the nurse paid no special attention until the two men left. They did not check at her station, but left very fast."

"Come on, man, what else?"

"When she checked Baumeister's room, she found the bed in a mess. Baumeister was dead on the floor, and there were signs of struggling. The police say he was attacked and his heart gave out."

I felt weak and sick. A sense of waste and uselessness was my only emotion at the moment.

"Do the police know why he was manhandled?"

"The assistant didn't know."

But I knew. I did not know who the two men were. It was unlikely that it had been Spinn and his silent partner, but it was a certainty to me that two men from the same team had come to find out what had happened to the Vermeer. They—whoever they were—knew that I had disappeared from the city, presumably with the painting. They would also assume, correctly, that Baumeister was the logical one through whom to trace the whereabouts of the picture. And in the process, they had killed the old man.

I started to curse. I cursed all the sense of waste and uselessness out of my system and replaced it with a rage. This was just as useless, but it made me feel a hell of a lot better. And, of course, Baumeister's death had been doubly useless. One, the Vermeer and I had since been spotted here in Rotterdam. Two, the Vermeer was a fake.

"Call that overseas operator back, will you, Mies? About the New York call."

He checked with the operator while I stood by the window, chewing my lip. Then Mies came over.

"Was he a friend of yours?" he asked.

"Yes. I liked him very much. Mies, listen to me."

"The picture is dangerous, isn't it?"

"Yes. We'll talk about that in a moment. Let's sit down." There was a window bench and we sat down there. It had stopped raining outside. Even if the sun had come out at that moment, I wouldn't have paid any attention. "Tell me everything you know about Swen."

"He was Elke's lover. I don't know anything else."

I took Swen's passport out. It was French. Border stamps covering the dates of two years showed that he had traveled extensively between France, Germany, Holland, and Belgium. At one point, the stamps stopped, apparently around the time when Common Market regulations made border checks less and less frequent. His occupation was given as import-export agent. In brief, there was nothing unusual and I learned nothing useful.

"Tell me this, Mies. How do you think Swen would know that Elke's father had just died?"

"He knew?"

"Yes. He said so today, at Elke's house."

"Perhaps she told him."

"No. She hadn't seen him before today, that is, since his return, and she never mentioned it."

"Perhaps mutual friends?" said Mies. He shook his head. "I don't remember their having any mutual friends."

"That makes it damn peculiar for him to know that a man died three thousand miles away."

"In a way, yes," said Mies. "But perhaps there is a simple explanation?"

"I'd like to have it. Let me ask you something else, Mies."

He looked at me very attentively, though I had the impression that he did not like the general topic very much.

"Did it ever strike you that there is a curious coincidence between Swen's arrival and disappearance, his movements in regard to Elke, and Ilja Kornbluth's trip?"

He became uncomfortable and did a few nervous things with his hands. They were large and they suddenly looked very awkward.

"What is it, Mies?"

"Do you know anything about his trip?" he asked me.

"No, just that he took sort of a sentimental journey to the place of his youth."

"Hm," he said and looked out of the window. "Yes, he did that."

"What are you leaving out?"

"Manny, this is very private. I don't know what it means, I am afraid to think what it means. Elke knows nothing about this."

"Go ahead. Tell me."

"It is like this. Ilja took a one-month trip, booked by Intourist. You know how they arrange everything ahead of time, the places where you are permitted to go, everything."

"Yes, I know."

"The Intourist trip was for one month, to Leningrad and immediate environs. Ilja stayed three months."

"How did he manage that?"

"He was sick."

"Is this what Elke doesn't know?"

"She would get postcards from him, picture postcards of Leningrad, saying the harmless little things one writes from a trip on a picture postcard. That's all."

"I didn't know Ilja Kornbluth," I said, "but it's plausible that he didn't want to worry his daughter. She's in Rotterdam, he's in Leningrad, and what possible good...."

"He was sick in Moscow."

"What was that?"

"Cards from Leningrad while he is sick in Moscow. Moscow was not on his itinerary."

"How do you know all this?"

"It is a little strange, and to me it was even frightening. I did not want Elke to know."

"What happened?"

"There was an international convention of physicians in Amsterdam one month ago. They came from everywhere."

"Including Russia."

"Yes. One night, a month ago, I get a call. It is a Doctor Loewenstein."

"A call, or you saw him?"

"Only a call, a hasty call, a frightened call. He said I should not interrupt, just listen. He gave his name and said he was a psychiatrist from Moscow, here for the convention. He has seen Ilja, he says, very briefly, and Ilja says not to worry, everything will be all right. But Elke must not see Swen."

"Did you ask this doctor why all the secrecy?"

"He would not discuss it. He said Ilja is in a hospital in Moscow."

"And the sickness?"

"He wouldn't say. He said psychiatric ward."

I got up. My scalp was prickling, which is a nervous symptom I have. It precedes an attack of anger. I prepared to control myself and succeeded in part. I reduced the attack to a quiver in my voice.

"Did you ever hear of anyone dying of a mental disorder, Mies?"

"No."

"No. Had Kornbluth displayed any sort of behavior which might be construed as disturbed, psychotic, bizarre, insane?"

"Of course not."

"Of course not! Do you know that something here stinks to high heaven and that I don't know what it is?"

The phone interrupted my yelling and I grabbed it. "DeWitt here. Who's speaking?"

She said something in Dutch, and then the New York operator came on, clear as a bell.

"I have your connection," she said. "One moment, please."

"Lobbe Industriel, Miss Moon speaking."

"Sunshine, this is deWitt. Give me the old man, and fast."

"Oh, Manny," she said. "You sound so loud."

You don't rush Miss Moon. She is Lobbe's executive secretary, New York office, and it takes her even temper to balance Lobbe's uneven temper.

"Where is the tub, Moon Maiden. I mean it!"

"He won't be back till tomorrow, Manny. Can I tell him something?"

"Yes. But you better not."

"When are you coming back?"

"Where is he, Moonshine? This is important."

"I'm not to tell anyone. But if you want me to reach him for you...."

"Tell him to prepare himself for a shock. That's my message, and I hope it worries him."

"Manny, you don't sound right."

"That's nothing. You should see me. I don't look right, either." I was about to hang up when I had a thought out of nowhere. "Moon girl, do you happen to know the quotation on Carbon and Allied?"

"Carbon and Allied? Strange you should ask. Wait a moment." I waited. She didn't take long. "85½, Manny."

"What was it yesterday?"

"91, Manny."

The Colossus had sunk another five and a half incredible points.

CHAPTER 21

I left Rotterdam that night. I took the shuttle from Amsterdam to London, and from London I caught a jet non-stop to New York. A few things took arranging first, all very important. Except for one which I no longer considered important. That was the fake Vermeer. It had caused a lot of grief over nothing, and I wasn't going to carry that dud along and maybe get jumped again. Orders were orders but I was intelligent enough to know when they no longer applied. Mies was going to repair the scratch, and then mail the picture to Lobbe's office. A matter of perhaps two or three days, he explained.

"Fake or no fake," I had told him, "somebody is still after it, thinking it's the real thing. You've got to get it out of here."

"Why?" he wanted to know.

"Because Swen saw it, Swen recognized me, and there's not much doubt in my mind that he's also after it. He saw me come to this building; he or an associate will undoubtedly be able to find out that there is one Mies Ruygrok living here who makes his living looking at Vermeers and such like."

"I'm not afraid," he said.

"Don't be stupid. For all intents and purposes, they killed a man trying to trace that picture. Where can you take it?"

"The Boyman Museum. I work in their shop. I can finish the repair there."

"And then I want you to disappear."

"What?"

"Until I have some better answers than I have now, I cannot tell whether you will be safe after my having dragged that—that thing in here."

"But I can't leave. My Anne is in the hospital!"

"And you must ask for police protection for her."

"But in the hospital...."

"You heard what happened to Baumeister in a hospital."

That's when Elke came back. The doorbell rang, which made both of us jump, but it was Elke and the taxi driver who had brought her to the door. I paid the man and pulled Elke into the apartment.

"What is all this?" she said and looked from Mies to me and then at Mies again.

I explained it to her. I told her that the Vermeer was a fake, but even though it was a fake, somebody was after it without knowing they were after a forgery. And I told her that these people played rough.

"I'm flying to New York, Elke. I want to see Lobbe on this. Among other things I want some explanations. Meanwhile...."

"You are leaving," she said. I had never heard her speak with such a small voice.

"Yes, Elke. I'm going to finish this up, and then I've got a vacation coming. Then I want to come back."

She didn't say anything.

"I'd ask you to come with me now, except there is a matter of safety. I'm known as the messenger boy who had the picture. That's why I'm going alone."

"I didn't mean to behave this way," she said. "We just met."

"Elke, what better reason to want to see each other more?"

She smiled and I wished we had been alone. I wished that, and also that there had been more time.

"Understand something now, Elke. You are connected with this chase for the picture. I don't want you to stay alone, or at home, or even in Rotterdam. You understand?"

"It's that bad?"

"Yes. I'll tell you about it some other time. Can you think of a place to go?"

"I know where," said Mies. "The Lobbe place."

"Are you nuts?"

"You don't understand. The Lobbe place outside Rotterdam is a monastery now. Lobbe gave it to the Carmelites and they have rooms there where you can go into retreat."

We arranged this. There was no getting Mies out of the city. Instead, he was going to try and move into a room at the hospital to be near his wife. And he agreed to ask the police for a guard, telling them as little as possible of this curious Vermeer situation.

Elke and I picked up some things at her house and then took a taxi to the Carmelite monastery. I saw no one following us. Swen, apparently, had not yet gotten through to his employer and he, himself, was undoubtedly still in the hospital.

I said good-bye to her in the giant hall of the old Lobbe place. It was very bare.

"Many beautiful things used to be here," she said. "How strange to come back now."

"Many beautiful things and a lot of troubles," I said. "And you didn't come back here. You're staying a few days and then I'll be back."

"I hope so, Manny."

A Carmelite monk with a beard took Elke away. But I did not come back for her as I had promised. It all turned out differently....

I made New York at ten in the morning all in one piece. I saw no one who scared me or upset me, but I stayed with the crowds. I wasn't carrying a box the size of the Vermeer, but I had my suitcase which might have held the picture. Perhaps the chase was off. I did not really believe it. Perhaps they had lost me again. That was the most likely explanation. But, as I have said, I was not scared or upset the way I had been before on occasion. Since Baumeister's death, I was angry.

Lobbe Industriel, New York, is a giant cube of glass and blue enamel. There are ten elevators. There are several tenants, all with different names, though most of them belong, in one way or another, to the parent company, Lobbe Industriel. My paternalistic employer, enthroned on the twenty-fifth floor, was about to receive a most irate son. He didn't know I was coming, of course. There had been no advertising of my whereabouts for the rest of the trip.

Miss Moon was just putting a rose into the vase on her desk. She was a sloe-eyed, rotund woman with an old-fashioned hairdo and looked more like a middle-aged teacher than a high-priced executive secretary to a slave driver like Lobbe. In fact, she had once been a teacher. I never learned if it had been languages or mathematics. She was good at both.

"Moon Maiden," I said. "Announce me."

She looked up and smiled as if I hadn't been away.

"Have a seat, Manny." You can't surprise her.

"He's in?"

"He rode in on a broom this morning."

"I might ride out on a rail, but announce me."

"At eleven-thirty?"

"At eleven-thirty. I don't care."

At eleven-thirty nobody sees Lobbe. At that hour he sits in his throne room with a code clerk and concocts edicts, missives, codicils, and proclamations which are then sent all over the globe.

"Did you tell him I called yesterday?"

"Yes. Your secretiveness put him in a funk that cost him half a million. He refused to see Stebbs who came in to have selling orders okayed, and by the time he got around to them the block he was selling had dropped half a mil."

"What block, Moonshine?"

"Carbon and Allied, Manny."

I thought about it for a moment, but decided to see Stebbs about it later. If I still had a head.

"So what's he like? Brief me."

"One chin," said Miss Moon.

This is a way we have of describing Lobbe's mood. One chin means he is angry. He sticks his jaw out and all the chins more or less disappear. Two chins is normal. He keeps his head just so and nothing much shows on his face. Three chins means he is in a thoughtful mood or asleep.

"You still want to see him, Manny?"

"I must. Give him a ring."

She rang and said into the phone that I was here. I could hear the immediate click at the other end of the line, and then came the explosion. The double doors to his inner sanctum flew open and Lobbe came galloping through. I had never seen him do that and I'll never forget it. At one point, I thought he might even soar off like a balloon. And he was laughing! He opened his arms, rushed me, and gave me a hug that made my ears sing. Miss Moon, for the first time in memory, looked upset. Then Lobbe gave me a wet kiss on the chin. He is shorter than I.

"*Mennekin*," he bellowed. "Do you know that I'm happy to see you?"

"Yes. The kiss spoke volumes."

"Strauss!" he yelled in the direction of his office. "Get out!"

Strauss, the code clerk, came out. He was shriveled like Scrooge and carried his paraphernalia in a metal box which was chained to his wrist. As he walked he clanked like a spook. Lobbe hustled me into his office and slammed the two doors.

It is an impressive office: oak paneling with little inlays of rosewood, Persian carpet repeating the red and brown hues of the wall, lamps with beige parchment shades as big as the roof on a doghouse, paintings on the walls, a Mayan stone god on the floor, a thirteenth-century altar cloth (Byzantine) draped over the grand piano on which Lobbe plays Telemann and Buxtehude. His desk, large as it is, was cluttered with papers and phones. He stopped in the middle of the room.

"Now, Manny. Where is it?"

"Sit down, Mister Lobbe."

Two chins. He did not want me to know how he felt.

"Answer me immediately," he said in a very even voice.

"I picked up the painting in Munich. The painting I picked up in Munich is a fake."

There was a couch nearby and Lobbe went there. He sat down on the leather cushions and folded his hands in front of his belly.

"Let me have it," he said.

"I haven't got it with me. Mies Ruygrok in Rotterdam made an identification and he's sending that picture to you by air. He'll send it tomorrow."

His face became dark red and his eyes glittered as if in a fever. He looked as if he meant to tear me apart. When he talked, his voice was hoarse beyond recognition.

"You left it behind—not here—"

"It's a fake! Didn't you hear me?"

"My instructions to you...." He actually could not go on. He just sat there and breathed and something like hate came into his eyes. I talked fast now. I suddenly had my anger back and to hell with his problems. He was going to hear about a few of mine.

"I was jumped by gunmen and a friend got killed. Lives are threatened because some maniac is after your Vermeer. And all this has been going on with the obvious assumption that I'm carrying the genuine thing. All this threat and confusion and danger while I'm chasing around with nothing but a fake! That makes not one iota of sense to me, Mister Lobbe, none whatsoever. Mies had to ask for police protection, Elke Kornbluth is in hiding at the monastery which used to be your place, I jump at every shadow, and you expect me to walk around...."

"Where is the Vermeer?"

"The fake. Mies took it to the Boyman Museum. He'll mail it to you tomorrow."

Lobbe got out of the couch with surprising speed. He went to his desk, reached for a phone, but just as rapidly changed his mind. He walked out of the office without looking at me. He was gone just long enough to have a few words with Moon, so it seemed, and then he was back, somewhat pale and very silent. His silences can be unbearable.

Three chins, and he was not asleep. He was looking down at his hands. Now and then, with a quick glance, he looked at me. It wasn't friendly.

"From the beginning," he said finally.

I started with Paris and got as far as Munich. When I came to the matter of Spinn, the fake Bonn official, I had to comment.

"If I had been less in the dark about everything, I could have operated with more efficiency. I register this as an instructional complaint because it almost cost me my life."

"So soon," he said. "Already in Munich...."

"Did you know somebody else was after the Vermeer?"

"Yes."

"You could have told me."

"I could not predict anyone would know as soon as Bonn made the announcement. Underestimated the situation. My instructions for speed, ordinarily, would have been sufficient. Clever. Had a man sitting in Bonn all that time, of course."

"Who had a man sitting in Bonn?"

He looked at me, bland as a fish.

"A collector. Some are mad as hats."

"Hatters."

"Continue."

I told him about the possibility of a fraud and my reasons for deciding on a stopover in Rotterdam.

"You violated instructions, deWitt."

"And saved you the shock of being handed a fake."

"That Vermeer is no fake."

"Listen. Ruygrok—you know his work?"

"Of course. Kornbluth's pupil."

"He is not only certain that it is a copy, he even knows that Ilja Kornbluth painted it!"

Lobbe looked at me without blinking.

"How is Ilja?"

I didn't answer for a moment, and then I tried it just as cool, watching him closely.

"Kornbluth is dead."

I am sure he controlled himself. The very absence of any reaction gave him away. Then he sighed and said, "I am sorry to hear that."

"He died in Russia. He went there on a four-week trip and came back three months later. They sent the ashes."

This time he blinked. I then told him of my meeting with Swen, and I told him who Swen was. But it was obvious that he did not want to hear any more. He looked at the clock on his desk and picked up the phone.

"Miss Moon," he said. "Are you done?" Then he listened. "Both of them?" he said next, and when he had the answer he hung up.

"Mister Lobbe."

He got up from his chair and looked at me as if I wasn't there anymore. But he waited for me to finish.

"If I knew a little more about...."

"You know enough."

"I assume you still want the original Vermeer, Mister Lobbe."

"I would have the original Vermeer if you had not left it in Rotterdam."

I tried to be patient, which made my voice shake.

"The painting in Rotterdam, I repeat, is a masterful copy perpetrated by Kornbluth. There are hints and indications, Mister Lobbe, which...."

"Forget it. You had the original." He leaned over the desk a little, his eyes very still. "I say forget it, I mean that literally."

"Just a minute."

"It is safer, deWitt."
"Safer? I've never felt unsafer in my life!"
"You are now out of it."
"What's that?"
"You are fired, deWitt. Out!"

CHAPTER 22

I had my bellyful of Lobbe and I certainly wanted no further part of his picture mania. If he wanted to delude himself about that fake in Rotterdam, to hell with him. But I stopped at Moon's desk on the way out. I remembered Lobbe's rage when I had told him where the picture was: he had walked out, and when he had come back, he had been calm. Lobbe reacts violently to disappointment, but then he has the capacity to make an almost immediate, corrective move.

I started conning Moon immediately.

"When will the picture be here, Moon girl?"

My guess was good and she went along with it.

"If it works as planned, tomorrow."

"Did you call yourself or did you give it out?"

"One of the girls placed them and he'll take them himself." She nodded at Lobbe's big doors.

"When?" I was still fishing because I didn't know what I was after.

"We got the museum almost immediately. But we haven't reached the monastery yet."

"Elke—" I said. I wasn't fishing now. I said her name because I was afraid for her.

"She'll pick it up and bring it," said Moon.

I went cold. He, Lobbe, with Buddha calm, cold as a snake, uncaring for anything but his obsession, was going to have Elke bring that fake with a curse....

My hate for the man was a cold, cold thing. I was surprisingly reasonable.

"Any other calls in that connection?"

"Manny, you're fishing."

"I was in his office when we planned it, Moonshine."

"Well, just the London call, to arrange for her escort."

"I wasn't sure on that point, whether she was flying over alone."

"Oh, no. The London office is sending two security men to Rotterdam."

Then I walked out. I did not want Moon to see how I felt, how I was full of relief that Elke had protection, how I was full of hate at the thought that

Lobbe was most likely thinking primarily of protecting his picture. The conclusion made sense. He was having Elke pick up the picture because she already knew of its existence. The men from London would only be told to protect the girl without having to know what she carried. I walked out. I was fired but I wasn't through.

My own office was on the eighteenth floor and I went down there for some quiet thinking. I thought for a while and then I called Stebbs.

Stebbs is a tall, friendly guy. He has the kind of friendliness which comes from being so tall that you are able to look down at almost everybody. He has a very small head but a very long nose. On it slide his glasses. Stebbs is investments and he works very close to Lobbe. He is close to me because only I can outlast him with martinis. And when Stebbs is impressed he is a friend.

He was out when I called his office and I left word that he should call me back. I thought some more and then I worked on my expense sheet. I was seeing to it that Lobbe wouldn't like it. Then Stebbs called me back.

"DeWitt to the rescue," I said. "You need a drink."

"Righto." And he hung up. Five minutes later, he walked into my office and five minutes after that, we walked into the bar on the other side of the street.

"How was Europe?" He grinned at me so I should know what he meant.

"They are beautiful, Stebbs."

"Tell me, tell me."

"I was too busy."

"You dog. I need a drink."

He waited, patient but disappointed. Two double martinis came which Rocco, behind the bar, had started to mix as soon as he had seen us.

"How was Lobbe?" Stebbs asked.

"He fired me."

Stebbs choked a little but worked the martini down valiantly. He doesn't give that kind of thing up so easily. "Why's that, Manny boy?"

"I'm buying the martini...."

"Martinis."

"Yes. I'm buying them so I can figure out why I was fired."

"I'm a patient man. Try and make sense."

"I think Lobbe fired me because I half stumbled into or onto something and he doesn't want me to figure it out."

"And once I've helped you figure this thing out, deWitt, to whom will you sell it?"

"Nobody. I'm just mad at him. He's used me and I don't like it. And just now he did it again, to somebody else."

He looked at me sideways and waved at Rocco for the second set.

"Manny," he said to me. "You sound like you're in love." Sometimes Stebbs can be uncanny, which is the reason why Lobbe has him in investments. "When do I meet her?"

"Once I know she's safe."

Stebbs, be it said, took me seriously. He didn't tell me I was sounding theatrical and he didn't try to pump me for gossip.

"What do you want to know?"

"I'll start at the beginning. You know why I went to Paris?"

"Yes, the merger that didn't come off."

"Do you know Sir Evelyn at Carbon and Allied?"

"Foreign exploitation, yes. He called from Tangiers not long ago."

"So you know he went there. Do you know why?"

"Sir Evelyn, Manny, has resigned under fire. He resigned under fire because he could not stop the tumble Carbon has been taking."

"I've been watching that. What happened?"

"Somebody was dumping big blocks through that Tangiers dummy outfit, Commercial Trust of Tangiers."

"Do you know why?"

"Mysterious are the ways of madmen and gods. No, I don't know why it was dumped."

"Do you know who was dumping Carbon?"

"I am one of the very few mortals, Manny, who does happen to know. I'm ready for another martini."

"Who?"

"He just fired you."

I think my mouth hung open. Stebbs laughed out loud, watched the martinis come, and applied himself.

"Stebbs, that doesn't make any sense, man! He stops the merger talks to send me on a cockeyed errand all over Central Europe, he sells Carbon at a loss, and on top of that he must have lost every voting share in that combine that he ever had!"

"That he has. Mysterious are the ways of madmen. I told you."

"And you don't know why he did this crazy thing?"

"No. Speaking of crazy, you know what he did while you were gone?"

"He went out of his head and gave you a free hand."

"You're close. Do you know Flood Research and Development?"

"Never heard of them."

"They are a highly specialized research organization, on a plane of specialization where physics and chemistry meet, hush-hush stuff, which is why I don't know anything else about it. They have a small manufacturing branch, otherwise mostly pure research. Very expensive operation...."

"What's the point of the story?"

"Lobbe just bought it."

"So?"

"Outright and with his own money."

"You're mad! I mean, Lobbe is mad!"

"He didn't want anybody in the banking world to know just exactly what was going on, so he did it the expensive way."

"This is the second time in five minutes that you've told me Lobbe has deliberately lost himself money."

"Strange and mysterious are the ways of the gods."

"I think I'm just a little bit drunk," I said, and Stebbs nodded to let me know that he thought so, too.

"Is any of this helping you, Manny?" he asked.

"Only the martini."

"Martinis."

"Yes, those. Forgetting about that Flood Research insanity, Stebbs, who's been buying all that depressed Carbon and Allied stock?"

"Carbon and Allied, some of it. The rest I don't know. But it's been going by and by. Not heavy though. Stealthily, it seems, so as not to wake the price up again. And then, I would guess, once it levels out at the bottom, somebody is going to gobble it. Carbon's in bad shape."

"They should talk."

We walked back to the office, Stebbs to try for an afternoon's work, and I to clean out my desk. I called our private travel and routing bureau and had no trouble finding out when Elke was due. She and two companions were booked on a TWA flight, to arrive at Idlewild at five a.m. the next morning.

I was done with my desk at 3 p.m. and sat woolgathering. I had irritable thoughts about Lobbe and I had confused thoughts about the fake Vermeer. And then I had a flash. This was not designed to get me back into Lobbe's good graces—I was not interested in that—but it was apt to give me some of the answers he had refused me. And if there was anything about the Vermeer matter which was not designed to meet the eye, this might help uncover it.

Just as Lobbe had had Kornbluth in Rotterdam, so he had a man in New York by the name of Talvini. Talvini was a restorer, primarily, and not an expert, as Kornbluth had been, but I thought Talvini might do. I had met him once, briefly, at Lobbe's Long Island estate.

I now called Talvini, helped him to remember who I was, and then gave him a cock-and-bull story about a rush job at the Lobbe place, something immediately necessary in order to get the picture off in time to a loan exhibit in San Francisco. Lobbe was a good client and Talvini swallowed my yarn. I took a company car from the basement garage and fifteen minutes later picked Talvini up at his Third Avenue workshop. He stored a lot of boxes in the back of the car, since he didn't know the specific nature of the job.

He was a white-haired old man who looked a lot like the stereotype of a musician. His Italian accent was lovely.

"He is a funny man, the Mister Lobbe," said Talvini. "Some pictures he wants cleaned, some pictures he wants dirty. Strange?"

"We shall see," I said as if I knew exactly what I was talking about.

We talked of food and of Tuscany and at four-thirty we drove up to Lobbe's house. It had three stories and a half-beam façade, and inside it was large enough to accommodate a small village. I rang and when the butler came, he looked surprised.

"Mister deWitt," he said, "I did not expect you."

"That's strange. Somebody must have fouled up at the office. No message from Mister Lobbe?"

"Only not to expect him before ten."

"I knew that, of course. Well, then, to work. You remember Mister Talvini."

"Of course," said the butler and helped Talvini carry his boxes into the hall. "Will you work in the usual room?" he asked Talvini.

"I guess so," said Talvini, who still didn't know what was up.

We went to the workroom and then the butler left. I told Talvini to unpack and then I left.

At first, I got lost. I had never been in the workroom or in the part of the house where it was located, but then I hit familiar terrain on the second floor and found my ugly duckling. She hung over the mantel in a little, dark room. She looked like Kornbluth's "Apple Girl" except that she was ugly. The colors were flat, and they lacked gradation. Their tone was vulgar.

I brought her to Talvini and he looked at the canvas with disgust.

"*Disgratiado*," he said. "Such a lousy copy."

"Look it over," I said.

"For what? For cleaning? It won't help."

"Look her over anyway."

He bent over the canvas and looked disgusted.

"She is tempera," he said. "I have to test the emulsion."

"What for?"

"Such a cheap copy," he said. "Perhaps the emulsion is artificial, made with gum. Then the tempera never sets, but is always water soluble. We'll see."

What we saw made Talvini's hair stand on end, and made shivers run all over me.

"A crime!" he stuttered. "A criminal, horrible overpaint!"

Then Talvini worked with the zeal of a Savior. From under the vulgar muck of the overpaint emerged, slowly, beautifully, an "Apple Girl" of which Vermeer would have been proud. I was quite sure, as a matter of fact, that Vermeer had been proud of exactly this one.

CHAPTER 23

I got to Idlewild at four thirty a.m. but there was something wrong. The big hall was too empty. I walked in, and then I saw them. There were eight men who all looked too much alike, who stood too still, who were too evenly spaced. The nearest one came over and asked me which plane I was taking. He was polite enough and spoke with a Boston accent. I told him I was waiting for the five o'clock TWA, which was innocuous enough, though my voice did not feel very safe in my throat.

"There is a special arrival shortly," he said. "I must ask you to wait outside. If you wish to go to the ramp, you may do so shortly after five."

Then he caught the look in my eye, some kind of jackrabbit flightiness, fright perhaps, something erratic.

"If you are thinking of calling the police," he said, "forget it."

I don't know how he meant to pull it off, but I could feel the gun. None of the other men had moved. I think he meant to march me off to someplace more private when the swinging door behind me flew open. I turned and Lobbe stood there. He was livid.

"Let him go," he said to the man with the gun in his pocket. "DeWitt, come outside."

They were all Lobbe men. They were all standing there holding guns, waiting for a forgery to show up....

I followed Lobbe outside. I suddenly felt cold in the morning air, and very tired. Lobbe stopped by a limousine which had not been there before. Front and aft was a very normal-looking car, each containing silent men.

"An army for a fake, Lobbe?"

"Shut up. Step closer, I want you to hear this clearly."

I stepped closer and his whisper was hoarse.

"I will have your head for this, deWitt. I will go so far as to have you thrown into jail."

"For stealing your Vermeer?"

"Where is it?"

"Stolen."

"Do not meddle, deWitt, I warn you!"

"Admit something, Lobbe. You want the fake, don't you?"

"Yes, I want the fake!"

"You want it so much, you'd endanger Elke."

"Do you see those guards, imbecile?"

I saw the guards. And looking at Hans Lobbe, I knew he would be as ruthless in holding his fake as the unknown collector had been in trying to get it.

"Who wants it, besides you, Lobbe?"

"Shut up!" And then, with a surprising catch in his voice, he said, "Here comes Elke...."

She and two men on either side of her came through the empty hall fast. All three carried identical suitcases. And then Lobbe rushed at Elke and, so help me, the old bastard had tears in his eyes.

"*Kleine meisje,*" he blubbered and gave her a hug, and she called him *Oom* Hans and started to cry, too.

Then it went very fast. The two men kept going to the limousine, the one who had talked to me took the suitcase from Elke, and all the guards in the hall disappeared. Elke and Lobbe came out, and she saw me. This time she didn't cry. She just ran over and held me very tight.

"I came because you were here...."

"Little fool. Do you know what you've stepped into?"

"Later, later, later!" Lobbe was frantic with haste and pushed us into the limousine. We took off before I was sitting down.

"Imbecile," said Lobbe. He was panting. "She is safe, *hein?*"

He, too, seemed relieved. We drove in silence. One car was ahead of us and one behind.

"She is safe," I said in a while, "with two carloads of armed men front and rear. For how much longer like that?"

He gave me a look full of anger, but said nothing. It was a tense ride, an ugly ride. I held Elke, but there was more fear than pleasure in our touching. We did not talk all the way to the Lobbe estate. The big house was lit, waiting quietly. Most of the men in the other two cars disappeared in the park and around the house. Three came inside with us.

The big hall was lit, but the butler wasn't there. The whole house seemed to be lit except for the upstairs. Outside, the dawn was lifting.

"Now you go to the room and wash, eh, Elke? Teck, you show her up."

Teck, who seemed to know the house, went up the steps with Elke. The three suitcases stayed behind. I watched Elke disappear around the bend at the first landing while Lobbe and the remaining two men took the suitcases into the library. I stood in the hall, to wait for Elke.

"DeWitt?" Lobbe was back in the library door. "Come here. We settle things now."

He was not angry anymore. He had apparently made another decision. He waved the two guards out of the room and told them to stand in the hall. Their feet shuffled on the marble floor, and then they stood still. But the sound had not stopped.

What happened next was faster than the telling of it. I saw it fall from the second story, but it did not register. The body missed all the railings and fell straight down to the marble floor with a sickening impact. And then the man's voice from above.

"He is dead. The girl is still alive."

"No!" I was screaming it. There was no rational meaning to my scream. It was simply meant to undo what was now a fact. They had Elke. They had been in the house, waiting for us. And then the voice again, talking from where two rifle barrels were poked through the second-story railing.

"You will follow instructions. Don't call for help, do not go outside. Bring the painting and we return the girl."

"Elke!" called Lobbe. "Are you all right?"

"Answer him," said the man's voice.

"Yes," she said. "Yes, *Oom*."

"I bring the painting," said Lobbe. "Please wait. I must open the safe."

"Five minutes."

"I need more time! The time lock is set."

"How long?"

"At least fifteen minutes before I can open it."

"Fifteen minutes."

I'll hand it to him, he was thinking on his feet. His face was bathed in sweat and he rushed into the library. There he fell into a chair.

"What's this time lock nonsense about fifteen minutes?" I asked him.

"Manny, I must think, help me think." His face looked like death.

"What's there to think, in heaven's name? You have to think whether to let them kill her?"

"Manny—may God forgive me—I can't let them have it!"

I thought he had gone mad. I stepped up to him and grabbed him by the front of his jacket. Heavy as he was, I shook his limp body back and forth like a rag.

"Manny, stop. Listen." I stopped and he talked fast. "You told me of Kornbluth in Russia. They held him for questioning, to find out what he knew of the copy he had made. He knew nothing. He thought I had it with me and had left the original behind. A mix-up in the haste. I took the original by mistake."

"And Swen was sent to Elke for the same reason?"

"More, probably. To be a threat to her life, to force Kornbluth to talk."

"Give them the goddamn cursed picture and be done with this insanity."

"I will tell you why I can't. They are agents of the Soviet Union. On the Vermeer copy are four separate ingredients. No written record of them.

Four compounds, Manny, which combined in a way I have in my head—oh, *Gott, Gott,*" he mumbled.

"Hurry up, Lobbe. Time!"

"It takes work," he said with a tired voice, "but the basic information is there, painted over the canvas. Four compounds, combined like I know, and a smart chemist goes from there on, and makes a stuff that can break down common compounds, silicas, break them down to be fissionable."

"Christ—*bombs out of stones!*"

"Wende told them what he knew. Not one of my chemists knew it all. Wende went over to them. I knew this. If they have the compounds, they can start!"

"Is that why you bought Flood Research? To develop it yourself?"

"Yes."

I was busy at the window bench. I could feel him watch me.

"And why I stopped talks with Carbon and Allied and why I dumped their stock. Through dummies in Tangiers the Russians had bought heavily into Carbon, enough control, enough hirelings to reach for the process. You understand everything now? *Hemel,* what next."

"Here," I said. "Take it to them."

I gave him the Vermeer which had been hanging in Lobbe's house under an ugly coat of paint until Talvini had cleaned it off. He got up and took the painting. He hardly glanced at it.

"I don't trust them," he said.

"I don't either. How can I get up there somewhere from the back?"

"I don't know. Think, Lobbe, think idiot-bête," he mumbled. "Of course," he said suddenly. "The chimney. Up like a rat in the chimney."

"I wish I had a gun."

"Time's up!" the voice upstairs.

"Coming!" yelled Lobbe and then he whispered, "I get you a gun. It is necessary. *Allons.*"

I followed him to the door that led to the hall. Lobbe's two men were still standing there, standing very still under the rifles that looked at them from upstairs.

"The gun," whispered Lobbe. "Throw it here."

The man understood him and knew what it meant. I could see him trying to swallow the dryness in his throat.

He was fast. He threw the gun into the library before the bullet from upstairs hit him. Then he fell down and lay still. I could hear his difficult breathing.

"Here!" yelled Lobbe. "I'm coming. No gun!" And he stepped out into the line of probable fire holding up the Vermeer.

They were going to let him come up. They felt safe up there, safe in the knowledge of getting another hostage if the painting was not already theirs.

I didn't watch him walk away. I was glad that the hall was so large and that Lobbe, as if fearful, was walking slowly. I had my shoes and socks off by then, and had stuck the gun under my belt. The rest was simple agony.

I don't know how long it took me to get up that chimney. It was long enough for everybody in the house to get killed, certainly long enough for me to die several times, several ways, inside that chimney. What weakened me immeasurably was the constant fear that I was crawling the entire length of the chimney, through the second floor, through the third floor, through the attic and up into the sky. And somebody down in the park, watchfully, would blow off my head as it came out the top. And then, out of nowhere, I met the joint where some second-story fireplace flue joined my own. I crawled in feet first. I hung by my fingers without touching bottom. I let go and died again.

It wasn't very far down, twelve inches maybe, but I caught on an andiron and thought my foot had broken off. Also, there was the noise the thing made, falling over.

I cowered there, afraid to breathe. I could see the room, and there were four servants on the floor, tied up and gagged. Perhaps that was why, on the other side of the door, they were not surprised by the sound I had made. Besides, Lobbe was talking very loud.

"I will not come one step further," he was bellowing, "unless you let go the girl, or I will destroy the picture. Then you can all go home and get shot by a firing squad."

They seemed to be thinking about it, or perhaps it was Lobbe's imagery which gave them a little pause.

I was out of the chimney and by the door. I don't remember if I ran, crawled or hopped. I had the gun out, some kind of .38 revolver, and then I opened the door.

I figured there might be three or four. One with the rifle covering the hall, the other rifle covering Lobbe, the third holding Elke, and perhaps number four talking.

There were only three, which was at least as smart an operation as Lobbe's useless army out there in the park.

I shot the one who was covering Lobbe because the one covering the hall would need time to get his barrel out from between the railings. In his haste, he dropped the rifle with a mighty clatter. That left the one who was holding Elke, the one who had been talking. I didn't know it then, but he was quick as a snake hauling a gun out of a shoulder holster. Lobbe rushed him. There was a shot and Lobbe dropped. But he is a heavy dropper. He tore and clawed at the man and dragged him down, too.

What helped with all this was the fact that the man who had been down in the hall had come bounding up as soon as he was no longer covered. He took care of the gunless one by the railing by throwing him over it.

Later, the army came in from the park, servants were untied, doctors were called, two dead and three wounded were counted. There was still some business to be taken care of before calling the police.

We were a grim and bedraggled tableau in the library. Lobbe, arm in sling, looked as if he might faint. Elke had soot on her face and hands. She had gotten that off me. I felt tired, and serious.

The man who had been talking was slim, with an intense face. He was the leader. He said his name was Domequ. He was not stupid and made no attempt to escape.

"This Vermeer is genuine," I told him, "and this one is fake. It's the fake which has the compounds painted over it."

They stood on the mantel and looked infuriatingly alike. "I can't tell one from the other," said Domequ.

"The fake has more glaze, you notice."

Domequ shrugged.

"For that matter," he said, "why go to the trouble of making a copy when the compounds could as easily have been applied to the original Vermeer?"

"I will tell you why," said Lobbe. "The old paint could not have taken the coating. We tried and it started to disintegrate." He blinked, either in pain or because he felt like crying.

"All right," I said to Domequ. "I have a message for your superiors from Mr. Lobbe." Domequ stared at me and then I went on. "We will let you go. We even hope you will make it. And when you get there, wherever they are waiting for you, tell them this."

I stepped away from the fireplace so that I could look at the fire I had built there.

"Tell them this," I said again.

And then following Lobbe's orders, I threw the "Apple Girl" with the deadly glaze over her into the fire.

It hissed and Lobbe's masterpiece of death curled, blackened, and died.

"And regrettably, because you do not believe me, tell them this."

That one really hurt the worst. I burnt the real "Apple Girl."

This time Lobbe did cry, and I could understand it.

But the curse which had hung above us all was destroyed.

Lobbe never mentioned his *bordelje* again, except once. He came to the airport with us, wearing his sling like a marshal's mantle.

"We will both try to forget the *Appel Meisje*," he said to me. "It will be easier for you, *hein?* A real *meisje* is best." He laughed and patted Elke's cheek.

Then he waved good-bye to us, and Elke and I went to a place where we could walk barefoot in the grass.

THE END

THE SPY WHO WAS 3 FEET TALL
by Peter Rabe

I have no cleaning woman except once a week, which has its blessings. I can stay in bed till late in the morning without interference should circumstances so demand. My circumstances, rose-skinned and helplessly asleep, lay next to me when the phone rang. I gave a start, as if someone were reprimanding me, and picked up the cruel instrument.

"DeWitt," I said, trying to sound as if I were not really in bed.

"Good morning, Manny. This is Miss Moon."

"Oh, God—"

"Correct," she said. "He wants you."

"Now?"

"*Instanter instantis*," said Miss Moon, who had once taught Latin.

I hung up feeling bleached of color.

'Oh, God' was Lobbe, my employer, and Miss Moon his archangel and exec-secretary. When she did the calling, Hans Lobbe really wanted you, perhaps on a platter and with a sour apple in your mouth.

I gave another start, as if the telephone were having a shrill afterthought, though this time the sound was different. Inge woke up. She always did this with the moan of a cat and a stretch of pure pleasure. Perforce of circumstance I turned away and reached for my robe.

"Traitor," she said behind me. "I wake up for you, and you are not even here."

"Take your last look, Inge. This traitor is to be shot at dawn."

"Dawn?" she said.

"In your case it is the time when you ordinarily go to sleep. In my case it is the time when I face the beginning of the end."

"Poor darling," she said. "Condemned men have one final wish, don't they, Manny? And the wish is always *granted*."

I groaned and got off the bed. I could see only her eyes, dark and shiny, like two cherries, one apple cheek, and her short nose, which moved in such a way that I could tell she was slowly smiling. Her honey hair was all around her head, and she stretched again. Gradually I could see more of her—her sweet, round arms relaxing above her head, her smiling mouth, her dimpled chin. There was nothing particularly sophisticated about her happy face—it looked too healthy—nor was there anything sophisticated about the thing that she did next. The sheet over her kept sliding down. The rest of her was as healthy as her face and even more distracting. I turned away like a madman and went to the bathroom.

"Traitor!" she called through the door. "Open up that door, traitor!"

I opened, and she stood there, marvelously naked, and tried to look forbidding. It was useless.

"Who was that on the phone, louse? Who is making you forget me?"
"The Almighty," I said. "My employer."
"Who?"
Inge, it need be said, had been brought up with all the advantages of a lot of money. One of those advantages is total ignorance about what an employer is.
"My employer, as you well know, is Mijnheer Lobbe, girl. Your uncle Hans." I dove into the shower.
When I came out again, I felt raw with cleanliness, which did not do a thing for me. Inge, in the mean, had put something on. It was one of those indescribable things that women wear in the morning before they decide what to do with their day. It did not really cover, it did not really reveal. It neither asked you to look closer, nor would it let you go. And it fairly demanded to be taken off to end the indecision. All of which she knew.
"Manny!" she said with disbelief. "You are actually getting dressed!"
I could understand her surprise. She was neither used to this kind of treatment, nor did she know about employers.
"This is your day off, Manny," she said. "What could Uncle Hans want?"
"He may be Uncle Hans to you, sweetness, but to me—"
"Wherever did you get those cunning shorts, Manny? Are those little ducks walking all around there?"
"They are little vultures walking all around there, sweet Inge. And you bought the shorts."
"They are awful, Manny. Take them off."
She herself was reaching for a secret device near her belly button that would almost instantly make her own garment take itself off. She smiled and said, "Uncle Hans won't mind."
It had been strictly the wrong thing to say, and I commenced dressing. "As I have vainly tried to tell you, he is not my loving uncle but my demanding employer, and I am only one of his allay of lawyers, not to mention part-time seducer of his favorite niece."
She wasn't impressed either with my description of her uncle or with the course this seduction was taking. She shrugged and went to the galley kitchen, where she plugged in the coffee pot.
"What does he want from you at this ungodly hour, Manny?"
"My head. In a brazier, with the flame lit underneath."
"He doesn't know about you and me. He's too busy."
"He is a Lobbe," I said. "Though it might have helped to nudge his intuition when you called him that time, for Heaven's sake, to ask *him*, for Heaven's sake, where you could reach me."
"He didn't mind. He said he'd like to know himself."

I knotted my tie tightly. Might as well get used to it.

"Shall I wait for you here, Manny, or will you pick me up at uncle's place?"

"Don't ask normal questions at a time like this." I went for the door.

"No coffee?"

"No."

"No kiss?"

"Yes."

It might be for the last time, so I kissed her good, and she replied in kind. It was no commuter's kiss by any stretch of the imagination, but it did make me feel somewhat married, leaving her behind like this in my apartment.

It had been sweet and now it would be short. Inge's visit to her uncle was scheduled to be over in a day, and she would disappear again into the upper world of Deauville, Cannes, Capri, and Positano. What would happen to me in much less than a day, I did not care to contemplate.

The Lobbe Building was like any other thirty-story structure in Manhattan. It was not so much a building as it was an achievement in glass. I looked at it when I climbed up from the subway and thought that it would make one hell of a tinkle if it fell over now. I devoutly wished that it would fall over now.

There were twenty plaques at the entrance, which identified the twenty tenants of the building. One of them read modestly, Lobbe Industriel, though you could safely guess that the rest of the enterprises in the building belonged to Lobbe, too. Lobbe sometimes claimed that the simple legend he used was an invention of his modesty; but when asked what the name stood for, he could describe a veritable octopus of connecting enterprises that covered the industrial spectrum.

Three hundred years ago the first acknowledged Lobbe dealt in spice. That is to say, he sailed out of Amsterdam as a sailor before the mast and returned five years later as owner and captain of the self-same vessel. It made the dockside sweet with odors of raw cinnamon and it made the first Lobbe rich.

For the next three hundred years the Lobbes kept that up. From spice they went to rubber, and because of transportation costs they added their own fleet. They branched out into anything they happened to transport, including a sample run of slavery. Hans Lobbe himself seemed the only witness to disaster. The war shut down the source of rubber, and the war's aftermath lost Holland most of its possessions. So Lobbe switched from kautchug to synthetic rubber and from that to synthetics altogether. DuPont sometimes worries about him.

Worrying about Lobbe, I took the elevator to the eighteenth floor. Here was Lobbe's inner sanctum, that is to say, the one he used in New York. I was sluiced with unpleasant speed past the floor receptionist, the Lobbe traffic-diverter receptionist, Moon's secretary, and then into the presence of Miss Moon.

Like Cerberus guarding Hell, she sits in her paneled room, where Lobbe's double portals are. But Miss Moon looks a sweet fifty-five, and her movements are pleasantly phlegmatic.

"Moon Mother," I said, "what does he want?"

"You buttoned your jacket wrong, Manny."

"Thank you. How do I look?"

"Dressed to kill, Manny."

"Don't say that. What does he want, Moonshine?"

"You."

"I knew that." And I sat down in a leather couch. It hissed and sighed under me in an expiring way, which is to say, exactly as I felt. Miss Moon pressed a silent button.

"Mister Strauss is still with him," she explained.

I knew that Mister Strauss would still be with him because it was not yet twelve o'clock. Between eleven and twelve Lobbe sat in secretive session with Strauss, who was the code clerk. Nothing interrupted that hour, except perhaps a matter of life and death. It was the important hour of lowering the ax on a competitor in Sweden, shaking up a government in Indo-China, bankrupting a syndicate in Africa, and other business activities like that. It was literally the eleventh hour, as Lobbe liked to say, and he seemed now prepared to give that time to me.

Strauss came through the double doors carrying his metal case, which was chained to his wrist. He looked ageless in an awful and preserved kind of way, and he rattled his chain like a ghoul.

"It is your turn," said Strauss, and passed from view.

Miss Moon smiled like a mother, but it did not help.

"Honeymoon," I said as I stopped at her desk, "how many chins? Just tell me that much."

"One," she said.

This was a code, a shorthand we had, describing the complexities of Lobbe's mood. Ordinarily he has two chins, which means normal, though normal in the case of Lobbe simply means ready to veer in any direction. Three chins means that he is sleepy or that he is thinking. He is very cagey about which is which. One chin is manifestly bad because it means that he is sticking his jaw out, and he does that only when he is angry.

"Good-bye, Miss Moon," I said, but I did not hear her answer.

I went into his office. Because of its size, I did not see him right away. But I heard him.

"DeWitt," he roared, "you're fired!"

Hans Lobbe was surrounded with deadly efficiencies, though this preference was in no way reflected in his office. There was a grand piano in the room because he sometimes liked to play gavottes by Telemann. A Byzantine altar cloth was draped across the lid of the piano. There was a small Franz Hals on one wall and a delicate Fra Filippo Lippi. Hung apart from these for reasons of theme and style was a Picasso ink of a lascivious goat. His desk was massively sculpted and reminded one of a palazzo. It was probably about as heavy.

He was not behind his desk. I found him under his Grünewald triptych, which hung over the bar. Lobbe was pouring schnapps.

He was short and round, like something drawn in slow motion. His thin hair was half yellow and half white, and his gentle, deceptive eyes, with their white lashes, were looking at me. I saw two chins.

"Sit down, mennekin," he said. "Want a schnapps?"

I did not want one. I needed one. "You just fired me," I said.

"Don't I know it. *Assieds-toi.*" And he waved me to a rabbit's-ear chair that faced his private view of the East River, framed by a window that was twelve by ten.

Lobbe, of course, was Dutch. As is the case with all Dutchmen who want to be understood in this world, he had to know some other languages. Lobbe not only knew a dozen of them, but often used them interchangeably. I have seen him speak Malay to an uncomprehending American and then apologize in German. Entirely as a matter of mood, he can stick to English quite flawlessly, and when that happens he is usually serious to a dangerous degree. So far, with schnapps glass in hand, he seemed unaccountably friendly.

"How does it feel, Manny, to be free like a dog?"

"I think you mean 'bird,' sir."

"I like dog better." And then swiftly, "How is Inge?"

"Inge? She seemed well, sir."

"She didn't come home last night and maybe she was dancing all the night with you. Therefore I ask."

"Er, yes. She was dancing all night."

"I did know this ahead of time because I know she loves to dance all night."

"Yes, sir, she loves it."

"In the décolletage she loves it."

"I beg your pardon?"

"Where they dance—discotheque. I was thinking of the wrong word."

"Oh, no—I mean, of course. I wonder, may I have that schnapps now?"

"Take it, take it." He waved at the earthenware jug that was sitting on the bar. He seemed distracted, which is the time when you watch out. He walked around a little, and then I could not see him anymore.

"Inge's father called from Rome last night," he said behind my back. "He wants to know when she comes home."

"I see." I saw nothing.

"There is the Prince Plozzi in Rome, who keeps asking for Inge, and my *Ezel* of a brother wants the sweet, innocent Inge to marry the *pazzo* Plozzi the lecher so *totalemente disgraziato* it is beyond my own and limited experience."

The last part was a lie. For the rest I only understood that Lobbe did not like Prince Plozzi. Sight unseen, I did not like him, either.

"So where is my Inge?"

"Don't know, sir."

"You dance with her in the décolletage all night and you know nothing about her?"

He was incredulous, but so was I. He had rousted me out of bed on my day off in order to ask me where his niece was so that he could tell her that her father had called from Rome because he wanted her to marry a disreputable Italian prince. And, coincidentally, he had wanted to tell me that I was fired. One thing had nothing to do with the other—a favorite Lobbe device for driving his listener into confusion and ignorance—but I was neither confused enough nor ignorant enough not to know that his real purpose for this entire meeting was something he had so far not bothered to mention. I did not enjoy his suspenseful little tricks, especially since he was no longer my employer. I noticed that he was eyeing me, and then he became immediately alert. But all he said was, "Have another schnapps, mennekin."

"No, thank you. However, I would like to know—"

"I will tell you why you are fired."

He padded his bulk over to the bar and poured himself a drink. He let me squirm a while longer, and I didn't like it.

"You are fired," he said finally, "so you are free to go elsewhere. *Prost.*"

And he poured down his schnapps.

I blew my top.

"Mister Lobbe, in view of the fact that you and I no longer have any official relationship whatsoever, let me point out to you that I am going to react to you entirely on the basis of personal feelings."

He turned his back to me and looked at the lascivious goat. "You hear?" he said to the picture. "A speech. A lawyer speeching at me from personal feelings."

"Mister Lobbe. I know you fired me and I know why you fired me, speaking of personal feelings."

He kept right on talking to the goat.

"It brays at me like an *Ezel*. It yells at me like from personal feelings of guilt."

"Mister Lobbe! My personal life and my business relationship to you—"

"Former business relationship."

"All right!"

"Sit down, Manny, and stop worrying about Inge. I asked about Inge because I have a message for her, but you don't know where she is because you only spend the whole night with her and not the whole day. *Basta.* Now stop speeching and listen to me."

I had been fired, of course, but not because of Inge—

"You are fired because I want you to build a road." He must have liked the expression on my face because he smiled like that goat. First he throws me out. What next? The road gang.

"I have a friend," he went on, "and he wants to hire you for that."

I took a deep breath and then I nodded at him, as if in thought. "I should build him a road. Of course. Is it a very long road?"

He looked at me with indulgence for a moment, which left me unprepared for the blast that came next.

"*Gott verdomme*, stop making me excited with little jokes."

"I can hear you, Mister Lobbe."

"I know you can hear me when I talk like to a deaf idiot, deWitt. Are you listening?"

"I am listening."

I watched him come away from the bar and sit down on the piano stool. There had been nothing fake about his unexpected burst of temper. This was serious, and I listened now because I wanted to know what it was.

"I have a dear friend," he said, "in some other company, and he and I are connected in a daisy chain together."

"A *what?*"

"Daisy chain. You don't use the word in business?"

"Not in this business, sir."

"But you know what I mean. All connected by company here, there, *und so weiter*. We have interests together, you understand."

"I understand that."

"I don't tell this to everybody, but in this daisy chain I own the company, and nobody knows it."

"I thought so."

He gave me a tolerant look and then went on. "The company is Sicherheitsnadelnmanufaktur—I am going too fast for you?"

"Not at all. I just don't understand it."

"A terrible German word. Like a speech by a lawyer." One side of his nose twitched, but he did not sneer. "The word means safety pin manufacture. Simple?"

"Oh, yes. And they build roads."

"*Dummkopf.* You know Bayer Aspirin? Made by Bayer-Leverkusen. They make aspirin on the side, like a spit in the bucket from the side of the mouth. The make film emulsions, insecticides, soil chemicals, paints, medicines, synthetics. They are big, would you say?"

"Yes. I would."

"Same like Sicherheitsnadelnmanufaktur. A hundred years ago, it is true, they make nothing but the pin."

"Before it was invented."

"Quiet. And now they make bulldogs, cats—"

"I'm sorry. Would you say that again?"

"They make the bulldogs to make the roads!"

"Of course. Bulldozers, caterpillars."

"Caterpillars? They got nothing to do with the worms, deWitt. You are thinking of Bayer and the insecticide. You don't listen, deWitt. They make all the machines to move the earth."

"Right."

"And now they got a contract in Motana to make a road in the woods, and I promised my friend in the company to lend you to him so you can handle the contracts with the Motana government. *Compris?*"

"Of course. And I think you mean Montana."

"You don't listen, deWitt! I say dog, I don't mean bird. I say cat, I don't mean worm. I say *Mo-tana* and I don't mean the other one. Montana was a state in 1889, but Motana was just made the other month brand-new in Africa!"

"Sorry. Seem to have missed that one."

"But not from now on, deWitt. I fire you from here so you can work over there for the pin company while they build the road."

"I see," I said, as if nothing else were missing. "However," I said, because a hell of a lot was missing, "why doesn't the Sickershnozzle company—"

"You got the name wrong. But go ahead."

"Why don't they hire a good road-loving lawyer right there in Germany?"

He looked at the goat for a moment but did not engage in conversation. Then he looked at me as if I were a goat. "Manford. Listen to me, darling. I am connected in a daisy chain, I told you, and I want my very own right hand to be right in there."

"You mean me, to represent you."

"No! *Idiot-bête!* You want the stock to go up right away when everybody knows the safety pin is connected with the Lobbe Industrie!?"

That part of his secrecy made sense. It still made no sense that he should send me over as his representative without telling me which of his interests I was to represent. I told him this and waited. He closed his eyes for a moment, smiled, and then looked at me with delicate admiration.

"I admire you," he said. "You struck unerringly at the weak link in my chain of truths, you know that, Manny?"

"Before you put it just that way, sir, I thought I was striking at—"

"Don't try to flatter me. I will now tell you everything."

This was unlikely, because I knew his habit of sending his men out on a most plausible errand that halfway through would turn implausibly into something else. I folded my arms, and smiled at him so that he would feel encouraged to do his best. He commenced to do just that.

"I want to kill two flies with one clod, and that is you, Manny. I want to pay up a favor by sending you out and I want you to go because Inge needs protection."

"Inge... needs *what?*"

"The call I mentioned was not from her father. It was from this *pazzo* Plozzi person, and he and our Inge have planned to go on safari. He called to discuss the travel arrangements."

Our Inge, he had said. I felt like a family member, though somewhat left out.

"And the safari is in Motana, I gather. She never mentioned a word to me. I thought she was going to Europe someplace."

"Yes. Rome."

"She didn't specify that, either."

"It is delicate of our Inge not to bring up the ex-lover, Manny. She is well brought up."

He had a point there, a Lobbe-type point, and I thought about the more positive aspects of all these new developments.

"I'll tell her," I said to Lobbe. "Might be fun traveling together."

"*No!*"

So much for the fun. Lobbe, of course, was thinking of the business again.

"Secrecy, Manford! In love and in war!"

"But I am neither—"

"But I am, dear. I love my Inge and I am at war at the bourse. You don't want to warn the Plozzi person he has opposition, do you? You don't want to warn the bourse I am in a daisy chain, do we now?"

"Forfend, Mister Lobbe."

He grunted and went to his desk, three chins showing. I don't think he knew the word "forfend." He sat down behind his palazzo of a desk, which changed the mood from that of a family affair to that of the Doge dispatching his page.

"You will be routed through Germany to confound the hound."

"I still don't see—"

"Quiet, Manford. Don't talk like an industrial spy. And you don't tell our Inge."

I made one last stand, based on suspicion. "I feel you might have told me about this double job involving my... involving your niece right from the start, sir."

He smiled, making it feel like a pat on the head. "I did not want to commandeer you into the role of... uh, the *chevalier*. I wanted to arrange you to run into our Inge and then let you protect her from your simple and natural instinct for always doing the noble thing, Manford."

I gave up and (so help me) I believed him.

I walked by Miss Moon's desk thinking of other things, rosy things, when Miss Moon called me back.

"Sign here, Manny, and take them to Personnel, won't you?"

She gave me a stack of papers that had to do with my firing and hiring. Typically enough, they had all been prepared for me before Lobbe had decided to tell me about the Motana assignment in three successive stages, each adding a little bit more when I caught him in an omission.

"And these go to Traffic. They've got your ticket waiting."

"Are they also going to tell me where I'm going?"

"Of course. You're going to Essen, and your flight leaves at eleven tomorrow morning."

"Moonshine," I said, "how come you know everything ahead of time, and I don't even get to know the half of it until it's too late?"

"Mister Lobbe said, 'Ignorance keeps deWitt on his toes.'"

I did not very much like that high-handed diagnosis, but there was no point in arguing with Miss Moon about it. I was getting ready to go when she handed me the third pile of papers.

"These are for perusal and study," she said. There was a brochure on the country of Motana, and there was a lot of material on the contractual requirements for the road building project. "That is the reason why you're going there, isn't it?" said Miss Moon, and she smiled less like a mother this time but much more like a madam.

"What keeps you on your toes, Moonglow? It can't be ignorance."

This time she laughed, because she liked me, and then she said bon voyage, and I left.

I went to the enclosure on the twelfth floor that passes for my office. I do my woolgathering there, my occasional paper signing, and I get the phone calls there that tell me my assignments. I had been given my assignment and was doing the paper signing when my secretary came in.

"There was a call for you, Mister deWitt."

It was her way of giving my calls importance. She would never say right from the start who had called. I waited.

"Your laundry called, Mister deWitt."

I still did not say anything because she would inevitably get to the third stage all by herself.

"They wanted to know when you're leaving so they can deliver your shirts on time."

I still said nothing, but for a new reason this time. I had to think this over. Then I said, "And did you tell them when I'm leaving?"

"Sure. Tomorrow at eleven."

"Smart girl. Take these to Personnel, will you, honey?"

"Yes, Mister deWitt. And bon voyage."

"Just a minute, honey."

She stopped and smiled at me. "That's French for fare-thee-well," she said.

"Thank you. How did you know I was leaving tomorrow, honey?"

She looked very nonchalant now, impressing me with her easy efficiency. "In the toilet. You know."

"Of course. Foolish of me to ask. I only ask because I don't have access to your toilet."

"I know that, Mister deWitt. You don't have to explain."

I then chased her out and sat woolgathering. There was no point in wondering how the female staff's grapevine worked. There was no sane explanation. But I was wondering how that laundry knew I was leaving before I myself knew I was leaving. The question was a corker because I did not have a laundry that delivered.

I cursed Lobbe, picked up the phone, and dialed the extension of my friend Stebbs, who works in Investments.

"Yes?" he said.

"Five minutes?"

"Right." And he hung up.

He and I understand each other. We know exactly how long it takes to get to Rocco's across the street, and no point wasting time on the telephone. We met on the street, at the red light, and then we crossed over in silence. We then passed the plate glass of Rocco's, nodded at Rocco, who stood there in the gloom, and by the time we sat at our table, the two double martinis were on their way.

Stebbs is tall, with a small head way up on high. He usually stoops in an accommodating curve that—so he claims—is designed to reduce the sense of inferiority everyone is bound to feel in his presence. I do not believe this is really true because if it were, Stebbs would not lard his conversation with such remarks as: "I see you are getting bald on top."

Stebbs' own small head is covered with a lot of sandy, unkempt hair, which makes him look professorial and basically preoccupied with otherworldly matters. It is true that the inside of that head is a welter of disconnected information. But in some mysterious way the bits and pieces join together and come out lovely and simple, like an intuition. That is why Lobbe keeps Stebbs in Investments.

Stebbs looked down at his martini, which caused the glasses on his nose to take their accustomed slide. He looked at me over the rims, grinned, and touched the stem of his glass with unerring precision.

"You are broke and you need a tip, and tomorrow Lobbe's empire will come crashing down with a Wagnerian rumble because of deWitt's market madness. Cheers." He picked up the glass, and then the martini was gone.

One reason for our friendship, so says Stebbs, is that I am unique. He does not know anyone else who can match him martini for martini. Since this was established we have usually stuck to three each, like two confident athletes who do not have to prove a thing to each other.

"Drunken advice I need like Lobbe needs another chin," I said.

He took my remark like a challenge. "Manny," he said, "you will pay for this."

"I know. I always get stuck with the tab."

"Cheers."

Of the second martini he drank only half in one swallow. I sipped on my own and watched his thin, nervous face turn calm, like a summer afternoon. I would not say that Stebbs ever got drunk, but he did turn very peaceful.

"Are you with it?" I asked him.

"The demonstration is going to cost you, Manford. I am immediately ordering another—"

"There's a cheaper way of finding out if you're with it. Pronounce the following for me: Sicherheitsnadelnmanufaktur."

He pushed at his spectacles and looked into space. "Sicherheitsnadelnmanufaktur is steady at forty-two and a quarter. Been that way for three years. You want any?"

"Should I?"

"If you like a conservative portfolio. Income is about three percent steady."

"I like them if Lobbe likes them."

"I don't know if he likes them. I don't think he even knows them."

"Stebbs, we can't be talking about the same man."

"He doesn't trade in them. Not through this office."

I sat back and sighed. So much for the way of deWitt, stock-schwindel investigator. If Lobbe was up to a finagle with the company for which I now worked, it did not show in his New York office. And nothing might show anywhere, simply because Lobbe was not finagling—unlikely as that might sound.

"For that matter," said Stebbs, "he hasn't been very active altogether. I mean, not counting the routine block trading."

"That doesn't sound like Lobbe, either."

"He's been busy. I don't know with what, but he's been in and out of Washington a lot."

"And London and Tangiers and Hongkong."

"But he wasn't summoned there."

I laughed and finished my martini. "I repeat, Stebbs, we are not talking about the same man."

"Your hero worship is disgusting, Manny. It is possible, for example, for the State Department of a sovereign power, such as the U.S.A., to beckon to a mere international privateer like Lobbe anytime, anyhow, and make him jump."

"Lobbe *jumped*? You just had your last martini, Stebbs."

Stebbs gave sort of a jump himself at that moment, but it did not seem to have anything to do with my announcement about martinis. "Preserve us," he breathed at me. "There is a female heading for this table."

It was an unlikely occurrence in Rocco's place, about as unlikely as the statement that Stebbs had had his last martini. But there she came, the female, my Inge, to our table and straight at me. She did not look helpless and rosy, as I remembered her at first sight in the morning, but displayed the shifting curve arrangement of her walk with bounce.

"Fink!" she said. "I'm sitting down here." And she did. She looked at Stebbs, who winced, and then she looked at me and my martini glass. She grabbed it up.

"It's empty," I said. "Unless you meant to eat the glass."

"I might, Manny deWitt. I just might."

"Rocco!" Stebbs' voice came like a cry for help.

"And why didn't you tell me you were leaving?" Inge said. "You are done with me in the morning after doing with me all night and then—"

"Inge, please."

"Thank you. And then you go away all day and make arrangements to disappear, and I—"

"Inge, we have a guest."

"I'll leave," said Stebbs.

"No! Your martini, Stebbs."

He sat down again. I made introductions and gave some benign explanations, and then Rocco brought three, unasked, and caused a welcome pause.

I said, "Who told you I was leaving, Inge?"

"Uncle Hans. He said you're going to Germany tomorrow."

"I just found out myself. How come he told you?"

"I'm family." She stopped looking at the glass Stebbs had just put down and looked at me. "Besides, I'm interested in you."

"Sure. So much so, you didn't tell me where you were going, either."

"You didn't care."

"I damn well care now."

"Then it might interest you to know I'm going on a safari to forget you."

"Hah!"

Stebbs made a mild interruption while Inge sipped from her drink. "Are you two married?" he asked.

I did not care to answer that but went at Inge again. "When did you find all this out, may I ask?"

"Uncle Hans called me."

"Called you? He didn't know where you were."

"He called me at your apartment, so he must have known where I was, no?"

Good old Lobbe.

"And how did you know I was here? He told you that, too?"

"Of course. I asked him, and he told me."

Stebbs winced before being spoken to.

"And you, too," Inge said to Stebbs. "He said you and Manny sit here every day like two industrial spies."

"Speaking of spying," I said, "we've got a lot to learn from Uncle Hans."

"Why?" said Inge. "Were you trying to avoid me? Were you trying to leave without so much as—"

"Now, just one damn minute, Inge."

"You are married," Stebbs mumbled, and waved at Rocco.

His cigarettes were on the table, and I took one. I rarely smoke cigarettes because they leave me dissatisfied in the extreme and produce a desire to keep smoking. But when I am highly dissatisfied to begin with, then sometimes I smoke somebody else's cigarettes.

"Listen to me," I said to Inge. "I was going to tell you."

"Is that why you drink?"

"Quiet, please. And as for the topic of leaving, I never asked you where you disappeared to for two days about one week ago."

"That's why I didn't tell you."

"*Gevalt*," said Stebbs, and studied his martini image in the glass.

"I'm asking now, Inge, dear."

"I went with Uncle Hans to Washington to be his hostess."

Both Stebbs and I sat up a little.

"Ah, yes," said Stebbs. "How I remember those marvelous galas Uncle Lobbe used to throw for his employees in Washington."

"He did?" said Inge. "He didn't this time."

"Oh?" I said, somewhat like a spy.

"Just old men," said Inge. "No women at all. Well, not all old men. There were two from the State Department, and they were quite nice."

"What you mean to say, I'm sure, you mean to say they were quite young."

"Nice. When I say nice, I don't mean quite young, Manny."

This was another Lobbe speaking, and she enjoyed the correction well enough to give me a smile.

"Tell me more," I said, "about the nice men."

She thought she was thwarting me with the dry recital that came next, but I listened very carefully. She said, "They explained that if they had known that Uncle Hans had such a lovely niece, they might not have been so hard on him."

Stebbs and I said it in chorus: "Hard on him—" but Inge looked at us as blankly as we were looking at her.

"That's what they said. It had to do with all the talks Uncle has been having in Washington. And then we talked about lobster."

"Rocco!" said Stebbs very loudly.

"You mean the little monsters from the sea? The ones we eat?" I asked her.

"Of course. Maine, North Sea, Pacific, African, and the little ones from Honduras. They all taste different you know."

"It depends on the sauce," said Stebbs.

"And you are the expert on sauce," I said, and then I tried to salvage the conversation. "Tell me about the other guests, Inge, the old ones."

This did not sound particularly jealous to Inge, therefore the topic bored her. She gave a very off-handed recital. "There was this old senator—"

"Name?"

"Kaufman, I think."

"Coughlin," said Stebbs. "Foreign Aid."

I said, "First time I ever heard of Lobbe having anything to do with aid to anyone."

"He gave me a Ferrari last Christmas," said Inge. "That helped."

"Who else was at the party, Inge?"

"Who else? There was a government man, but nobody said from what part of the government."

"That is most un-Washingtonian," observed Stebbs.
"And what did he talk about?" I asked.
"We talked about lobster."
I looked at my watch because the conversation was getting nowhere. But Inge, consistent with her affluent upbringing, neither understood about watches nor liked what they did.
"You don't want to hear the rest, I gather." She said this while looking straight past my left ear, which is something I detest.
"You mean there's more?"
"There was the man from the UN, wearing a big shirt down to the feet and a skull cap with little teeth hanging down all around."
"Manny," said Stebbs in a gloomy voice. "I'm never coming to Rocco's anymore."
"And this man," said Inge with a touch of defiance, "was the most beautiful looking person, with nut-brown skin and gleaming, gorgeous teeth."
"Hanging all around the rim of his hat. I know. From what country was he, darling?"
"He spoke French."
"Congo," said Stebbs.
"And he spoke English, German, and Hindustani. He talked to Uncle Hans in all of them, trying to be polite. You know how Uncle Hans is in a conversation sometimes."
Stebbs groaned and got up. "I am going back to the simplicity of beating the market. Also, I got to pack. Leaving town."
"Coincidence," I said, trying to be polite.
Stebbs frowned and had more to say. "You know, funny thing happened to me on the way to the Traffic division. My secretary stopped me with the entirely too personal intelligence that my laundry had called up to ask when I was leaving so that they could deliver my underwear in time."
I sat up but did not act eager. "And the funny is," I said, "that you don't wear any underwear."
He sneered at me. He glanced at Inge briefly and then he talked, cool and condescending.
"The point, Manford, is simply that I wash my own."
Inge ignored all that and asked, "Where are you going?"
"Ellsworth, Maine. Lobbe wants to know if he should merge that Maine Production outfit with his United Processors." Then Stebbs said good-bye and left.
"How dull," said Inge.
"Maine Productions," I said to Inge, "cans lobsters," and I thought to myself that in the midst of all this dullness there was something distinctly fishy.

Essen is one of the Pittsburghs they have in the Ruhr Valley. A lot of steady money is being made there, but the city itself is insistently ugly. I took a taxi at the airport and slept all the way to the safety pin company. The driver woke me, and there was the plant. If this place made safety pins, they made them big enough to clamp the Straits of Gibraltar together.

My instructions were to meet with two men in Essen. The first, Herbert von Beck, was a small man with a very large skull, a parrot nose, and a mouth like a line. He seemed to be lost in his oversized office—easily fifty feet long. He shook my hand, handed me a spool of tape, instructed me to play it on an appropriate recording device en route to Motana so as not to waste time, and advised me to follow its suggestions. Then, having a minute to spare, he related the gist of the tape. There were two men to deal with in Motana, the President and the Prime Minister. The President was a figurehead, said von Beck, but he was keen on having roads, parks, schools, and other such trivia added to his and his country's glory. The Prime Minister was a power-juggling opportunist with a streak of radicalism obtained at a school called Oxford. "*Das ist alles.* Good-bye." And I began the safari away from his desk.

The second man had the lowlier name of Otto Braun, but his office, though smaller than von Beck's playing field, was fitted out with a banquet table. It was ten in the morning, and I found Braun, not at his desk, but by this table.

While von Beck was all head and no body, Braun was a lot of body with hardly any head. He was a fat man, and no other details of description could possibly add anything. He watched me come in and smiled, giving me time to take in that table. It was on rollers, I noticed, and it was covered with many plates of food.

"Mister deWitt," he said in a surprisingly tiny voice, "will you join me in it?"

I walked to the table and found that his usage was apt. That sight was engulfing. There was sausage (four kinds), bread (three kinds), and ham (two kinds, to wit, Polish and Westphalian). There was cake (one kind; was the man on a diet?), and there were mysterious salads in five different bowls. I had no idea which meal of the day all this was meant to be.

"I am sorry I cannot offer you a chair," said Braun, and, in fact, there was not a single chair in sight. "I must have the exercise."

He demonstrated the meaning of his comment throughout the rest of our meeting. He walked around and around the table, eating.

"You've seen Beck?"

"Yes. Just now."

"Too bad. Take the smoked eel with the black bread."

"Thank you."

"He told you about Motana? He has never been in Motana. But I have."

"He told me briefly whom to see."

"Take the pickled carp and the yoghurt sauce."

"Eh—thank you."

"He told you about the two headmen, and one is a figurehead and one is a radical?"

"Yes. That's what he said, in brief."

"All wrong. He gets his information from the *Spiegel* and the *Time* magazine."

I put my plate down, but he immediately gave me a fresh one.

"Take the pheasant *en gelée* and the mushroom salad. The *gelée* is made by squeezing the—"

"That's all right. I'll take it."

"Instead, one is an idiot, one is a bum."

"Rather a young and inexperienced nation, I understand."

"And already an idiot and a bum run it. Now you take the blood sausage with the radish there. On top you add this. You see this, what it looks like?"

"Thank you, no. I'd rather—"

"Eat, *Kind!* When you get to Motana, you know what the national dish is there?"

"No, thank you. Mister Braun, the reason I'm here—"

"Right. Just a minute. I always have to sit down after the walking."

He sat down on a wooden chair behind his desk, a very prosaic chair designed only for normal use. It made an agonized sound, but it held.

"The reason you see me," he said after some heavy wheezing, "is to learn what goes on when you build a road. Just enough so you know a road from a river bed, you understand, and the rest is the problem of the engineers. Then I tell you the difference how it is done in Motana."

He did and handed me mimeos to make it clearer. What it amounted to was that normally you make a firm bed and then you put on something smooth. In Motana, he explained, consider yourself lucky if you can make the firm bed and forget about the smooth.

"And most of all," he finished, "remember you got a deadline."

I had not known about any particular deadline, aside from Lobbe's chronic illusion that the mention of his wish was the same thing as its fulfillment.

"There is a rainy season, you know."

"I see. And your safety pin—your equipment doesn't work in the rain."

"Right. It sinks in. It sinks in and comes out in China."

"And when is this flood?"

"We need three months to do the road for the good people there, and the rainy season starts in two months. So we got to hurry. And we don't dare start till you have the contract sealed up."

I felt full of indigestibles, and it was a toss-up what was the cause of it. I understood why Lobbe had been in such a hurry. I understood that there was probably competitive bidding on the road project, though I was told to get the details once I got to Motana. That sounded like a Lobbe touch. I did not understand how I could do a Lobbe-type job in minus-time.

Otto Braun, quietly dwarfing his desk, looked at me through the folds where his eyes ought to have been.

"Don't worry, *Kind*," he said to me. "There are no other bidders, really. The others don't think they can do it."

And on that Lobbe-type assurance I left Essen.

My next stop was Rome. The Lufthansa prides itself on an exceptional cuisine, the likes of which might satisfy an Otto Braun. I was not, however, any sort of Otto Braun, in fact even less so after having been with Otto Braun. I had two astringent glasses of a stomach tonic and waited anxiously for Rome. Inge was waiting for me there.

All Inge knew was that I had been on business in Essen and that dear Uncle Lobbe might tack a vacation on the tail end of a job well done. So the plot was that I would see Inge for one day in Rome, the one day between my arrival and Inge's departure for Motana, and that my one-day Roman Holiday would drive me into such helpless longing and foolishness as to make me dash off to Motana with her.

In fact, much of this was true, for I had just learned that I did literally have to dash off to Motana. I spent six hours flying over the lovely Rhineland, the stupendous Alps, and then the antique quiltwork of Northern Italy. I paid little attention to any of it. Once over Rome the only thing I could identify was the Colosseum, a large, broken bowl. Tell me it is astounding as an engineering feat. Tell me that architecturally it is aesthetic. Tell me the sight is ominous with history. I believe it, but from above it is a simple, broken bowl.

Lufthansa went punctuality one better and arrived at the Rome airport fifty minutes early, and knowing my Inge, who is never anxious enough to get anywhere ahead of time, I just stood around in the flat, yellow sunshine in the square between the airport buildings and felt very much alone. What heightened my sense of strangeness and abandonment was the black hearse. Where does a hearse go at the airport? Perhaps to the freight entrance? It moved slowly along the angle of two main buildings, and neither the busy-bee sound of the Vespas nor the cackle of disoriented tourists could make a ripple in the pool of dead, still air that moves with a black hearse. This one was motor-driven, but it had a body like a coach. It slid around the angle of the two buildings and, yellow sunlight notwithstanding, brought a heavy aura of gloom. It stopped at the bottom of the stairs where I was standing.

The driver, with a macabre touch of consistency, was a very black Negro. The man next to him was blond, but he made up for his high color by seeming to be in deep melancholy. The back doors of the hearse swung open, and an active little man jumped out, dark hair curly, black eyes nervous, olive skin shiny.

"*Piercere*," he seemed to say, and waved at me.

"I don't speak Italian."

"Is okay. Help me, please? For this job you do not have to talk."

I had fifty minutes to kill, so why not? I went down the steps and to the back of the hearse. There was a coffin inside.

"Go in and push the thing my way, please?" said the curly-haired man.

I climbed into the hearse. The coffin, of walnut wood with brass handles, seemed light, and I remember wondering if there was anyone in it. Later I was sure that no one had been in it because that is where I woke up.

Like Dracula arising from a bloodless sleep, I first saw a vast and stony ceiling and then the columns that supported it. They were, I noticed, a lot like those in Lobbe's Fra Filippo Lippi, which meant I was reincarnated in the early Renaissance.

"He rises!"

This much was true. I could not place the voice, but it seemed human. I could not tell the emotion, but I knew mine. I felt terrified, as if I were the one who was witnessing a corpse rise from a coffin.

When I was sitting up, I became aware of how much my head hurt. My bones seemed made of lead. It was a toss-up whether I wanted to be dead or alive at that moment. I became a little dizzy—the columns of the basement chamber seemed to be pulsing in and out of shape—and then I saw the apparition.

It was Archangel Michael, and I was Saint Manford. There was the white and flowing robe, the mighty sword, casually used like a walking stick, and there was the halo, which was like a jeweled cap. Archangel Michael was as black as the chauffeur of the hearse. Why not? However, I noticed that he had no wings. Therefore, I was real, and he was not.

"Mister deWitt," said the robed Negro. "I did not expect you up so soon." The accent was British, and the melodious quality of his speech was like a song.

"Who's up?" I said, and then I climbed carefully out of the coffin. It sat flat on the stone floor and presented no problem, but I moved awkwardly, anyway. I straightened up, feeling faintly drugged. I waited for the Negro to walk up to me. He came slowly and smiled. When he was within reach, I swung fast and hooked him hard in the stomach. He kept smiling.

"In view of the drug in your veins, Mister deWitt, you delivered a powerful blow."

I, too, thought it had been a powerful blow. My wrist felt as if it had snapped, and his stomach had felt like boiler plate. I got a little dizzy again, but this time that only made me mad.

"What's this all about, Michael?"

"The hearse and so on?" He gestured. "A convenience for abduction. Progress is slow, but, as per local convention, a hearse's progress is totally uninterrupted. Also, many people will turn away. By the way, Mister deWitt, my name is not Michael. It is Torquet."

He bowed from the waist, and his large, strong face looked remarkably mild when he closed his eyes as if in deference. He performed the gesture beautifully. There was really nothing deferential about it.

"And if you were in Motana," he said when he straightened up again, "you would call me Torquet Two."

"What do you mean, if?"

"Because my father is alive, and his name is Torquet One."

"I didn't mean that, Mister Torquet Two."

"Just Torquet is fine here. I hope you don't still have the illusion that you are going to Motana? Clearly you are not, Mister deWitt."

I did not answer. I looked around the vaulted stone chamber. It was windowless and large enough to hold my coffin, the hearse, and some rows of shelves with large wine barrels. They looked dry and dusty. In one wall there was also a large double gate. The wooden planks and the iron fastenings looked medieval.

"Yes," said Torquet. "It leads to the outside, but we are going this way."

Torquet turned, walked through one of the arches, and waited for me at the bottom of a flight of stairs. I followed.

The staircase curved up through what seemed like three stories, and we stopped on a landing, where Torquet opened a door. We went from sullen stone into a lovingly paneled room. It was a study to please a prince, all warm intimacy for conversation with friends. Two lamps at the ends of a carved library table gave a shadowed light, and two leather couches faced each other in front of the big vault of a stone fireplace. It was sandstone carved so that mythological animals seemed to support the mantel. All this was either the damnedest imitation this side of the movies or the room was pure quattrocento. There were also three deep windows, and through the leaded glass I could just see the night shapes of the trees outside.

"It is ten in the evening," said Torquet. "I thought you would sleep till midnight, which is to say that no food has yet been prepared for you." He waved me to one of the couches and smiled. "But you showed more stamina than I would have anticipated from your—er, civilized life."

"You think I'm decadent, perhaps?"

He smiled at me in a benign way and changed the subject. "And now, Mister deWitt, you are undoubtedly full of questions. Please ask them now because I do not have much time."

"Ask? I was sure it would be the other way around."

He raised his eyebrows and dropped them again. It had the same effect as if he had been shrugging his shoulders. "I'm sure I know more than you," he said.

"I don't doubt that. But simply because I don't know why I'm here, what I'm doing, and why I'm doing it—all of which happens to be true—none of that, I'm sure, is going to prevent you from being very clever with me, is it?"

He ignored all that and said, "You asked three questions. I will answer each of them so that you will be more tractable while you are here. Why are you here? Because I don't want you to go to Motana."

"You don't want the road."

"We do want it, but not from you."

He had given me a free gift of an answer that had been obvious since I had woken up in a coffin with an uncomplicated view of a hearse, dry wine barrels, and Saint Michael grinning at me.

"Your next question," he went on, "concerned what you were doing. You were about to negotiate with the Motana government for the German construction company whose name I cannot pronounce."

"I knew that. Including the name."

"It seems that this is all you know."

"You mean there's more?"

"Since you're not going to Motana, the rest does not matter. The next question was, why you were doing all this."

"Because I'm hired to do it."

"Is that why Mister Lobbe fired you?" '

I was rather amazed at the extent of his information but tried to cover it. "I thought you knew all the answers, Torquet."

"No. I said I knew more than you."

"And would you tell me how you know?"

"It would not be ethical to reveal sources, but industrial espionage is for sale, and personal leaks of information are always available."

"The laundry call to find out when I was leaving. A leak in the traffic department to find out where I was going."

"I think our agents called everyone who was known to be going on a trip. It was wasteful, perhaps, but necessary. From then on, it was simply a matter of following the three or four potentials, of which you were one."

"But why did you look into Lobbe Industriel in the first place? The road is not a Lobbe project."

He shrugged and got up. "Apparently there are matters you were not meant to know."

That sounded a lot like Lobbe, and I felt my loyalty flag badly. However, something else worried me. "You had me followed on the plane?" I asked.

"Of course."

"And in Essen?"

"As much as possible."

"And that, Torquet, was not enough for you to know when I would get to Rome."

He smiled and played with his walking stick for a moment. "I know what worries you, Mister deWitt. It was unlikely that anyone followed you into the plant, since it is not open to the public. And you are mindful of the fact that neither you nor anyone else had known when you would leave the plant and when, therefore, you would take your next flight to Rome, as it turned out."

He was getting to it. I was worried, and he kept smiling.

"You made a phone call after you left the plant," he said.

"To the airport."

"I did not know that, Mister deWitt. I do know that you called a number in Rome."

There it was. I had called Inge, and only she had known exactly when I was to arrive in Rome.

"You called, I'm told, from a booth somewhere in the streets of Essen, and it seemed to have been a simple matter for our man to listen from the next booth, separated by a sheet of glass."

"Nice of you to tell it that way, Torquet. It protects your private leaks."

"Unnecessary in this case, Mister deWitt. Our agent in the next booth understood nothing. He only knew that it was a Rome call because he checked with the operator. Your arrival here in Rome was covered by the simple expedient of continuing to follow you."

Perhaps Inge was really not involved. I could not tell. But, in any event, the simplicity of their methods depressed me and made me feel disgusted. It must have shown clearly on my face, because he said, "I understand your feelings, Mister deWitt. But do not let our easy ways upset you."

"And why in hell not, may I ask?"

Torquet had moved back to the door from which we had come. "Perhaps it has not occurred to you," he said, "that your Mister Lobbe's measures of secrecy were not directed against us at all."

The thought was new to me. If Inge had informed on me to Torquet, who represented some faction in Motana, or if that faction had operated as Torquet had explained, then it was truly scandalous how little Lobbe's preparation had guarded against a leak. It was entirely likely that he had ignored this direction of a leak while guarding against some other, perhaps more dire interference. But since I, typically, did not know Lobbe's game, this clever thinking led me nowhere.

"Good-bye, Mister deWitt. We shall not meet again."

"See you in Motana," I said.

He had the door open but stopped a moment. "You would not like it in the rainy season, Mister deWitt." He waved at the pleasant room. "You will stay here in comfort until it starts." He closed the door behind him, and I could hear him use a key to close the lock.

It was a lovely study, but I did not appreciate it now. On the contrary, violently angry at the song and dance I had been led, I stood up and started cursing in a loud voice. The results were fine. First of all, it relieved me immeasurably and secondly, it seemed to activate a portion of the paneling. It did not creak or slide in some eerie way, but simply swung open like a door. Then I saw a serving cart on wheels, loaded with food, and the curly-haired Italian pushing it.

"*Mange, mange!*" he called, as if that explained everything.

He also left the door open, though that meant nothing. The blond man who had sat next to Torquet in the hearse came in and closed the door behind him. He also locked it and put the key in his pocket. He stayed by the door, looking handsome in a cool, disdainful way.

The Italian was something else entirely. His nose was too large, his voice was too loud, his curls were too shiny, but somehow this ugly man managed to be attractive.

"*Mange!*" he said again. "You know what that means? Watch me. It means eat!"

I watched and saw that it was true. He ate a chicken leg, two pickled cauliflower buds, an apple, and a chunk of cheese.

"Good, eh?" he said.

"I haven't tried it yet."

"Hurry up, man."

I took a chicken leg, roasted, and when I ate it, I could taste the Parmesan.

"Where'd you learn English?" I asked him.

"Red Hook. My name's Joe, which is short for Giovanni, and now you try the little fishes, deWitt."

Giovanni Braun, I thought. I took some fish on a fork and when I ate them, I could taste the Parmesan.

"And then one day," said Joe. "I got throwed out."

"The Mafia let you down."

"There was nothing they could do. I was born in Messina. Try the onion and tomato salad. Made it myself."

I ate some, and it was good. "You seem very fond of Parmesan," I said.

"Very. I put it on everything. Hey, Horst!" he called to the blond man by the door. "*Mange, mange!*"

There was not too much light by the door, but I could tell that Horst reacted with something like disgust. I did not like him very much.

"He's an ex-American, too," said Joe.

"I didn't know they had blonds in the Mafia."

"Not Mafia. The Bund. They're worse than us, you know that, deWitt?"

"What's the difference? You're both jailers."

Joe thought that very funny and laughed hard for a while. Then he explained the difference to me. "The difference is," he said, "that Horst over there, he is a fanatic. Look at that face. No fun. Just fanatical thoughts. Me, I'm not fanatic. I'm just greedy."

I poured some dark wine into a water glass and drank. It tasted a lot like vinegar and was very refreshing.

"Dear Joe," I said, "I would be delighted to bribe you."

"And I'd be delighted to accept. That's why they hired Horst over there."

I could see the point. If I wanted to get out of this intimate study for conversation among friends, it would have to be over the dead body of that SS man by the door.

"You two were hired just to keep me here?"

"And we don't get the money if you get out before two months are up."

"Do you know why?"

"And I don't want to know, either," said Joe. "Eat."

"If you knew, Joe, you'd see that it doesn't make sense. Did the black man hire you?"

"That's it."

"He doesn't want me to build a road in his country, but as soon as I don't show up to do my job, the company that sent me will send somebody else. So you might as well let me go. As a matter of fact, that way you can earn your pay immediately, through me, and no waiting around for two months of this nonsense here."

He thought about that for a moment; in fact, he stopped chewing while he was doing it. But then he looked at Horst and shrugged with resignation. "I'm a reasonable man," he said, "but that one isn't." Then he grinned and leaned closer. "Besides, look at it this way. Two months of nice company, nothing to do, good eats, a good woman if you want—you name it, I provide."

I would have felt very guilty if I had accepted without a struggle. I said, "They are going to a lot of expense for nothing, Joe. Villa, guards, food, females notwithstanding—if I'm still missing a week from now, it'll all be wasted because somebody else will be sent in my place."

"Not my worry, friend. Besides," he added, "the black man said they may have the whole thing fixed long before then. And don't ask me how or what. He didn't say."

It made a limited kind of sense. Torquet had said, in effect, that he wanted somebody else to build their crazy jungle road. Crazy or not, that would be Lobbe's lookout. I had only one job for the present and that was to get out of this place.

"You are thinking again," said Joe. "You stopped eating."

I gave him a smile, like between buddies. "Well," I said, "I've had food, I've had conversation—and what was that other thing you mentioned?"

He got it immediately and slapped me on the leg. "You dog! She's gorgeous, deWitt. Sit there. I'll get her right now."

"You mean she's in residence?"

He had to think about that word for a moment. "I'll tell you. What she actually is, she isn't a regular hoor, you understand, but she's a friend of mine who sometimes likes to make a little extra."

"I meant, does she live here, too?"

"No, I was just thinking ahead a little and asked her to be here."

"Very nice," I said, and I meant it, too. It was nice to know that there was somebody who could come and go whenever asked, more so than Joe and Horst, and much more than myself.

"I'll send her right in," said Joe. "Her name is Manuela."

"Where are you going to be?"

"I just ate," he said. "I always got to wait a few hours afterwards."

"But what about Horst? I mean, a little privacy might be just the thing, you know?"

"Manuela don't care," said Joe, "and you don't have to worry about Horst."

I did not quite follow the reasoning and most definitely continued to worry about Horst.

In a sense Joe turned out to be right, and had I known more about Horst, I might have been very much more clever about it. But a pathetic thing happened, which shook me up for a while, and it was not more attractive simply because it turned out to be useful.

Joe took the serving cart with him, and Horst closed the door after him. Horst had not said a word so far, communicating a mood simply with lowered lids, crossed arms, and legs akimbo. The stance was fitting for a number of things, all of them unpleasant. It was good for silent terror at interrogations that last through the night. It was good for that helpless feeling that comes when you do not know your enemy's strength. But it somehow was not good enough to instill respect.

After Joe had gone, Horst came forward, and I could see him in the light. My impression of him did not change except that it got somewhat worse. I had never before seen a face that was truly handsome and repellent at the same time. Horst leaned against the library table and looked down at me where I sat on the couch. Apparently there was going to be no talk. He would simply stand there and fulfill his built-in function, to guard and to intimidate. But he had barely started with this act when the door in the paneling started to rattle. He looked at the door but made no move.

"It's for me," I said. "Would you mind opening the door?"

He did not like that at all. But it was obviously not Joe at the door, since he had a key, and Horst's concern with all irregularities got the better of the situation. He went to the door and opened it. The girl who came in was most certainly Manuela.

Her hips said so, her breasts said so, and her small, painted face said so, too. She tossed her long black hair, and that said the same thing. All of it said, I know you are looking at me, you cannot help but look at me, and you can have every one of my three dimensions if you can bear to be transported into the fourth. And I dare you.

She came straight for the couch, and I got up. She liked that. She smiled, promising a fifth dimension of transport. "I don't speak much English," she said with a shrug.

"Not essential. Please sit down, Manuela. My name is Manny."

"That is a name?" she said, and lowered herself on the couch.

I say advisedly that she lowered herself. The act was partly a function of a dress that was not meant to give anything but her shape, and it was partly due to her natural inclination to lie down flat on her back. I sat down next to her without trying to encourage her abandon. I did not very much feel like an animal, what with Horst in the shadows, the hearse in the basement, and Giovanni waiting for his turn. This reluctance must have somehow transmitted itself to Manuela, because she sat up, tugging at her dress as if that were going to make her bodily presence less evident.

"You Americans," she said. There was no disdain in her voice, just lack of understanding. "Why don't you at least take off your tie?"

"Later," I said, and smiled at her with something of a cocktail smile. She obviously did not understand its restraint.

"Manuela," I said, "are you going to come often?"

"I can come anytime you want, Americano."

"You live far from here?"

"In Ostia."

"Oh," I said. "I thought we were in Rome."

"We are in the *campagna*. With the scooter I come from Ostia in half an hour. You are interested in geography, Americano?"

I had a corrective answer for that, but Manuela was at the moment looking at a little watch she had on her wrist. In or out of bed, that little gesture is apt to rattle me.

"Giovanni says," she told me, "that I should come and see him when we are done. And he never sleeps more than two hours after he eats."

Back to business. I clearly felt that I was not going to reach this woman through her mind—conversation was not going to be the avenue of progress.

"I'll tell you what we do, Manuela," I said, and ran my hand down her naked arm. It started out as a calculated gesture, but it did not end up that way. I could now readily have become caught up in further calculated gestures, but at that point she killed it.

I have this thing about someone looking at a watch in my presence and I have another thing about people looking straight past my left ear, as much as to say: I thought Manny deWitt was here someplace, but I must have been mistaken.

My hand on her arm had reached the wristwatch when I turned around to look in the direction of the thing that seemed to fascinate her. I am sure my stare became as blank as hers.

Horst had moved to one end of the library table. The lamplight on his face was full and sharp. And now his Apollo's head was running with sweat. His hair had turned darker, his fine nose looked gross with sheen, and his classic mouth had turned into a mere repository of large teeth. His hands were trembling.

There is such a thing as having a convulsion. Horst, staring at us, was having a revulsion.

While this reaction in the man still puzzled me, Manuela reacted. She got up slowly and, though her body was all softish curves, she managed to convey a very hard and ugly tension. She glared at Horst and said one word. "*Pederaste—*"

That is a pretty harsh thing to say to a beautiful young man, even though the choice of the word may be obvious. Horst, assaulted, took one stiff step back. This gave him a measure of courage, enough to speak another word in a manner in which I had never heard it spoken before. He said, "Female—" And he pronounced it as if he were throwing up.

Manuela had true pride in herself and a lot of presence. First she stalked Horst and then she punished him. She and the man, he backing, she advancing, performed a weird sort of dance of death, a veritable immorality play to which they both seemed fated.

Manuela said a lot of things that I did not understand. She spat the words, which seemed to leap at Horst like black tarantulas, and all the while she jerked at her clothes. She kicked her shoes off. She kicked her dress off. She unsnapped her bra and let her breasts bounce out. Then she slithered out of her panties and threw them at the man. She attacked him with the sight of her uncompromising body as if daring him to deny it, as if challenging him to match what he could not admit existed. To Horst the challenge was too much.

His breathing became like the sound of plumbing noises behind a wall. His eyes forgot to blink the sweat away, and then his hands remembered that they wanted to kill. It would take very little more for the panic to leap out of him and turn into murder.

Manuela did not see any of this or perhaps she did not believe it. Her great female confidence made her stupid. Horst took a leap at her with all controls gone, the fear smothered.

It was a sort of leap of triumph, but then I moved very fast. I literally flew into the girl to get her out of the way. I almost did it clean.

Actually I was the only one who fell down. Over me there was a sharp sound of impact. Then Horst stumbled past me, and Manuela bounced into a wall.

She had been hit in the side of the head. I could tell by the way she shut her eyes. Strangely, the first thing she did was to look down at her breasts. She held them tenderly, then bent into a crouch. Now there was a lot of fire in her face. But I had no time to think about this. My head got an awful jolt.

The impact had felt hardly human, and when I rolled over, or fell over, I could clearly see why. Horst wore short black boots and he was hauling back for the second time to make the next kick better than the first.

I had seen this done in the movies without understanding how it worked and I did it without knowing just what I had done, but I caught the boot in two hands—I know that much—and then Horst was all over me. He was a hectic fighter and lousy. It was a mauling and squeezing of ribs, and perhaps this was not fighting at all, but his kind of love. His eyes were shining, and his face was deeply flushed.

I am rarely inclined toward mayhem, so that when the thought of it does occur to me, I am apt to take advantage of it before the moment passes.

He was holding me in a hug when all at once I dug at his Adam's apple. That made him give way enough for me to whip one elbow across his face.

His nose caught most of it, and that pain is instantaneous. I had caught him across the bridge of the nose and not from below, or else he would have passed out. But he curled up with shock, and I got free.

I was much too mad to stop now and I decided it was best that he should not be conscious for the rest. I put the two reasons together—though either one of them would have been enough—and I improved on his own technique and kicked him solidly in the head. I do not remember the sound, but I do remember the way he jerked. It looked very conclusive. I got quickly down to him again and put my hand in his pocket. Manuela was still by the wall and did not seem to have moved. Her face was the same, and she was still in a crouch. It was weird.

"Get your clothes," I told her.

"Americano—" She seemed hoarse and hardly moved. "Now, Americano!"

"The clothes, damn you!"

She gave a start, as if coming out of a trance. "*Va bene, va bene,*" she said very fast, and picked her clothes up.

She picked them all up but did not put them on. She held them in her arms, but I was much too busy to give her further instructions. I had found a small-caliber automatic, one blackjack, and two bunches of keys. I stuffed these into my jacket pocket and left the rest of Horst's possessions lying on the floor: one very dirty handkerchief, a neatly folded sheaf of lire, a very messy ball of string, and a snapshot of a fat baby, encased in celluloid. In some combination these things might have told a lot about Horst. But I had no time. I ran to the door through which I had come with Torquet and started to try keys.

Manuela, slow like sleep, came closer. "You are leaving me?"

"Get your clothes on. You're coming along."

"Oh?" she said, and again did nothing about the clothes. "But Giovanni said that he wants me afterward."

"Screw Giovanni."

She did not know slang and could make nothing of that ill-chosen word but instead started to protest again.

"But he said that when I am done with you—"

"You're coming. You can tell him later I dragged you off and raped you."

"He won't believe it."

"You're right. I forgot."

Then I got the door open. I grabbed Manuela and shoved her through because I was not going to leave her behind to stimulate Joe into premature wakefulness. He had another hour of natural sleep coming, and I needed that hour, too.

She was already padding down the stone steps when the sound behind me made my insides flip over.

Horst was up. Rather he was crawling on all fours, weaving a little, but staring me straight in the face. Perhaps his skull was made of stainless steel, but I could not have him staring at me while I was leaving the paneled room in which I was meant to stay for two months. I came back toward him just as he was sitting up.

His eyes were none too steady, and I saw that they were full of water. He raised his face to me and then one hand, as if begging for something. His other hand had somehow found the photo, and he was holding it carefully.

"Please—" he said.

I stopped walking and realized that it was the first word he had said since "female."

"Please," he said again. "Is she gone?"

"Yes."

He mumbled something that I did not catch and closed his eyes. Then he fell over sideways rather slowly, curled on the floor, and did not move anymore. I touched him, and he stayed asleep. The small picture fell out of his hand.

In the wine vault that was now a garage there was the choice of Manuela's Vespa or Torquet's hearse. When I opened the gate, which sounded as if the hinges were dying, I saw that it was raining outside. Manuela and I decided to take the hearse for that reason, though the Vespa would have moved us much faster. I tore a few wires on the Vespa, but this machine is so simple that there is not much you can damage. I hoped it would be enough to discourage Joe from pursuit, and we drove into the night.

It had been true when Manuela had said that the house with the paneled room was in the *campagna*. It was a three-story stone structure with columns for ornamentation. Both neglect and the size of the place dated it. The building sat in a park that I could not see clearly, but I felt it had probably long gone to seed. The hearse, without lights, bumped over cobbles, and the thin tires made singing sounds. Under the trees on both sides of the drive the rain was dripping.

"Whose place is this, Manuela?"

"It is called the Plozzi Lodge," she said. "You can sometimes see the beach to the left of the road, but there also used to be heavy woods and of course the marshes. This place was for hunting."

"Plozzi," I said, and thought about it.

"He owns many villas and palazzos. The *principe* comes from a very old family."

"*Pazzo* Plozzi is the name he goes by in some circles," I said.

"He is," she said seriously. "He never married." Manuela had put her dress on but was holding her underwear in her lap. She was playing with it absently.

"He is," I repeated. "What does *pazzo* mean?"

She put her finger to her temple and made the European gesture of twisting the finger around, which is to tell you that you are nuts.

"Crazy," I said to the road ahead. "Crazy like a fox." It was all clear and ugly. Plozzi, the old lecher, gets into the innocent Inge. Social connections, if not money, take care of that. He sics the girl on me because there is monkey business going on with Lobbe and some road in Motana, and I am the uncanny idiot-savant who will run errands for Lobbe while totally in the dark. Then Inge spies on me, no matter how unknowingly, and Plozzi intercepts at a convenient point where he can stuff me behind the paneling of one of his stately mansions. If I had stopped in London, he might have locked me up in his Mayfair flat; in Paris, in his *intime* chalet in the Bois; in Hongkong, on his double-decker saipan. I was going a little bit out of my mind with visions of the ubiquitous *principe*.

"When was he here last, Manuela?"

"Who?"

"The *pazzo principe*, the one who held me prisoner here."

"Oh, that one. Giovanni said he would leave today. Didn't you see him? He drove your hearse himself."

"What's this?"

"I saw him from a distance," she said. "He is beautiful." She rubbed her arms and cocked her head. "I have never had a black man."

Torquet, then, was a prince, too. I should have known it by his multilingual, overbearing kindness. Torquet the Second, yet.

I gave Manuela—she was lost in her own frustrations—a fairly aggravated look. "I realize it has been a harsh and empty day for you, woman, what with a pederast, no prince, and Joe left asleep, but would you just please try and remember when Plozzi was here the last time?"

"I don't know. I have read in *Oggi* that he was in Deauville to watch the horses."

I happened to know that no races were being run at Deauville during this particular time of year. "When did you read this?" I asked.

"Yesterday. At the dentist's."

I could check that off. Her issue of the magazine could have come out at the turn of the century when Plozzi had been a mere youth. For that matter, my own source of information on Plozzi's whereabouts was probably entirely reliable except for the interpretation. He was undoubtedly in Motana, the safari story an effective cover, his real purpose in the country whatever scheme he and Torquet the Second were concocting against

Lobbe. And if they were determined enough to intercept Lobbe's handyman and desperate enough to lure Inge into the very heartland of their scheme, then Lobbe himself must really be into something far-flung in wickedness.

But none of this heady stuff helped me forget for a moment what Inge had done in the meantime and whom she was spending time with while I was groping my way through the black rain in a black hearse with a black-haired *bambola* by my side, approaching God-knowswhat black fate.

"Americano," she said in the dark, "don't turn on the lights."

"I have no intention of turning on the lights. If I knew where I was going, I might need lights on a dark night in the rain to help me find the way, but since I have no idea where I am going—"

"Because I think he fixed the Vespa and is following us."

There was no rearview mirror. Perhaps because a hearse is accorded unimpeded progress everywhere, there never is one. I could have turned and stared out the cut-glass window in the back door, but it seemed wiser to orient myself in the landscape. I was driving on a road, a country road, but now I wanted to see the country as well because I had to get off the road.

"Look out the window on your side and tell me if there is a ditch," I said.

"A what?"

"*Fossa, fossa!*" I said. It was one of those odd, far-between words of foreign origin that you have heard and you don't know when, that you remember and you don't know why. I also knew such a word in German—*Hexenschuss*—and I thought of it then for no good reason and without being able to remember what it meant.

"No *fossa*," she said. "There is no ditch."

"Excellent," I said. "Here goes!"

"But there is a wall," she said.

"*Hexenschuss!*"

It sounded impressive enough for a swearword, so I used it. I think it was more the magic of that word than the skill of my hearse maneuver that kept us on the road. I could see the stone wall about flush up against Manuela's window, and then suddenly the wall ended. There were now some spooky trees and some undergrowth.

"*Avanti!*" I yelled, and crashed into the unknown.

There was no problem about stopping, because it happened by itself. The hearse stopped, the motor stopped, we stopped up against the dashboard. All was still under the trees except for the whisper of rain touching the leaves. There were leaves in the oddest places. The windshield was covered with them, so that they looked mounted under glass. A drippy branch had grown into my window, and Manuela wore some leaves in her hair.

"*Pazzo Americano*," she said, and scratched her head.

I did not get out but climbed into the coffinless rear, where I sat by the big window in the back door. I could see the road well enough. On one side the broken stone wall cut it off, and on the other the glistening road wound itself into a curve.

"I can hear him," said Manuela next to me.

In the distance I could hear the waspish sound. I could also hear Manuela breathe next to me.

"What will he do if he finds us, Americano?"

"If it's Horst, nothing. Because I'll shoot him." I took the automatic out of my pocket and worked the slide back slowly and just so far. I stuck my finger in the open breech and felt the bullet there. "And if it's Giovanni, also nothing. Because I'll bribe him."

"Americano, you are wonderful."

"Don't push like that."

"I am not pushing. I am built like that."

"Don't breathe like that. I can't hear the motor."

At that point it was not necessary to hear the motor because the light of the Vespa began to show on the other side of the wall. It moved fast, a jittery reflection on the rain in the air, and then the single eye of the lamp whipped into view and passed. I could see the hunched form of a man in silhouette when the light was pointing away, and then the Vespa leaned through the curve and was gone. I could hear Manuela breathe again. I noticed there was moisture on my forehead and I sat down on the floor of the hearse.

"Put away the gun, Americano."

"I did."

"Why are you shaking, Americano?"

"I get that way afterward. After I'm tense."

"Oh. What is tense?"

"Excited."

"You are no longer excited?"

"Manuela, you are blowing in my ear again."

"Why do you say you are no longer excited? I can tell that you are lying."

"I am aware of that. What's this?"

"Me, Americano."

"It's a leaf. How did a leaf get there?"

"Take it out."

I took it out. I found no more leaves anywhere, though I surely would have found them had there been any more. I lay in the hearse once again, but this time I knew every minute of the time I spent there and never again as long as I live will I look at a hearse and feel completely gloomy.

The rain stopped, and it was very quiet. The clouds in the night sky shifted and now and then let the moon through. There was no longer the thick, low blanket of darkness overhead, but there was now a view of blue masses and silver spires that continually shifted their shape and moved in unhurried ways. The countryside was very much blacker than the sky and it was sharp the way a miniature is sharp and defined. I saw rows of cyprus, which stood still under the moving sky, and there were squat houses in the rolling fields, precise and immobile under the moon, reminding me of a steel print.

Manuela showed me the way to Ostia, a town that looked ramshackle and dead in the night, and when I dropped her in front of the house where she lived, she told me which road to take in order to get back to Rome. She lived on a street that I think would be as depressing in daylight as it looked in the night—paper drifting in the wind, rows of stone houses with cracks like scars and with posters that flapped where the glue had dried away. From there I drove the hearse around the outskirts of Rome so that I could get to the airport more quickly.

I did not drive the hearse all the way to the airport but abandoned it on a side road when I could see the blue light of the control tower well enough. From there I walked to the airport in fifteen minutes.

There were a few Fiats parked by the buildings, a Mercedes, two Maseratis, and a scattering of Vespas. There was no way of telling if Manuela's Vespa was one of them. I took my time and looked for Horst or Joe in the buildings and in the shadows outside. I found neither. It took much more time to arrange for the rerouting to Motana. The clerk was half asleep, I was soon fully irritated, and the business of rerouting my direct flight to the capital of Motana over Malta and Tangiers for an earlier departure was fully as complicated as trying to amend the Magna Carta.

While this was going on at five o'clock in the morning I placed a call to Long Island, New York. Even if the ticket clerk never mastered my rerouting to Motana, an immediate talk with Lobbe was imperative.

I reached him at his Long Island place, not because I was one of the few who had the private number, but because I knew the first name of the butler. He did not have a name like a butler, nor did he look like one. He was called Kalopidos, and he had a black handlebar mustache that twitched.

Kalopidos did not get Lobbe out of bed at five in the morning (it was one o'clock in the morning on Long Island), but he had to go and holler for Mijnheer Hans Lobbe from the dock of the estate. Lobbe was rowing a six-foot dinghy in the midnight waters of Oyster Bay. This was a secret habit of his to lose weight.

When he came to the phone, he yelled as if he had to reach me without benefit of the instrument.

"Mennekin!"—his voice reverberated—"you call me at this most private hour either because you are an utter success or because you are as usual."

"I am still in Rome, sir."

There was silence at the other end, which was probably a polite omission of a profanity. I used this moment to jump right in.

"I am calling to give a report and to obtain information. It turns out that there seem to be a number of things I know nothing about."

"That's all right, mennekin. I don't expect you to be perfect."

He was still calling me mennekin, which meant that he was still in a fairly good humor. But I did not expect it to last.

"Mister Lobbe, in connection with this routine contract job I was to handle, I have, since my departure, been spied on, abducted in a hearse, held prisoner in a deserted castle, and been forced to flee for my life."

I thought it was a good speech. Lobbe was paying for the call, and I had a few hours till flight time. When I was done, I expected him to be silent with shock and guilt.

"Are you still a prisoner?"

"No. I'm calling from the Rome airport. However—"

"In other words, you will be in Motana one day late. Not bad. Not bad. Why are you calling, Manny?"

If I had been talking to anyone other than Lobbe, I would now have turned into stone just from sheer surprise. But it was no good to allow Lobbe to arrest you like that unless you wanted to enter a perpetual state of suspended animation. Instead, I cursed. Lobbe allowed this for a while, at something like five dollars a minute, but then he got miserly.

"When you get to Motana," he started to say, but I was four thousand miles away from him and mighty aggravated.

"*If,* Mister Lobbe. *If* I get to Motana. The plot surrounding this prosaic road job in the jungle includes, among others, Gabriele Plozzi."

"At what it's costing for this phone call, mennekin, I cannot afford your jealous imaginings."

"Mister Lobbe, my prison was his hunting lodge right outside of Ostia."

"*Quatsch.* The Plozzis have not held property in Italy for a hundred years. All they got is their name on some buildings and parks."

"But he does know Inge. And in view of the coincidental nature of—"

"Jealousy is a form of devotion, mennekin, but it is a lousy one. Don't cloud the brain because of a woman."

The phone booth, though of clear glass, was giving me claustrophobia. My own skin was giving me claustrophobia. No miracle of telephonic engineering can substitute for a snarl, face to face, and that is what I dearly would have liked to give Lobbe right then and there. Instead, I responded mildly, like a man of reason.

"If a clouded brain is all that's behind my difficulties, Mister Lobbe, then would you please explain to me why a total stranger, some dignitary from Motana by the name of Torquet, drugs me into insensibility, hauls me off in a coffin, locks me up with a glutton and a pervert and a debilitating female, and—"

"*Vat, vat, vat?*"

"—and then returns to Motana, where he is undoubtedly prepared to do the same thing all over again should I show my face in that country."

"What's this about a debilitating female?"

Lobbe has a selective mind. It shuns the commonplace (gluttons), the morbid (coffins), the ridiculous (perverts), and goes straight to essentials. But I decided to hell with his interests and a little bit more of mine.

"Torquet is his name. If I am to operate safely in Motana—"

"Which one, Torquet One or Two?"

It irritated me that he should know of not only one Torquet but the two of them and that neither he nor the tapes I had collected in Essen had made any mention of their menace. I must have sounded fairly peeved when I told Lobbe that the black prince in the hearse was Number Two, because he got fatherly with me in a foolish way.

"Don't worry, Manny," he said. "I will take care of them."

"Why now? Why not before?"

"I did not know they were involved."

"You did not know. May I ask why it was not known that a six-foot-plus menace, who is known as Number Two, and somebody else, who is known as Number One and must therefore be at least of a size that—"

"You are jabbering, Manford. Torquet One, for your information, was head of the most important tribe in Motana. Under the present governmental setup his position is meaningless and his importance is nil. However, his son, educated in Europe, seems to have entered national affairs. Did he say anything to you?"

"He wants somebody else to build the road."

"You are sure."

"Mister Lobbe, he not only said so, but he reinforced the point by the use of—"

"You told me. She was debilitating. Now you will please get off that subject and listen to me, Manford."

There was no question that he was serious. His English had become increasingly correct, and he was calling me Manford again.

"I have a certain amount of influence in Motana," he said, "and I will bring it to bear."

"I am not entirely reassured, sir."

"Damn it, deWitt, I have strong ancestral ties in that part of the world. Haven't I told you the story of great-grandfather Mies?"

"Several times, sir."

"Then perhaps you remember it."

"I certainly do."

"Good. In other words, you will be able to enter Motana safely because I will immediately get in touch. Before I hang up, are there any other worries?"

This one was difficult. It was about Inge. As far as I was concerned, the girl was under a cloud. As far as Lobbe was concerned, she was a family member and for that very reason embodied truth, beauty, and love. Whatever doubts I had about the girl's loyalties, Lobbe would not believe, but I had to bring the matter up somehow.

"I am worried about Inge," I said. "In view of my suspicions about Plozzi, her hanging around with him bothers me."

"Then, take her away from him, mennekin, which I already asked you to do here in New York. You also have to ask me how?"

"In a way, yes."

"Because she is in Motana with that Plozzi? I told you I will fix your safety there, and you are still afraid?"

"No."

"Then, go!" And on that theatrical note he hung up.

I left that phone booth feeling slightly like Don Quixote, as noble and as ineffectual. I had given him a lot of information, and he had promised me help. He had given me hardly any information, and the source of his help, I decided, approached the ridiculous. Great-grandfather Mies Lobbe, indeed!

As a businessman, old Mies had been a failure. From a moral point of view Mies had been reprehensible. But in the eyes of Hans Lobbe old Mies had done a wonderful thing. Mies Lobbe decided to become a slaver. On his first trip out he fell in love with one of his cargo, turned the ship around in midocean, and returned to Africa a liberator.

"He had style," Hans Lobbe would say. "He had largesse! There is today not one important native clan on the West Coast of Africa that cannot claim ancestral relationship with the Lobbes. That is largesse!"

And so, with a promise of help based on a debauchery one hundred years old, I went back to the ticket counter. My clerk explained that everything had been arranged. Translated, that meant that it would be another few hours before he knew when I could leave for Motana.

I called Inge's number in Rome on the off-chance that she was still there. I learned, after much ringing, that she had in fact left on the Motana flight that I had missed on the previous day. It made sense because that had been the plan. My coming along with her seemed to have been strictly a take-it-or-leave-it proposition. I hung up and felt almost glad that she was not there.

I went to the travelers' bar, which served mostly espresso and vermouth. The espresso tasted too strong, and I switched to vermouth. I sat there for quite a while, and the longer I sat, the more my current preoccupations seemed to disappear, and I began to feel at peace. In the middle of this euphoria there came a slap on my back that felt a lot like the blow of a hammer. I smelled Parmesan.

"Don't let the friendly greeting fool you, deWitt. I got a gun in my pocket, and it's looking at you."

I sat up slowly on my stool, as far as my backache permitted, and turned to look at Joe.

"Christ," he said, "you been drinking. I can smell the coffee all the way over here. Easy now. Don't move."

"I can't. You broke my back."

He became solicitous and took my arm to help me off the stool. Then we walked to the long benches, where we sat down in the vast privacy of the empty waiting hall. I carefully put my hands into the pockets of my jacket. I now had Horst's gun in the palm of my hand and felt very clever.

"You got one, too, huh?" said Joe.

"Yes," I said.

We looked at each other without moving.

"This ain't the way I learned it in Red Hook," said Joe.

"Or in the movies."

He nodded and seemed to be thinking.

"What do we do now?" I asked him.

"I don't know. You want to kill me?"

"No."

"Me neither."

"You want money."

"*Ecco*," he said, and took his hand out of his pocket.

"How much did Plozzi pay you for the kidnapping job?"

"Would you mind taking your hand out of your pocket?"

"Sorry." I took my hand out and said, "How much?"

"I don't know from Plozzi," said Joe. "My deal is with Torquet."

"Did he get the villa from Plozzi?"

"Naw. The place belongs to the State, and the State rented the place to the Motana embassy. That's how come Torquet was using it."

I considered that it looked indeed as if Plozzi had nothing to do with any of this.

"And I always used to think," Joe was saying, "that Motana was kind of a sheep country between New York and California."

"They seceded. How much, Joe?"

"How much you got, deWitt?"

"Look. Maybe you saw me make some phone calls a little while ago."

"And now they're all going to come busting in here to arrest me."

"They're not cops, but they're coming for you."

Suddenly Joe's hand was back in his pocket.

"Pay me, and I disappear. Don't pay me, and there's trouble."

I kept bluffing him. "How's Horst?" I said.

"I know you can hit," he said, "but I'm not your enemy like Horst was. One thousand dollars and we're friends."

It was Lobbe's money, but I did not like to pay something for nothing. "Does Torquet know I got out?" I asked him.

"You nuts? I don't want to lose my two-month meal ticket."

"I didn't think so. But if you take me back, you will lose it. Just in case you showed up, Joe, I had the villa staked out. Take me back there—in fact, walk me out of this hall—and the men I've called will haul you in."

He thought about that for a moment and then he figured that he saw the hole in it.

"You don't make sense, deWitt. How come I'm still sitting here making a kaffeeklatsch? Looks to me there's just us mice. Get up," he said, and got up himself. "We're leaving."

I sighed and stayed where I was. "The reason we're talking is because I need your help. If you help me, nobody is going to touch you."

"You talk like a shyster, deWitt."

"I happen to be a shyster—sufficiently high class, I might add, to bribe you with one hundred dollars."

"Two hundred," he said, and sat down again. "What do you want me to do?"

"Can you get in touch with Torquet?"

"Sure. Through the embassy."

"Send him a wire that says that you got deWitt safe and sound but that deWitt is the wrong man. You got that out of him, tell Torquet, when whiling away the time with a few persuasion exercises you learned in your youth. Tell him that deWitt is a decoy and that the real man is Plozzi."

"The *principe*? You're nuts."

"Two hundred dollars' worth."

"Me, too," said Joe, and when he had called his contact at the embassy and I had paid him the money, we had a few vermouths, which he paid for.

I had ample time to get over the sweet vermouth headache because the trip to Motana took two days. It sometimes takes one day by jet from Rome to Ville-blanche, on the coast of Motana, but sometimes it takes two days. I stayed soothed during most of the trip with the information that it can also take four days. What delayed us was a refueling stop in Adrar. They were having an untimely sandstorm close in on the field, and our pilot kept us on the ground till he felt that the air had cleared enough. He did not want sand in his fuel system. Also, he did not want sand in his jet engines, and the job of blowing it out again took several hours.

I never saw Adrar. Part of the time I slept in the terminal building; part of the time I looked at the landscape from the terminal building. The view was of something left over after one thousand years of sunshine. The sun, I was sure, was several light-years closer to this port of call than to any other place on the globe. I was afraid that if I went outside, I would bump my head into the fireball.

My first view of Villeblanche was beautiful. The town, as the name suggests, looks white, a sloping expanse of flat buildings with veins of green marking the run of the streets and round eyes of green where little parks dot the town. All this goes down to a very blue sea. Only the land's edge shows the angular gray and black shapes of commercial installations.

We set down on the inland side of the town, where the jungle seemed in active motion, leaning and bulging toward the tarmac of the landing field. When I walked from the plane to the terminal building, I smelled what is technically known as rot, but it made me think of heavy earth, fleshy flowers, and juicy fruits. So Paradise might have smelled.

Why build a road here? I thought. Who would want to leave?

The terminal building was white stucco inside and out. Inside it looked as if someone were in the process of moving in but with little conviction of staying. Three rows of wooden benches were unevenly aligned. The ticket agent's counter held a litter of papers and also cups, glasses, and plates. Besides handling reservations, the counter dispensed coffee, wine, and French rolls. A brown telephone booth stood at an angle, and there was a three-foot space between it and the wall. A half-naked baby was yanking on the cable that connected the booth to a junction box.

I decided not to call Government House first because my rush was not theirs but only mine, and I wanted first to check out Inge.

Her local address was Place de Safari, Bureau, Villeblanche. The address seemed a little strange, but then I also found the benches in the hall a little strange, the baby on the telephone cable, and the buns and bottles on the ticket counter. In the booth I picked up the receiver and heard a sound like the wind in the willows. Through this sound there now came something like a wild mating call. I looked at the baby on the cable, but it was not saying a thing. Then the mating call changed to a melody in English.

"You don't understand Motanesque?" said the male operator.

"Is that what it was?"

"Since you don't understand Motanesque, and I was speaking something that you did not understand, therefore it must have been Motanesque," said the operator.

I was to get used to this argumentative approach to life in Motana, but at the moment the lecture startled me. And there was more.

"Do you speak English?"

"Yes."

"Then why do you not speak in English to me instead of worrying about the fact that you cannot speak Motanesque?"

I told him that I was startled by a talking operator altogether but that I would now like to speak to Inge Lobbe, and I gave him her address.

"Since you have an address but not a telephone number, don't you find it strange that you should be using a telephone instead of a taxi?"

I took a moment to recover. His answers were as tricky as a Zen story, and I did not have the customary ten years to work things out. I said, "I conclude from your cleverness that you don't have the telephone number I asked for, and since you are an operator and don't have this number, I am led to believe that there is no such number."

"You are new here," said the operator.

"You find that strange?"

"No. Not after listening to you. But since there is no number at the Place de Safari, I do find it strange that you ask me...."

Before this sophist at the other end of the line persuaded me into insanity, I hung up and got out of the booth. The baby, I noticed, had stopped swinging on the cable and was looking at me. "I know where it is," the baby said. "For one hundred francs I will drive you there."

I stared down at the baby and felt that the operator of a moment ago had been downright commonplace in comparison.

"It's all right," said the baby. "I am tolerant of foreigners. Next you want to know how old I am."

"You find that strange?"

"Not from you. I am thirty. You have heard of pygmies?"

"Of course!"

"Then, why do you look surprised?"

I was not going to get involved. I was determined about that and walked to the baggage counter, where I found my suitcase and the gladstone, and then I went outside.

There was a lush miniature jungle surrounded by a circular drive, and on that drive, close to the entrance, there stood—or rather, there listed—

a vehicle that could have been a car. It could have been several cars. The wheels were larger in front than in the rear, the hood was olive drab and seemed to belong to an army two-and-a-half-ton, but the tonneau was black lacquer and basket weave. One door opened, and Baby climbed out.

He had changed. Perhaps my knowing that he was thirty emphasized the maturity of his face. He was coal black, round-eyed, and had a flattish nose. There was a serious cast around his mouth, and he moved his head with authority. The position of his eyebrows suggested boredom. He now wore a kind of fez and a jacket, tailored, of course, because it fit him. It was a buff chauffeur's jacket. The only thing that distracted from its elegance was the fact that he wore no pants. His shorts were not visible now.

"This," he said, "is my taxi, the 'Spirit of Friendship.'"

"Of course it is a taxi."

"If you know that it is a taxi, then why do you act surprised?"

I decided to put a stop to that kind of talk right then and there.

"I am staring," I said, "not because I don't know it is a taxi but because the fact of the taxi and the fact of the stare are both facts, and since a fact is a fact, therefore my stare and the way that taxi looks are the same thing. Don't tell me you find that strange."

He smiled, showing teeth like porcelain.

"That," he said, "was beautiful."

Clearly I had just spoken Motanesque.

"Fifty francs to the Place de Safari," said Baby, and then we climbed into the car.

There was no ordinary seat in the front but a thing like a high chair. Baby climbed up on that and started to work the controls, which were all under the steering wheel.

The ride through town was colorful. The very sameness of the white houses emphasized the variety of everything else. There were statuesque natives wearing the long shirt and skull cap I had first seen on Torquet. Some of them were carrying staffs. There were Indians in their cheap Hongkong suits, dealers in currencies and experts in complicated banking transactions. I saw the Chinese, the traders of the Pacific, who were apparently moving in on Africa with accustomed acumen. The pace was not hurried. The white-helmeted policeman directing traffic moved about with the grace of a dancer. The darting children in the street were the real controllers of traffic. Suddenly there was no more town. There was a road of packed dirt, a tunnel under trees, and everything in green shadow. Then the trees opened to make a large clearing. Rocky ground kept the growth away and gave room to a view I had not expected. There was a row of three panel trucks, four Land Rovers, and two pickups, which had seats in the back and a seat each on the front fenders. There were stacks of crates, a row of wooden cages, and a low bungalow.

"Place de Safari," said Baby, and pulled up in front of the bungalow. "And this is the *bureau* for the safari company."

As I got out of the car a man in the image of Noah came out on the porch. He seemed dressed for jungle warfare, and even his gray beard looked more fierce than kindly. He came down the few steps from the porch and immediately grabbed my hand in a crushing token of friendship. The event was particularly unnerving because I had the strong suspicion that this might be Plozzi. The only similarity between him and my image was that this man was old. Aside from that he was strong, fierce, and very vital. Knowing Inge, I thought that this man made sense and perhaps I was the freak.

"You come for me?" he boomed. "You want something I got?"

The content was disturbing, but the delivery was hearty and warm. And if this was Plozzi, then an Italian spoke with a Dutch accent.

"As a matter of fact," I said as I took back what was left of my hand, "I came for Miss Inge Lobbe."

"The pretty *meisje!*" He grinned. "And then you are the deWitt she talks about. I am van Voos, of van Voos Safaris."

My hand did not hurt anymore. My image of Plozzi remained securely intact.

"She got the mail here," said van Voos. "But now she is in Villeblanche at the Central till safari time."

"I take you there," said Baby, but I was not quite done.

"Are you the one with whom Miss Lobbe will go on safari?"

"No," said van Voos. "I hire out the equipment and the guide. Both bush and jungle."

"Of course," I said. "She is going with Plozzi."

"I don't know any more. He is now in jail."

The sun grew and kissed everything, and the jungle hummed with life and love. I gave silent thanks to Joe and his phone call and I stood in adoration of my own underhandedness.

"How strange," I said. "Would you know why he is in jail?"

"No," said van Voos. "It is a young country. They do not always know why they do things. Like the crazy road."

"Road," I said, and let it hang there,

"Let your man drive you past the road they are making in the jungle. But you know the road. Miss Lobbe said that you might come to see her because you are with the project of the road."

In very short order he had hit me with a number of things. Somebody was already building the road, and Inge had assumed I was coming to Motana because of the road project.

"Who did you say was building the road?"

"You, no? Of course the Motanesque started it, but you came to finish it with the machines that sit in the harbor, no?"

"Yes, of course," I said. "All I meant was that I just came in on the project. I don't even know where it goes."

"I don't, either," said van Voos. "It starts at the harbor and goes through the jungle."

"It must go somewhere," I said.

"In Motana?" He laughed. "It's a young country, you know. Roads mean progress, so they build a road. How come you don't know where it goes?" And he looked at me.

"I don't have to know where it goes. I'm just a lawyer, doing contracts."

He thought that was very funny and he was still laughing about it when Baby drove the car and me back into the jungle road.

Baby took a left fork back to town, which took us down the same kind of green tunnel through which we had come. But then we came to The Road.

It was a wide strip of raw earth that could have accommodated six lanes of a highway, though at this point of work the cut through the jungle had a surface a lot like a badly plowed field. All this uprooting and plowing was being done by a tumult of half-naked workers, who glistened with sweat in the sun or who looked buff with bark dust and dry mud. They felled trees, burned underbrush, cracked stone with hammers, filled holes with shovels. They carried the debris of their work in round baskets and then dumped it into wooden carts. All the while they chanted.

"Stop the car, Baby."

He did and turned around. "How did you know my name?"

"You're famous," I said, "even where I come from. Now I'd like to see what's going on."

Not all of the men were working. A few had sat down wherever they happened to be, and the rest simply worked around them. This friendly habit was apparently one of the reasons why Motana needed outside help with the monster road. I looked both ways. At the end leading toward town the wide slash in the jungle curved out of sight. Going inland, the road seemed truly to lead nowhere. It stopped in the distance against a primeval wall of green, and then came only jungle again. Not too far beyond was a rise that became a mountain. It was not high enough to carry snow, but it was bald on top, where no jungle reached. I listened to the workers for a while.

"What are they singing, Baby?"

"It is Motanesque," he said. "They are talking."

I had an idea how the talk was going, having been exposed to the manner myself, and there was undoubtedly another reason why they needed help with their work. Baby, I noticed, was leaving me. He walked to a truck that I had not noticed in the melee of people and equipment. The open bed held a coffee urn and boxes of food. The catering establishment was run, as might be expected, by a group of Chinese. They wore suits in the style of the early thirties, wide lapels, fabulous shoulders, and pants legs as wide as the distance from heel to toe. In contrast to the lively faces of the Motanesques those of the Chinese seemed to be plastic masks. Behind them, undoubtedly, ran thoughts of profit—how the Motanesque franc stood at the Tangiers exchange, whether to exchange for Formosa yen, Hongkong dollars, or good German marks. Baby came back eating a rice ball.

"I eat here every day," he said. "The rice is strange, but I am getting used to it."

This comment left him wide open for a Motanesque gambit, which might run: If you are eating because you are hungry and also because you want to get used to the food, then the Chinese will be the first to charge you twice, while the price is further increased by the car trip. In addition, rice is not native to Motana, which makes your eating the balls a slur at the Motanesque economy. Therefore, somebody here is stupid.

"How much did you pay, Baby?"

"Do you think I am stupid? Nothing!"

I looked at the truck and watched the Chinese hand out coffee and other things.

"Baby," I said, "what you say is contrary to the natural laws of commerce."

"This is not commerce," he said, and got on his stool. "This is a cultural mission."

"Just one damn minute," I said, because I was now thinking ineffectively. "You mean these Chinese are doing all this out of love?"

"Yes."

We bounced across the new road bed and then continued with the dirt road on the other side.

"This is ridiculous," I said. "I know about cultural missions, and this isn't how they work. And I know about the Chinese. The Chinese can't afford love. They're too poor."

"They just exploded an atomic bomb, which proves that they are not poor. Anybody who can afford an atom bomb can afford love."

I was new to this argument and gave up the pursuit of more familiar logic. However, I managed to hang onto the idea that this Chinese venture was paying for something. If Motana was not the target for a rice ball profit, then it was most certainly the target for some other kind of profit.

The Hotel Central was in the style of much colonial architecture. The façade made no concessions to the locale but suggested a nineteenth-century bank. It had heavy walls, the cheapest type of insulation when labor is cheap. The windows were tall because otherwise the high ceilings would be in perpetual gloom.

I told Baby to wait by the tree-lined curb while I carried my own bags into the hotel. I registered at the desk, and while somebody carried my things up the open staircase I used the house phone to call Inge's room. She was not in. I left a note for her at the desk and went back to the taxi. Baby was asleep.

"Baby," I said, "Government House."

He opened his eyes enough to recognize me and then closed them again. "Not now," he said.

"Now."

This time he only opened one eye. "Sleep time," he said. "Later I will take you."

It was barely the afternoon, and I saw no reason for sleep time or baby talk, for that matter.

"What was in those rice balls, Baby?"

In a most un-Motanesque manner, he said nothing at all.

"Baby. Wake up. It isn't sleep time, and therefore you can drive me to Government House."

He opened an eye. "You talk like a Motanesque, except no Motanesque talks during sleep time." And he turned away, curled into a ball.

If I needed more proof of this statement, I found it at Government House after a fifteen-minute walk through empty streets. The seat of government was the very soul of silence. Downstairs the information booth was empty. On the second floor all the office doors were closed. On the third floor one office door was open because it had a broken hinge. The room behind the door turned out to be empty, anyway. On the door it said Fiscal Department. If the broken hinge of the door meant that somebody had run off with the treasury, then this was obviously the hour to do it.

I took a walk on the empty streets—even the trees seemed to be sleeping in the sun—and passed many closed doors and many open stores that had no attendants.

Excluding myself, I encountered only two phenomena that suggested life. One was a Chinese who was walking rapidly and seemed to be talking to himself. The interesting thing was his suit. It was the Chinese Republic civilian suit of blue. It was cut to a national standard and naturally did not fit. The other exception was the Colonial Club.

The front was ornate, with plaster columns and a Grecian frieze, and the brass plaque that identified the building had not been changed since

Motana had ceased to be a colonial territory. Inside, the place was like an English club: leather chairs, mahogany bar, silent reading room. I went to the bar and had a Scotch and soda. I also bought a cigar, which is something I like to smoke when I am dead certain that there will be no interruption.

The bartender was a corpulent Frenchman who had the kind of complexion that is usually only acquired on my side of the bar.

"Have one with me," I said.

He looked around the visible part of the paneled room and then smiled at me. "*Avec plaisir.*" He smiled. "The members are asleep."

Three elderly members in armchairs seemed indeed asleep, but a young man in khaki shorts was not. He sat near a window, and his glass, siphon bottle, and decanter of whisky were on a small table next to him. He sipped and stared out the window.

"He is not a member," said the Frenchman. "He does not count. *Salut.*"

We chatted about the weather, but there was not much to chat about because the weather was always the same. We chatted about the new state of the nation, but there was not much there, either. Motana had existed only for a few months. We could not gossip about anyone because we did not know anyone in common. But, then, perhaps we did.

"Friend of mine is in town. I wonder if you know him."

"I wonder. *Salut.*"

"It's empty. Why don't you have another one."

"*Merci,*" he said while doing the honors with great dexterity. "My friend is your friend. Who is he?"

"His name is Plozzi."

The bartender stopped the drink in midair and looked at me steadily, as you might do when your child comes home one day and says his first dirty word.

"I gather you know him," I said.

"I do." He took a drink and then put down the glass. "Do you know him?"

"Why—it seems you know more about him than I do."

"Indeed. For instance," he said, "I know what he looks like," and he nodded past me at the three members.

I pulled on my cigar too hard and got a mouthful of very hot smoke. I tipped my glass and got a windpipe full of very hot whisky. It is a harsh method, but it counteracts the feeling of being caught with your pants down.

"As a matter of fact," I said, "I have not seen good old Plozzi in a very long time. He must have aged considerably, considering his kind of life."

"Some, it rejuvenates; others—" And the bartender shrugged. Then he nodded past me again. "The one who is sunk in his chair, the chair with the little round table nearby."

I turned and saw the creature immediately. He looked worse than I had imagined. He was a sunken heap of dissipated bones with wrinkles hung over it. Even his seersucker suit looked like nothing but wrinkles. Teetering on top of this heap in the armchair was a vulgar head. The bony skull had a number of hairs on it, like strands of stuffing coming out of a doll. But there was nothing doll-like about that face. The bags under the eyes were bigger than the eyes. The nose was bigger than the chin. The nostrils were bigger than the mouth, and if there were teeth in that mouth, they had to be mouse-sized.

Inge, of course, had been putting me on. It was out of the question that she had ever wanted this thing. And yet she had said so; and this carrion fit my image of him.

I went to him, intending to start out polite. "Plozzi," I said, making it sound like a spit.

He gave a start, as if he had been asleep. His eyes rolled up at me and they looked like something half gone that floats under water. Dorian Gray at the end.

"I am deWitt."

He did not let me know right away how he felt about that. The marine quality of his eyes kept me guessing, and the nasty cast of his mouth remained the same. Then he said, "So what? If I had the name Dimwit, I'd change it."

That did it for me. That concentrated all the meandering dislike for the man into a simple wish for destruction. The wish was pure and unadulterated. I could feel it in my hands. I had to hold them, one in the other, and while I talked I could hear my knuckles crack.

"I am here about Inge Lobbe. I am not here concerning you and Inge, but I am here about myself and Inge." As I talked his eyes occasionally lit up and then receded again into idiocy. He was not watching me as much as my hands. "I want you out of the way," I said. "I don't want you within sight, sound, or smell. I don't want you to answer, argue, or plead. I just want you to run as far as death permits you. And if there is any doubt...."

His jaw had started to shiver. His eyes tore themselves away from my hands, and he said, "No, no—" Then he hoisted himself out of the chair and scurried out of the room with a walk like a crab.

I was still horribly tense, which accounts for the fact that I jumped when I heard the laugh.

"Bravo!"

I turned and saw the young man by the window smile at me.

"Have one," he said, and pointed at his whisky bottle.

I went over to where he sat and did not care that he poured it for me straight, without ice, and into his own glass. In fact I loved him for it. I sat down and drank the whisky, which felt warm and smooth. His tanned face was handsome and friendly. His dark curls were springy with youth. The view behind him was a peaceful street. I put the glass down and smiled at him. "Sorry about that unpleasant business during siesta," I said.

"Don't be sorry," he said. "Most unpleasant fellow, and there are many of us here who wish they could have such an effect on him."

My new friend had a melodious voice with an indefinable accent of remarkable charm.

"The only thing that shakes him up," he was saying, "is what you did to him. Never seen it done so well."

"Is that the truth?" I said, wishing he would tell me just what I had done.

"Would you do it for me?" he asked politely. "What's that?"

"Crack your knuckles."

DeWitt, sure scourge for scurvy lechers, was now reduced to a talented knuckle-cracker. I deflated, but my friend did not seem to notice. His face lit up, and he looked past my left ear.

I have mentioned what this does to me, but this time there was more to come. He got up, opened his arms, and received the lovely shape of a smartly dressed female.

"Darling!" she said, and gave him a kiss on the cheek.

"Chérie," he said. "Meet my new friend."

She turned and looked beautiful. Inge always looks beautiful.

"My God!" she said. "You mean you and Plozzi are friends?"

It was difficult to hate the real Plozzi immediately; his kindness was too recent. But when Inge let him go and was done scolding me for not showing up in Rome, I tried for the properly hostile footing.

"I thought you were in jail," I said to Plozzi.

"I was. Some kind of mix-up, it seems. They let me out after twenty-four hours, about the same time that young Torquet was called away. Do you know him?"

"Hardly. I have heard some unpleasant things about him. But you seem to know him, *principe.*"

"Call me Gabriele. Yes, I knew him socially in Rome. Very pleasant fellow. Helped him find embassy quarters at the time. I think they rented a lodge that used to be in the family, though I don't know why. Wonder if they use it."

"They use it."

"Do they? Should be difficult to make it livable again."

"They had no difficulty whatsoever."

"That's nice," said Plozzi. "Torquet seemed pleased."

"Oh, yes."

"And then," Inge put in, "Torquet arranged this job for Gabriele as a return favor."

"Job?" I said, waiting for the skein of intrigue to unfold.

"The poor darling is very poor," said Inge. With great versatility she was smiling at me while stroking Plozzi's head. "But he is an experienced hunter," she went on, "and Torquet got him a job with van Voos Safaris."

"It was nice of him," said Plozzi. "Of course, then he very quickly put me in jail." He smiled, since the whole thing seemed highly amusing to him.

"Makes no sense to me," I said, meaning every word of it.

"The favor was personal," explained Plozzi, "and the jail thing was political. For a young country they are already well compartmentalized. The only strange thing was that I got out so soon."

I had a dawning notion that it was not so strange at all.

"Torquet, you see," Plozzi went on, "wanted to prevent someone from building their road. I have no idea what goes on in their little government, but somehow Torquet got the notion that I was a spy of the opposition, and I was pulled in for interrogation on the matter. In the middle of my innocent denials they let me go, and young Torquet went, too."

"Where is he now?"

"He got a royal command from his father, Torquet One, to return to the tribal seat. It's called Miesville."

Inge brightened up and said, "There's a funny thing about that. Did I ever tell you the story I've heard from Uncle Hans?"

"Not now, *cara*," Plozzi said. "Let us first ask our friend to join the safari."

This bronzed idol of women on many continents seemed to be totally ignorant of the meaning of competition. He even smiled at me, his enemy, as if I meant him well. This reduced my repartee to a sullen murmur.

"I can't go. I'm busy."

"Then I won't go, either," said Inge.

She looked at me and did not seem to notice that Plozzi's fingers were walking around on the back of her hand like a tomcat stalking.

"I'll stay with you," she said to me, "till the road is done."

It was that simple, and Plozzi was out. Torquet was out of the way, and Plozzi was leaving. He said this arrangement was just as well, the trip would be rough, and we would have fun when he came back in a few weeks.

So Lobbe's admonition to save Inge from Plozzi had turned out to be most certainly a ruse. But how did Inge know about me and the road? I asked her straight.

"Because Uncle Hans said that you went to Essen to take a job with

Sicherheitsnadelnmanufaktur. And they are building the road here, aren't they?"

"How do you know?"

"Everybody knows. The harbor is full of their equipment."

Somebody, somehow, was awfully certain I would be successful with a job I had not even started yet. And Inge had been awfully certain that I would show up in Motana.

"This needle outfit," I told her, "handles jobs all over the world. How did you know they would send me here?"

"It was a good guess, don't you think?" And she smiled.

I waited for more stunning logic, and it came.

"You weren't at all worried about missing me in Rome and, therefore, you were very sure you would see me in Motana."

"After one day in Essen on a new job?"

"Why not?" she said. "You must have known all along that your job would be in Motana, you fink."

"She talks like a Motanesque, don't you think?" said Plozzi.

Inge ignored the compliment and seemed more interested in the thing she saw outside the window. "What in heaven's name," she said, "is that?"

"That," said Plozzi, "is locally known as the Spirit of Friendship. It is half brute, half beauty, wedded together. The front is an army truck. The rear is a Rolls Royce."

And there, nose raised haughtily in the air, my taxi came bobbing down the street. It pulled to the curb at the front of the building.

"What in heaven's name is driving that thing?" said Inge. "It runs on radar?"

"You might say that," I told her.

"I don't see anything in the front seat."

"It is very small."

Baby got out of the car, and in a while we watched his fez meander toward us around the chairs and tables.

"I am awake," he said to me. "It is time for your appointment."

Inge looked at me as if she resented my having a life of my own, but I ignored her.

"Thank you," I said to Baby. "How did you know I was here?"

"Yum Lee told me."

For a Motanesque reply, this one was very short, but like a Motanesque argument, the meaning was not clearly apparent.

"Yum Lee," said Plozzi, "is the head of the Chinese Cultural Mission."

I left for Government House to start earning my keep. There was to be a second siesta three hours later, and Inge and I would see each other then.

On the way to Government House I would stop at the hotel to pick up my papers, and I had to tell Baby that.

"Since you went to Government House once before without papers," he said, "why do you want to go there now with your papers?"

"The first visit was meant to be just formal. This one has got to be business."

"No," he said, "that won't do. Since you did not succeed in your formal visit without papers, and since you are now going with papers, therefore you will not succeed with business this time but instead will succeed with a formal visit. But since you no longer want a formal visit—"

"Stop that!"

"I am trying to help you."

I breathed deeply a few times and then I acted very calm. "I am glad you are trying to help me. I am glad Yum Lee is trying to help you help me. How did he happen to know where I was?"

"Because Yum Lee likes to know everything."

I had the feeling that Baby was babying me with those short sentences, even though they were losing none of that Motanesque quality of leaving out a lot.

"And how did Yum Lee happen to tell you where I was?"

"Because I did not know where you were, and he knew where you were."

"That was very good, Baby. Now, let's take this one step further. What, may I ask, is your connection with the Chinese Cultural Mission?"

"I eat their rice balls."

He had, of course, given me more than his name, rank, and serial number, but the simplicity of his answers was, nevertheless somehow more devious than my questions.

"I recall"—I started over—"that you are trying to help me. If you are trying to help me, Baby, but at the same time indicate that you would rather not take me to the hotel from where I can then commence to do my business here in Motana, I therefore conclude that you are most certainly trying to help, but not me."

"Very good," he said. "That was much better. However, I am trying to help you because you seem to need it. You are not as clearheaded as I, and therefore I must do what can be done in such a case."

I was not a fare; I was a case. He was not a chauffeur; he was my therapist. I tried playing it that way.

"Since you are more clearheaded than I, and since I only think I know why I am going to Government House, would you therefore tell me why I am going to Government House?"

"Yum Lee asked me the same thing."

"I thought he knew everything?"

"It helps if he asks me."

"Did he also ask you not to take me back to the hotel, Baby?"

If I thought I had sprung something on him, I was disappointed. He answered immediately and—relatively speaking—straight to the point.

"Since he knew I would know his intentions, and since he does not know my intentions, therefore he did not bother to ask me to help him with what he would do, anyway."

"So the bastard went and searched my room."

"He should be done by now," said Baby.

He was right, of course. The maid had put all my things in their proper places, and Yum Lee and his men had left everything in the proper places. There had been no effort made to overdo anything. All the contract papers were still there, and they had even left the folder open so that I could note at a glance that they were not interested in theft. They now knew as much as I did. It was perhaps fortunate that I knew so little.

Government House was in full activity now. The large entrance hall resounded with the bustle and action, the conning and agonizing that one finds in the corridors of a hall of justice, where decorum exists only before the bench. I went to the information booth, and there sat the only Motanesque in the hall who did not seem busy. He was chewing on a rice ball. I presented my credentials and asked to be directed to the office of Patel, Premier of Motana. While he had no specific advance knowledge of my arrival, the Premier had been informed from Essen that a final negotiator would be there at any moment. My man in the booth picked up a phone and talked Motanesque. Then he hung up and talked to me in English.

"You will be received in Room three-thirteen. You will be directed from there."

I thanked him, made the turn around the booth, and almost fell flat on my face. Baby was standing in my way below eye level. I caught myself and then Baby's gesture. He was looking at me and he briefly put his finger over his mouth. Then Baby walked away and sat down on the fifth step leading to the upper floors. He sat close to the central railing without looking at me, and when I walked up to the other side of the railing, my head was on a level with his. We did not look at each other. "He did not speak with the office of the Premier," said Baby.

"What did he say?"

"He said you were coming up."

"Somebody was expecting me?"

"It seems so."

"Whom did he talk to?"

"I don't know. But he did not talk to the Premier or to the secretary of the Premier. The secretary was called to his native village."

"And his name is Torquet."

"Yes."

And somebody was taking his place in one way or another.

"Baby," I said, "if I'm not back in half an hour, send someone after me."

"I will be there myself."

"Listen to me. I know less than you and am less clearheaded about it, we have discovered, and that makes me generally suspicious and—"

"Never mind that kind of talk now," he said, to my vast surprise. "I will take care."

I did not argue with him. I knew no one who might be better to send if I needed help.

"How come you happen to be listening?" I asked him as I started up the stairs.

"We agreed that I am the clearheaded one and that I must therefore do what is missing in the more dimwitted—"

"Never mind that now." And I went upstairs.

I had no problem finding Number 313. I had been there before. The legend on the door read Fiscal Department.

The door was no longer hanging, but that was because the latch was engaged. If I had been Baby, I might have thought of a way of getting through the keyhole, but instead I opened the door. It collapsed immediately into its former ghost town position of disrepair. The room beyond was the same, too. No furniture. Nothing.

They had waited behind the door. One wore blue and was Chinese, one wore white and was Motanesque, and the third wore brown and can best be described as an ape. He was a Caucasian ape conditioned for survival in the dives of Hamburg, the underworld of Marseilles, or in the ring of some tank town, U.S.A.

The Chinese wore no glasses, but his eyes looked like black glass. His face was delicately boned and immobile, and his hair was shaved down to a five o'clock shadow. I had the notion that he was the brains of the outfit. The Motanesque simply stood by. He was uniformly well-shaped, but he was not Torquet. Torquet had looked alive instead of sullen.

I turned to the Chinese. "Yum Lee, I presume." And I gave him a little bow.

He spoke English with somewhat of a nasal intonation, but he was perfectly fluent.

"Doctor Yum Lee," he said, "is head of the Cultural Mission. We, on the other hand, have another function."

I looked at the ape and then at the Chinese again. "You don't have to explain it."

"Very well. In other words, you will be quiet."

"I have nothing to add to your information. You've seen my papers."

"Of course."

"Then, why am I here?"

"You were detained once before. However, for some reason not yet explained, Torquet failed. First in Rome and then again here."

"He was called by his father," said the Motanesque to the Chinese. "In our country that is important."

"Such a young nation and such old notions."

There seemed to be no love lost between those two, though that did not alter the program.

"Take him," said the Motanesque, and nodded at the ape.

I figured that when an ape "takes" something, he may well ruin the object in the process. I thought of this very quickly but not quickly enough. The ape took me by the arm with surprising agility. To my further surprise, I remained all in one piece. This was, perhaps, a gentle and highly trained ape. He said, "Walk this way, please," and with only the lightest directional touch led me, unresisting, to the far side of the room.

There was a door, and we went through it. There was another room, and we went through it, too. There was enough furniture in the second room to supply the empty room as well. Another door, another room. It soon became apparent that the entire third floor was vacant. Either Motana was young enough to lack bureaucratic proliferation, or perhaps the young ministers downstairs did not know yet that there was this other floor above.

The latter guess proved wrong; the last empty room we entered was in the process of being painted. There were no painters, but there were buckets and ladders, and a pile of coveralls lay in a heap by one window.

"Put one of these on," said the Chinese.

No Chinese torture, it seemed. Perhaps they were going to put me to work.

"Like this," said the ape to me.

He put on one of the splattered coveralls and did not bust a seam. In fact, unlike the coveralls I had seen on real painters, his fit. When I was finished dressing, I watched the Chinese get into his working clothes.

"Is it part of the torture," I asked him, "that you don't tell me what goes on here?"

"Torquet failed," he said. "Therefore we must finish the job."

If he was referring to the room that had not been finished, I did not believe him, and when the Motanesque saw me look at the walls, he gave me what he thought was an explanation.

"For the duration, or as long as you survive it, you will be kept in the *quartier intérieur*."

It sounded ominous, but I convinced myself that anything this sullen man said would sound ominous. I tried to remember what the *quartier intérieur* was, because it had been mentioned on the tapes I had been given in Essen. I remembered only that it was an uncultivated area of Motana. I watched the ape open a window.

"Look at me," said the Motanesque, and just as I turned he slapped me in the face with a paintbrush.

I now looked like the least experienced painter of the lot, even after the rest of them had also splattered themselves. The old battleship trick of odd paint patterns on the hull worked just as well on the face. We were not easily recognizable. Then we went out the third-story window.

The feat was less heroic than it sounds because there was a scaffolding built up against the rear wall of the building. Apparently the Motanesque government did not want its front façade marred by the contraption of wood and twine, but this also meant that the rear side of the building, which faced a wooded hill, would first get the paint job, which nobody could see. We all climbed down, and I kept looking for Baby and I kept looking for a cordon of armed police to close in. In fact, I did not give up looking, even when they pushed me into the rear of a delivery van. Then the doors were shut, and there was nothing in the van but a long wooden tool chest, myself, and the ape.

"You understand," said the Chinese from outside, "that you will be severely manhandled by your compatriot if you should scream or attempt anything else unscheduled."

I understood that. I had not known that the ape was a compatriot of mine, but then his English had not sounded like the standard Americanese you would expect from an ape. He had been polite and articulate. The rear door slammed, and the van drove off. For a while the ape and I sat eyeing each other in silence, hearing the rattle of the truck and the occasional bounce of the toolbox lid.

If there are tools in the box, that might equalize us....

"Now, then," I said, "let's chat."

"Are you nuts?" said the ape.

Obviously, he had a well-developed sense of context. This was no time to chat. This was fright and gloom time, and I ought to have known better. I leaned one elbow on the box and idly fiddled with the open latch. Mighty tools would be inside. The box was almost as long as the truck was wide.

"Your Chinese friend," I said, "mentioned that you and I"—I wormed a finger between box lid and rim—"are both Americans." I took the elbow off the lid. "Doesn't that give you any sort of feeling of—OUCH!"

I yanked my hand away and shook it. I could have sworn that the lid had snapped at me and I had one throbbing finger to prove it.

"I don't get you," said the ape. "What's a feeling of ouch?"

I had shifted my weight while doing the job on the lid, or perhaps the truck had bounced at the wrong moment, but in spite of these reasonable explanations, I felt thoroughly disgusted with myself. It was a good thing that Baby had not seen this. He would have evolved a stupidity theory to put deWitt in a subclass all by himself.

"The box bounced into me," I said to the ape.

"Excuses."

He and Baby should get together, I thought. But in the meantime, as if by way of confirmation, I lifted the lid once again. I lifted it enough to get a quick glimpse at the tools and then I dropped it.

The ape and Baby should get together? They were together. The ape was in the van, and Baby was in the box. I had seen him lying on his side, and he seemed to be sucking his thumb.

I looked over at the ape, but he had apparently not seen a thing. Nor did he seem interested. He scratched his hind quarters and blinked his eyes as if thinking of something else, of something dreamy and soothing, and then, suddenly he rolled over and went to sleep.

Baby came out of the box and stuffed a short blowgun into his pocket. He retrieved the needle dart from the ape's thigh and put that away, too.

"I think I'm going nuts," I said.

"Do not worry," said Baby. "You have me."

Baby did not know the drug's chemical structure, but he knew the plant from which it came. One dose produced healing sleep, another deep coma, and a stronger concentration was the lethal amount the Motanesque had used in war and which they still used on the hunt. Baby did not tell me which dosage he had used, but he would not bet on more than fifteen minutes' sleep.

I was at the back door and opened it up a crack.

"If we jump, that car in back there will hit us," he said.

"I'll wave at it. That'll bust their caper."

"The car is there to guard the door," said Baby.

"We're still in traffic," I told him. "I yell and wave, and somebody who isn't guarding the truck will see us, too."

"In that case they might shoot."

His brief statements were no more flattering to my intelligence than his long ones.

"We'll wait, and maybe they'll drop back enough for a jump," I said.

He acted as if that had been a foregone conclusion. And we waited. I had no watch on me. Fifteen minutes happened on every second breath I took while watching the car in back follow us closely.

"How did you know enough to set this up like a cheap movie?"

"I am clearheaded."

"I didn't ask that."

"You could only leave by the front hall or by the scaffolding in back. I asked the information clerk to watch the hall while I watched the rear."

"You mean you asked the son of a bitch who set me up for this?"

"They had bribed him. Since he was bribable, I bribed him. Therefore, since—"

"Enough already."

"While he did not come to tell me you were leaving by the front, I saw you leaving by the window. And the empty truck was waiting."

"What if there hadn't been the toolbox?"

"I would have followed in the Spirit of Friendship."

"And later collected the fare."

He ignored that and said, "They are falling back."

It was true, but it did not last. They caught up again very quickly. Then I looked at the ape.

"Only half the time is gone," said Baby.

"And by what stroke of providence did you happen to have your ray gun with you?"

"Blowgun. Not ray gun."

"And by what stroke—"

"I always carry it."

"Of course. Stupid of me to ask."

"Yes," said Baby.

We waited. I felt that time was racing for the sleeping ape and that it was dragging for me. I got tense and started to sweat. Baby got tense, too, but he did not sweat about it. He took out another needle and sat down next to the ape. He watched to see if the ape's eyelids were beginning to flutter, and I watched the car in back. No change.

"They want to take me to the *quartier intérieur*," I said. "What is it?"

"The hunting preserve of the interior. It is larger than the part where we civilized people live."

"Who's back there?"

"There is Miesville, and there is the wild part with the animals. Except for the hunt, they are protected."

"But a human being is not."

"True. In the past a youth would be sent there with a knife and nothing else. He had to stay for six months, and if he came back alive, then he was a man."

"You mean to tell me that's where they're driving?"

"No. They intend to drop you at the Place de Safari, which is the best way into the preserve. From there it is a one-hundred-mile trip."

"By safari," I said to myself. "Via friend Plozzi." Then I turned to Baby, who was gently blowing on the ape's face. The face stayed asleep. "Do you know when the next safari leaves from there for the preserve?"

"Plozzi leaves in two days," said Baby.

"Hey! They're stopping for that truck!"

Our guardian chariot had been cut off. A big, brand-new yellow truck came rumbling across the intersection we had just passed. On the door of the cab was a black design of a safety pin. Then a flat bed with two caterpillars on top came into view. Each of the vehicles was painted yellow and carried the safety pin emblem.

"I jump first," said Baby. "Then I catch you."

"To hell with that," I said, but very suddenly I stopped myself and did not jump first.

I knew a lot more by now but still not enough and I felt reckless with safety while I had Baby around. On a less carefree level I still felt that two days at the Place de Safari would certainly not be lethal and would also provide ample time for Baby to bring on help before I was carted to the interior. And during that time my captors, feeling safe and successful, might find nothing wrong with telling the condemned man what his agonies were all about. In back of this reasoning was the fact that there had been no attempt made to kill me but only one continuous effort to keep me out of the way.

"You jump first," I said.

"No."

"Since you will have to follow me in order to find out where I am so that you can rescue me tomorrow, it will not do for me to jump first and for you to stay here."

He got ready to jump immediately. Just before he did, he looked up at me and smiled. "You are getting better," he said. Then he winked. "Also, I am getting better when it comes to understanding you."

I got the door closed behind him after he had jumped and then I went quickly back to my seat by the toolbox. Soon the ape started to flutter his eyelids, pushed himself up, and then looked confused.

"I was asleep?" he said.

"Yes."

"And you're still here?"

"I was afraid you would wake up. I spent an agonizing fifteen minutes."

"Must have been those rice balls," he said.

Visions of relative comfort while chatting with my captors turned to nothing when we got to the Place de Safari. When the Motanesque opened the rear door, I could see where the truck had parked. We were right by the side of the bush, and a row of crates cut us off from the clearing where van Voos had his bungalow. I could see parts of the house through a space between crates and I could also see an armed guard in the clearing, nodding his head while the Chinese was talking to him. The Chinese was saying, "We will bring the rest later and put it over there," and the armed guard was saying, "I will tell Mister van Voos when he comes back."

If I can hear the guard, I was thinking, the guard could hear me.

"The pressure," said the Motanesque by my side, "is slight, but the pain is stabbing. Then you pass out."

I felt the very light-fingered touch of the ape from behind me. He had all ten fingers up on both sides of my neck. I was not even to know where he was going to press.

"Tell him not to," I said. "I won't yell."

I was allowed to step away from the truck.

"I would like to see your boss," I said.

"You will."

While the Motanesque said that, I found myself handcuffed from behind. That ape was a marvel of gentle speed.

"I have a number of things to say to him that might be of interest to him," I said.

"You may speak to him later," said the Motanesque. "He will also accompany you on safari."

While this was said to me I suddenly had a wad of a rag in my mouth, and then the gag was secured with a swift slap of tape over my lower face.

But this time the change in expected program was too much for me. I am not a good fighter when I can't yell and when I am handcuffed from behind, but I kicked the Motanesque in the stomach, hit the ape's shin with my heel, butted his nose with my head, and somehow got into position to groin him. The end result of all this panicky heroism was that the Motanesque lay flat on his face, and the ape was the same as before. It is true he was panting a little, but that might have been because of the slap he gave me across the side of my face. It had been, after all, a resounding slap. It careened me across two yards and into the side of a crate, where I fell down.

When I was ready to get up, I could not. I was jackknifed into a foetal position, and the entire effect was secured by strategic windings of rope. I was secure enough for long-distance shipping. Then the ape stuffed me into a box in the lower tier of the row of crates. He moved me around a little bit so that I would sit on my behind instead of on my head, and that was the extent of the human touch. The ape nailed the open panel shut, picked up the prone Motanesque, dropped him into the rear of the truck, and then drove away. I could see all this through a crack between boards. Next the truck showed on the other side, in the clearing. It stopped to pick up the Chinese, then drove off. The guard sat down on the stoop of the bungalow. Next came my agony.

I could move my head and I could move my limbs. I was secured so marvelously that I could move all my muscles without permanently altering my basic position. I used this marvelous freedom to pound against the walls of my box as best I could, but either it only sounded loud because I was inside my own echo chamber or the guard had been bribed not to hear. I gave up with a headache, which continued the pounding I had done, and I stared at the guard through the cracks. He sat on the other side of the clearing and looked straight at me. I was sure he was looking straight at me and yet not sure. This voiceless and soundless encounter had something terrible about it. I felt the panic rise in me as at some menace beyond my control, like the tide, like the wind, like fire. If this was what it meant to return to the womb, to hell with it. I screamed without sound and I struggled without motion and I was soon exhausted. In a while I slumped into my own black nothing, something like sleep.

Twilight in Motana is quick, like a moving shadow, and then it is dark. When it is dark, it gets pleasantly cool—pleasantly when you can move. The cold woke me. I flexed and hitched around for a while until I felt more alive. Not too alive. That would have been unbearable. There was light in the bungalow, and there were two lights in the clearing, high up on poles. While I had been out three more pickups had come to the Place de Safari. Black, shadowed men were standing around, and then I could tell by the voices that one of them was Plozzi. He moved around the vehicles and waved a clipboard in one hand.

"All this junk? What does this have to do with a safari?"

"It is one of the functions of the cultural mission," said the voice of somebody short and round, "to bring progress not available through your own efforts."

"I don't live here," said Plozzi. "I just work here. That is an American expression. It expresses the limits of my interest, and my interest is confined to getting the safari into the bush and out of the bush. This—these machines are too heavy for transport on raw ground."

"As head of the Cultural Mission, I assume full responsibility for success as well as failure of our gifts to Motana."

The voice had been gentle, and the silhouette was round. This was Yum Lee, kindly giver of gifts. I arched in my box and looked at the pickups.

Their loads, against the light from the bungalow, were gawky, spiky, chunky, metallic.

"And the safari is my responsibility," Plozzi was saying.

"Will you want to be known as the man who has prevented us from drilling life-giving wells in the wilderness?"

"*Por Dio!*" yelled Plozzi. "This is a safari, not a construction trip!"

"I know," said Yum Lee. "We will therefore only test-drill between the moments of sport you have planned for us. We will build the wells later."

Plozzi cursed so fluently that whole sentences came out like one word, while Yum Lee stood by in patience.

"All right," said Plozzi after a while. "Reload your love machines on five trucks instead of three, and I will take you."

"Of course," said Yum Lee, with a soothing sound. "Of course, signore."

The Chinese Cultural Mission was wooing not only the townfolk with rice balls, but also the backwoods natives with wells. It would all make a very good impression, though wooing gifts never guarantee the complexion of a marriage. Nor was any of this display of love consistent with my own predicament. I had come courting, too, but had been spurned before I could show my presents.

For a while I watched what I could see of the reloading. I noted where they left the equipment that would require additional trucks. But soon I had to concentrate only on all the minute things I could do to keep my blood flowing and keep my rear end from turning numb like stone. It was bad going, but at least I no longer felt the panic.

In a while all activity ceased in the clearing, shadow men got into a car and drove off, and then the lights in the bungalow went out. The two lights on tall poles stayed lit, and instead of one guard there now seemed to be three. They walked around and around, and whenever I could see one, I imagined that I could tell one from the other. It seemed that none of them knew I was here. It was probable that one of them knew and that he might slip me some water in the night. Then I would yell. And then he would slap the tape back on my mouth and explain to the others that he had startled an animal. As time went on I knew that I would be an animal yelling. The feeling got worse when I smelled the fire.

I could not see it, but I could see all three guards run in one direction. They disappeared toward the far end of the clearing. I tried to relax and perhaps I could have made it, except that then I hallucinated the voice.

"How are you?"

Now I screamed like an animal, and no one could hear me.

"I came in the spirit of friendship," said the outside voice.

Then my box creaked. One side opened, and I fell out. I looked up and saw a Baby who was taller than I.

Before we could leave the clearing, I first had to grow up again. Growing up is a painful process under any conditions, but when you do it within five or ten minutes, the growing pains are terrific.

When I was fairly myself again, I became aware of my resentment. Like the pains, this may also be a symptom of growing up.

"Where in hell have you been?"

But Baby was more grown up than I and he did not bother to answer. He said, "Was it worthwhile in the box there, or would it perhaps have been better if you had stayed with me?"

The guards, I noticed over the top of the boxes, had beaten the fire out. It was time to leave.

"Where's the Spirit of Friendship?" I whispered.

"Right here."

"I mean the car."

"Right here." And he pointed to the end of the clearing, where the road to town disappeared in the dark. And there, true enough, she stood with her nose up in the air.

"And the guards don't mind."

"Of course they did. I had to bribe them."

We started toward the car, along the dark side of the row of crates.

"That's going to be some bill if my stay here keeps on like this."

"Yes," said Baby. "I had to bribe them twice. Once to park the car after hours without explaining why and a second time so they would tell me where you had been packed away."

We were almost at the mouth of the road when I decided to make further use of the guards' cooperativeness.

I stopped and said, "Baby, go back there and bribe them into the bungalow."

"Why?"

"I'm going to where the machines are lying on the ground."

"I cannot bribe them if you are going to steal."

This seemed to be a principle, and I promised that I would leave everything as I had found it. Then Baby went to the bungalow, where the guards were now standing around, and I went back the same dark way we had come. Bribe or no bribe, there was a decorum to be observed.

I did not know anything in detail about well-digging machines, but I had seen the gawky things on occasions behind a farmhouse or on a field. The thin-looking equipment would rear up like a praying mantis, and the drilling part of the machine would be a strong, heavy rod with a bit at one end and a provision for jointing at the other. Sitting next to the drilling rig, there would always be a powerful motor.

In the dim light by the crates I found what I was seeking. But it was all a little different.

The three portable gasoline engines did not look very strong, and they had a power pickup for one belt only. I worked the gear levers carefully and could discover only neutral and a single speed. This did not give much leeway for variations in the work load that the motors could carry.

I found the dismantled parts of the upright rigs, which were, fortunately, always tied together. I paced these off, added the footage, and came up with an estimated "tower" size of six feet. That was a far cry from the twenty-foot rigs I had seen in barnyards.

I found nothing like the sort of boring rods I had expected. Again the sections were surprisingly short, but the most wondrous thing was that some of them were hollow. The hollow rods were the only ones with a bit attachment. I was impressed, but I felt that something was not kosher.

Baby and I drove back toward town through the tall walls of the jungle. They looked dark and silent, as if the night sounds in the air came from somewhere else. There were long, never-ending sounds from the jungle, small startled ones, and the sharp kinds that were clearly interrupted. It did not sound like paradise at all.

"Take me down to the harbor," I told Baby.

"It is large."

"Where all those yellow monsters are parked."

I had not yet looked up the local representative from Essen who was to handle the actual road-building job and I had not seen any of the working crew either. I was especially interested in that crew. Baby's clearheadedness was all well and good, but obviously I also needed some muscle.

"Will anybody be down there with that equipment? I've lost track of time."

"It is not yet nine, but the second siesta is just over."

I had been boxed for an incredibly short time. For the rest of Motana the last phase of a workday was just starting.

"What did you learn from those crates?" Baby asked.

"Do you know anything about wells?"

"They are the veins of the earth opened, and we accept them as a gift for which the earth sacrifices herself. Since this gift is a sacrifice, therefore, we never break open a well ourselves."

This was a more poetic answer than most of Baby's replies, and I suspected that it was a part of the country's lore. I also suspected that Yum Lee might not know about the taboo.

"Did you know that Yum Lee means to join the safari that leaves in two days?"

"Of course. Except for the white hunter and the bearers, the whole safari is Chinese."

This was news to me. "Do you know why Yum Lee is going, Baby?"

"He says he wishes to meet the land."

"What a gentleman."

"And he says he wants to bring the land a gift."

"You know what it is?"

"He didn't say."

"I didn't ask that, Baby."

"I think he means to drill a well, or so I heard."

"You told him what you told me about the digging of wells?"

"No. He did not ask."

And if that was the general attitude of the Motanesque, Yum Lee would continue to walk in ignorance, then.

The lights showed first through the trees, and then Villeblanche lay in full view. Baby skirted the town and came to a wide quay that arched and bent around the deep contour of the harbor. By the show of lights on the water there did not seem to be many ships, but on the landside there was the usual mess and confusion. There were slips, cranes, dolly tracks, stacks of bales, crates of things, and even penned cattle. Then there was a big row of road-building equipment that looked as neat and clean as a toy window display.

"Find me the man who's in charge, Baby."

"You."

"Since I do not feel very much in charge of anything whatsoever today—"

"Never mind. I will find him." And Baby sighed like an old man.

We left the taxi by the fence that enclosed the long compound of equipment along the dock. We walked through alleys between the toys, and I felt like a midget. We found the project engineer and two of the foremen in a trailer that was fitted with drawing boards, blueprint racks, two desks, and a table. Everything looked very orderly in the fluorescent light, and nothing seemed to have been used except the deck of cards. It was dog-eared and greasy, and the three men were playing Skat. I introduced myself and showed credentials, and then Hengstman, a foreman, offered me a warm bottle of beer.

"When do we start, Mister deWitt?"

"I don't know." I gave the bottle of beer to Baby and asked if I could have one, too. Hengstman, who reminded me of the ape but with a black mustache added, gave me another bottle. I sat down. "How long have you and all this equipment been here?"

I looked at the other foreman, whose name was Luft. He was small and quick like a bantam and he waved his hand at Podolski, the engineer. He was the only one of the three who looked like the stereotyped German. He had wavy blond hair, serious, ice-blue eyes, and those unbearably regular features. Curiously, he was the only one of the three who spoke English without a German accent; his accent was Polish.

"We and everything else came during the past month," said Podolski. "Luft and I came directly from Essen; Hengstman had been in Afghanistan. Some of the crew had been in Egypt and in Liberia, and the rest were hired in Germany."

I had not asked for all that, and he had also left out what I really wanted to know.

"How long has the equipment been sitting here?"

"One week. Why do you ask, Mister deWitt?"

"Because we don't have a road contract, and all this stuff, which looks brand-new, has been shipped here on no more than a gamble."

"If we do not get this job," said Podolski, "we will move everything to the Central African Republic. The next job is there."

All this made a slight amount of business sense, but I was still left with the suspicion that my superiors in Essen had some foreknowledge about their good chances for getting the Motana job. Apparently they had not known that their final-phase negotiator, deWitt, was prone to disappear into old houses, hearses, and crates.

"Tell me, Podolski," I asked, "do you happen to know how the equipment would be shipped to the Central African Republic if it had not been shipped here first on a gamble?"

"It would be shipped to Villeblanche the same way, and then we would take it to the Republic by land. It is the best way, since the C.A.R. has no access to the ocean."

So much for the Essen gamble.

I summoned Baby, wrote a note on a slip of paper, and gave it to him. "This is for the manager of my hotel. Ask him to prepare the items I have listed for you to pick up. Then go to Government House, third floor, the half-painted room, and see if you can find the thick folder of papers I left there. On your way back here pick up the stuff at the hotel and bring me everything as quickly as possible."

Baby left, and in a short while we heard the Spirit of Friendship grumble off into the night.

I watched the men play Skat for a while and drank beer. I considered that I had so far spent my time on this job with people who either had only partial knowledge or who had given me only partial information. First on the list was undoubtedly Lobbe himself. He had another phone call coming, though first I would finally make contact and get the official view at Government House. Because of the local workday arrangement, I could still get my foot in the door by ten o'clock. My recent experience there dictated that there must be no advance notice of my arrival, my departure, or even my present whereabouts—not until I was properly prepared. The three men at the table continued playing.

"Boring job, so far," I said to them.

"Not the most efficient operation I've ever seen," said Podolski.

"Might get worse," I said. "It might never start."

Luft, the bantam, looked up at me. "Isn't it true that you are here to see that it starts?"

"True. Though I was not told that there are people here who do not want me to start it."

They all looked polite and waited.

"One hour ago," I said, "I was tied hand and foot and ready to be shipped out into the wilderness by the Chinese you see walking around in town."

"*Unglaublich!*" said Hengstman, and stared at me.

"And how does it happen," asked Podolski, "that you are now here?"

"My friend who just left us got me out. But that doesn't guarantee he'll get me out of the next attempt. As soon as they discover that I'm gone, they are going to try a little harder."

"*Schweinehunde!*" said Luft with feeling.

After a proper pause I said, "How many men do you think you could lend me?"

According to Luft and Hengstman, I needed only Luft and Hengstman to rout the Chinese army, but Podolski thought it was just as well and certainly more spectacular if I moved about town with, say, a couple dozen brutal-looking specimens, preferably ones who had not shaved in about a week. We discussed this idea for another minute, and then Luft and Hengstman dashed out to recruit my troopers.

Podolski and I had another beer each.

"What," I asked him, "do you know about well-drilling?"

"Nothing. Ask me about dams or something like that."

Instead, I described to him what I had seen in the clearing, the machinery the Chinese were going to take on safari.

"I know this much," said Podolski, "they are hoping for a water table no more than three meters down. With that kind of expectation you can do the job with a shovel. But, then, you most certainly do not have to take core samples."

"Very interesting."

"It is as interesting as cracking a nut with a drop forge."

"Then, you and I must have it wrong. Maybe they are not drilling for water."

"Ore? Ridiculous."

We had no chance to pursue the subject, nor did it seem vital at the moment. Baby came back with my things. He gave me the Homburg, the frock coat, vest, and striped pants. He laid out the shirt with the starched front and also the silver tie, which was a four-in-hand. And he had not forgotten the silk socks and the black pumps. I changed at one end of the trailer and when I was newly dressed, I was also newly oriented. A civilized quality would now mark my underhandedness. My appearance would make duplicity almost spiritual. I walked to the door of the trailer and watched the men of my honor guard arrive. Beside them Hengstman looked like a sage, and Luft seemed like a fly. They were a fitting complement to the new me.

I marched through town under my Homburg and in the middle of a fore-and-aft flying wedge. Surrounded by this lozenge of stubble-jawed animals with mean elbows and big feet, I was impossible to overlook.

The Motanesque appreciate decorum and they also love fun. They stopped dead in their tracks and then they clapped their hands. The Indians barely saw us, being busy with spiritual and financial matters. The English saw us but, being tolerant of foreign customs, they behaved as if we were not there. The French looked at my clothes, and the Germans looked at the formation. And then two cars came rapidly down the street and when they reached us, they swerved hard to get out of the way.

The lozenge was making a left turn at the time in order to short-cut through a little park, and because of this, I could see that the two cars had stopped abruptly. Blue suits came jumping out into the street, and then we were around the corner and in the park.

"Hengstman," I said, "Luft. I think we did not discourage them. I think we attracted them."

They smiled and told their men.

We kept walking through the park. It was not large, and there were a few lamps along the paths, but the shrubs and trees, like the native jungle, were very dense. The jungle quality did not distract from the genteel air of a park in Europe. There was even music. There was a rotunda in the center of the park, and when we got there, we could see the small group of Motanesques who sat by a lamppost and played their instruments. There were drums like bongos, there was a flute with an oboe sound, and there were three string instruments that had to be plucked. Except for the uncomplicated repetition of the melody, the music made me think of jazz. Some Motanesques were clapping in rhythm, and a few were dancing in pairs. Beyond them, where a path continued on the other side of the rotunda, stood a phalanx of three blue marionettes.

"I'll send a man," said Luft, "and then we'll just walk on."

"That's very nice," I said, "but maybe we can't spare the man."

We stopped and looked at all the six paths that led away from the rotunda, and there were blue marionettes at each one of them.

I looked for Baby and saw him near the players. He was snapping his fingers and bobbing a little with the rhythm. I walked over to him and started to snap my fingers, too. I forgot about my Homburg because I had to do something casual now.

"Do you see Yum Lee anywhere?" I asked him.

"No. He is probably waiting for them to bring you to him."

In how many pieces, I wondered, but at that moment I saw Yum Lee.

He walked alone into the rotunda and looked like his silhouette from a few hours ago but very much fleshed out. Contrary to stereotype, Yum Lee was not yellow, but pink.

One's impression was of pastels. His hair was gray, his suit was beige, his shoes were light charcoal suede. When he moved his little hands, his nails flashed roseate. The only decisive color tone in the man was in his lacquer black eyes. Though Yum Lee came toward me with a comfortable smile, his eyes suggested something different. I was reminded of the perfect glass on a shuttered lens. Those eyes made his smile suspect and gave his gentle voice the lie.

"We have not met, Mister deWitt," he said.

"You did not check your luggage."

He liked that, and we shook hands.

"It is pleasant to walk in the park," he said. "Shall we go and discuss our differences?"

"I would rather stay here and listen to the music."

He looked at the musicians and at the dancers as if he were taking me literally.

"They seem to be so young," said Yum Lee, and smiled like a father.

"And you are here to help them grow up?"

"Our own poets, Mister deWitt, could not have formulated it better."

"I didn't know you had any poets left. I thought they had all become speech writers."

His smile changed character. It looked a little tired.

"Mister deWitt," he said, "let us stick to matters that we both understand."

I looked toward the periphery of the rotunda and at his men standing there. I noticed that my own animals were slowly, surely forming an ever-expanding circle. Yum Lee looked, too, and then he nodded.

"Yes," he said, "but when I am threatened, I tend to become brutal."

"Threatened by what, Yum Lee?"

"You. I have tried to contain you twice, to no avail."

"Rome?"

"Yes."

"And the Place de Safari."

He nodded, as if apologizing for his failures.

"Might I ask why?"

"Of course, Mister deWitt. I don't want you to implement your chances of building the jungle road."

I listened to the music under the lamppost and felt that it said more than Yum Lee had said. At any rate, it said something less complicated.

"Yum Lee," I said, "you are a liar."

He was startled. Perhaps it was for that reason that he changed the subject.

"They are going to break them in two," he said.

I looked where he was looking and saw that his blue marionettes were no longer standing in the half shadow of the paths but were moving toward us. Luft nodded at me, but I shook my head.

"Wise of you," said Yum Lee.

"Yes. The longer my men wait, the more effective they become."

"This time you are the liar," said Yum Lee. "And you know why I call you this, but I do not know why you called me the same."

"Because if you wanted to prevent my company from building the road, then it would do no good simply to remove me. And if you wanted to remove me, then you could have done better than to lock me up in a villa or to cart me in a crate to the hinterland."

He cocked his head at me and waited. "You are not finished," he said. "You have not given me your conclusion as to this mystery of my methods."

"If you wanted to prevent the building of the road, you have acted stupidly. You may be inefficient, but I don't think you are stupid. At best, Yum Lee, you have only delayed us."

"Beautiful," he said.

"But why?"

"My relatively gentle tactics," he said, "sustained for you an illusion of progress, though it was progress against odds. In this way, Mister deWitt, I did not provoke you too much while causing you to waste a great deal of energy."

"That," I said, "was admittedly beautiful."

"Also it worked."

I was about to ask him more, but just then there was a distraction. Two of my men, it seemed, had started to dance with two of the blue Chinese. It was a rather slow dance, the faces somewhat too stiff to suggest true enjoyment, the handholds a little grotesque. And then the two Chinese stepped back, and my men went down on their knees.

"It is a new dance," said Yum Lee. "We intend to teach it more universally."

"Do you know that one?" I asked him.

Another of my crew had stepped in. He embraced both the Chinese, and very swiftly their heads collided. There was the solid sound of bone, and the two Chinese weaved apart with no regard for musical rhythm. All of the Motanesques stopped dancing and started to clap their hands.

"As a matter of courtesy," said Yum Lee, "let us join in the local custom." He began to clap his hands violently.

The explanation for his peculiar action appeared at once. Baby stepped into the rotunda from one of the paths with three white-helmeted policemen following. They came, so to speak, as observers. Their hands were folded behind their backs, and they simply stood there, looking around. It did not seem strange to them that the music became louder and the beat more hasty, as if conveying a message. They did not marvel at Baby's starting to hop around among the Motanesque dancers, nor did it surprise them when the Motanesques came whirling about the rotunda, grabbing themselves a blue Chinese each, and then continued to whirl and stomp with much insistence and little ceremony.

And then the dancers were all disappearing into the dark of the paths. The clapping Motanesques returned without their partners to find themselves Chinese who had so far been neglected. My own men, I noted, were also vanishing. The policemen, nodding and smiling, stalked slowly across the rotunda, pleased with the sight of so much simple gaiety. They passed us, and one of them bowed to Yum Lee.

"Your Cultural Mission enjoys our culture?" he said, and walked on.

The music stopped.

"Was that another dance," I asked Yum Lee, "with which your men were not familiar?"

The dancing Motanesques had all returned, but of the Chinese and my men, only Hengstman and Luft were in evidence.

"It wasn't quite the way we had planned it," said Luft.

"You mean it's over already?"

"They don't want to dance anymore," said Luft.

"Who is the pygmy?" Hengstman wanted to know.

I told him that Baby was my choreographer and then I turned to Yum Lee and bowed the way the policeman had.

"Next time, Yummy, it won't be this polite. Next time our inscrutable Western impatience is going to get the better of us, and there's going to be no cutting in by the local talent. We're going to hog the whole floor to ourselves, and your little boys blue are going to be led a dance with a much more devastating tempo."

Yum Lee bowed, too. "Your arrogance is only matched by your skill at double-talk," he said. "And now that we are enemies, Mister deWitt, let me confuse you with a warning of my own: if you fail with your road, it will go my way. If you succeed with your road, it will lead nowhere. I wish you befuddlement."

He left and had his wish.

There was a protocol about seeing the President of Motana, but I did not feel that I had the time. My arrival had been announced through the Essen office, but the various interferences I had experienced since coming to Villeblanche had kept me from making a proper appointment. I would simply see how far I could get by walking into Government House half an hour before the close of business. It was really no more unusual than everything else that had happened so far.

Properly speaking, the room was not an office at all. It was an ornate reception hall of proportions adequate for a cotillion. Two large chandeliers were reflected in the parquet, and rows of Empire chairs lined two walls. A secretary's desk looked insignificant near the double doors, which seemed to lead to the President's inner office. I never got into it.

Phone calls on three different instruments established the following: President Matan was busy; he was not in; he was on the point of leaving. I tried to make my position clear to the secretary, who was like a lovely cat and just as distant.

"In answer to all three replies," I told her, "please tell His Excellency that I have just come to an agreement with Yum Lee that affects the interests of Motana vitally."

The girl did not relay the message by phone but by intercom, and the language was Motanesque, though brief. Then she clicked off the intercom, ignored me, and picked up one of the phones again. The language was Motanesque again, but I understood one word—Patel. That was the name of the Prime Minister. She hung up and then looked at me.

"This time there is only one message," she said, "and it would be the same on all the other phones. You have an appointment with President Matan tomorrow at one in the afternoon."

I noted that the appointment was in the middle of the first siesta of the day. "I get up early," I said. "Couldn't I see him in the morning?"

"There is a meeting of the Diet," she said, "and the President will be attending."

"And this evening?"

"The office is closed."

I took a stab at it and said, "Does the President always visit the Prime

Minister in his chambers after the business of the day?"

"No," she said, "they are meeting at the Prime...."

And then she stopped. She knew instantly that I had been fishing and she acknowledged it with a smile. "You think like a Motanesque," she said. "It will surprise them."

I thanked her for the compliment with a bow, and then she told me where the Prime Minister's residence was. I rejoined my entourage of construction workers and went to visit the two heads of the state.

There was a lush garden behind a wall with a gate, and at the gate were two guards. They looked at us and came to port arms, but then the maneuver got sloppy. The muzzles of their submachine guns started to point our way.

From the tape I had received from von Beck in Essen I had learned that Patel, in order to stay close to the people, kept his doors open to visitors at all times. If this was true, I had nothing to fear from the guards unless my men started something.

There was some grumbling when I told my protectors I didn't now need them, but one by one they melted away and went to wait at each end of the street.

Then I turned to Baby. I told him to go to the Club and give my apologies to Inge, who had presumably been waiting for me these several hours. He argued that my protection was more important than my good manners, but I insisted that a total of a dozen men at either end of the street would give an effective illusion of safety until he was done delivering my message. Then I went to the gate, tipping my Homburg, while two submachine guns did not seem to know which way to look and sunk down in resignation. One of the guards tapped me for weapons, and then they nodded me through the gate.

Patel's official residence looked vast and white. It was a cross between a Southern mansion and a Northern bank, but it was clearly lit neither for business nor for pleasure. There was a light under the portico and there was a light in the entrance hall, which I could see because the front door was open. A phone call from the gate seemed to have alerted the butler, who stood there and peered into the dark. I remembered how Kalopidos used to look in Lobbe's doorway on Long Island. When you were not expected or not wanted, he would stand there like a mountaineer who had just heard a strange footfall on the other side of his still. Patel's butler stood there in the same way. I sidled away from the drive and stood under an elephant tree to think. In that new position I could see past the main house, toward the back garden, and in the back garden I could see the garden house. It was lit up.

It was a funny little structure that duplicated the front of the main house but was only large enough to contain one room. I stepped through the portico and looked into the room through a window.

Patel, I decided, loved chintz. Curtains, couches, and chairs were covered with chintz. A certain New England quality of the room was disturbed only by an elephant head on one wall, a stuffed thing noble enough to deserve a room of its own. Patel stood under that head, and it hardly dwarfed him.

He was an enormous man. He had no more color than could be acquired in a weekend of skiing. His clothes were conservative Bond Street, a style designed to make the wearer inconspicuous—that is to say, if the wearer did not happen to be two hundred and eighty pounds of live muscle stacked six feet and seven inches high. The fact that Patel wore a pince-nez did not make him look more bookish, and the fact that he affected a high, starched collar did not make him look old-fashioned. He was young and quick-moving, and he did not try to build an impression on his light color. The starched white shirt darkened him, and the stitched cap identified him as Motanesque. He had a fairly dark-looking drink in his hand, and while I was watching him he downed the glassful, including the cubes of ice. I did not get a good look at President Matan until I was in the room.

Patel opened the door almost as soon as I had knocked, having covered the width of the room, I imagined, in something like two casual steps.

"Did you send him...." He stopped in midsentence and looked at me, Homburg to pumps. He did not smile or bow, unlike the average Motanesque. "Uhu," he said. "You must be you yourself."

"When at my best, yes, Mr. Prime Minister," I said. "May I come in?"

"You are here," he said with a shrug. Then he stepped aside and let me into the room.

President Matan sat sunk in chintz. He was a very black and a very severe-looking man. His hair was graying, and his skin was wrinkling, and his belly, I noticed, was getting away from him. He glittered at me through steel-rimmed glasses.

"What the hell!" he exclaimed.

The young Prime Minister had spoken with the usual British intonation, but President Matan sounded American. I put my Homburg on the table and felt immediately less diplomatic.

"My thought entirely, Your Excellency," I said to Matan. "Why are you trying to avoid me?"

Matan looked at his Prime Minister briefly but seemed to get no help. Patel was by the bar, filling two glasses with whisky. He tonged ice into each, which brought the liquid close to the top.

"I'm not trying to avoid you," said Matan.

I have always felt that a direct denial settles nothing. It does not resolve the doubt that inspired the question, it does not win an argument, it does not advance the plot. However, it does throw the discourse back into the lap of the questioner, and I started over.

"Originally I came here simply to obtain signatures on an agreement between Sicherheitsnadelnmanufaktur, the company I represent, and your government. We build you a road; you pay us over a specified period of time—that was my understanding before I got here. It is now my firm impression that delaying the building of the road is more important to you than completing it. I am here to ask why."

"Because," said Patel as he handed me one of the glasses, "we are not sure that we want you to build the road for us."

"Do you want Yum Lee to build it for you?"

"That has not been settled, either."

"Why not?"

"I need not explain to you, Mister deWitt, that any utilization of foreign help from a large power by a smaller power entails unwritten commitments and obligations by the smaller power. These bear scrutiny and multiple decisions."

"I don't represent a 'power,' Your Excellency. I represent a company that builds roads."

Patel looked at me for a moment, but his face was without the usual Motanesque mobility. I could not read his expression.

"Are you serious, Mister deWitt?" he said.

I looked from one man to the other, but neither volunteered anything.

"Why else am I here?" I said finally.

Patel considered me as if he were choosing a tie and I wouldn't do.

"You have apparently been hired to finalize a contract for a road. Cheers." He raised his glass, and then he and I drank.

Then his whisky was gone, and my throat seemed to be gone. When I was capable of sound again, I said, "Yum Lee, as head of his country's cultural mission, has manifestly more interests at heart than the building of a road."

"Of course," said the Prime Minister. "He wants to gain our friendship."

"Pardon the crass note, sir, but how will he pay for your friendship? With rice balls?"

Patel laughed with the sound of a subterranean earthquake. Then he was silent for a while. "He is paying for it, Mister deWitt, with a road," he said finally. "With a free road!"

I took up the whisky glass again and did not care what would happen. I drank, and this time my tongue was incinerated.

This piece of news was entirely new. My briefing had been simple enough: Obtain final signatures of authorization. This will entail no more than a little possible skirmishing about the payment plan. Everything else will have been done before your arrival.

Obviously nothing had been done about Yum Lee.

"When did Yum Lee raise this possibility?" I asked.

"This evening, Mister deWitt."

I had arrived this morning.

I had not been expected, what with the plans they had laid for me in Rome. When I did show up, Yum Lee had quickly made up for the failure of his European help by attempting to abduct me and then by attempting to do it a second time in the park.

After his most recent failure, Yum Lee had most likely picked up his phone, played his trump card, and effectively knocked my safety pin company out of the running.

There was little else I could do. I tried to think. Small personal things can sometimes open a gap in the opposition, which sometimes shows where a weakness may lie. I paced around the room and then I stopped by the bar, from which I could see both Matan and Patel.

"You are aware, gentlemen," I said, "of the events in Rome."

There is something very special about the form of address that assumes that the listener knows what you are talking about. One who knows what you are talking about is more apt to stay with you, simply waiting for you to go on to the news. In contrast, one who does not know what you are talking about has to make an effort to catch up. He either tries to remember what he might have forgotten or he tries to read meanings between the lines. In either event, he feels obliged to disguise his ignorance.

The Prime Minister smiled for the first time. It was the Motanesque smile that appreciates the opponent's finesse, that admires a good thrust and says touché. President Matan had turned his head slightly, as if to hear better, as if to take a cue from Patel.

"President Matan does not know," said Patel.

Then he turned to the older man and explained it. "Torquet took matters into his own hands," he said. "Since it was his conviction that more was to be gained from an affiliation with the Chinese, he attempted to undercut the proposals from Essen by the simple expedient of holding their emissary, Mister deWitt, in confinement until matters were settled according to our best interests."

There was a silence of injured vanity, of importance endangered.

"Damn it all!" yelled Matan. "Why wasn't I told?"

"I admit I kept it from you," said Patel. "And as you know, I dismissed Torquet immediately upon learning of his high-handed methods."

"You dismissed him!" said Matan with a good deal of spite. "His father called him back!"

All was apparently not well between President and Prime Minister. As my tape had made clear, the office of the President was by no means an honorary post only. It was executive in function, while the Prime Minister's office was largely legislative. Both posts were, furthermore, political, and each was vulnerable to popular pressures.

"That was a shame," I said to Patel. "Torquet must have been a great disappointment to you."

He shrugged as if the topic no longer had any interest for him. "I hired him as a matter of courtesy to his father, who used to be titular king of one of our *quartiers*."

"*The quartier intérieur?*"

"The hinterland, so to speak."

"Which," I went on with studied disinterest, "comprises three-fourths of your land area and contains almost half of your population."

"My friend the Prime Minister," said Matan, with an expression like a prune, "thought it wise to be friends with the former king's son. I can understand that."

"So can I."

I could almost see more, something like a plan, but it was not yet clear. Unthinking, I took a sip from my glass, but it seemed that all possible damage had already been done—I did not feel a thing this time. Instead, I was suddenly struck with an almost blinding inspiration.

"Did you know, Mister President," I said, "that not only Torquet, but also Yum Lee tried to remove me from the scene?"

"No!" He glared at the Prime Minister. "What else have you and that—that cultural missionary been doing?" he said loudly.

Patel did not like that. He took a deep breath of threatening proportions, but then he spoke very mildly. "I have been exploring the possibilities of cooperation," he said, "which have at present resulted in the free gift of a road to our country."

He was very good at twisting the causes of events, and before Matan could catch him up on it, he bowed to me and said, "I apologize for the display."

"Nothing new among statesmen."

"I'm sure, Mister deWitt, that with experience it will undoubtedly occur less often."

"It would seem to depend on the pressures," I said. "And speaking of pressures, Mister Prime Minister, would you know what the purpose of Yum Lee's safari is?"

"Trophies," said Matan, instead of his Prime Minister.

"Is that what his drilling equipment is for?" I asked.

Patel took over again, underplaying. "Publicity for the masses, I believe. In fact, the phrase is Yum Lee's. He intends to take core samples for possible mineral exploitation."

Patel meant me to believe that he did not think much of Yum Lee's gesture. He seemed to regard it as one of the minor concessions one makes to a giver of free gifts. No six-foot drilling rig was going to do a consequential job of exploration for anything—or so he implied.

I played it his way for the moment because soon, now, I meant to set him up and move in. I sighed, put my glass down, and showed altogether that I felt I was through.

"It is clear," I said, "that I cannot compete with goodness that asks for nothing in return. As the loser, gentlemen, grant me the favor of asking for one farewell concession." I felt so nervous at this point that I grabbed for my Homburg as if it were an anchor, and I had to restrain myself from putting it on. "I would ask," I said, "that you grant me the right, gentlemen, to address your assembled Diet for five minutes. Without rancor, in a gesture of friendship that asks no reward, I wish only to save face by showing that I have at least tried my best."

"Why are you so nervous, Mister deWitt?" asked Patel.

"I get nervous when I don't do my best."

"You're doing pretty well, I'd say."

"You have the generosity of the victor. Allowing me to bid you farewell in front of the Diet would make your generosity manifest to more than the three of us. It would please you, it would please me, it would please Yum Lee, and it would please my own people to have been treated thus."

"Might even leave the door open for future friendship," said the politician Matan.

"Oh, yes, Mister President." I meant that most fervently, though he did not know it yet.

Once back on the street I gathered my *Schutzstaffel* and took them all to the Club with me. They were not dressed for it, but they were entitled to it. I also had a notion that they might afford some distraction when I saw Inge again. She would be sure to be in a rotten mood after waiting for me for over six hours. I need not have worried. When I got to the Club, Inge was not there.

My men made horrible noises on the parquet with their boots, so I took them into the library, which had a carpet. A waiter wheeled in a cart with bottles and glasses.

"When," asked Hengstman, "do we start the road?"

"I'll tell you tomorrow," I said. "I have roadwork of my own to do tomorrow. If it works, you work. If it doesn't work, we'll all be through waiting just the same."

They all drank the first round to road builder deWitt.

"How are you going to do it tomorrow?" asked Luft.

I did not want to tell him in detail—as far as that went, I did not know the details myself. But I told him in general. "Looks, luck, and lies," I said.

They all drank the second round to my Homburg.

"Do we keep worrying about Yum Lee?" Luft wanted to know.

I wanted to know that myself. The man had won a victory that for all intents and purposes was irreversible. But in the face of such success he might get doubly irritated with unexpected interruptions in his master plan.

"We most definitely," I said, "continue to worry about Yum Lee."

The third round, accordingly, went to Yum Lee. In the absence of roadwork he kept the men alert in the pursuit of street brawls.

He was keeping me alert, of course, with his plans for a safari with drilling equipment. That and rice balls and the road—they undoubtedly all hung together.

"You haven't finished your first," said Hengstman. "You don't like to drink?"

"I do, except it tastes like water after the stuff I had at the Prime Minister's house."

So they drank the fourth round to my jaded tastes.

I was getting nervous. Inge was gone, and there was no sign of Baby.

The men drank round number five to the *Tanzmeister*, whoever that was. It turned out to be Baby, who at that moment walked into the library looking glum and full of disapproval.

"I took Miss Lobbe home," he said to me. "We don't approve of you."

"I don't, either. Take me home, too."

"Since I took Miss Lobbe home with my full approval and since I do not approve—"

"Just shut up."

This time it was easier to dismiss my bodyguards, who were downing round number six to the tune of "Schnitzelbank." But Luft insisted on following Baby and me out. When we passed the French bartender, he had a glass in one hand and a bottle in the other and he was pouring crème de menthe over his left cuff.

At the hotel I parted with Baby, asking him to come back at eight in the morning and to bring Plozzi along.

"Anytime," he said.

"No. At eight."

We parted on that kind of surly note. It was not so easy to get rid of Luft. He followed me as if I were an important gangster and he kept looking around with a clear wish for disaster.

The night clerk wasn't much help, either. "Miss Lobbe left word," he said, "that she is not in her room."

I went to the stairs, and Luft was still following me.

"You can go now," I said. "I'm safe. You heard the man."

"First," he said, "I inspect your room."

"You do nothing of the sort."

"Mister deWitt, since you are going to—"

"Don't you start that kind of talk, now!"

He said nothing else and simply followed me upstairs. I felt I could get rid of him and inform myself all at the same time, so I led the way to Inge's room, which was a few doors from mine. I would insert the key, find that it did not work, and then send Luft to the desk while I found solitude in my own room. It almost worked as planned. I got the key in the lock, tried the door, and it opened. I looked in and found the light on and found the bed empty.

"Safe," I said. "Just as I told you." And in that way I informed myself and got rid of him.

When Luft was out of sight, I went to my own room, slammed the door shut, and just stood there in the dark for a moment, festering. As I went to the bed I was wishing that I had some of that stuff the Prime Minister had been serving. But even before I got there, I knew that I was not alone in the room and I knew, with a strong touch of desperation, that Luft was too far away to hear my call.

"I said I wasn't going to be in my room," said Inge.

Then I forgot about Luft.

All told, I do not think that I slept for more than two hours. Part of it was pure pleasure. Part of it was pure worry. I had nightmarish dreams of roads leading nowhere, of roads leading right through my bedroom, of Chinese marionettes bashing their skulls into each other, and once I saw a hairy ape towering over my bed. I woke at five in the morning and could not go back to sleep. I just lay there and worried. After a while my fretting must have disturbed Inge, for she woke with an unaccustomed start, stared at me for a moment, and then slowly smiled.

"Oh," she said, "so it's you."

I let that go by. A thin light was beginning to show through the slats of the shutters, and I just lay and watched it.

"What time is it?" said Inge.

"Five o'clock."

"Good heavens!" she said, and jumped up. Then she leaned on one elbow and down over me in her Inge fashion and smiled again.

"You are a beautiful lover," she said. "You are very special, Manny, because you made me sleep away the whole day."

Then she got up and stretched. She rubbed her head and mumbled,

"What a lover. I'm still tired."

"Inge," I said, "come here a minute."

She immediately jumped back on the bed and put herself close. "You old goat," she said. "Again?"

"Inge—"

"Wait," she said. "We've got the sheet between us." She corrected that with alacrity. "Now, then, what was it you were going to do?"

"I was going to say, sweetness, that it is five in the morning."

This did not produce a chill, but a further heat. "Goat!" she said very loud. "Very old goat! Is that why I'm tired?"

"Since your sleeping habits take you habitually way past the hour of five in the morning, I would say that you are tired because—"

"Don't you talk Motanesque to me! And I'm not *that* tired!"

I was not that tired, either, and I pulled her closer. In a while we lay in a rosy peace we had made together. But she did not go to sleep again, and neither did I. She smoked a cigarette and tried to make rings.

"Did you ever see Uncle Hans make smoke rings?"

"Smoke screens only."

"I forgot to tell you," she said. "He sent me a telegram."

"When? Why? I mean, what did he say?"

"What do you mean, why? Because he loves me."

Which perhaps explained why he had not sent a telegram to me.

"He sent it," she went on, "while you were making a display of yourself in town, which I heard about, and he asked how I was getting along."

"How are you getting along?"

"I was getting along miserably at the time, thank you. And he asked about you."

"What?"

"Are you fine, he asked, and then something I did not understand. 'Ask mennekin—' he said." She interrupted to look at me. "What does that mean?"

"That's Dutch."

"I know that's Dutch because I'm Dutch. Why does he call you that?"

"Because he loves me."

There was a better answer. Lobbe did not want the telegraph clerk or anyone else to know whom he was addressing.

"How did you happen to know he meant me?" I asked Inge.

"Because of the rest of the message: 'Ask mennekin when will he need Stebbs.'"

If there was anyone I did not need at this point it was Stebbs. But the reference would hardly be a joke.

"Are you sure he said Stebbs in the telegram?"

"Of course. It's in my room. And since there is nobody here who knows Stebbs except you, therefore Uncle Hans must have meant you when he said mennekin."

"Brilliant."

"So you know what it means?"

"Not a glimmer," I said.

"Well, at least you know it must have to do with investments. You introduced me to Stebbs and said that he was in investments."

Of course, I thought. But so what?

"Give me one of your cigarettes, would you?"

She gave me one, and I lit it. But I was thinking about business now, and there seemed something very wrong with lying in bed next to Inge and thinking about business. I got up and walked around the room.

"This looks very funny," she said from the bed. "I have never seen you smoke a cigarette naked."

I put the cigarette out. "There is something very funny going on around here altogether," I said. "Tell me, Inge" —I sat down on the bed—"do you remember what we talked about when we had martinis with Stebbs?"

"Washington and the party."

"Tell me again what you remember about the party your uncle gave there."

She crossed her arms behind her head and looked at the ceiling. "Well, I was telling you about those two young men from the State department, and you got very jealous."

And they had said to her that they might not have been so hard on Uncle Lobbe if they had known his lovely niece. What mattered, perhaps, was that State had been hard on Lobbe.

"Tell me who else was there, Inge."

"You were only jealous about those two."

"I am vastly jealous! My jealousy includes every man-jack at that so-called party!"

"I was the hostess. It was *not* so-called!"

"Listen. That was a business meeting. When Lively Lobbe has a real party, he invites musicians, bookworms, fishermen, and maybe Kalopidos. He invites happy people, not career men and politicians. Once more, now, who else was there?"

I remembered who had been there, but I wanted to check it out for a new view. I could no longer escape the impression that Lobbe's being summoned to Washington, Lobbe's wining and dining officials who had been hard on him, and Lobbe's packing me off to Motana on a totally nonsensical emergency mission to get a fully negotiated road contract signed all had to hang together. As puny as his explanations had been, that's how really big his real reasons had to be. He had always been secretive, but never to the extent of sending out a total ignoramus. That was not the way he worked. It could only be explained by some outside pressure. That's when I remembered Torquet's cryptic remark in Rome.

"Perhaps it has not occurred to you," he had said, "that your Mister Lobbe's secrecy measures were not directed against us at all."

And last night I had asked Patel why he thought I was here in Motana. His silence had been too long, and then, as if discarding a thought, he had said, "You have apparently been hired to finalize a contract for a road."

The price of keeping your own negotiator in ignorance is high. He might negotiate for the wrong thing. That price was apparently no consideration to Lobbe. And it was also no consideration to the heads of the Motanesque government, or else they would not have brushed me off in the Lobbe fashion.

I still did not know what had been hidden from me and why it was so important to hide it from somebody else.

"About the rest of them," Inge was saying, "they were all in the government. Except for the cultured Negro in the skull cap from the UN."

"The Motanesque."

"I don't know that. He spoke so many languages and he did not have this country's accent or any other I could distinguish."

"You said he wore a skull cap."

"So do the Moroccans, the Egyptians, the Libyans, the—"

"All right. And the government men?"

"State Department, Foreign Aid, and one who wouldn't say."

"CIA."

"He didn't look anything like a spy."

"Naturally."

"I'm getting hungry, Manny."

It was a much more sensible comment than mine about the man who would not say. He could simply have been an introverted house dick.

We got ready then and went downstairs for a breakfast of sautéed fish in a lemon sauce and had raw figs afterward. It was all very good, but throughout I kept juggling Investments, State Department, Foreign Aid, and the UN. It meant almost nothing. No road led anywhere.

I expected Baby and Plozzi, but Luft showed up first. He had some very strange news.

"After you went to bed," he told me, "I sent over a man, of course."

"What do you mean, of course? Sent him where?"

"Here. To the hotel."

I looked at Inge on the other side of the table, but she was still eating.

"Why are you telling me about this unnecessary nonsense, Luft?"
"Because of the repercussions, Mister deWitt. You should be prepared."
"All right," I said in a low voice. "Give me the repercussions."
"At three in the morning," said Luft, "my man on the second floor—not the man in the lobby—he sees these two Chinese come down the corridor."
"Don't stop now, Luft."
"And he watches. He sees these two Chinese try a door."
"Did it all go this slowly?"
"How slowly?"
"Never mind. Go on if there's more."
"There is more, Mister deWitt." He hesitated as if bracing himself for the worst. "The point of the matter is, Mister deWitt, that my man went on duty up there after coming straight from the Club."
"Schnitzelbank," I mumbled.
"Yes. He was a little bit drunk, you see, and so he made a mistake with the doors."
"You're going too fast, Luft."
"I mean, I know your door, you showed me your door, I showed the man your door, but, then, he was too drunk to remember it right and he followed those Chinese right through the wrong door."
"Right through it."
"It was open. The Chinese were already inside, and my man he took their two faces—"
"I think it was their heads."
"Yes, heads, and banged them together till the Chinese left. That was fine by him."
"I understand that."
"But then he discovers the awful mistake!"
"He is sober now."
"It sobered him when he saw it was not you in the bed there, but this man and woman, he says. They were lying in bed there together!"
I looked over at Inge. She was looking at her fingernails.
"Is there more, Luft?"
"No. My man ran right out. But just in case there is a complaint in the hotel, and they describe my man, there may be repercussions."
This time when I looked at Inge, she was looking straight back at us.
"I'm sure the people in that room were not disturbed, and thank you for watching out for Mister deWitt." She smiled, but then she looked immediately past my left ear. "Gabriele!" she called. "Over here!"
Luft escaped while Baby and Plozzi came over. But before business, there had to be more Inge.
"Gabriele," she said, "sit down. Listen, the funniest thing happened to

me last night while I was—"

"Inge!" I said. "I have an important matter to attend to at the Diet, a most *public* matter in which a hell of a lot hangs on impeccable, irreproachable—" I hesitated, trying to decide how to make this both delicate and strong, when Plozzi cut in.

"You mean the thing about the truck driver in your room?"

"Plozzi," I said, "how in hell...."

"I forgot who told me. Most amusing. But you wanted to see me at eight."

Inge, deprived of her amusing anecdote, fell silent, and we all got into the Spirit of Friendship, where I was able to talk business with Plozzi and Baby along the way. I was glad to find that Plozzi was cooperative. Inge said not a word.

We parked outside the Motanesque Diet Building. Most of the people who entered had come on foot, but there was a goodly row of old Citroëns, vintage Bentleys, brand-new surreys with donkeys in front, and single donkeys with wild-colored blankets over them.

In the entrance hall I turned where the arrow directed me to the Chamber of Members while my companions went up to the visitors' gallery. The President's receptionist, whom I had met the night before, then seated me near the front of the Assembly Hall.

It was like Westminster Abbey except that the ornate woodwork, which contained the stepped seats and the galleries, was made of a white wood with dark grain markings. This made for a zebra effect. Nothing else distracted from the Victorian Gothic quality of the place, neither the ornamental spears, or the tribal emblems, or the lion-skin shields. Members took their seats, some dressed in mufti, some in the native gown, and in a while one did not look any more unusual than the other. The President took his seat behind the Chairman's rostrum, and the Prime Minister took a seat in the auditorium, where his party was grouped.

Parliamentary procedure is the same everywhere. Usually the creaky progress of its machinery bores me, but now it set my teeth on edge. There was a presentation and arguments concerning a new loan for commercial developments. The issue, because of questions concerning interest rates, was sent back to committee. Next came a tariff discussion that was so complicated that I soon lost track of it. But I did understand that the proposed rulings concerned exchanges between the *quartier intérieur* and the *quartier principal*. In other words, the dispute was confined to the same country. The interesting thing was that the weight of representation from the hinterland went against the President's recommendation and—as would be true with any good politician—this development disturbed the President quite a bit. I tried to relax with this piece of information, but I could not.

I was not sure enough myself about what was to come.

Then the Prime Minister addressed the Chair in order to drop the bombshell of the day.

"I have good news today!"

Then he let everybody hang while he went through the formalities of thanking everybody for everything. He even looked at me and made a slight bow. I looked back at him with the proper expression of brave resignation. It did not take much faking.

"... so that our patience—the same staunchness of purpose that some of you have seen fit to call fearful hesitancy—has now borne fruit. Our road, which will yet lead to the affluence and stature for which we all strive, will now become a reality!" He paused, secure in the knowledge that everybody was with him.

"But you might ask," he went on, "at what price will all this be ours?"

"I'm asking," called somebody from the opposition party.

"I'm glad you asked that," said Patel. He drew himself up to full size, which was quite a spectacle. "At the price," he suddenly roared, "of our most abundant commodity! At the price of the one thing that we always give away free!"

Everybody started to look worried.

"Yes," said the Prime Minister, as if soothing a child, "we shall have our road—for the sole price of friendship!"

Immediately they did not look worried anymore. They laughed and clapped, but then an opposition member got up.

"You mean the road will be for free?" asked the delegate.

"For free!" boomed the Prime Minister.

Again there was concord, and when a second delegate got up, they paid him no attention.

I can only explain what he did by assuming that he was so full of love he simply had to find an object for it. He looked at me, grinning, and left his seat. By the time he reached me, he was no longer alone, and then I was hoisted aloft like a helpless football hero.

"Not him!" bellowed the Prime Minister.

They put me down and drifted back to their seats.

"Members of the Assembly," said the Prime Minister, "you have just now shown your friendship to the loser. I hasten to say that this was very admirable of you. However, the one who will build us the road, the one who will give us the gift of prosperity, is our kind friend Yum Lee!"

Perhaps everybody was a little exhausted now, because the applause was merely polite. The Prime Minister took up the slack with self-serving generosity.

"And now"—he addressed himself to me—"in the spirit of friendship,

Mister deWitt, we give you this opportunity to bid us farewell."

I was presumably prepared for this, except that I did not feel like it. I walked to the lectern below the President's seat and looked at the assembly. All I seemed to see were white eyeballs. The sight unnerved me, but I found my voice.

"Mister Chairman, members of the Assembly," I said, "I am a man with thoughts of profit and I therefore regret that I cannot give you your road. But I commend you to the profitless friendship of Yum Lee. I had only a road for you, but Yum Lee has other plans for you. I have yellow machines, and they can do only one thing. Yum Lee has machines, and I am told they can do many things. Today in the wilderness of your *quartier intérieur* there roam the wild beasts that you hunt. The land has lain useless since time began and seems fit only for animals. But Yum Lee will change all that. He will drive the beasts into hiding with the powerful roar of his machines. The machines will tear up the land and shovel dirt to the surface in order to find, so he says, hidden minerals that might make you rich. But do not think that he will transform your lovely veldt into an ugly wasteland. Far from it. I do not know how he will build you a road because I have not seen his machines for such work, but I have seen the machines with which he will go into your hinterland, and the harm they do will be of another kind."

A number of the delegates were now grumbling. I was going to make it unanimous.

"He will perform his search in a new way, a way for which you yourselves do not have the daring. Friendship makes Yum Lee risk this fearful way!" I now reared up and bellowed the way Patel had done it. "Yum Lee will bore and tear into the veins of the earth because friendship makes him stop at nothing! He will force the earth to pour out her blood for you. He will drill wells!" I lowered my voice. It was very quiet in the house. "And that, gentlemen, is the way of Yum Lee's friendship, which now is yours. Farewell."

The continuing silence in the house told me nothing. I walked slowly back to my seat.

"Just a minute!" Patel was livid. I returned to the lectern and looked at him in a gentle way.

"A question, perhaps?" I said.

"What is this nonsense about Yum Lee?" he yelled.

I knew this was only his opener, but I could not let it get by.

"I don't know," I said. Then I gave it to him in Montanesque. "Since you understood me enough to ask your intelligent question, I could not have spoken nonsense, and by the same token I would not expect you to understand the nonsense of Yum Lee. You must therefore simply learn to accept Yum Lee's nonsense as the quality of his friendship. Are there any other questions?"

"Yes," said the President above and behind me. I did not turn around to look at him, but I could hear the tone of worry.

"If you are telling the truth, Mister deWitt, I wonder why I do not see it."

"Understandable," I said without turning. "You were not there when Yum Lee explained what he means to do with his vein-punching machines in the hinterland."

"But he said this to you?"

I turned around and looked up at his worried face. I smiled at him, giving him no comfort. Then I said, "No."

Now he felt comfort. I could see it grow and take over his face. But just before he got too much of a good thing, I gave him pause.

"Baby!" I called up to the gallery. The President looked startled. "Tell your President, Baby!"

Baby stuck his head over the railing and gave a straight delivery, just as we had planned it.

"Yum Lee confided the vein-draining purpose of the machines to me. I did not explain to him that he was planning to violate a taboo, because he would not have planned to violate it except from ignorance or perversity. I despaired of informing such abysmal ignorance and who was I to counter such perversity? I have since not eaten any of his rice balls." Then his head disappeared.

"Just a minute!" said the Prime Minister again. "I know him. He drives a taxi, and the machines he describes are said to be in the *intérieur*, but we all know that no taxi, not even the Spirit of Friendship, can move in the *intérieur*. Therefore—"

"Plozzi!" I called loud and clear.

Plozzi jumped up and nodded down at the Prime Minister with a courteous smile. "Allow me to save you from error, Mister Prime Minister. I have been charged by Yum Lee with the transport by safari of all those machines. They are at present still at the Place de Safari for all to see."

The Prime Minister took only a moment to recover. "And the purpose?" he said. "Yum Lee has described a different purpose to me. Nothing about wells, only minerals!"

"Different stories for different ears?" I interrupted. "We call that duplicity!"

"We, too!" yelled somebody from the opposition party.

"Are you forgetting about the free road?" Patel yelled back.

"That's in this *quartier* only," said somebody who, by his costume, was apparently from the hinterland.

"Well put," I said quickly, because this would now have to be the kill. "You must always remember that the act of friendship that offends the taboo is directed only at your backward hinterland!"

Now came a great deal of shouting, and anyone not familiar with parliamentary practice might have thought that nothing was getting done. I turned to the President's rostrum and leaned close. "President Matan," I said for just his ears, "there are an awful lot of votes back in the hinterland, isn't that true?"

His face became transfixed with fervor. He stood up for the first time and spread his arms like a conjurer. "What shall it be?" he declaimed. "The yellow machines or the yellow menace?"

He was a good politician. He only asked a question to which he already knew the answer.

I felt like Talleyrand after Vienna, like Bismarck after Versailles—deWitt after the Rout of Yummy. I wrestled my way out of the Assembly Hall and waited for my entourage from the gallery. The President's secretary came up to me while I was waiting around and told me that the road contracts would be signed in special session that afternoon and would I be interested in any further discussion of them before the signing took place. I am generous in victory and said that no further discussion was needed, the signatures would be enough. Then I saw Inge in animated conversation with a white-robed delegate. Plozzi was standing by, laughing. I walked over to them to listen to compliments.

"Oh, it's you," said Inge unnecessarily. "This is Kamatur," she said, introducing the delegate.

He bowed, and I bowed, and then he said, "We were discussing your speech, Mister deWitt."

"Thank you," I said, and nothing else because I did not wish to interrupt his further comments. For once I was looking forward with pleasure to some Motanesque long-windedness.

"It was an unusually delicate speech," said Kamatur. "In view of what had happened, it was remarkably free of rancor."

I had no idea what he was talking about.

"Of the many qualities that Yum Lee possesses, only one is really unpardonable. He is indelicate—quite the opposite of you."

"Oh, well," I said, "he'll learn about the customs of others."

"I don't think so, Mister deWitt. He is too indelicate to understand our feelings."

"Even after my speech?" I said, and laughed politely. This time Kamatur seemed to be the one who went blank. "Our decision," he said, "had little to do with your speech. It was good oratory, but we had already decided against Yum Lee."

"You what? Since when?"

"This morning. You know."

"I do?"

Everybody looked as if he were the only one who knew anything, and Baby looked disappointed in me. "Surely," said the delegate, "you know as well as anyone else that Yum Lee sent two men to disturb you in bed last night."

I looked at Inge, and she looked right back at me, as if she were used to this sort of thing. "He heard it on the street," she said.

"And that," Kamatur went on, "was an unforgivable act of indelicacy. Well, Mister deWitt, when we learned of that, Yum Lee really had no chance anymore."

He bowed and withdrew, taking with him a good deal of the sense of accomplishment that had buoyed me.

"You will forgive me," said Plozzi, "if I rush off after such a beautiful speech. But I must ready the safari."

"You're not leaving till tomorrow," I said.

"Yum Lee sent word to the gallery," said Plozzi, "that he would like to leave with all speed."

"He's taking those damn machines?"

"Of course," said Plozzi, and then he left.

Yum Lee was not through. He had lost the road contract, but he had further plans—

I looked around the large hall and at the construction men that Luft and Hengstman had stationed there. I was wondering whether I would still need them when I saw Luft come in through the front entrance. The little man spotted me almost immediately and came over fast.

"Luft," I said, "I've got a message for Podolski."

"He has a message for you."

"Mine's bigger. Tell him to roll out those machines and dig!"

His weather-beaten face lit up, and for a moment I thought he was going to salute, but then he just shook my hand as if I were a pump, grinning. "And now the message for you," he said. "Podolski received this wire." He handed it to me.

It was not signed, but the form of address identified the sender: MENNEKIN PHONING YOU THIS DATE TWO PM YOUR TIME C/O VILLEBLANCHE AMERICAN CONSULATE STOP URGENT STOP URGENT.

I was looking forward to this one. When I have finished a job—and I had just finished a tricky one and I felt I had, after all, done it well—then Lobbe can come on as urgently as he likes, and I remain calm and infinitely secure.

I took Inge to the Club for some lunch, and then we had Baby drive us to the consulate.

It was a one-story bungalow with a porch all around, very much like van Voos' house at the Place de Safari. Inside, however, it was something else again. Inside, it was Grand Rapids Baroque, Iowa Conservative, and a little bit of Sears Roebuck Modern. The consul—he was a vice-consul actually—opened the door for us himself and led us into his museum of doilies, linoleum, and heavy furniture.

His name was Bliss. He was an elderly, serious man who seemed to have polished his bald head for the occasion. He had been informed, he told us, of the forthcoming call and he was happy to extend the government's assistance to fellow American tourists and travelers. He apparently did not know who I was, and quite possibly he did not even know about the road project.

He sat down behind a metal desk and bade us sit down, too. Inge sunk into a maroon armchair, Baby disappeared into a green one, and I sat down on a very hard white and blue couch. It was stuffed with horsehair that felt like nettles.

"What unusual furniture," said Inge politely.

The consul's old face doubled all its wrinkles, and he showed two rows of plastic teeth.

"They don't make 'em like that anymore," he said.

"I believe you," said Inge. "It looks ageless."

"Brought it along when I first came here," said Mister Bliss. "Near forty years ago."

"That's before there was a Motana!"

Mr. Bliss nodded and told us about it as if somebody had finally asked him a question he had been waiting for. He had come as representative for his father's firm, Bliss Pipes, when the country was still a native kingdom. He had sold lengths of plumbing to the king's army. With Mr. Bliss' wares an attempt had been made to establish an artillery on the principle of the blowgun. When the propulsion problem proved to be beyond the average capacity of lung power, the left-over pipe was used to fashion a picket fence around the king's private game preserve. Next Mr. Bliss operated under a series of colonial governors, and a new use for the pipe was found: to catch the water of the clear mountain streams and convert it into rust-brown tap-water for the population centers of Motana.

"But now that I've entered the diplomatic service," said Mr. Bliss, "I've been letting the business slide. I'm studying the language. I don't hold with sign language for a member of the diplomatic service."

I was going to commend him on that when the phone rang. Mr. Bliss handed it to me, and I put the receiver to my ear.

First there was the sound of ocean waves, and then the lengthy mating call that all Motanesque operators seem to emit. And next, fading in and out, the voice of Lobbe.

"DeWitt? Answer me!"

"Here I am!"

"I know *you* are there. Is Stebbs there?"

"No," I shouted back, "Stebbs is not here. I was not expecting him."

"So what? I sent him."

"Here?"

There followed a sentence or two that I would not write down, even if I could spell it. That sort of language from Lobbe is always followed by an exhausted silence, and this one was significantly longer than most. At over ten dollars a minute it was a very significant silence. I waited for the sense of it all.

"I sent Stebbs to Tangiers," said Lobbe. "After the business in Tangiers he was to come and see you in Villeblanche. You understand so far?"

"No."

"Nevertheless. When you see him, I want you to tell him to go straightaway back to Tangiers and cancel everything."

"I see. And he knows what you are talking about?"

"Manford," he said, "you mean you *don't* know what I am talking about?"

This irritated me no end. Since childhood there has been no one who has ever called me Manford except with intent to reprimand. Lobbe was no exception. But, above all, his line of attack completely skirted what for me was the real issue, the local issue, the victory for which I was being denied my recognition. I did not answer him but changed the subject.

"Mister Lobbe," I said, "I have been sent here on a matter that seems to have nothing to do with this conversation. I specifically came to the phone to report that during the past twenty-four hours I have succeeded in completing my business and that in the face of a number of unscheduled and unspeakable obstacles. We are now building the road, Mister Lobbe. I got the contract!"

My sense of accomplishment dissolved in another silence. Perhaps Telstar was not functioning—or worse, perhaps Lobbe was not functioning.

"Do you have a scrambler there?" I heard him say.

"No, sir. I am not using a scrambler. What I said was in plain English."

"I know what you said in plain English, deWitt. I am asking you whether or not the consulate there happens to have a scrambler of the manufacture that you have seen in my office."

"No scrambler, Mister Lobbe."

"Unfortunate. Just tell me one thing, deWitt. Do you know yet where the road is going?"

"No. I haven't thought to ask."

"Sorry," said Lobbe. "My fault. All my fault."

"I don't understand, Mister Lobbe."

"I can tell. But I cannot tell you on the phone. Ask Stebbs when he comes. And drop everything, deWitt."

"There's nothing to drop, Mister Lobbe! We've got the road!"

"DeWitt," he said, "this is why I call. Do not build the road." And then he hung up.

After I hung up, there was the sort of silence that is not measured in time, but only in depth. It does not matter how long it lasted. I knew only that I stood in a room where nothing seemed to have changed since the day forty years ago when pipes were stored there. The first one to speak was the one I thought would have the least to say.

"Mister deWitt," said Bliss, as if he were thinking. He tapped his too-white teeth with a pencil and said my name again. And then, "Aren't you the young fellow who came down to build us a road?"

In view of the phone call I had just received, I was tempted to say No. But I was not really used to the thought yet.

"Yes," I said.

"From Essen, Germany?"

Our consul, it seemed, was not living entirely in a vacuum. I nodded. He opened his desk and pulled out a note. He read the reference number on it and then found a file in a cabinet drawer that was marked: SPECIAL, EXPEDITE.

"This is about you," he said while he brought the file back to the desk. "Wire came in the middle of the night sometime—let's see—ten p.m. Was going to deliver it to your Mister—what's that?—Pa-derewski?"

"Podolski. Why to him?"

"Because it says here—I'll read it to you."

"Please do."

"It says here: TO ALVIS BLISS, VICE-CONSUL—"

"Would you mind getting to the message?"

"Don't you want to know who it's from?"

"All right."

"All right, listen."

Mr. Bliss did not sound folksy anymore. His voice was like something you turn on with a switch.

"DEPARTMENT OF STATE, PASSPORT DIVISION, WASHINGTON 25, D. C. PURSUANT DIRECTIVE SW-4521-F, THIS DATE, UN-

DER MEMO SIGNED P. MCFUNTY—"

"I don't get the relevance of any of this, Mister Bliss. I don't even know who McFunty is."

"Well, I had to look that up myself right here in the directory we get when we enter the diplomatic service. He's listed there under State Department and he's Assistant to the Director, West African Desk."

"The message, Mister Bliss."

"I'm coming to it. Here we are... FOR IMMEDIATE ATTENTION YOUR SERVICE." He looked up to explain. "That means I have to act on it."

"Please do, Mister Bliss."

"It says here: CONTACT MANFORD DEWITT, U S PASSPORT NUMBER...." He looked up again. "You got your passport with you?"

"No. It's at the hotel."

"That's right. They've got this new custom here, leaving the passport at the desk."

"I don't know my passport number by heart, Mister Bliss. Could you continue without it, please?"

"Guess you're the fellow all right, since you admitted all those things I asked you. Now, it says here: 'DEWITT' we got that—it says to contact you 'c/o HERMAN PODOLSKI, SUBJECT WEST GERMAN REPUBLIC, ENGINEER SUPERVISING MOTANA PROJECT SIKURHEETS—"

"You can skip that, too."

"Guess I'll have to. 'CONTACT THROUGH HIM—here that is, Villeblanche—OR THROUGH LOCAL CONSTABULARY FOR COMMUNICATION VERBAL FOLLOWING: MANFORD DEWITT ON PENALTY OF PASSPORT WITHDRAWAL TO CEASE ALL ACTIVITIES IN BEHALF OF LOBBE INDUSTRIEL AND OR SICKER—'you know the word—'IN CONNECTION WITH GERMAN CONSTRUCTION PROJECT VILLEBLANCHE, MOTANA. SUGGEST TWENTY-FOUR HOUR DEPARTURE AS EVIDENCE OF COMPLIANCE WITH DIRECTIVE. ADVISE SENDER. EXPEDITE.'"

He looked up as if he had not understood a word. "I just gave you the communication, verbal. Right?"

"Right."

"Have to ask that."

I sat down on the horsehair couch and tried to think. This was the second time that the State Department had figured in connection with Lobbe. Lobbe had been summoned to Washington, where he had not gotten his way. And then he had sent me to Motana ostensibly to represent an enterprise that seemed to have nothing to do with Lobbe Industriel. But State had found out, and once again an effort was being made to stop Lobbe.

I took a deep breath and thought about the twenty-four hours I still had left.

"Mister Bliss," I said, "do you know why I am being ordered out of the country?"

"Well, now, Mister deWitt, it's not as if we could order you out of somebody else's country, you understand. All we do—"

"I know what you do. Do you do it so that I cannot build a road?"

"That would be my understanding. It says so practically right here."

"And do you know why, Mister Bliss?"

He gave me the bureaucrat's blank eye. "Because it says so right here, right from the desk of McFunty."

Of course.

"And what," I asked him, "happens if I refuse to budge?"

"In that case," he said with awe, "the violation can go all the way to the top."

I don't know if he had learned that expression in the galvanized pipe business or in the diplomatic service, but it obviously covered an abyss of ignorance. Nevertheless, I made one more attempt to get information from him.

"It seems clear that this road is important, Mister Bliss. Would you know why?"

"Nope. And I won't ask, myself."

"Do you know where it leads?"

"'Course not. I wouldn't meddle in the internal affairs of the country that's the host. Rule right here in the book of directives we get when we enter—"

"Yes."

He sensed my disappointment in his performance for the first time, and this, I think, prompted him to toss off the next remark.

"I don't know any of this officially, you understand, but I can put two and two together like the next fellow. So I think it's really got to be something big, Mister deWitt, real big. You know why?"

"Because I'm going to lose my passport."

"Peanuts, Mister deWitt!"

"Not to me."

He ignored that.

"Would you say, on the other hand, that the Seventh Fleet was peanuts?"

"I beg your pardon?"

"It's in all the papers! The Seventh Fleet just happens to be nearby!"

I neither had seen any papers nor did I really understand what Bliss was driving at. I looked at Baby, who had been silent all the while.

"There is only one paper in Motana." Baby spoke. "It says that anyone who wishes to witness a spectacle of unusual beauty against the sunset tomorrow evening might stand on Cape Sif and see the fine silhouettes of many ships passing along the horizon. They are going to the Mediterranean and they are part of your navy, it says."

I got up. "May I use your phone once more, Mister Bliss?"

"You mean long distance?"

"No, Government House."

He was impressed. I dialed with hope. Since having come to Villeblanche, I had asked van Voos where the road was going, and he had not known. I had once asked Baby, and he had not even cared. Just recently Bliss had given his own explanations for ignorance. The only ones who knew for certain what the road was all about sat in Government House.

I fought my way past the operator, through the Government House switchboard, and up to the President's secretary.

The conversation was brief. First she told me, without being asked, that the road contracts had been signed in behalf of the government and in favor of the Essen company. That was no longer a consolation to me. She then told me that the President and the Prime Minister had taken the government helicopter in order to make a formal visit to Miesville in the *quartier intérieur*. They would there obtain Torquet One's *pro forma* signature in connection with the building of the road.

Clearly for once everything was going in opposite directions.

It was only when I dropped Inge off at the hotel that I realized I had not let her talk to her uncle—this was the reason she had come along with me. I told Baby to drive to the harbor, hoping that Podolski was not taking the local Hour of the Sloth seriously now.

He wasn't there. He and his trailer and practically all of his equipment had already moved out, moved to the jungle road. Baby drove me there.

It took longer than expected because Villeblanche was suffering its first real traffic jam. The tail end of Podolski's monster caravan was still lumbering through parts of the town. The front end, I soon discovered, was already clawing its way into the wilderness.

The leisurely ways of labor on the unfinished road were no more. Loaded dump trucks were chasing each other toward the harbor, and empty ones were clattering in the opposite direction. Earthmovers were leveling the uneven ground, and scrapers were shaping it. A phalanx of bulldozers up front was destroying like Juggernauts whatever lay in their way. The racket of the diesels was like the sound of war.

I found Podolski on the raised scoop of a cat. He looked happy.

"Look good?" he yelled at me when he saw me.

"Bad. Sorry," I yelled back.

"That's good," he shouted. Then he had the scoop lowered and came over to me.

"You and me are going to have a quiet talk," I yelled in his ear.

"Very funny. Ha, ha!"

"Actually not, Podolski. Where can we go?"

"If you can wait just a little, we can go right up the mountain," he yelled back.

"The mountain may have to wait."

"If you'll just wait a little," he yelled louder, "we can go right up the mountain."

"The mountain may have to wait."

By this time he took me seriously and led the way to his trailer. It was pulled into the old road that went to the Place de Safari. We got in, and he brought out the beer.

I took the offered bottle, drank a little, and looked out the window. Where the roads crossed, I could see the Chinese canteen truck. Persistent bastard, that Yum Lee. But there were no customers now. The three Chinese in attendance were standing by the truck, arms folded. Sometimes they waved at the equipment passing by and sometimes they smiled. The sight was rather odd.

"You know what one of them told me?" said Podolski next to me.

I turned around and sat down at the table. The beer did not taste good.

"He said, 'Herr Kaiser'"—Podolski laughed and sat down, too—"because he thinks I'm German. Well, he calls me that and then he says, 'Do you know where your road is going?' And then he answered for me. 'Nowhere!' After that he just laughed, as if that was very funny."

"It's not funny," I said.

"I did not think so, either. You are not drinking your beer, Mister deWitt."

"It is not funny, but it is serious," I said.

He looked at me for a moment and then he could feel my mood. "All right," he said, "tell me."

I told him. I explained to him briefly and seriously that the road project had been canceled and that this meant as of now.

He did not like what he had heard, but he finished his beer calmly enough. Then he took the empty bottle and threw it out the door. He waited till the glass broke before he swore. Then he came back and sat down again.

"It is the first job for me, Mister deWitt, without pride. People laugh at us, people hold up our work, and I am altogether beginning to feel like a puppet with strings that go someplace I don't know. I don't like that, Mister deWitt."

"I don't, either."

"And I will not call off my crews, Mister deWitt. Not until I hear it from Essen. I know you represent Essen, but your information did not come from there. I am sorry."

"So am I. But I am telling you all I know, and what I told you will happen."

"When I hear from Essen."

In that way he tried to keep a little of his pride. I would not take it from him.

"All right," I said, and got up. "But, for the record, if it comes up, please remember that I told you."

"I will, Mister deWitt."

He got up, followed me to the door of the trailer, and, to my surprise, put his arm on my shoulder.

"You are a good man, Mister deWitt, under the jokes you make with the Homburg and so forth. In your job it must be very much harder to keep the pride. I and the others like you."

"Thank you, Podolski."

We walked out of the trailer and we said nothing until we came to Baby's car on the other side of the new road.

"*Sauhund*," said Podolski to the Chinese who was grinning at him. Then he turned to me. "What did he mean about the road going nowhere?"

"He meant that Yum Lee is not through. He meant that Yum Lee had something to do with the phone call I just told you about."

"Bah!" said Podolski. "What is this? A political road?"

I looked up the length of the road to where it ended just short of the mountain. "Where is it going, Podolski?"

"To the mountain. We have to get there to finish the job."

"Why the mountain, Podolski?"

"Well, that has to do with the way you build a road," he said. "The bed of the road—this type for this sort of weather and then with a rainy season—needs a great deal of crushed rock and gravel. We will get that out of the mountain."

"And then what will they use the road for?"

"I have no idea."

He was a builder of roads, no matter where they led, no matter what the reason, he must have thought, because this led to his next remark. I was already in the car, and Baby had started the motor.

"You remember you asked me about the drilling equipment?" he said.

"The stuff the Chinese are taking into the hinterland?"

"Yes. I looked at it this morning before they left."

"You recognized it?"

"I did not recognize it from your description, but now that I have seen it, the matter is simple. I have used it myself."

"I see. It makes potholes."

"It is a ground sampler. We use it to get the necessary information about the soil before we can decide how to build a road properly."

The puzzle, it seemed, had grown by another piece.

Back in Villeblanche I called Government House and learned that the President and the Prime Minister were still away and would probably not be back until the following morning. I was not looking forward to their return with unmixed feelings. I went to the Club to sit awhile and think a few matters over.

First I stopped at the bar. The bartender did not yet have a hangover. He was still freshly drunk. His eyes were hooded, and his hands moved like something ominous in a bad dream. In that condition I would not trust him to mix me a glass of water.

"You are not alone, monsieur," he said.

Since I was alone, the man was obviously seeing double.

"And now, monsieur, I drink I am ready for you. *C'est à dire*"—he corrected himself—"I ssink I am ready for you."

"Forget it. I'm not ready for you."

"Halt!" he said, and held up his hand.

I have seen many a bartender humor a customer, but I have never seen it the other way around. I thought perhaps the time had come now and I sat down on a stool.

"You're bombed out of your skull, *copain*. *Ivre mort*. You understand?"

"Not only that—I know!" He then took a deep breath and came hand over hand along the bar. "Since I am now ready for you, please *regardez le fruit de mon travail*."

The demonstration of the fruits of his labor was not easily followed. A shaker was variously filled with red vermouth, crème de menthe, gin, a prune, and a slice of tomato. Together with a cube of ice this mixture was then thrown away, shaker and all. The next step was similar to the first but with slight variations in the ingredients. I lost track. The process was repeated, perhaps with improvements. I can't really say. As long as he was happily busy, I started to think of other things.

"Drink it!" he said.

As a matter of fact, a champagne glass had materialized on the bar.

In it was a liquid that I did not care to contemplate, even though it looked almost like water. I had, after all, become acquainted with his technique.

"Drink it," he said again, somewhat more plaintively.

"*Copain*, I want to live. Thank you, no."

To say that he was offended does not cover the spectrum of his emotions.

His anger roiled, his grief boiled, and his sorrow uncoiled before me.

"Look at me," he said finally. "I am *ivre mort*, correct?"

"I would say so, yes."

"I have never been like this before."

"You would say so, perhaps."

"Correct. I endure this state after the laborious process of learning how to perfect this drink."

"It was difficult."

"And now it is perfect. Drink!" His eyes crossed with emotion while he waited for me.

A sacrificial feeling came over me. I lifted the chalice in the manner of Socrates and drank. Then, *mutatis mutandis*, it was suddenly a most excellent martini! I smiled with warmth and said, "*Copain*, I love you."

He shrugged his shrug, now that he had gotten his due, and then he said, "It is perfect, yes, but it should not have taken this advanced state of occupational drunkenness to achieve the masterwork. You must, however, thank your friend, who with infinite patience sat with me through all the trials, sample after sample, until perfection was reached."

"Just one damn minute," I said.

"I told you when you came in that you were not alone. He waits in the salon."

No other man on earth— I went to the salon and it was true. Stebbs was there.

He sat in the chair by the window where Plozzi had sat not so long ago, to witness the start of my job in Motana as Stebbs seemed to have come to witness the end.

Stebbs looked cheerful enough. "Just got here," he said.

"But with enough time left over to send one perfectly adequate human being to the snake pit."

"A weak person. You know what he and I did?"

"I just saw him."

"Weak, those wine drinkers. Nevertheless, through him I will now have left an indelible mark on Motana. Here he comes now. Watch it, *garçon!*"

The indelible mark was moving in a manner unpredictable toward us. He held aloft a deep metal tray marked Cinzano on which were the predictable martinis. Stebbs, anxious now, took the tray from the bartender and then put the glasses on the table.

The glasses were empty. Stebbs poured the contents of the tray into the glasses, turned the bartender around, and asked him to return in ten minutes. The bartender looked as if he had a complete anesthesia of eye, ear, nose, and throat, but as his trip to the bar and back would take at least all of ten minutes, I turned to Stebbs with the hope of no interruptions.

"How did you find me and why are you here?" I said.

"I asked at the best hotel, since you are on expenses, and they told me where you do your drinking. Here I am."

"Now, why?"

His martini was going down, and he started to look in the direction of the bar. "Because you're building the road, naturally. What's the matter with your mood, Manny? Something wrong?"

"Nothing that some information won't cure. One question, Stebbs. Where is that road going?"

He blinked at me, and I had to think of all the teaching he had been doing across the bar in the other room.

"Do you know or don't you?"

"Of course I know! Why in hell do you suppose I went to Tangiers to help set up the Motana Industrial Company?"

"So help me God, Stebbs, I don't know."

"Inscrutable Lobbe," he mumbled. "That road will run straight into the most magic mountain of this continent."

"And when you say the secret word, a thousand dancing girls will come out, each wearing two precious jewels."

"No," he said. "What's in there is uranium."

I had my surprise. And then I had the satisfaction of seeing a lot of things fall into place. Not all of them, but most of the puzzle was gone.

"And besides Lobbe," I said, "there are the Chinese. You know about them?"

"Lobbe told me just before I left."

"Then why in hell all that secrecy with me?"

"Because you, and not I, shlemiel, were going to do the negotiating for something Lobbe was forbidden to do. Remember Washington?"

"They told him not to touch the mountain. I finally gathered that. And I still don't know why."

"Because the Chinese were after it, too. The policy decision was made way up on high, designed to avoid premature frictions. What they worried about was an encounter between the U.S. and China on a level of internal African politics, about international propaganda and the world-wide deterioration of the U.S. image. Lobbe was warned off on penalty of severe sanctions. You know they can hurt him and you know how he hates to lose one penny. Where's that waiter?"

"In delirium tremens. Tell me something."

"The only acceptable cure—"

"Not that. You mean to tell me we were going to cure our deteriorating image by letting the Chinese grab that uranium?"

"Not quite. So far they cannot exploit that mountain."

"Guess again! They are going to build a road of their own to that mountain and they knew ahead of time that Essen was not going to finish that road for Lobbe!"

"They knew? Inscrutable."

"They knew Lobbe was after the project. I've been followed and I've been delayed by them since New York—in Essen, then in Rome, and now here. And when I suddenly outmaneuvered them, I just as suddenly got the word from Lobbe to cancel all efforts and advise you that you should dissolve whatever you started to do in Tangiers."

"Christ!" he said. "And just before I left, Lobbe told me he'd cancel out only if the U.S. Government got tipped off. The Chinese sent the tip-off."

"Who else? Only thing I don't get is why they are building an inland road instead of letting us finish ours and grabbing it with the same maneuver they used just now."

"Not inscrutable. You don't read much, do you?"

"I haven't read a Doctor Fu Manchu in years."

"Then, maybe you ought to. Look, we built Motana's harbor in Villeblanche under Foreign Aid. Wrapped around the gift was the usual proviso that no Communist power could use, exploit, etcetera, the facilities that we had given for free."

I thought that over for a while and realized that Yum Lee had therefore never intended to build or complete or snatch the road from Villeblanche to the mountain. He had stalled me, interrupted me, and finally pulled out the rug from under my efforts for some entirely different reason.

The contracts between Essen and Motana contained one formerly obscure provision: whoever completed the road received prior and/or preferred use of its facilities for any commercial or industrial purpose that might be negotiated separately or severally to the mutual advantage of the people of Motana and the builder.

"And if the U.S. government thinks that the Chinese can't deliver with exploitation equipment," I said to Stebbs, "then they're wrong! Dredge your sump of a memory and tell me what country lies southeast of here, what kind of government it has, whether or not it possesses a deep-water harbor, and whether that harbor is not open to the People's Republic of China."

"The way you ask the questions, Manny, you seem to know the answers."

"I do, but before just now none of those questions would even have occurred to me. The country has an industrial loan from China, it has a big harbor, it's about two thousand nautical miles closer on the Cape of Good Hope route from China and, for all I know, it has the mining equipment already stashed in the various industrial developments that have been built up there."

"Sir," said Stebbs to me, "are you imputing stupidity to the actions of my State Department?"

"Forfend! But ignorance, yes. It has a representative here whose claim to fame is that he once sold rusty pipes to the natives, and this without benefit of any knowledge of their language. It has no diplomatic posts of any sort in the country to the south because we don't even recognize its existence. It would sooner tell Lobbe to stay out than to try to get them in!"

"He has been known to be devious," said Stebbs.

"He's got a better reputation for straightforwardness with a clear profit motive than many a government I can name that claims to have nothing but a pure love motive."

"You seem angry, Manford."

"Shut up. Whatever happened to that zombie you created?"

We got up and found him behind the bar, where he usually worked. He was not working anymore. He was leaning there as if one of his legs had sunk into the ground.

"Every ten minutes," he kept mumbling.

The evidence of his labors was on the bar, a row of several trays, each holding two martini glasses. For a while Stebbs and I just sat there and did what we could to eliminate the evidence.

Somewhere along the line I got up. If I did not get up, I would never get up and also I would soon forget the idea that had come to me.

I left Stebbs and the bartender conversing in primitive French and went to the office of the club to use the phone. There, in an infuriating conversation with the operator, I learned that a call to New York would take upward of twelve hours to complete, whereas a call to Tangiers could be placed in less than one hour.

There was a holding company in Tangiers that maintained intimate relations with Lobbe Industriel. It was the company through which Stebbs had initiated the issue of stock for the Motana Industrial Company, and I knew that it had a direct line to Lobbe in New York. It could place a call there almost instantly.

The connection was completed in forty-five minutes, and as soon as Lobbe got on the line, I wondered why I had taken the trouble.

"Sir," I told him, "I have a plan."

"*Klootzak!*" he yelled. "Are you trying to ruin me?"

"No. I've spoken to Stebbs, which means that I finally know the situation. All I want—"

"*Klootzak—*"

"Mister Lobbe, don't use that word again. There is no scrambler here. Listen."

This time he kept still, though it seemed to me that I could hear his breathing.

"Have you told Essen to cancel yet?" I asked.

"Of course! *Instanter instantis!*"

I had thought so. The machines would be idle by now, and I would have no further authority with Podolski.

"I need some of the equipment to go into the bush. Will you authorize?"

He thought for a moment, presumably about the way it feels to be treated with Lobbe-type secrecy.

"Why, deWitt?"

"There is no scrambler here, Mister Lobbe."

"I see. How long?"

"A few hours."

"It is—unrelated?"

"It is safe."

"How do I know what you think is safe?"

"Listen," I yelled, "even the U.S. Government has given me twenty-four hours!"

Then he was very quick. "The Essen equipment for a few hours in the bush?"

"I'm going on safari."

"I will authorize instantly," he said. "Good hunting!"

We hung up.

I had a surprisingly difficult time getting Stebbs off that bar stool. All the evidence on the trays had not yet been eliminated. However, he sprung up immediately when I accused him of being drunk, insensible, and bombed out of his mind. We walked outside.

Then he saw Baby's car by the curb and he started to shake. "Manny," he said, "be honest with me. Tell me quickly what you see."

"Stop that and get in."

"Get in? Manny, you must help me, not taunt me, for heaven's sake!"

"What are you, one of those weak men, those wine drinkers?"

He plunged into the car, but when he saw Baby on the high chair behind the steering wheel, he immediately scrambled out the other side again.

This escape, however, produced further proof for Stebbs that his senses were disintegrating. A goat walked by, stepping right over Stebbs, who was now holding on to the ground. The animal's udder slapped Stebbs in the face.

"Manny!" he yelled, "how in heaven's name can she also have a beard?"

"A local custom," I said, pushing him back in the car. "You'll just have to get used to it."

"I don't want to get used to it." He collapsed on the seat.

"Look at me," I said.

"No. I keep seeing that other thing."

Baby turned around to take a hand in Stebbs' rehabilitation. "Do I still look the same?" he asked Stebbs.

"Heaven forgive me, but you do."

"So do you," said Baby. "And since you look still the same, and I still look the same, and since I am still in sane health with no fear of being overcome with idiocy, therefore your idiocy cannot exist because you exist and are the same as when you first appeared."

"Stop that!" said Stebbs with some vehemence. Then he looked at me. "Is he nuts or something?"

He was rehabilitated and, breathing a sigh of relief, I told Baby to drive to the airport.

"Who is flying?" Stebbs asked.

"You are. To Tangiers."

He did not want to go until I reminded him that Lobbe wanted him to stop all the stock issue arrangements that had been planned for the new Motana Industrial Company.

There were regular flights to Tangiers twice a day, and the next one would not leave for two hours. Before then Stebbs had to be functioning, and even longer before I wanted to be off on my remaining errands. I bought him a ticket from the man who also sold liquor and cakes.

"Let's have one for the road," I said.

Stebbs turned away as if he no longer considered me his friend. I decided that his attitude was promising. "I will explain this to you stepwise," I said.

"I don't want to hear about it. There is only one cure—"

"I wasn't going to talk about that."

"Thank God."

"Now, listen. I'm going through with the Motana project."

"Hah!" he said. "You and who else?"

"You."

He was now, in terms of his own body chemistry, more than halfway sober. I could tell by his patronizing sneer.

"And with whose money, since it isn't going to be yours and most certainly not mine?"

"Lobbe's."

"You know something, deWitt? I think you are trying to drive me to drink."

"There is nothing underhanded about it, by the way. He will accept and agree—if you make sense."

"Insults will get you exactly nowhere."

"All right. I'll have to ask Lobbe for a better man—somebody who can hold his liquor."

"All right, you son of a bitch. Let's hear it."

"In Tangiers, Stebbs, go immediately to the holding company and call Lobbe. This needs straight-line and scrambler."

"Gadgets don't impress him, deWitt."

"Only what you will tell him with the gadgets." I noticed that he was getting interested and went on. "Tell him that I am getting a bona fide franchise from the Motana President for the digging of rocks. Specification: rocks for making the roadbed. This is supportable because Essen will substantiate it, or else they would never have taken the job."

"You're serious?"

"Completely."

"And uranium comes in the shape of rocks, too, I seem to remember."

"Don't worry about the switch from one kind of rock to the other. So far we are only interested in continuing the road project without interference and in obtaining the franchise. State will change its mind about pushing Lobbe around once they learn that the Chinese are ready to move in. I'll fix that end of it."

"Don't worry me like that, Manny!"

"Don't worry."

"It is my distinct worry, however, that Lobbe will not want Motana Industries to exist in any shape or form whatsoever."

"Then dismantle it. It's only a paper outfit so far, anyway, indicating intent. Tear up the paper, and there's the evidence of your intent—I mean Lobbe's intent—to pull out of the Motana operation."

"For real evidence that will convince State, shyster, he will also have to pull Essen off the job."

"Which means I cannot get a mining franchise, since that is contingent on the agreement and performance of building the road."

"Exactly. So how are you going to go ahead without Lobbe's dying from government sanctions?"

"Tell him I can get him a franchise for digging rocks. The price is small. The price is safe."

"But that would be a bald-faced lie."

"Quiet. In return for the tremendous gain of obtaining the franchise he must do only two things. He must under no circumstances pull Essen off the job."

"*Gewalt*—"

"The road is for digging rocks now, rocks for a road!"

"Now hit me with the other one quickly."

"And Essen must transfer—for services rendered etcetera—their option on the mining franchise to me."

"*What?*"

"Private U.S. citizens like me could not care less to be hit with U.S. Government sanctions. Therefore, let Essen give me their option, and I will get the franchise from Motana, while Lobbe is safe."

"With these stakes," said Stebbs thoughtfully, "Lobbe might bite."

"Look at all the safeguards I'm giving him."

"But for how long are they any good till they're shot full of holes?"

"Tell Lobbe I need only twenty-four hours. If he keeps Essen in, if he transfers the franchise to me, then all I'll need are twenty-four hours."

"You're insane!"

"Lobbe understands that. And he'll be thinking of the stakes. Got all that clear to make a strong argument?"

"Got it."

"Try hard."

"I am built of iron."

"I know. Except for the liver. In terms of getting to Tangiers, calling him, talking it up, you should be able to wire your answer to me no later than eight hours from now. All the paper work can be postdated. But I must have Lobbe's Yes or No in eight hours. Send it c/o President Matan. I'll be with him."

"Will do. And what will you be doing while I do your work for you?"

"Get up enough confidence to do the rest of the job."

I left him sipping a cup of coffee, and then Baby barreled me back into town because I had to find Podolski.

We found him sooner than I expected. His yellow jeep was parked by the telegraph office, and a big snake of his equipment was moving slowly toward the harbor. His cancellation from Essen had already come through.

I walked into the telegraph office and saw him arguing with the clerk. They had no language problems. One was yelling in Motanesque, and the other was yelling in Polish, but they were not listening to each other. They were trading insults. When Podolski saw me, he started yelling at me from sheer momentum.

"Five hours ago I get a cancellation from Essen!"

It dovetailed. He had been told to pull out at about the same time Lobbe had told me to pull out on the phone in the consul's office.

"And," he said, "the same message said you were fired."

"I was. But I'm hired again."

"That's what it says right here in the radiogram—no, it says I should lend you my equipment in order to go on *safari!*"

"You don't believe it?"

"That clerk made a mistake, I tell you! It makes no sense!"

"That's why I was looking for you. We both got the same message, but the only mistake was that Essen sent you the order in code. Come outside. I'll explain it to you."

He breathed as if he were running a race and was losing it. We sat down on the steps of the building, and I pointed at his equipment, which was moving by in the distance.

"When they sent you the cancellation, they didn't tell you to move your stuff out, like to the job in the Central African Republic?" I was sure they had not, because they simply passed on Lobbe's instant stop order. The timing told me that.

"No," he said.

"There you are. The confusion, as you once suggested, Podolski, is political. Hence the code. What they should have simply told you in this second radiogram is: COUNTERMAND, DEWITT REINSTATED—the bit about lending me equipment implies that—AND UNDER NO CIRCUMSTANCES MOVE YOUR EQUIPMENT OFF THE JOB."

"But I got an order to stop work!"

"Right. Just leave the equipment sit on the job."

"This sounds like madness. You see that, Mister deWitt?"

"Yes. It is not good for your pride in the work. Now, the reason you got the second telegram is to move gradually back from madness and into the regular work-a-day again. For the moment it won't look much like building a road, but that's where we're going. You want to hear about it?"

"Just tell me what to do, please."

"Fine. First of all, get all the equipment back on the road."

He nodded and looked patient.

"Then I need a jeep so I can drive to Miesville."

"You can take mine."

"And then I want you to take several bulldozers and some of those things with the big belly and the airplane wheels into the bush. You know what the bush is like here?"

"Yes."

"How fast can you move that kind of equipment—traveling, I mean, in that terrain?"

"Earthmover, empty, can do about sixty kilometers there. Bulldozers on flatbeds, maybe forty. Smaller wheels, you know."

Yum Lee, I considered, had about half a day's head-start. Since he was traveling with overloaded pickups and would certainly stop for the night, the timing was not bad. Besides, Yum Lee was supposed to be stopping to drill holes.

"By this evening, Podolski, I want you and a goodish line of that equipment to catch up with Yum Lee's safari. Get a guide from van Voos. When you reach Yum Lee, tell him this: Since he caused us to lose the road job, we would be interested in selling him some or all of the equipment at a very cheap price. Understand?"

"No. But I can remember."

"Fine. Then tell him that you have brought these samples—"

"Why so many?"

"Not your worry, yet. Tell him you brought a generous amount of equipment for his inspection and for his men to try out. They won't be operators, but you will have one for each machine along, to act as teachers. Tomorrow at nine o'clock I will come from Miesville with others to join you, and at that time I want a Chinese at the controls of each vehicle. You carry a two-way?"

"In the jeeps."

"Take one. I will look for you by air and will talk to you then about how to carry out the details."

"What details?"

"I was just coming to that." And I told him the story his men should tell and then I told him a story that reminded him of the Polish Blitz. Except this time he laughed about it.

Before I left for Miesville in Podolski's jeep, I made a phone call to Inge at the hotel. She was out but had left me a message, which the clerk read with obvious relish. It's gist was that if I preferred to spend a drunken afternoon with a creepy friend who had been seen to fall through cars in order to attack native goats, then she, in turn, would spend her time in the company of unspecified friends of her own and in occupations that didn't seem to be of much interest to me, anyway.

Not exactly cheered by this message and with a foreboding that much more had to be done than I would ever have time for, I left word that I hoped to be back tomorrow and drove with Baby to the Place de Safari. There I discovered that the exit road toward the hinterland had been widened into a big, untidy gash. Podolski and his equipment, at any rate, seemed well on their way.

Once in the bush country, we had a thin moon overhead. Its light made an otherwise boring monotony of bushland quite charming. Sometimes there were strange trees and low thickets, which Baby advised to avoid.

How he found Miesville I don't know. Three hours out of Villeblanche we came over a rise, and there was a red glow below us, as if a house had burned down.

"It is the way the king seals a bargain," said Baby. "He burns his house down."

"Expensive custom."

"He does not seal many bargains. His subjects don't want him to."

"Democratic king."

"The subjects have to build the new house. The custom insures that new agreements are not made rashly."

When we came through the trees behind which Miesville lay, the custom appeared even more benign. Most of the houses along the dirt road were made of woven fronds, tied poles, and similar year-round harvest materials. There were two obvious deviations from this prehistoric norm. One was a compact little power plant that hugged the near side of the eternal mountain. The source of water power for the plant was not visible, but the plant's presence explained where the prospective Lobbe mine would derive its power. The mountain itself would provide for its own degutting.

"Very good machine," said Baby. "It hums all the time."

"Much too big for Miesville," I said. There were only occasional houses that had electric wiring run into their roofs.

"It was a present to the king from a rich relative in America," said Baby. And when Lobbe had put it there, he must have discovered the uranium.

"Generous man, that rich relative," I said to Baby.

"Very. It is a family custom for the king to send a present to the relative every five years. Mats. Carvings—one time he sent a statue of stone."

"Stone from the mountain?"

"Yes. And that time, out of gratitude, the rich relative sent the light machine as a return present."

Dear Uncle Hans. He gets a present of carved stone and he discovers that the stone contains a goodly amount of uranium. Right away he gives a present big enough to run a mine.

"Who is this generous relative, Baby?"

"Family taboo to talk about him."

The other out-of-character sight was the house where Baby told me to stop. It was a smaller version of Government House in Villeblanche and presumably it duplicated the other one's function for the *quartier intérieur*. At first sight its function seemed to be to offer a flat roof for the landing of the government helicopter.

The present function of the front hall was something else. Hung by its heels were the charred remains of a cow carcass of some sort, and the litter on the floor showed that guests had been eating there. An open double door at one side showed a room bare of furniture but full of prone bodies. Some of them moved, some of them burped, and a number of them were steadily snoring.

"The civilized guests," said Baby, "always go upstairs after a function."

We went upstairs. In the equivalent of the President's chambers there was a little fire on the parquet, just a small, ceremonial fire, and some mournful ceremonial dancing was going on. After seeing the remains of the feast downstairs, I could understand the low-key mood.

In the counterpart of Room 313 of Government House I got my first glimpse of the civilized guests Baby had mentioned. The room was brightly lit, there was Western furniture, and the crush of people and the din of their talk was like any *de rigueur* Washington party. I looked immediately for President Matan, but my search was unpleasantly interrupted. Yum Lee, as pastel as ever, came toward me with his whisky glass.

"You seem surprised, Mister deWitt," he said, and smiled.

I was also disappointed. A lot of the safari plans for tomorrow had been directed at him. And then I had a ghastly thought. What if he had brought his safari party with him and Podolski was trailing it right into town!

"I thought you were on safari," I said with great effort to sound normal.

"They will slowly continue on, and then I will rejoin them," said Yum Lee. "But I could not let the opportunity go by to join this sort of gathering. It is more informal than your day at the Diet, I grant you, but its function, for me, is similar." He smiled, inviting my understanding.

Slow-moving, soft-sell Yum Lee had, quick as a fox, taken this opportunity to do some spadework of his own. I had no idea how to handle this surprising situation.

"You are late for the formal festivities," said Yum Lee. "May I show you where the drinks are?"

"Cup of hemlock? No, thank you. You were not late, I gather."

"Never. I always anticipate you, have you noticed?"

"I certainly have, Yum Lee."

"But it is clever of you how you always outguess me just one step behind."

"Not this time," I said. "I did not know you were here."

"But you know why I am here."

He was enjoying himself. He took my arm most affectionately and guided me to a niche with a love seat in it. It was an inappropriate setting, but Yum Lee wanted seclusion.

"You knew that I sent your government the evidence that has caused them to persuade your Mister Lobbe that he should drop all plans for a road."

"I'm surprised you did not send it sooner."

"It was not convincing enough until the Essen contracts were actually signed."

He enjoyed the talking, and I needed time to think.

"Though it seems," he went on, "that at the time of your impassioned speech in front of the Diet you did not know that I meant to build a road through the hinterland."

For the moment I did not have to answer because President Matan and a small entourage were coming our way. It now struck me that with Matan in the conversation I might get my sights up again and then let go with both barrels.

There were formal greetings, which were disposed with quickly because I was not the only one who wanted to get down to business.

Matan was quite irritated. "What, may I ask, was this nonsense about well-drilling equipment, Mister deWitt?"

"Yum Lee just explained to me for the first time what the real purpose of the machinery was. You too have finally been told?"

"He brought one of the pieces along to show us," said Matan. He was disgruntled about having been so much in the dark, and I could understand that. But his obvious displeasure was not with Yum Lee, but with me.

"You and I signed a contract," he said, "a contract with a franchise clause attached. I assume that you know by now what that road is for?"

I bowed and said, "Now that secrecy from my government is no longer an issue, I too have been told."

"Of course it's no longer an issue," said Yum Lee. "His government is no longer deceived and has forbidden the honoring of the contract."

"Most awkward politically, you know that, Mister deWitt? I blame that on you! I had no idea you were under governmental pressure not to build that road. Do you realize we have Foreign Aid relations with your government and must act grateful?"

"I know, Mister President. However, you do not seem to know that I am under no governmental pressure whatsoever."

"What's that?" said Yum Lee.

"And in that case," asked the President, "why did you stop work?"

"It was not our government that temporarily disrupted work progress." I paused for the vacuum that the listener cannot fill. They all had to hang on my explanation. "I am prepared to finish the road. I am prepared to fulfill all franchise conditions, and, Mister President, my government is prepared to *protect* my contractual interests with a show of force!"

"Your government—protect—" Yum Lee did not know whether to laugh or to cry. For a fact, I did not know either.

"You are aware," I said to Matan, "that our Seventh Fleet is even now off your shores? I am confident of their assistance."

"A moment, a moment, please!" said Yum Lee. He took a deep breath and said like a teacher, "Is it or is it not a fact that you had to stop work on the road?"

"Yes. A fact."

"And that cancellation was due to your government's intervention?"

"Sorry. Not a fact."

"Then, what in the devil is all this?" said Matan, much too loud for politeness.

"Sabotage," I said.

It meant nothing to anyone until I looked at Yum Lee.

Yum Lee, not knowing if I were a fool or a madman, started to giggle with indecision. When he was through, I turned back to Matan.

"Mister President. I have road machines; Yum Lee does not, to say nothing of the fact that he cannot use your harbor."

"I am aware of all that."

"But he must build a road to obtain the mining franchise."

"He will if you cancel out on your road contract. He will build in this *quartier*."

"When?"

"When he gets his machines."

"He has got them, Mister President! He has, under threat of arms and with falsification of fact to you and my government, found the time and opportunity to obtain machines. He has stolen mine!"

"Preposterous—" said Yum Lee.

"In a way, yes. But even now several of the stolen machines are following in the path of his so-called safari! Do you think, Mister President, that I would claim all this if I could not show you the proof?"

There was a great deal more—mostly loud sounds from Yum Lee, but one half hour later I was on the roof with the still unconvinced Matan.

"The proof will be in the presence of the machines," I stressed again. "And the proof of my government's cooperation with you, Mister President, and with me as a threatened American citizen—that proof is in your hands alone."

He still hesitated about the last part. I could see the sweat on his forehead. It glistened in the light from the cabin as we stood next to the helicopter.

"Why don't you call the Admiral of the fleet yourself?" he asked.

"Because he does not know me and because he has not had reason to ask for clarification from Washington. He would have to do so in my case, and it would take time. He does not have to do so if you, President of a friendly power, invite him." I had to take a deep breath before adding the threat. "On the other hand, if it later came out that you, host to an American who is threatened, that you, head of a government that is recipient of American aid, that you delayed, in behalf of a Chinese conspiracy—"

There was more of the same on the trip to Villeblanche, but I did not have to say much else once the pilot had found the campsite on the safari route. Below us was a veritable herd of construction equipment, which dwarfed the other parked vehicles.

"I want to go down," said Matan.

"And get shot at? That's why we must make the plans for nine o'clock tomorrow morning."

It was actually already tomorrow. It was three in the morning. Shortly afterward, in Villeblanche, the President of Motana spoke to the Fleet via the government transmitter.

He did it well. He beseeched a friendly power; he shuddered with the thought of a foreign take-over. He asked for a demonstration of intent.

The answer was positive.

With this demonstration of intent by the fleet, he reciprocated with proofs of his own good faith. He signed Yum Lee's deportation order, and he drafted a franchise permitting me to dig rocks once the road was cut through.

It was now about five in the morning, and the main part of my work was over. Nonetheless, the show of force in the bush four hours later was satisfying to watch.

As seen from the ground, where government heads and some delegates were also emplaced, the jet fighters seemed to scream with anger as they passed at eight hundred feet. They made five passes. Chinese were running every which way, and after them came Podolski's men, shouting like liberated POW's. The story they had to tell was suitably harrowing. How they had been forced into the cabs, how they had driven at gunpoint.... And when that was over and after the Navy had left, the construction workers got themselves a bonus when they took the Chinese on.

The franchise was ratified the next day, but I was no longer in Motana. Plozzi had received an accidental cut on his head and Inge's solicitude told its own tale of what had happened while I was besting Yum Lee. There were no angry words. I was grateful to Plozzi for helping me and I told Inge I hoped we would meet again when she came to New York.

I left Motana, even before Mister Bliss could have counted my twenty-four hours.

He called me mennekin and gave me a schnapps. He did not talk to the goat on the wall but relaxed both of us with a song by Buxtehude. He is in a holiday mood when he plays the piano in your presence.

"Relax, mennekin. Everything worked."

"*I* worked."

"I pay you," he said, and laughed.

It is hard to resent him when he laughs like that, and then he talked about the road going well and he laughed again when he explained how the State Department had changed its tune after the Navy Department had proclaimed its proud intervention.

"And now," said Lobbe, "a little something like from a father."

"That sounds like you are about to pull me up short," I said. "I felt throughout that I was following your example of finesse very closely, Mister Lobbe."

"You tried. I am flattered."

"You are welcome, Mister Lobbe."

"But, then, it becomes unbelievable to believe," he said across his folded hands, "that you make little mistakes."

"Like how little?"

"Like the telegram you asked Stebbs to send and you never asked for it."

I was speechless for a moment, but of course he was right.

"You know that could have been such a gigantic fly in the ointment that there would not be enough salve left to salve anything?"

"It was an omission. I don't think it was any riskier than most of the commissions."

"That is bad, too. I am coming to all those now."

"It was part of the entire complexion of the job, Mister Lobbe, since everything had to be done on the spur of the moment—because of my ignorance of the darker facts."

"*Toi, toi, toi,*" he said. "Does that crock hold water? What kind of crock is this, Manny?"

"That crock is my considered point of view."

"I am not talking schwindel," he said with a straight face. "I am talking good business. You listening?"

I nodded, hoping he would run down before too long.

"I ask you, do we go around and finagle a friendly power? Do we go around and irritate hostile powers? Or is it normal practice, I ask you, to dumboozle your own country's naval power into a conspiracy?"

He might have gotten away with this guilty speech, but then he had to top it. "I ask you, Manford."

I blew. "You're damn well going to make money on it!" I said.

And then he yelled, "I damn well will make money on it!"

I got up, feeling calm, and it felt right and good to slip it to him. It had not occurred to me before.

"The franchise, Mister Lobbe, is in my name."

"*What's that talk like from a counterspy?*"

"I said, the franchise happens—"

He was way ahead of me. "You are in my employ, and anything you—"

"I was not in your employ, I remind you, when I obtained *my* franchise."

It was Lobbe, and I should not have been surprised when his face creased up and he burst out laughing.

"I love you, Manny," he said. "That was good!"

I began to wonder if he were pulling my leg.

"You want cash or stock?" he asked.

I had not thought about it.

"Take stock," he said. "I have more stock than cash, and the stock will be more than cash."

We had a friendly talk about it, all very straight, and then I agreed to take stock.

Lobbe can be happy about seemingly opposite things. He had been happy when I had pulled the finesse, and now he was happy because he had come back with one. I did not know it at the time, but the stock was almost worthless and would be for quite a while.

But that did not matter then in his office. I felt damn good about the deal except that something else was still bothering me. I could not put my finger on it.

"Damn it!" I yelled when it came to me. "I completely forgot to pay Baby! Do you know that?"

He turned to the picture window so that I could not see his face. "I know that, Manny. I took care of it." Then he looked at me over his shoulder. "You did not know he was a Lobbe?"

THE END

CODE NAME GADGET
by Peter Rabe

CHAPTER 1

The man for whom I work, Mijnheer Hans Lobbe, is the head of an enterprise which is modestly known as Lobbe Industriel. The modesty ends with the name. Since World War II Lobbe Industriel has been very big in synthetics, but in view of the company's three hundred years of existence, this preoccupation is only one of a great many. In the Lobbe tradition, there are many pastures but, in the same tradition, nothing is let go of that has once been acquired. I was in Honduras renegotiating the lobster-bed rights which Grandfather Gaenserich Lobbe had acquired in 1888. How Gaenserich had managed that little deal in the midst of a bloody revolution is a tale to curdle the blood of any ordinary robber baron. My own job, on the other hand, was much simpler. It consisted of a six-hour siesta per day and one courtesy visit per day to an official whose rank, name, and influence shall remain obscure, and since that visit never occurred until five minutes before his office closed I would take him and his family of eight to dinner with monotonous regularity.

As a matter of procedure, this rapprochement went on for five days, once every year. Then one talked business. This business, so ran my briefing, consisted of an argument about the size of the bribe.

None of this made any sense. The bribe never varied more than one hundred dollars either way, the lobster-bed franchise brought in less than the amount of Lobbe's monthly Manhattan telephone bill, and my talents as one of Lobbe's lawyers were allowed to remain in disuse. But Lobbe had been very fond of old Gaenserich. I, for my part, was perfectly willing to enjoy the fruits of his sentimentality. Six-hour siestas were new to me, but I was learning. On the second day I could sit on the balcony of my hotel room and not fidget for an entire hour. I knew the rooftops of Tegucigalpa better than the city itself. On the third day I was preparing for a no-fidget marathon to shame the previous one, arming myself for the ordeal with a supply of rum, lemon, and a bucket of ice, when the phone rang.

I had not known that this phone could ring. Room service, for example, was obtained by hollering down the resounding stairs of the hotel. I knew this for a fact, because that is how I had got the rum. But now the phone rang.

"*Dígame!*" I said with the proper impatience used during siesta.

It was the overseas operator, and she did not bother to test my Spanish.
"Mister Manford deWitt?"

"*Aquí.*"

"I have a collect call for you from Miss Moon in New York, U.S.A. Will you accept the charges?"

"No." Then I hung up.

If this seemed like rudeness, then my next move must have looked like insanity. I walked out of the room and never came back. I was in New York at six o'clock the next morning.

It is a reflection of Mijnheer Lobbe's personality that there are few ground rules for the guidance of his employees. The very few standard procedures which do exist are not found in print. The collect-call-telephone procedure, for example, was explained to me by Miss Moon, Lobbe's exec secretary if not his more benign alter ego, on the occasion of my first overseas job for the company.

I was to go to Beirut at that time, negotiating mightily over oil rights and barter arrangements all the way down there on the plane, and as soon as I had reached my hotel there had been this phone call. It meant: Leave instantly with a minimum of fanfare.

Five hours after my departure from Beirut two of the men I was to meet—one a minister of commerce, the other the brother of a king—were bombed to bits by an unemployed postal clerk who had been imported for the occasion from Yugoslavia.

The telephone signal had saved my life. Lobbe, upon my return, had put it the other way around. "You saved me the embarrassment of a lot of explanations by not getting killed over there, mennekin. I like the way you run fast."

But now, at Kennedy Airport at six o'clock in the morning, I felt safe, bushed, ignorant, and totally unconcerned with further procedure. I knew that my replacement would already be in Honduras. Still, it is part of the telephone bit that you check in, regardless of the hour, upon arrival. But it had been a harrowing night flight. It had been the untimely loss of a wonderful, undemanding assignment. As I shivered in the four a.m. April cold, I thought I would damn well use this zillion-dollar installation for at least one cup of coffee before I made my call.

"Martini," I said to the man behind the counter. I would look for the coffee shop later.

I do not ask for a martini at four o'clock in the morning as a matter of course. But it is different at an airport. The customer might have had a harrowing night flight. He might be on his way home and to bed, time having lost its reality in flight. Besides, he is not likely to see the bartender again.

The bartender shrugged dully when I gave my order. He was a big middle-aged man with the standardized nondescriptness of most terminal servants.

"Takes all kinds," he said.

I let that go by. I would of course never see him again. He brought me the martini and said, "I got a message for you."

"You what?"

"Your name's deWitt, isn't it?"

I had the glass halfway up and set it down again. "Would you repeat that, please?"

"Why? Don't you know your own name?"

I picked the glass up and let him wait for his answer. He did not wait for it.

"She calls up and says I should look for a guy with a tan like he's been on vacation and wearing an ice-cream suit, probably wrinkled. And if he's wearing a tie it's hanging out of his jacket."

I tucked the tie in.

"How come your ice-cream suit's wrinkled?" he asked.

"Because I detest synthetics."

"You maybe feel there's something unnatural about them?"

"I work for the man who makes them."

"He knows you work for the cotton lobby?"

"Look," I said. "I don't want to seem pushy about this, but you did say there was a message."

"That's right."

"Were you supposed to give it to me?"

"She said you'd show here right off the plane and you should wait."

"Of course. Till doomsday. Just long enough, it would seem, for you to get to the point."

"Kind of jumpy, aren't you?"

"That's right. I go to pieces when somebody calls me up at six o'clock in the morning. What if I had been asleep?"

"I think you need a drink."

"Of course. However, that has nothing...."

"Her name was Moon," he said. "That make you feel any better?"

It did not. I felt spied upon, put upon, and no longer safe in my ignorance. It occurred to me that the telephone procedure might not have been a move to save me from assassination but instead was preparatory to sending me off somewhere else, unbriefed, without luggage, my only qualification that I was not expected. The high-handed manner of removing me from my earlier scene of inactivity was typically Lobbe. I reached for my martini and saw that now there were two.

"Typically deWitt," I heard behind me. "Two martinis at six o'clock in the morning when for everybody else one is quite enough."

I turned around and looked at Stebbs without a hint of approval. I know Stebbs well and he is my friend and it is because of this knowledge and friendship that I try to avoid him except when we are able to drink together.

Stebbs works for Lobbe in the Investments Division. He looks like an assistant professor of higher mathematics who finds himself substituting in a class on woodcraft. The hour and circumstances this morning enhanced the impression of inappropriateness, and I would not have been surprised to learn that he had kept on his pyjamas under the tweeds he was wearing.

"Ah well," I said. "How important can it be," and turned back to my two martinis.

"I'll tell you," said Stebbs and sat down next to me. "After breakfast."

One of my martinis was gone and Stebbs sat there making a face. He had grabbed up the first one, the warm one.

"Would you like another one?" asked the bartender.

"Bullshot," Stebbs said to him.

The bartender looked at me, as if for help, but in view of his opening remark to me I looked right through him. He pulled himself together and said, "Sir, I'd just as soon give you what you said, but you can't use any of that crazy language around here."

Stebbs looked at me, but on account of his introductory remark to me, I gave him no help. Stebbs is very long, and when he leaned on his elbows and toward the bartender on the other side, they were almost nose to nose.

"A bullshot," said Stebbs, "is hot bouillon with a shot of vodka in it. Then you drop a raw egg in."

"O great day in the morning," said the bartender to the ceiling, and then he went away to make the thing.

"Now that you're here," I said to Stebbs, "why don't you tell me why Lobbe sent you."

"Moon sent me. Lobbe is in Spain and you're going to London in forty-five minutes. I'm here to give you the stock-transfer authorizations you'll need there."

"London? Right now?" I laughed sort of a laugh, not knowing what else to do. Then I tied it all up with, "I left my luggage in Honduras. I got no clothes."

"I mean to ask you," said Stebbs. "How come your suit is wrinkled like that?"

"Harrowing night flight."

Stebbs looked up from the sleeve of my jacket and grinned at me.

"Rat fink," he said. "That's pure *cotton*."

The bartender dropped the raw egg on his shoe.

"In any event," I said, "an ice-cream suit in London in the middle of April...."

"Will have to do."

"I was pulled out of Honduras to dash over to England where McEvoy in Lobbe's London office is perfectly capable of swinging any local deal all by himself."

"Precisely," said Stebbs. "Which is why Lobbe picked you from Outer Obscurity. Nobody knows you in London, nobody knows you left Honduras, should they care to ask, and last but not least you don't look like a negotiator."

I did not ask him what I looked like but I asked him what I was buying.

"You are buying," he said, "the Gadget."

The bartender dropped another raw egg on his other shoe.

What I knew about the Gadget undoubtedly did not do the invention justice, though for me it was a sufficient yardstick of its importance that Mijnheer Lobbe had been trying to buy it for a number of years. So had duPont, whose name, in Lobbenese, was mud, and also I.G. Farben, whose name, in Lobbenese, was *Dreck*. The electronic apparatus could be programmed to record the relative purity of any compound contained in commercial compositions. It could be keened up to detect the presence of chemical elements. It could save Lobbe Industriel nine million dollars per year in quality control alone; not to mention the reduced competitive price Lobbe could charge for his products; not to mention that he could prevent his competitors from doing the same thing to him.

"Who am I," I said to Stebbs, "to buy a gadget which the inventor has refused to sell for these many years?"

"Old Crevassette is dead," said Stebbs.

"Oh. That was clever of Lobbe."

"Crevassette died in Spain, on vacation. Lobbe was there at the time."

"Fiendishly clever, wouldn't you say?"

"He was negotiating."

"Knowing Lobbe...."

"Shut up a minute, will you, Manny? Anyway, Crevassette's brother was there and you know how relatives are, because as soon as old Crevassette died...."

"I know how relatives are. So what's the rush with London?"

"The Crevassette outfit is incorporated there. And the option which Lobbe was able to buy is good for only twenty-four hours."

"I guess I did *not* know how relatives are. Who else is after it?"

"You know. Mud and Dreck. But they don't know of the death yet."

At that moment the bartender stepped up.

"Here," he said, "is your bull thing."

The drink was in a soup plate and looked like scrambled eggs *au brun*. I cannot repeat what Stebbs said at that point. It covered the spectrum from Mud to Dreck.

CHAPTER 2

I left Kennedy Airport around seven in the morning with a folder of stock-transfer authorizations under my arm, some nutty explanations by Stebbs in my head, a martini inside of me, and the one consolation in all this Lobbe-type suddenness that I had a reservation at Claridge's and would commence the pleasure of that stay in about six hours. I never got to Claridge's.

It was part of the proper navigational procedure when London Airport shuts down on account of the fog. The intervening delay was spent in Shannon, Ireland.

I consider that place the most inhospitable stopover point in the world, aside from a seat on a picket fence. You are assaulted with an incomprehensible language disguised as English, with useless souvenirs disguised as authentic merchandise, and with hard plankings disguised as benches. After much shivering in the customary afternoon winds of Shannon comes nighttime. It is an Irish *Walpurgisnacht*. The wind shrieks and howls and the sky rains Druid swords. The lights turn dim, the people on benches turn into black, inhuman shapes, suggesting death and menace. The bartender, who had two little eyes, sharp as icepicks, kept darting loving glances out at the roiling weather, as if he were just longing to be out there. Maybe he did have a date with a warlock and I was keeping him from it.

"Hola," I said. "I do want another drink."

What he saw, what he heard, was beyond mere human ken. An unearthly excitement shone at the points of the icepicks and his black, Celtic locks danced about.

"Hola," I said again, "when shall we two meet again? In thunder, lightning, or in rain?"

He looked at me as if he had just come up from fifty fathoms and I shoved the martini glass at him.

"Another one ye be wanting?"

I did not know the first person counterpart to "ye" so just nodded. Then I heard what his elfin ears must have been picking up in that witch-brew weather out there, the frantic whine of two jet engines coming down.

"Some wild Irishman landing in the spring weather out there?" I said conversationally.

He jabbed at me with the icepicks and pushed the drink at me.

"You don't like martinis," I guessed at him.

"Naw."

"That's because of that foreign-type olive, I bet. But have you ever tried it with a raw potato in it?"

"Really now," he said.

The jet was clearing its throats at the end of the runway, wherever that was, and then came rolling our way with the sound of a thousand fifers fifing. It swung smartly into the aura of wet light from the building and stopped. I could not tell the make because it was a sleek, private job, possibly owned by some insane Argentinian beef baron who liked Ireland in April. I turned back to my bartender.

"Does he come often?"

"Who?"

"The beef baron."

He said something which I was just going to ask him to translate into English when he pinpointed his eyes ever so slightly to one side of my ear. I particularly dislike that look. It is as if the observer does not acknowledge my presence; in fact, tells me that I am not really there. His eyes widened to their widest possible dimensions, which gave him a wide-awake look. Also his jaw sagged. I felt a violent gust of wind lick me across the back of the neck and now, I thought, the warlock was coming to fetch the bartender bodily.

"*Vat, vat, vat* do I see loafing around when I am not expected?"

I whirled around, though I did not need confirmation. That was Mijnheer Lobbe Himself, with jokes to mislead you into thinking that he felt benign, with his unspeakable accent to mislead you into thinking that he did not know English very well. He wore a large loden cape and came flapping rapidly toward the bar.

Lobbe is not very tall, but he is very round. He has thin hair, both white and blond, which he wears long enough to make you forget that he is a militant executive, if not executioner. He has mild blue eyes with very light lashes. This makes him look like a barnyard animal, which is also misleading. He has a Buddha mouth, denoting a state of grace and inner calm, and that too is a deception. He has furthermore several chins, their number varying with his mood.

"I thought you were in Spain," I said.

"I know you thought I was in Spain," he said. Then he pulled two barstools together and sat down, one cheek on each.

"Offer you a drink, sir?"

He looked at my martini and made a face like a Javanese demon mask.

"*Pfui*," he said and looked up at the bartender, who was standing right opposite. "*Wirt!*" Lobbe said, very loud. "I want some Focking!"

Lobbe tends to have a petrifying effect upon the help at any time, but what he did to the bartender was positively biblical. The man turned into a pillar of salt.

"Well?" said Lobbe after one second of patience. "You maybe stand there like that because you are trying to tell me something? You never heard of it, *peut-être?*"

"Sir," said the bartender with caution. "I am a worldly man, but I am not used to such language around here."

"*Vat, vat, vat?* In Holland we have it all the time!"

"I believe that."

"Mennekin," Lobbe said to me. "Explain to this native what I want. Maybe he doesn't master the English so good."

"A double shot of Wynand Focking," I said. "It's a gin."

As the bartender left, muttering, Lobbe hitched himself around on his stools.

"Mennekin," he said. "I come all the way from London to tell you how glad I am you are here."

"I am here because London Airport is closed," I pointed out to him.

"I know. Only an absolute madman would fly me out, but I knew you were stuck here, so I came."

I was convinced this largess was only half the story, but he was not yet through conning me. He drove one massive elbow into my side and said, "You like the plane?"

I looked at the sleek thing and nodded.

"You'll love it," he said.

"What's that?"

"You and the madman are going back to London."

"What are you saying, sir!"

"*Wirt!*" bellowed Lobbe. "What happened to my...."

"We don't have it," said the bartender very rapidly. "It seems it is an off-brand."

"I've never heard it called *that* before," said Lobbe. He pitter-pattered his fingers up and down on the bar. "I think," he said, "now you give me bullshot."

The bartender slowly closed his eyes.

"It's all right," I told him. "It's a drink."

"Yes." He kept his eyes closed. "Like the other one."

I explained that it was not like the other one and, for the second time that day, told how a bullshot is made. Lobbe sat there with surprising patience.

"Mennekin," he said with suspicious calm, "it is very nice of you to come all the way from Honduras to explain to the natives here at great length and at no small cost to me what it is I want from this man."

"Sorry, sir."

"I will now tell you why you are really here."

"To buy you the Gadget," I said.

"*Hemel,* I hope so!" I was surprised at the concern in his voice. Then he leaned closer. "Something is wrong!"

His breath smelled faintly of cloves and his pink jowls smelled of bergamot. It was rather a pleasant combination.

"I am in Algeciras," he said, "to negotiate once again with that *crème de la merde* Crevassette, when *pfft*, he dies."

"That is rather bad."

"I am in Algeciras," he said, "to negotiate once again where he goes for the crazy experiments he likes to do...."

"Like the Gadget?"

"Something else this time. He hides there under the rare name of Smith in his villa and then he goes *pfft*. Across the bay in Gibraltar they point all the guns at Spain. You know how nervous they are."

"You mean he blew up?"

"He, house, everything, leaving me stunned, leaving the grieving brother also stunned."

"Is that how you managed to convince...."

"I had to work fast. I did not want the other cutthroats to start in on him with their influences."

"I understand you not only worked fast but well."

"I right away console the grief-stricken brother in his greed...."

"I think you mean grief."

"... with three million pesetas option money."

"He must have been numb. Didn't he know he can't get fifty thousand dollars out of Spain?"

"He asked me to put the bribe on deposit with Barclay's in Gibraltar."

"He mourns well, that grief-stricken brother."

"He is the smart Crevassette. You know why the dead one would not sell me his invention?"

"You wouldn't pay him enough."

"Bah! Because I am a capitalist, he says in his lousy English. I argue with him who else but a capitalist can afford to buy his Gadget and you know what he said?"

"No."

"Never mind," and Lobbe sighed. "He is dead and now I think well of him."

I could understand that.

"What's bad then? The short option period?"

"No. That's good business and that brother, that unspeakable *pedazo de carroña*, he knows very well there are other cutthroats around. What is bad is when I go to London."

"Miss Moon never mentioned that I should meet you in London."

"I did not come to meet you. With the lucky break in Algeciras I have a day to spare before I must be in Mexico City, so I fly up to London just to look at my Gadget."

"I didn't know it had been built."

"The model, *Dummkopf*."

"And how did it look?"

"Ha!" he said. "I stand out there in the rain and the place is locked up!"

The place, I assumed, was Crevassette's small manufacturing plant. Under the name of Special Developments Company, Ltd., and with the aid of about twenty employees, Crevassette had developed and built custom-made electronic equipment.

"You don't think that's strange," he said to me. "No. After all, the owner goes on vacation...."

"He went *pfft*."

"You said that."

"And already, Manny, I see somebody sneaking around the place, with that poor *crème de la merde* Crevassette still flying around up there in little pieces."

"You got back to London pretty damn fast yourself."

"But I am buying the place!"

"The whole place?"

"I was going to tell you. This other one, the grief-stricken one...."

"The *carroña*."

"The same. He insists. After all, he knows nothing about electronics."

"Only about money."

"Ah, mennekin, you will like him, that brother!" and Lobbe laughed unpleasantly.

"But now that you are here, Mister Lobbe...."

"I am leaving. I was going to be there in London for an innocent little look but now I am afraid."

"Which is why you are sending me into the fray."

"True. So, I am standing there in the rain, I knock on the *verdommen* door. No answer."

"Typical of empty buildings."

He groaned with patience.

"Inside," he said, "I see the man. He moves around with a flashlight. I knock, out goes the flashlight."

I waved at the bartender, who was standing near the back with arms folded. I pushed my martini glass at him and then Lobbe remembered about his bullshot.

"Where is it?" he said to the bartender.

The man first finished the martini and put it in front of me.

"It will take a moment," he said to Lobbe.

"*Why?*"

"I don't have an egg. I must get the egg from the owner of the restaurant in that other part of the building. The owner of the restaurant does not have a liquor license and wonders if it is legal for him to let me have the egg for the bull thing. He went home, to discuss it with his wife. It will take a moment."

Lobbe and I looked at each other, saying nothing. I pushed my martini over to him and he had some.

"Mennekin," he said very low, "never mention this to me in the future."

"Never."

"It did not happen."

"I understand."

"Good. Where was I now?"

"You were at the point where you started to run away from the burglar."

He looked at me and suddenly there was only one chin. He was angry and now his English would be precise and uncluttered with foreign phrases.

"Manford," he said, "you are about to do business for me to the tune of five million dollars down."

"Stebbs gave me the stock authorizations which I am to use for...."

"Don't interrupt me with what I already know."

"Yes sir."

"You have about eighteen hours of option time until filing and initial deposit. Of this time I want you to use only ten hours in all."

"Before the burglar walks off...."

I was lightheaded with lack of sleep but I should have known better. Lobbe turned white. It was his sign of exerting considerable self-control. He finished up, sharp and serious.

"The burglar," he said, "followed me. In a Morris Minor. I want you to remember that car, deWitt. A blue Morris Minor, One Thousand. When I left my car at the hotel he was still there, discreetly. I went inside and made a phone call. Fifteen minutes later—you understand my connections are good—the answer came back. The man in the Morris is one Rodney Ramsey. He is an officer in British Intelligence."

CHAPTER 3

No further explanation for Lobbe's haste was required. He wanted his deal sewed up before there was a chance of complications with—to use his words—the most high-handed branch of the British government. Any branch of anything would be the most high-handed, if Lobbe ran afoul of it; however, none of this explained why he himself had left London with a homicidal pilot in the middle of a purblind fog.

"What's behind all this, I am sure," he said to me, "is some kind of Radford plot."

He finished my martini and then he had a double vodka without the bull. The Radford he had mentioned was not one of the major cutthroats but another electronics firm, very much like Crevassette's, and they had sometimes worked together on the same projects.

"That Radford," Lobbe breathed heavily. He no longer smelled of cloves. "That unspeakable finch—"

"I think you mean fink, sir."

"He is consultant for the British government, did you know? He tells their spies what to look for, did you know?"

"No."

"I know! So here perhaps it is in the nature of a return favor for that Radford rat robin—"

"Fink, sir."

"—to weave a plot with official help now that I am about to take possession of Crevassette's little hole in the wall!"

"Radford knows you?"

"He detests me!"

I said nothing. To know Lobbe was not necessarily to love him, but to detest him was something else again. I myself rather liked him, which accounts for the fact that I had managed to work reasonably well with him. On the other hand, it was quite conceivable....

"The fact is," said Lobbe, "I once robbed him blind."

"Hard to believe."

"Don't lie to me, mennekin. But now, you see, I must not alert Radford until you have entered the papers."

"Miss Moon sent along papers to show that I'm buying for Gorgon Manufacture."

"A little *Schwindel* which does not hurt. Especially now that Radford worries me."

"But didn't you get a firm option in Spain?"

"Paper. If Radford finds out in time—and I'm worried he will—if he finds out soon that his friend is dead and I have bought first refusal, then he will *give* to the *pedazo de carroña* the fifty thousand to hand back to me!"

"What about this Ramsey person?"

"*Vat, vat, vat!* You find out something too, huh, mennekin? I myself think he was looking for papers. He works for the government. He has ways and secret methods. And for a little money on the side, for a little better than government pay, why wouldn't he peddle something of value to a man like that Radford who is looking for anything that can hurt me where it hurts? Something to hold up the sale so I lose option time, and the Gadget, and my fifty thousand too? Aha! Here comes the lunatic!"

He was already upon me. He dripped water on me from the visor of his very crushed cap—he was, in fact, wet all over—but nonetheless smiled at me as if we were having the very best of flying weather.

"This," said Lobbe to him, "is the very valuable Mr. deWitt. Be careful with him. And this," he said to me, "is Max Garten. You better be very careful with him because he is your pilot."

We shook hands without particular feeling, though Max Garten was still smiling with a faraway expression on his face. At first flush he did not look like a madman to me, his fog-bound takeoff and his perfect landing in a shower of Druid swords notwithstanding. His face was languid, with a rather Lincolnesque charm. Indeed, his profile seemed to have been pried off a coin. Only the mooning eyes suggested possible madness.

"Let's go," he said, "if we're going to make Soho by eleven."

"Soho? There's no airport in Soho!"

"I know," said Garten.

"He will take you to Soho after you land," said Lobbe, "to the place where Meghan Bushmill lives."

"Of course. How could I forget where Meghan Bushmill lives."

"You know her?" said Max Garten.

"No."

Max Garten looked at Hans Lobbe and then they shrugged at each other indulgently.

"She is," said Lobbe as to a child, "Crevassette's private secretary. You go see her instantly. I want the keys to the safe where the plans are, I want the inventory...."

"Tonight?"

"In Soho," said Garten and smiled at me. "Do you get airsick?"

"Most definitely yes!"

"You won't with me. I go too fast."

I said, "Listen, Mr. Lobbe. If you think...."

"If we don't hurry up," said Garten, "we'll have to crash regulations. Radio says they're closing London to *all* traffic."

"Mr. Lobbe, if you think for one minute—" But then I turned rapidly back to Garten, who had just come through to me. "What do you mean, *crash?!*"

"He means that figuratively," Lobbe explained. "Break a few simple regulations."

"You mean safety regulations, don't you?"

"I have a beautiful safety record," said Garten. "Would you like to hear about it?"

"I would love to hear about it. As a matter of fact, I insist on hearing about it!"

At this point he had me by one arm, Lobbe had me by the other arm, and while I was clutching my sole piece of luggage—the briefcase with papers—Lobbe went so far as to drape his loden cape over me.

"I won't need it," he said, as if giving up his parachute. The rain was starting to knife at me.

"What about that safety record, Garten?"

"You see a scratch on me? Any scratch whatsoever?"

"I'm not seeing much of anything at the moment."

We had started to run over the tarmac, on account of the rain.

"Not a scratch," said Garten. "Eleven crash landings and I walked away from each and every one of them!"

I was on the first step leading up to the cockpit and when I turned around there was Max Garten right behind me. He smiled, looking dreamy. There was no scratch on him, but perhaps, sometime, somewhere, he had severely fallen on his head? He nudged me and I did not want to get him excited. I went on. Lobbe waved at me from the distance.

"*Hals und Beinbruch!*" he yelled, which was his perverted way of wishing me the best by mentioning the worst.

I was convinced that I had fallen severely on my head, somewhere, sometime....

Garten waved me to the copilot seat. Sitting next to him was a mistake. I had to watch him do frightening things to switches and buttons while he kept up a volley of explanations.

"Now this little bugger here—hello there, where is it? Ah yes. Was thinking of the later model in which they moved—ooops! That was rather unexpected, wasn't it. I say there, deWitt. Let's strap you back in, shall we?"

I think he had offered to let me sit next to him so that he could strap me into the seat himself, having undoubtedly been bribed by Lobbe to throw a particularly obstinate knot into the webbing which only he, Max Garten, could undo.

"I would rather it were possible," I said to him, "for me to be thrown clear."

"Haha! That's the spirit. Now, let's see. Actually, we have two engines here. So we better find the doodad which turns on the other one too, I imagine."

From that moment on I tried to pay as little attention as possible to anything he did. It is my claim to courage that I gave up without a whimper when overcome by the inevitable. I have had a lot of training in that and this was the time when it paid off. The next thing I recollect is that it had stopped raining and we were standing still.

"Where are we?" I said.

"Fifteen thousand feet up."

Of course. The engines had died.

"The nacelles," he said, "are both at the tail. Rather pleasant, the silence, don't you think?"

"Like the grave."

I noticed that our airspeed was five hundred miles per hour and that we were losing altitude at a staggering rate.

"Without trying to be technical," I said, "would you show me where the landscape is?"

"Below. Actually, you are looking at fog."

"I see."

"Haha! Capital!" He breathed deeply a few times. "Zen," he said to me, "helps calm the nerves. If you'll let go of that particular lever for a moment, I think we'll manage the approach fairly well now."

I was petrified and he unclamped my hand himself. Most disturbing was his religious breathing.

"May I ask what we are approaching?"

"Damned if I know," he said. "You wouldn't happen to have any chewing gum on you, by chance? Helps with the Zen, you know."

I did not have any chewing gum. I promised myself that if I ever got out of this seat alive I would send great globs of chewing gum to all the Zen monasteries in the world as an act of thanksgiving. At that moment Max Garten made one of his alarming remarks.

"I say, what's this?"

"Good heavens, where?"

"It's gone now. Looked for all the world like a chimney, and here we are at eight hundred feet. Ridiculous."

"*Eight hundred feet!*"

"Landing approach. Don't try to smoke now. Quite hazardous at the moment."

I closed my eyes because there was nothing to see anyway.

"We *are* landing in London, I assume."

"You don't think I'd turn back, do you?"

"Never."

"Right you are. Now, if you'll just flip that little switch there, deWitt."

"*What* little switch, for heaven's sake!?"

"Never mind. For the present, much more important—actually *de rigueur*—to get this landing gear to respond."

I closed my eyes again. I kept them closed even when my vertebral column jarred into the top of my skull and even when Max Garten stopped breathing in that disturbing Zen way of his.

I heard the engines screech and then I heard them die. I felt him fumble with my harness and I still did not open my eyes.

"It's all right now, deWitt. I just undid you."

"That you did."

"It's London!" He sounded surprised.

"Even without me flipping that little button?"

"Never mind that now, deWitt. That was the ON button for the ejector seats."

In a while he got me to his car which was parked in the yellow fog near the hangar where he had left the plane. It was not a Morris Minor, though I would not have been surprised if it was. I will leave out the terror of his drive to Soho, always on the wrong side of the street. I did not really become properly alert again until we stopped in front of the house where Meghan Bushmill lived, because there, at the hour of midnight, stood the blue Morris Minor by the curb.

CHAPTER 4

The fog in front of Meghan Bushmill's house was surprisingly yellow, and the two street lamps which illuminated the thick sea of billows were only visible as diffuse auras of light. The blue Morris Minor was beaded with moisture and the little drops would shoot down now and then, making veins of water.

I looked at the car for a moment but the sight made no sense. A British agent was spending the night with Miss Bushmill. Was it assignment or assignation? There were solitary footsteps in the street. They came and went. It was Jack the Ripper weather.

"Garten," I said to my pilot, "have you met this Bushmill before?"

"Fact is, no. Your Mister Lobbe just hired me. But speaking of Bushmill, a nice tumbler of the Irish...."

"Garten, if you think you're going to get drunk while I depend on you for safe transportation in this yellow split-pea soup—"

"DeWitt," he said and smiled his reminiscent smile. "The day I bagged three Messerschmitts I was sloshing with the sauce."

"What did you do, ram them?"

"Just the last one," he said, while I went into the building entrance.

The stairwell started almost immediately behind the door and gave the impression of a damp elevator shaft. The mailbox at the bottom said that

Miss Bushmill lived on the third floor and that she did not care for solicitations. That part did not worry me, but I felt somewhat apprehensive about busting in on her past the hour of midnight. I did not know her, of course, but would imagine she might get fairly nasty when rousted out of bed, especially if Ramsey of the Morris Minor was holding her enthralled there. It never occurred to me that the blue Morris' owner might be in some other apartment.

In any event, I need not have worried.

There was no problem about getting in. The door to her apartment was open. And the next door behind that one was open, too. There was a lot of light in the two little rooms and there were more people than two little rooms can conveniently accommodate. In fact, the party threatened to make the building top-heavy. The problem was, which one might Meghan Bushmill be?

The girl in the Edwardian suit turned out to be a man, and the one in the ruffled blouse and velvet stovepipe pants left doubt about its gender even after the most critical gaze.

"This," said Garten, "is not what I'd call a party of secretaries. Ola! I see someone I know."

Garten was much taller than I and had spotted the table with bottles at the other end of the room. He now swam his way in that direction and left me by the door.

I had been just a little bit worried about the way I was dressed—Tyrolean loden cape and Bloomingdale seersucker suit—but the ensemble proved no handicap. I was adopted without the bat of an eye. A most shapely little thing who seemed dressed mostly in hair took my arm without any introduction.

"You're the one Bunny brought," she said.

"No. As a matter of fact...."

"I can tell by the clothes. Revolutionary." She tugged at my arm, as if she knew where she was going. "Come on. Bunny won't mind."

"Just a minute." I pulled my arm away. "Bunny does mind. In fact, Bunny wants me to meet Meghan. You know where she is?"

"Bunny? But Bunny brought you."

"No, Godiva. The stork brought me."

"Excuse me," she said, because somebody had grabbed elsewhere and she instantly responded by clutching at the intruder.

I turned elsewhere, too.

"Excuse me, I'm looking for Meghan Bushmill."

"Go right ahead." He wore a beard and sunglasses. He paid no further attention to me.

"I have to talk to Meghan Bushmill," I started with someone else.

"Could you help me find her?"

He had a heavy peasant face and wore his hair like Napoleon or like a yokel.

"Who is Bushmill?" he said.

Max Garten, I noticed, was with the person of the frilly shirt and the velveteen pants.

"I would say, in all modesty, that I am probably the only man who at forty thousand feet and replete with oxygen mask...."

"How was it?" asked the frilly one.

Somebody tapped me on the back.

"Didn't Bunny bring you?"

This one was a decidedly masculine youth, or sought to create this impression by the manner in which he was attired. The imported Levis were tight to the point of obscenity, and the black leather jacket had shoulders like those of a football player in full gear. There was no hint where his own shoulders ended.

I said, "Would *you* help me find Miss Bushmill?"

"Right now?"

"Instantly."

"What are you, some kind of voyeur?"

"I beg your pardon?"

"Meghan is getting dressed in the bedroom."

"I see."

"You do?"

I said, "Look, Galahad...."

"Gilliam."

"Look, Gilliam. I don't give a damn what she's doing in the bedroom...."

"Gilliam Ramsey," he said.

I took another look. I now saw that he was only a youth because he looked youthful, though the boniness of his jaw and the well-muscled neck suggested a man most likely in his thirties. His sandy hair was longish in the British manner, by which I mean to say that it was rather full on the sides of his head. I decided that the aura of youth was largely created by his guileless blue eyes. Naturally, like the getup he was wearing, that impression was most likely fake too.

"And who are you?" he asked me.

"DeWitt. And Bunny did not bring me."

"Of course. The stork did."

If there was going to be an end to this I would now have to say something official.

"I'm here on business," I said. "You may gather, in view of the hour and the circumstances, that it is rather pressing business."

"Crevassette business?"

He gave it no special inflection, nor did he bat an eye. As a friend of Meghan's he would naturally know for whom she was working.

"Crevassette business," I said.

"I see." This time he looked at me with a little more interest. "And you are an American."

The discovery did not need the talents of a spy. There was my accent, my haircut, and possibly the harassed look of a man whose responsibilities interfere with his pleasures and whose pleasures are continually undercut by an awareness of duties yet to come. Ramsey looked at my clothes.

"Clever of you," he said. "Your entirely fitting getup threw me off. But if you don't know Meghan, how did you know enough to come properly dressed for her party?"

"That, Ramsey, is an extremely long story." Then I smiled my in-crowd smile at him. "How did you come upon your own disguise?"

"I've cultivated Meghan's acquaintance for some time," he said.

I bet he had, at that, though without Lobbe's hysterical coaching I would never have given Ramsey's remark a second thought. Nor did he encourage it. He turned and waved at me to follow him.

The distance to the bedroom door did not exceed six yards, but I briefly lost Ramsey along the way. Max Garten exploded between us.

"DeWitt!" he said rather breathlessly. "It's a girl!"

"Congratulations. And how, just as a matter of medical curiosity, did you accomplish a nine-month happening in nine minutes?"

"She was quite frank about it, not to say demonstrative. Her name's Bunny, by the way."

"That figures."

"Excuse me. She awaits."

He churned away and I made the bedroom door. Ramsey was waiting there.

"Your friend," he said, "seems to have met Bunny."

"Old warrior type," I said. "*Veni, vidi, vici.*"

"I know he is," said Ramsey. "Used to be one of our aces, you know. Spitfires at eighteen, Victoria Cross at nineteen, innumerable bail-outs—"

"I know about that part. But how did you know?"

"The papers."

"I meant, how did you know him?"

"I don't. I merely recognized him."

Ramsey was either very innocent or very knowledgeable about everything, such as how to dress for Meghan's party, how to explain things most casually, how to look innocent under my stare, which must have been ominous with Lobbe-inspired suspicions. And then the door opened behind him.

Meghan Bushmill surprised me. First of all, as the pacesetting hostess at this particular party I thought she might emerge from her bedroom wearing Gestapo boots up to the knees and sackcloth down to mid-thigh. Instead, she was recognizably dressed. Her skirt had big folds and the blouse was without ruffs or mad cuffs. She had lovely legs and fine ankles which were unconcealed by military footgear of any kind. Since she was Irish I thought of the adjective *comely* to describe her.

She had pitch-black hair, combed back loose and straight, which I mention because of what it did to her face. It exposed her face, giving it a look of such terrible and innocent vulnerability that I was confused as to how to begin.

She looked me up and down with wide blue child's eyes as if I had come from Honduras in a Tyrolean loden cape.

"Miss Bushmill?" I said.

"Yes?"

I let the sound of her voice go through me without interference. It was a lovely voice.

"My name is deWitt," I said. "I represent Lobbe Industriel. I would not ask to see you, if it were not critically urgent."

"What is?"

"A company matter regarding the Crevassette interest."

She eyed me, and all that innocent wonder I had seen in her eyes somehow turned to ordinary, cool, sober, and very businesslike speculation.

"I know of the Lobbe correspondence, of course. But after midnight?"

"I'm afraid that can't be helped, Miss Bushmill. We have only about eighteen hours' option time left and under the circumstances...."

"Gilliam," she said, looking right past me, "is this someone Bunny brought?"

That did it. I seldom feel severe and I rarely get severe with a woman, but now I heard my voice come out like a crowbar clanking along an iron fence.

"Pursuant to the death of Mr. Crevassette, my employer obtained a written commitment from Crevassette's next of kin, his brother, and under the terms of the—agreement...." The word came out like the dying sound of an engine conking out.

I had nearly forgotten how vulnerable she could look. But what in fact stopped me much more than her expression, I think, was Ramsey's reaction. He stared at me as if I were something that goes bump in the night, and then he said with an insistent and steadfast voice, "God damn it all to hell and back!"

Meghan, on the other hand, just closed her eyes and reached for the doorknob for support. With her free hand she made a fist and pushed it against her mouth.

Neither of them, it seemed, had known that Crevassette had been blown all to hell and back less than twenty-four hours ago.

CHAPTER 5

We sat her down on the bed and then Ramsey closed the door.

"He was such a sweet old man," Meghan said. "So sweet, so distracted."

"I'm sorry," I said. "I totally overlooked the possibility that you did not know."

"How did it happen?"

I told her what I knew, that he had been working on something and that it had all blown up.

She couldn't have cared less about triggering devices or the guns of Gibraltar, but she just sat there on the bed, looking down at the hands in her lap. She cried very quietly. I did not know that she was crying at all until I saw the slow tears fall on her hands, which she rubbed listlessly, one over the other. I put my hand out and touched her and started to say, "Is there something...." But she shook her head.

"Maybe we had better just leave her be for a moment," said Ramsey.

I nodded and we went to the other end of the room.

I was in London because Lobbe felt that at least the initial moves in the Crevassette matter should not come from McEvoy's office. Anyone interested would expect them to come from there. But the main reason with Lobbe—as always—was the matter of speed. One man moves faster than a whole office. And now, it seemed, my midnight blitz was turning into a midnight wake. It was true, that as a matter of personal delicacy as opposed to routine office procedure, the Crevassette business could be sewed up by me in a matter of hours. Or it could get lost in eighteen.

I rarely smoke, finding the experience just an unpleasant goad for something more, something which the next cigarette never supplies, but I had a cigarette with Ramsey while he and I stood by the narrow window which faced the street. I assumed it was the street. There was actually only the opaque muddiness of the end of the world outside, a swill without definition, except for the submarine sheen of light where the street lamps would be.

"Were they related?" I asked Ramsey. He and I smoked, talking quietly.

"Meghan and the old man? No. Just the love of the old for the young, and the devotion of the young for the old."

I had expected less than poetry from him.

I turned around to look at Meghan because she had made a sound—a very deep breath and then an exhalation that was like the dropping of a heavy burden: She was finished crying. Then she left the bed and went into the bathroom. When she had closed the door I said, "She took it hard."

"Always been terribly grateful to the old man." Ramsey looked out of the window at nothing. "Not too many years ago, you see, Meghan's father accompanied Crevassette to a trades fair in Halle, East Germany."

"How so?"

"Old Bushmill is an engineer. Worked for Crevassette. Vast surprise when the Commies in Halle arrested old Bushmill for spying."

"Had he been?"

"Doubt it," said Ramsey. "We—I mean, the British Government—is relatively powerless in that sort of circumstance. But old Crevassette—a man of no mean connections—worked hard and got Bushmill out."

"I can understand why Meghan was grateful. But why did she go to work for Crevassette?"

"After that Halle incident her old man just quit. He retired to Shannon where he sits in his windy room, so I'm told, doing nothing. Meghan had to pick up the threads, and Crevassette offered her the job before she asked for it. Another reason why she has felt grateful. You saw how she reacted. Not one touch of interest as to what blew the old man over the Rock; only grief that he was gone."

"Yes," I said. It seemed my turn to look out the window. I could almost feel the moist air reaching for me.

"Just what did blow him up?" Ramsey asked.

"I don't know." I thought of who Ramsey was supposed to be. "Don't you know what he had been working on?"

"I? Not the foggiest."

"I thought you might know. You're apparently close to Meghan."

"Socially...." He let that trail off, as if in thought. "I remember! Something to do with gunnery?"

"I thought he worked exclusively...."

Meghan came back into the room. She had washed her face and brushed her hair, or whatever it is women do which makes them look both fresh and exhausted at the same time. I thought she looked well enough to get back to interrupted business, but I decided to let her show the way. She did, immediately.

"I never allowed you to finish, Mister deWitt. Something about an eighteen-hour option...."

The next five minutes were devoted to paper rattling, to legal phrase rattling and explanations. I did not have to explain very much to Meghan. My authorization to represent Lobbe in the ownership transfer of Crevassette's lock, stock, and barrel, as authorized by the sole heir Bartholomew Crevassette, brother of the deceased, as per blah sales agreement of blah blah—all that she understood well enough. But....

"Why now?" she asked.

"Because, Miss Bushmill, pursuant to the written...."

"Just say it, Mister deWitt, won't you?"

I had no idea where I had gotten the impression that Meghan Bushmill was vulnerable, soft, and helpless.

"I want the stuff that's in the document safe. You have the combination and I want the stuff now."

"Why?"

I could not fathom how I had missed seeing Bushmill's recalcitrant black-Irish soul. At any moment now I expected her quiet eyes to turn into silent icepicks and her tongue into a Druid sword.

"Because," I told her, "it says so in the contract."

She was ready to say something again, but I held up my hand in a small, elegant gesture, a restrained warning, which looked like a get-set for a karate blow.

"And because," I went on, "I damn well didn't come flying nonstop from Honduras into the middle of a medieval fog just to get hung up at this *Walpurgisnacht* gathering in your chambers. I came for those papers in the safe and I need them because I've got to process them before legal submission tomorrow. Can you understand that, Miss Bushmill?"

The explanation was hogwash. Lobbe simply wanted a physical transfer without having to wait for the slow grind of the legal mills. Meghan Bushmill blinked and bit her lip. Wild with legalistic emotion I didn't think for a moment that she might actually be trying not to laugh. When she spoke at last, the mildness of her tone took me by surprise.

"Speaking of *Walpurgisnacht*...." and she pointed at my tropical ensemble. "It's a long ride to the plant. Wouldn't you rather wear something warmer?"

"Uh—"

"A different jacket, at least."

"As a matter of fact—"

She was not listening so I did not bother to finish. She went to her closet, though I had no idea what she meant to do there for me. Then she showed me.

"Think any of these might fit you?"

I found that I had acquired a stiff upper lip. I did not flinch at all when I discovered there was indeed more than one man's jacket hanging in Miss

Bushmill's closet. I studied a tweed and a blazer and a worsted that hung between her taupe sheath and her plaid jumper.

"Gilliam," she said to Ramsey. "I don't think Milos minds but would you ask him?"

I apparently did not look as if I understood. While Ramsey left the room Meghan said to me, "They belong to Milos."

She folded her arms in a way that made her breasts prominent. My appreciation of the view must have registered in my face because Meghan frowned, looked down at herself, and then dropped her arms.

"Really, Mister deWitt. You *are* an American, aren't you."

It was a rhetorical question and therefore did not require an answer. I sighed and took off my loden cape.

"Have you ever been in Italy, Miss Bushmill?"

"Yes."

"Have you had an Italian lover?"

"I don't see what business that is of yours."

"No business. But it makes no difference. Your exposure to the social climate was sufficient, I would imagine, to help you appreciate this tableau—"

"Which tableau?"

I had not gotten used to her interruptions, I was still merely getting acquainted with them.

"Stop talking for a minute and listen. All right? Fine. Now. The Italian lover stands in front of you and stares at your bosom. What does it mean? The male animal wants the female animal. Now, if the man were American, the look would mean, of course, the repressed Puritan stealing a lecherous look. The Italian comes into your bedroom and sees men's clothes in the signorina's closet. He stares! In a most flattering way, he is obviously being possessive. But if he were an American, the look would mean, of course, that he censors you for your disregard of conventions."

"My goodness—" she said.

"Is not at stake," I said. "And my goodness, or its opposite, is not at stake either."

"My—you *are* a lawyer, aren't you."

"Of course. I am a type. An American type, a lawyer type. Do you type everything, Miss Bushmill?"

She did not like that one little bit. I did not get the ice-pick eye. The look was more like fire. Perhaps she had seen me for the first time and that's what the sight did to her, though I prefer to think that I'd hit home. She remained speechless, and that—I think—meant that she suddenly did not know what type I was.

Party babble hit the back of my head and what came into the room now might very well have been something Bunny had brought.

It wore English clothes, about the size of the jackets in the closet, but these didn't look so good on a monkey. It had black hair, the familiar lanky sort, but surprising because it was growing out of an egg. The face was humanoid. It seemed especially bizarre because the eyes were lively with intelligence and the voice which I heard was warm and articulate.

"Mister deWitt. I am charmed to meet you. My name is Milos Ort. My jackets are yours."

We shook hands. My startled first impression was now entirely wiped out by the second, that Milos Ort was simply a somewhat jumpy arm dangler with a bland face and mobile eyes. However, it next occurred to me, Ort must have had some fabulously redeeming features to be a closet-mate of Meghan Bushmill.

He stepped back, tossed his head to get the hair off his face and said, "So you are the young man from Lobbe Industriel who will now, *pro tem*, run the remarkable Special Developments Company for us."

He had a velvety accent which I couldn't at the moment pin down. His first name was possibly Slavic, his last name possibly Germanic.

"For us?" I said.

I felt quite overcome by his knowledge. I had not made mention of my name, connection, or mission to Milos Ort, though Gilliam Ramsey, for reasons of his own, might have quickly briefed the man. But I most certainly had not explained to anyone that under the transfer arrangements I would indeed be President *pro tem* of Special Developments. It was merely a matter of papers, but the papers had not even been drawn up yet.

Ort proceeded to explain what he had meant by "for us" while I, remembering my rush about getting to that plant, picked a jacket, discarded my own, and put the tweed loaner on.

"I am a salesman for the company. I love to work with people."

"So much for your types," I mumbled to Meghan. "Only American car salesmen can say that with honesty."

"And," Ort continued, "I also represent other manufacturers from Sofia on the Bosporus to Frankfurt on the Main."

"Not that jacket," Meghan was saying. "All the buttons are gone."

"They manufacture all the varieties of the machines," Ort was declaiming, "for which the genius of poor Crevassette supplied the final perfection and the impossible improvement."

"I was right," I said to Meghan. "He apprenticed in Los Angeles where they sell cars for nothing and get very rich."

"He is Czech," said Meghan. "And he is not a salesman. He is a manufacturer's representative, and not very rich."

I had the heavy tweed jacket on and was patting myself. Ort had fallen silent. He was sitting on the bed now, looking at me with attention. I caught a whiff of his appeal. He did not care how he looked to others, but when he looked at you he gave you all his concern. I could imagine how he might come across to women.

"You look nice, Manny," he said.

That was the biggest surprise: he even knew the diminutive of my name. However, I let it pass.

"Thank you," I said. "Would you mind getting up off that cape you are sitting on?"

"Oh! Apologies! Is that the beautiful thing in which you came flying in?"

"Yes. I had it made in Transylvania. And now, if you will excuse us, Miss Bushmill and I—"

I let the rest of it dwindle away because Ort's bland face, with its occasional strange quirks of animation, now seemed to go entirely dead. His eyes, still as stones now, were looking past me.

Ramsey had come back into the room. The way he looked back at Ort was the human counterpart of the Czech's unearthly expression. Clearly, these two did not like each other.

The explanation was no problem. They were both gone on Meghan. The only thing that struck me as peculiar was the curious concentration of talents around the young woman: a dead inventor who used to heave real pull in East Germany, a British agent who worked for a manufacturer who had also been one of Crevassette's friends, a business representative who moved back and forth across the Iron Curtain.

For the moment I decided on saner pursuits. I swung the cape around me and left the room in search of Max Garten.

CHAPTER 6

When I found him I took one look and I knew that Max Garten would fly no more. He was in the third room of Meghan's apartment. In the States such a room would be called a dinette, since it adjoined a small kitchen. However, in view of the absence of table and chairs I did not know what Meghan used the room for. I was certain I knew what Garten had used the room for, though then again, not certain either. Item, he was not on the cot but the cot was on him. It had been turned upside down and on top of it sat the slim, close-cropped young thing known far and wide as Bunny.

"Is it working?" she said very loud.

Mumble, mumble from the fallen Max. He was alive.

"What," I said, "are you two doing?"

She looked at me with the flat eyes of a fish. The sole source of animation in her face was her remarkably mobile and voluptuous mouth.

"Shh," she said. "It's Zen."

I gave up on her for the moment. Fish eyes alienate me.

I bent down low to define the position and possible activity of Max, but this was impossible. In addition to being surrounded by the upside-down canvas belly of the cot, he was almost totally swathed in several blankets. What I could see of his face was wet and darkly discolored.

"Garten," I said, "you seem to be forty thousand feet under."

Mumble mumble from the blue Max. I was not sure just how alive he was. I straightened up and turned to Bunny again.

"Get off him instantly and help me remove this sarcophagus."

"No."

"Why not?"

"He ended up completely exhausted and begged me to help him with this restorative exercise."

"I know, Zen."

"He said he was in charge of your well-being and had to force recovery by drastic means."

"Is he chewing gum?"

"I beg your pardon?"

"Bunny, for the moment you are in charge of his well-being. Keep him here. By force, if need be."

"I won't need it."

"Er, quite. And tell him I'll be back here in an hour."

I found Meghan in the tiny entrance hall, dressed to go. And Ramsey, dressed to go, and Ort, dressed to go, too. They could all tell by the look on my face and the flap of my cape that I did not like what I saw. I wanted Meghan to come with me, but nobody else; not Ramsey, for obvious reasons, not Milos Ort, because the scope of my suspicion of him was widening. I was even glad that Max Garten was not able to come along, but only for reasons which involved the risk of my life.

But I could tell that Ort did not want Meghan to creep through the night unattended, and Ramsey did not want Ort creeping off attending to Meghan. Still, I knew that Lobbe would not care to have even a few millions of his money jeopardized by somebody else's sentimental squabble, and it bugged me that they would not be shaken.

I shrugged and the four of us left the giggle and chatter of Meghan's party and walked into the quiet fog.

We would drive in Ramsey's car. We stood by his Morris, each wrapped in his thoughts, the only sound the tiny scratch of Ramsey's key as he tried to unlock his door. The tiny sound and the tiny horizon made a little world which had, for that moment, the fairy-tale quality of a secret game played by children in a snug room while the wind outside roared.

It roared. We all gave a start and Ramsey dropped his key. The roar was deafening. Then we could see it flail into view.

Max Garten emerging from the fog seemed a monstrous thing. His longish hair was awry and his scarf flapped about him. He was taller than any of us, but the way he came weaving through the fog was an overpowering sight, regardless of size. I would have to ask him about that recent Zen experience.

"DeWitt?" he roared. "Aha! There you are!" And then he fairly fell on me so that it was hard to tell whether he was giving me a brotherly hug or the death grip of a drowning man.

Ramsey had found his key in the gutter and started for the door lock again. Milos Ort was holding Meghan's arm. They both looked appalled.

"Do not, I repeat, do not," said Garten, "do that again. Strict orders, you know. Not to let you out of my sight."

"Get off me."

"Sorry."

"And I don't need a bodyguard."

"You lack my special training, deWitt."

"I know. Zen."

"Zen karate."

"Just recently, I've seen you laid out by considerably less."

"Eh?" he said and leaned entirely too close.

I stepped back.

"Bunny said that you ended up totally destroyed."

He straightened up, very calm and disdainful now. Some of his characteristic vagueness showed again.

"The arrogance of the female," he told the fog over my head. Then he looked down at me. "I was merely bombed out of my skull. Hence the sweat and thought exercise."

Now he was no longer flailing or leaning but had resumed his usual calm, upright stance, although he was listing about somewhat, as if wafting with the fog.

"Well now," he said, watching Ramsey open the door of his car, "I'm fit again. Come along, deWitt."

"I'm going to the plant with these people."

"Quite. And I'll drive you."

"*Now just one damn minute!*"

I am reluctant to unravel the details of what followed, but it was all about who would drive with whom. I would not drive with Max and he would not let me go separately with the others. He also refused to let anyone but himself drive his dangerous machine. I have failed to mention that it was a long-snouted, two-seated Austin-Healey which had undergone some kind of major surgery. It had to do with shaving the block and lowering the head, or shaving the head and lowering the boom—Max's explanations were never very clear—so as to shorten the stroke or the strike zone; in any event, all this head surgery had made a howling beast out of the machine, and with Garten at the wheel even the London fog would be no tranquilizer.

To be brief about the rest, when Max had stuffed me into the seat next to him, he also resumed his solicitude for me.

"You'll feel more confident, Manford...."

"Don't call me that. What are you doing with my knee?"

"Knee? What knee? Why—I'll be deuced. For just a moment there I did miss the gear stick, didn't I."

The motor was already anxiously roaring in neutral and something near the dashboard glared at me maliciously like a basilisk.

"Compass," said Garten in order to soothe me. "Compass, for heaven's sake!"

"Can't do without it, deWitt, don't you realize. Well now, let's see—"

I abhorred this last remark when Garten made it. It always suggested that he was probably blind.

"Cylinder head temp getting cozy, pitot pressure—*oops*, forgot for a minute that I'm not in a plane."

"By all means, Garten, let us not forget *that* again!"

"DeWitt, I say. Would you mind letting go of that stick?"

"Stick—"

"The brake, you know. Fine. And now the wrist, please. Mind letting go of my wrist?"

We took off as my head snapped off, and then we left our sound and all sanity behind us too.

We were instantly nowhere, though progressing rapidly, I gathered from the tigerish way in which the fog shredded my face. Garten was craning his neck over the top of his windshield. He did not like the moisture on the glass.

"Comfortable?" he asked. "Eh? Won't talk, is that it? Very well. As I started to tell you, deWitt, so that you may feel more at ease, when I was on instruments...."

"Garten, we just passed something—"

"Naturally. Take a look at the dash, won't you?"

"I cannot see the dash, Garten."

"Haha! Capital."

But he did not finish telling me whatever it was he had wanted to say in order to comfort me. Instead he now crouched low over the wheel, peering about.

"Afraid something might whip your head off up there?"

He went Haha again and said Capital.

"Just checking the instruments. It seems...."

"*Garten!* You are *not* driving on *instruments*, are you?!"

"Well, well now, what's this?"

"*That*, von Richthofen, is my wristwatch!"

"I'll be deuced. Well, let's see now, I think we better bear...."

"Garten, if you say 'let's see now' one more time, I swear I'll kill myself!"

"No need," he said while concentrating straight ahead.

He had made a point. I said nothing more for several minutes but merely trembled. Meanwhile, his concentration had not slackened and his Lincolnesque profile sharpened into that of a hawk—correction—vulture.

"I smell rot," he said. "Do you smell rot?"

"The word, Garten, is Death."

"And the sound of water lapping."

"Flapping, Garten. The proverbial wings of."

And then the arched gate of Hell shot into view, devoured us, and we thundered down the vaulted passage where the River Styx must flow. Like Dante's hero, Max the Madman never turned back or slowed down.

"Garten," I said, "the meaning of that water...."

"No question about it. I can see it right next to me."

"I hope it's merely the Thames and not the Seine, for godsake."

"We're still in London."

"Which you gather from the fog."

"Didn't you recognize the bridge we're under?"

At that instant Garten jammed on the brake, and then he actually stopped.

I said, "Did you lose your nerve, Garten?"

He did not deign to answer. He merely pointed ahead. Now I saw that the pier under the bridge ended just slightly in front of us and next came water. Garten was grabbing my knee again, but before I could point this out to him he had found the shift lever, and I was instantly smacked against the windshield as the machine went into reverse. He immediately found one of the forward gears, or perhaps his rocket boosters, and I was glued into the back of my seat on the rebound. By the rise of the hood in front of me I deduced that we were climbing back to the level of the street on which we had been driving and then, by the virtue of centrifugal forces which pitched me hither and yon, that we were changing streets many times. Garten didn't talk. He was obviously worried we would miss the others on account of that wrong turn under the bridge. I didn't talk, because the more recent forward thrust had caused me to partially swallow my tongue.

When Garten stopped at Crevassette's small plant there was no one else in sight. We had arrived first, of course.

CHAPTER 7

As far as I could tell in the dark fog and by the auras around the street lamps, we were in a low-building neighborhood. There was nothing of the high-backed, and somehow tubercular, appearance of the typical English industrial street. There was none of the eternal dark brick which characterizes for me the working-class quarter of England. Crevassette's building, for example, was built of gray cinder block and looked like an overgrown garage at the outskirts of New Jersey. Two similar buildings lined the street further on.

"Looks fairly new here," I said.

"Courtesy of the Blitz."

When away from the objects of his madness—cars and planes—Garten soon reverted to his gentle, vague self.

Architecture was not among the things that interested him.

We huddled inside our clothes and I strolled along the façade of the building. The front door was locked. The big casement window through which Lobbe must have seen the light of his fabled intruder was dark and heavily beaded with fog. There was a locked gate to one side of the building, large enough to admit a truck. Toward the back there seemed to be a field. I returned to Garten, who now looked asleep on his feet. It was time to establish a working relationship.

"Max," I said, "are you awake?"

"I think so." There was no appreciable change in his expression.

"Listen," I said. "As long as you take Lobbe's orders seriously, I would like to know what they are."

"To protect you, deWitt." He smiled, as if he were thinking of something else.

"Do you know why? I mean, do you know what's involved here?"

"Skullduggery," he said.

"No. Big business."

"As I said."

"Look, Max. Ever since I met you, I've had this sinking feeling that my wishes are not your command, that your protection amounts to interference with the normal course of my business, and that your and my relationship...."

"Mr. Lobbe warned me that you would attempt to finagle me into a position of ineffectuality."

"Finagle" was one of Lobbe's words. Max Garten, quite clearly, had been brainwashed into ignoring my demands. Instead of trying to reindoctrinate the man, I decided to try something else. He had, quite clearly, no personal pride which I could use as a lever to convince him that he should think on his own, under my direction, of course; but he might well be more pliable if I appealed to his lust for daring and speed.

"Max," I said, "I don't think I would be undercutting your loyalty to the man who pays you, if I asked you to do a number of unusual things in the name of speed and efficiency."

I waited a moment, watching him start to grin slowly.

"You are finagling me, deWitt. But I'm with you."

Then he sneezed abruptly. Sweaty Zen and clammy fog were a bad combination.

"The first unusual thing I would ask of you, Max, is that you take your damn rocket ship and blast off for Claridge's where you and I have rooms. There I would suggest...."

"Preposterous," he said without any emphasis whatsoever. "I must point out," he went on, "that your stratagem to get me out of the way with the heartfelt motive of getting me into bed on account of a cold in the nose is misguided and unnecessary. I have ditched in the icy waters of the Channel, off Jutland, and once amongst the Shetland Islands. Never quite understood how that happened," he mumbled. "Entirely off course from any action, don't you know. But to continue: I spent fifty percent of the time under water, fifty percent on the water, and all of the time in the water. In the case of the Shetland event, it is true, I contracted pneumonia or some such affliction, but nobody tried to put me to bed." He looked off into the shrouded distance and smiled vaguely. "That's not quite true. There was this remarkable cure which an old man in the Shetlands perpetrated on me. He had, you see, two daughters. I hesitate to recall their age, though I hasten to say that they were both nubile. Now, the theory of the procedure...."

"Never mind that."

"Very well. What we actually did...."

"Max. Some other time."

I looked at my wristwatch and wondered where Meghan was. The thought recalled forcefully that I was trying to rush a deal before an option expired and that while I was stamping my feet in the fog, Meghan, who held the key to my success, was in the company of two unknown quantities.

"Max," I said. "This Ramsey person. Do you know him?"

"No. For that matter, I doubt whether I would want to."

"How's that?"

"I suspect," he said, "the man who is in disguise. That ridiculous rocker outfit of his hardly conceals the fact that the man is some sort of government person."

"What?"

"It's an instinct, don't you know."

"I know. Like instrument flying."

"Quite. The man hangs around where he isn't wanted. Typically governmental, don't you know."

"How do you know so much about him?"

"Bunny told me. And, I might add by way of further damaging evidence, he has in the past consistently refused to sleep with her."

"Maybe he's queer."

"No. Bunny has an instinct for that. It's more as if he did not want to subject himself to influences which might cloud his judgment, which might be construed as alliances of a non-governmental nature."

In the evidence-and-speculation department Max could apparently not tell one from the other, and this in spite of the fact that, according to Lobbe at any rate, Ramsey was indeed a government man.

"What about Ort? You know, him?"

"Oh yes. I know quite a bit about him."

"From Bunny."

"Right. It seems this Milos Ort is quite phenomenal in bed."

So much for that source of information.

"Max," I said. "Let me explain the situation briefly. I am here to buy a company, which is worrisome enough. But in addition there is this man Ramsey, reputed to be a British agent...."

"I told you!"

"... who might be doing a moonlighting job for a competitor."

"What's the nature of this job he's doing?"

"I don't know. Presumably to interfere with the transfer arrangements in general and with my acquisition of certain plans for a—uh, a gadget in particular."

"Which is why we are standing here in the fog."

"Succinct of you. Furthermore, there is the ingratiating Mr. Ort."

"Bunny says that when he...."

"Never mind, Max. As I was saying, there is also this Ort, who crosses borders freely, who represents many manufacturers, so it seems, and who has attached himself to the confidential secretary of Crevassette."

"Being a bit spooky, aren't you, deWitt? I mean, to attach oneself to the likes of Meghan Bushmill requires no ulterior motive whatsoever."

I wrapped myself into the loden cape, thinking that I might now look inscrutable. Actually, I was cold.

"I will waste no more time. Just be sure that I get what I want without interference."

"Do I kill someone?"

I had learned by now that Max did not make jokes. He was not an extremely serious person, but he had the straightness of someone remarkably naïve. All those crash landings, undoubtedly.... At any rate, I took him seriously in turn.

"We do not kill anyone, Max. Possibly a show of strength, if need be, but nothing else. As it is, the plans I've come to acquire are significantly incomplete. The supplementary information—as a matter of safety—is in the hands of Crevassette's brother."

"Clever," said Max.

"Yes, very, very clever."

And all this time we stood all alone in the fog and nothing was happening. I would even have welcomed a frightening sound inside the building and a mysterious light at the window.

The sound, when it cracked the silence, was frightening all right, but it did not come from the building, but from down the street.

"Bad landing," said Max as he strained to see.

"You should know."

"There are people," he said, ignoring my comment completely, "who should not be allowed to drive."

"Or land."

He gave me a tolerant smile. Then we saw the Morris Minor follow after its cloudy beam.

There was only one headlight. For that matter, there was only one front fender. The invalid pulled up to the curb, climbed up on it, then bumped down again. Having in this manner established its whereabouts, the vehicle stopped.

Ramsey, Ort, and Meghan all climbed out, each and severally reflecting the damage which the Morris had sustained. Meghan, the sweet, helpless one, was intensely angry. She slammed the door behind her, in spite of the fact that Ort was just trying to crawl out. By the sound of it, the door hit him in the head. He then emerged cautiously, smiling in that awful way of someone who must either smile or scream. Ramsey seemed too embarrassed even to acknowledge his situation, but looked instead as if he were vastly bored with such things as lost fenders, smashed headlights, hysterical passengers, meteorological miasmas, bare survival, and the insanity of Americans.

"Well now," he said and put his hands in his pockets. "I see you made it."

"Hah!" said Meghan. Then she turned on me. "Mr. deWitt!"

"Yes, Miss Bushmill."

"You will be good enough to instruct your driver on the return trip—I am assuming there will be a return trip—to contain himself and his driving habits sufficiently so that incompetents like Gilliam Ramsey here are not drawn into suicidal attempts to follow the leader—a leader, I might add, who seems bent on defying every natural law of survival."

"Yes," I said. "He is unusual." Then I turned to Ramsey. "Were you trying to follow the glow of our afterburners?"

Ramsey gave a slight laugh.

"Did you take a short cut of some sort?" he asked Garten.

"I don't know," said Garten.

"Now that we're here," I said to Meghan, "why don't you and I complete our business so that these gentlemen won't have to stand around in the fog too long."

It did not work. Ramsey suggested they all wait inside, Ort insisted on going with Meghan, and Max, quite tacitly, attached himself to me. The most interesting performance, however was given by Ort.

While Meghan worked the moist lock and then let Ramsey push the solid door open for her, Milos Ort stepped up next to me and slowly, almost shyly, put his arm through mine

"Mr. deWitt, you have not had a very easy, a very smooth reception."

I thought I was getting one now, but I nodded.

"Perhaps your work does not take long, perhaps it is easy, but if I can be of any assistance to you...."

He did not finish the sentence, assuming apparently that I knew what he meant.

"Very nice of you," I mumbled. "Thank you."

"Not at all."

We walked into the building and followed Meghan and Ramsey down a long corridor. The various doors, I imagined, led to the workshops in the building.

"There is always that lag," Ort was saying, "if not a complete interruption, of the normal business when there is a change of hands."

I stopped to look back briefly. Max, closing the front door, winked at me and then followed.

"I can help you minimize the dead time," said Ort. "The inevitable loss of business in a case like this."

"Well, I'm not really familiar with Crevassette's operations," I said to him.

"But I am," and he smiled. And then, "Besides, you are the head *pro tem*, are you not? I would have to do business through you, would I not?"

"You are well informed, Mister Ort."

"Milos. Please."

I nodded and thought for a moment. Ort was right. The transfer process should not really preoccupy me much longer, what with McEvoy's staff doing the leg work. And wouldn't it be a fine feather in my cap if I could walk up to Lobbe when all this was over and not only hand him the company he wanted, the Gadget he craved, but also some going business for Special Developments Company, Ltd., deWitt, Pres. *pro tem.*

Meghan was unlocking the door at the end of the corridor. Ramsey stood by with an expression on his face which did not go with his fierce leather jacket. There seemed to be something aflutter in his eyes, there seemed to be a touch of worry around his mouth. He looked at me and then he looked away, as if to make the point that he really did not care. About what? He had been jealous of Ort over Meghan. Was he now also jealous of Ort over me? The thought was ridiculous, but there it was.

Meghan flipped a light on the other side of the door and lit up a room which had undoubtedly been Crevassette's own place of work. There was a desk whose neatness implied the solicitude of a good secretary. There was a table against one wall, a large sheet of thick plywood resting on three simple sawhorses. The top of this expanse was an unspeakable welter of notes and books, a coffee pot, tiny tools, a slide rule, an abacus, a pair of large scissors, and a pot of glue. The wall over the table held a collage of slips of paper—in blue, yellow and white—all tacked there in esoteric disorder, bearing penciled formulas, spidery drawings, cryptic notes. Crevassette, it seemed, had communicated with himself in various colors and in several languages; mathematics, German, English, and French. One note read: *Gurken kaufen*, a reminder not to forget to buy pickles.

"The plans," said Meghan, "are here."

She stood by a commodious safe. It was taller than she and it rested not on the worn, wooden floor of the room but on a slab of concrete. The safe was painted black, adorned with scrolls in gold paint, and bore the legend, "Monolith, Krupp Werke, 1893." So much for the old-fashioned touch.

Meghan opened a thing like a fuse box on the wall next to the safe. She inserted and turned a key in the appropriate manner, flipped three levers back and forth in a particular order, and when a little light blinked on she went to the safe. There was a bit more hocus-pocus with a lever, a key, and then with the combination dial.

"I would like a witness present," she said. "I know, Mr. deWitt, that your instructions don't require this, but I would like a third party to witness and sign for the transfer."

"Max Garten, my assistant," I said, and then I looked at Ort and Ramsey, who were both standing there in separate attitudes of curiosity, Ort smiling his disturbing smile, Ramsey starting to sweat at the hairline.

Max went to the office door and opened it. He stood there with all his blandness, his foolishness, his other worldly six-foot-five insanity shining from his face, but somehow he also came across with a clear, unquestionable authority.

"Miss Bushmill said a *third* party," he said quite simply.

Ramsey and Ort looked at one another, hesitated a moment, then left the room.

Meghan waited till the door was closed. Then, with businesslike efficiency, she opened the two successive steel doors, pulled out the thick, labeled leather tube which contained the long roll of specifications and blueprints for Gadget, signed with Max and me the prepared memo transfer and receipt, and closed the safe again.

"According to my briefing," I said, "there is a model of the Analyzer."

"Yes. In the vault room."

"And according to my instructions, which you have read, I am to have it disassembled and crated for shipment to New York."

"You want to look at it now?"

"Just a look," I said.

Before we had the look, the three of us in dead Crevassette's quiet office kept very still while we listened to an unexpected exchange on the other side of the office wall.

CHAPTER 8

"You understand deals," Gilliam Ramsey was saying.

I don't know whether the intervening wall softened his voice or whether he was actually trying not to be heard.

"All my life," said Milos Ort. "I am good at it."

"Not this time," said Ramsey. "Unless you listen to me."

"Ah—" said Ort. He could just have been finishing a glass of liqueur.

"I want you out of the picture," said Ramsey.

Meghan made a sudden move but I put a hand on her arm.

"If that's about you," I said to her, "then I want to know about it."

"Why? What possible business...."

"Quiet."

She blinked at me and, surprisingly, did not say a word. Then we listened again.

"What are you after?" Ort was saying.

"Not you," said Ramsey. "But if you don't give me what I want, I'll go after you too."

"How threatening," and then Ort giggled.

"Not really. But I am offering you a deal. For your testimony," Ramsey said. "I will arrange immunity for you."

"Idiot," said Ort. "I can destroy you and your effectiveness with one simple statement to, for example, the naïve Mr. deWitt."

Max, who was half sitting on a window sill, yawned. I did not know it at the time, but when Max yawned it had nothing to do with being tired. It was something like the muscle stretch which a jungle cat performs in preparation for some vast, lethal leap. For the moment, however, his yawn merely irritated me. And so did Meghan. She looked up at me and nodded slowly, just once, but in a most deprecatory way. But then what galvanized her was nothing that came from me.

"I could tell Meghan," said Ramsey.

"She does not matter," Ort said.

There was just the slightest slump in Meghan's posture, and though I was not looking at her at the moment I knew that she was looking at me. If I had looked back I would undoubtedly have felt like comforting her in some small but genuine way. But these are afterthoughts. Actually there was no time.

"Then it's no deal?" I heard Ramsey saying.

"Idiot," said Ort again. This time the disdain in his voice could have melted steel.

Nothing else was said after that, nothing clear, though I thought I heard Ramsey say something like, "Out—". Mostly, we heard sounds which were muffled. They meant nothing to me. But they apparently meant a great deal to Max. Without benefit of machinery he suddenly streaked across the room, yanked the door open, and was gone.

By the time Meghan and I reached the passage beyond, the scene in the hallway had petrified.

Ramsey was in a heap on the floor. He was holding his wrist. There was a gun which had slid against one wall of the corridor and Milos Ort was eyeing it as if he had never seen anything like it before. Max was taking a deep breath.

"I don't know what it means either," he said. "But Gilliam here was holding a gun on the foreigner."

Ort ran one hand across his forehead. His skin was moist, his face distracted. But in the middle of his helpless gesture he stooped to the ground very swiftly. What kept him from picking up the gun was Max's foot. The rather large shoe was now entirely on the gun and partly on the tips of Ort's fingers. Ort waited patiently until Max shifted his weight. Then he stood up slowly and with a show of composure smiled at Meghan and me.

"We were quarreling over Meghan," he said in a tired voice.

The explanation, in view of what we had heard before, was a patent lie.

Ramsey got off the floor and said nothing. I looked from him to his enemy and then back at him; but Ramsey was clearly in no mood to explain, to excuse, or to further lie about whatever the fairly important thing must have been which had caused him to commit an act of extremity that had completely misfired.

Under the stress of this sort of situation the simplest act is to commit yourself to one side or the other. Curiously enough, I could side with neither Ort nor Ramsey. To me, they were equal unknowns. I bent down and picked up the gun which Ramsey had dropped. It was a small-caliber automatic. I ejected the clip from the butt and dropped it into my pocket. I jacked the slide back and found that the chamber was empty. Then I tossed the empty at Ramsey.

He caught it and then he finally said something. Or, rather he tried to say something.

"DeWitt," he said, "the way things must look to you at the moment, I'm afraid you're going to make a rash mistake."

"How?" I said, but I felt mostly rhetorical about it, not caring what his excuse was going to be.

"In judgment," he said. "It is true, I had a quarrel with Milos...."

"Over Meghan," Ort said again.

I looked at him, but only got his desperate smile. I turned back to Ramsey, who was just slipping the empty gun under his black leather jacket as if he had practiced the move a great number of times.

"Why the quarrel?" I asked him.

"Because I hate Milos Ort."

I turned to Max, who was leaning against the wall, eyeing Meghan.

"You're a lover," I said to him. "Does this sound like a quarrel over a woman to you?"

Max pushed away from the wall and sneezed. He apologized with a bow in Meghan's direction and said, "The young woman is worth it, but the idea of a quarrel over her at this time, under these circumstances, is preposterous. For example, I had occasion at one time...."

"Thank you, Max. Exactly what I think. You lovers are peaceful enough at the party, but you wait until I take Meghan Bushmill to the plant here before having this shoot-out. Why, I wonder?"

Ort sighed, and Ramsey put his hands in his pockets.

"I think I had better go," he said, and went to the door.

"I apologize," said Ort. "For both of us."

Max sneezed.

Meghan gave him a look of concern, then watched her two suitors go out the front door. She searched her purse for a key and opened one of the corridor doors.

The room beyond was windowless. It had work benches along all the walls, tables with electronic testing devices, and trays full of minute electronic components. Low hanging neon lights illuminated the work benches when Meghan flipped the switch. We walked past them to a far door.

"Please don't sneeze again," she said to Max. "We try to maintain a relatively constant humidity in this room."

The door was steel. Meghan opened it with Max's help and we walked into what I supposed must be the vault room.

According to the information I had received, a full-scale Gadget was of the approximate size of four telephone booths stacked together; the model, designed for test and demonstration purposes only, was to be not much larger than a steamer trunk. This reduction in size was said to be partly due to miniaturization, partly to the omission of parts. Nonetheless, it had been executed in sufficient detail to serve as an effective guide in the making of the real thing.

This was all the information I had been given about the Gadget. It was sufficient for the present. Because when Meghan turned on the light in the room I was immediately able to grasp one pertinent fact: the model was missing.

CHAPTER 9

The room was bare except for a work bench against one of the walls. There was a double-winged door at the back, an efficient-looking affair, also made of steel. The cement floor was streaked with black skid marks which went from a point by a wall to this second steel door.

Max was already by the door, rattling it, fingering it.

"Locked," he said. "And judging by the draft down here"—he looked at his feet—"this leads to the outside." There was nothing deceptive about Meghan's reaction. She was so surprised that she did not seem to hear Max's remark. She stared at the wall, at a complex arrangement of electrical outlets which might have supplied the model with power, and then at the steel doors through which the model had apparently been taken away. I swore an oath, nothing fancy as I recall, but of sufficient loudness to revive Meghan. She looked at me as if my presence on the scene explained everything.

"Do something!" she said, with all the single-minded logic of a field marshal.

"Right. I want you to call the police." Then I turned to Max. "Run out to the back and see what you can see."

"I think it's rather foolish to assume...."

"So do I, but just go and do something foolish once in your life, will you, Max?"

I did not wait for an answer but ran to the front of the building. Max's footsteps followed me. When we got to the street Max continued running until he turned a corner of the building. I stayed in front, looking for Ramsey and Ort.

There was one car and one man. The car was Max's rocket ship and the man was Ort. He came toward me through the fog slowly, simian arms dangling, humanoid face grinning. He looked like a man who was about to sell you dirty pictures.

"He's gone," said Ort.

"Where did he go?"

"He didn't say. He was quite offensive, and then he just left."

"Offensive about what?"

Ort shrugged.

"You know," he said. "You have seen how he acts."

It was true, I had seen how he acts. What I did not know was why he acted the way he did.

There was a sneeze in the yellow fog and Max came back. He gave a thoroughly uninteresting report of having seen nothing but locked doors, an empty yard, a fence beyond, and an alley on the other side of it.

"And the fence is intact," he said. "But it isn't high. How much does the model weigh?"

"About six hundred and fifty pounds," said Ort.

If he had not seen my look he must have felt it, because he beamed his simian grin at me, as if to apologize for talking out of turn.

"An interesting detail," I said to him, "considering that we are dealing with a secret device."

But then he had me again. The Gadget might be secret, he explained, as far as its electronic refinements were concerned, but neither the general principle of the device, nor its existence, was unknown. As for the weight of the model, that had been mentioned to him when old Crevassette himself had shown him the machine.

Meghan came out to join us and said that the police were on their way. Her call must have had the absolute punch of efficiency because we could already hear the awful wailing of a police car in the distance. Max sneezed and Meghan gave him an anxious look.

We listened to the approaching yammer in the distance and then heard it expire. The police car had stopped nowhere near our own place of mystery.

Somehow, that expiring, faraway sound made me feel abandoned and lonely. I had become sensitive to a whole list of unknowns. Each, separately, was of minor significance, but their aggregate had the weight of a great, hopeless helplessness. Max's disregard of the elements and the basic laws of survival had made me feel unsafe to the degree of worrying about my survival. Milos Ort, with his uncanny knowledge of little details and his patent desire to be friends with the temporary head of Crevassette's gave me cause for nothing but nameless suspicion. And his apparent liaison with Meghan added to my dislike of the man. Meghan herself, who was apt to rankle by her way of completely ignoring me, except as a bearer of bad news and a disruptive nuisance, was no comfort. As for Gilliam Ramsey, the inconsistency of his conduct was perhaps the most bothersome item. An agent who wore Levis and leather jacket, he had pulled a gun in the heat of an argument and then drifted off into the night. The gun play had been so half-hearted and inept that it could only make sense in a context which I knew nothing about: some entirely desperate business. Only an extremity would have made Ramsey's improvisation absolutely necessary, it seemed to me. And the performance had failed so miserably that the man had had to bolt the scene in order to recoup in some other way.

The police siren started pulsing again.

"They stopped to read the street sign," said Ort, "and now they are coming this way."

"Primitive," said Max. "If I had to rely on signs in my business...."

"You might have a more modest record of crash landings," I told him.

"Your scarf has come undone," Meghan said to him. And then she wrapped it around his neck solicitously.

The police car shot into view very fast, a performance which made Max's feverish eyes glisten even more. The black little vehicle jammed to a stop right behind Max's roadster and two bobbies jumped out. They treated me to a performance for which my experience with policemen on the roads of America had not prepared me. They apologized.

"Bloody accident down the road," said one of them. "Sorry for the delay," said the other.

"How bloody?" I asked.

The heavier of the two, who looked like a benign spirit on a Christmas print, smiled.

"There was no blood, actually."

"But the bloody car," said the other policeman, who looked like a mole, "was fairly smashed."

"Blue—" I said.

"Blew? Nothing blew. Driver safe and sound and unconscious behind the wheel. Cracked a rib or so, by the looks of it."

"Was it a blue Morris Minor?" I asked.

They looked at each other, and the Spirit of Christmas nodded.

"How do you know?" he said.

"Because he's a friend of mine. Named Ramsey. He just left here."

"What did he hit this time?" Meghan asked.

"He didn't. It hit him. By the looks of the gouging he got it must have been a lorry."

It had been Ramsey. They had lifted him out, called an ambulance, and had left him with the third policeman in their team at a corner under a street light. Ramsey had come to just before they had left and had told them his name.

"Didn't talk so good, but he said Ramsey, all right."

"Did he say anything else?" Ort wanted to know.

The heavy policeman gave him a look but no answer. He then wanted to know about the report of a theft.

We did not get away for nearly an hour, and not even Max's sneezing, sweating, and shivering caused the law to alter its pedantic pace. I tried to hasten procedural matters by identifying myself as the *pro tem* victim, but it was not until an Inspector had arrived from the Yard, together with a team of robbery experts, that we could leave. After that it still was not Claridge's.

We went back to Meghan's house. I sat in my old seat next to Max, but with Meghan on top of me. Ort had to sit on the luggage rack, facing backward. Max, of course, drove.

When we arrived, in a state resembling suspended animation, the place was absolutely quiet. It was now five o'clock in the morning, and all the party people had left. The main room, except for the disorder, was rather attractive. Bookshelves covered one wall, the multicolored spines suggesting both serious intent and leisure. There was a low bent-wood table in excellent condition, a Chippendale couch which looked like an heirloom, and a breakfront with leaded glass and wood inlays which had a lot of Biedermeier charm. There was a cast-iron radiator under each of the two tall windows. Someone had painted one yellow and one blue. The blue one was softly ticking to itself. The low light came from a hanging lamp in one corner. It was amber satin on top and had a tasseled fringe. It looked like another heirloom. Only when I had sat down did I realize that the mood suggested by the room did not reflect the mood of all its occupants.

I did not know what it meant, but Meghan's usually quiet face with the vulnerable eyes had become still as stone. She was staring at Ort. When she spoke, finally, her tone was low and even.

"Milos," she said. After one last look at him she turned away. "I want you to get out."

I thought she looked positively dangerous, and I had to admire Ort's courageous giggle.

"But what is it, my dear?"

"Get—out! Now!"

"But why?" said Ort. The sudden excitement in his voice had just the faintest touch of panic. There was no anger.

Meghan turned to him again. She was apparently over her anger. Her face showed nothing but cold disdain. I would have been wilted by that look, and I had to marvel again at the way in which Ort received it with his almost habitual, conciliatory grin.

"You made a phone call before we left."

"It was nothing."

"At midnight?"

"Since we were leaving unexpectedly, I called my service. You know that I sometimes get business calls at very odd hours, darling."

She flinched at the last word, but did not take it up.

"You made a very odd call, Milos," she said. "You talked low and fast and the only word I happened to overhear was 'Westminster.'"

"That happens to be the name of the young man who handles my night calls."

The disgust on Meghan's face hardened, then totally disappeared. It was as if she were quite herself again, somehow entirely on her own, and Milos no longer mattered.

"You know what I know and I know what you have done. Why discuss it? And now you will leave this very moment."

"But my dearest Meghan...."

"Or I will ask Mr. deWitt to throw you out."

I reacted with mixed feelings. I am not beyond throwing somebody out, particularly for someone like Meghan Bushmill, but I did not have the faintest idea what was going on or where, indeed, my own interests lay. I had the uncanny feeling that everything was happening precisely because I had appeared on the scene.

But I was spared making a decision. Garten blew his nose, put the handkerchief back in his pocket, and at the same time coiled an incredibly long arm around Ort's neck in the manner of a purposeful boa constrictor.

"I will leave," said Ort. It did not sound like his normal, mellifluous voice, but it was distinguishable.

"Let go of him," I said to Max.

While Meghan went into the bedroom I took off the loden cape and then Ort's jacket. But first, out of habit, I ran my hands through the various jacket pockets. Garten let go of his victim, patted Ort's suit, and straightened his tie. While this was going on I found the slip of paper. It was no more than a small, torn-off corner and it had a number on it.

"May I have that, please?" said Ort.

I gave him the slip and also his jacket. Meghan came back from the bedroom, carrying a small canvas bag and an armful of clothes. Ort took these also and walked to the door. Then he turned and looked only at me.

"With your permission," he said, "I would like to call on you tomorrow—or today, as it were. A matter of business, you remember?" With that he left.

Undoubtedly he knew where to reach me. He knew altogether more than I did about anything.

As soon as the door closed the phone rang in the bedroom. Meghan went to answer it and then called through the door.

"It's for you, Mr. deWitt."

It was now five-thirty in the morning.

CHAPTER 10

In the course of my labors for Mijnheer Lobbe, I have acquired the reflex of assuming that behind the new, the unexpected, and the vexatious, that worthy may be found. The assumption is based more on feeling than evidence—except the circumstantial evidence that he remains invisible until matters are approaching a catastrophic head. Then with a great leap out of the void he materializes on my back. So when I went to the bedroom, where Meghan was holding out the phone to me, I fully expected that Lobbe was now going to reveal himself.

"DeWitt here."

"One moment please. I will connect you."

"With whom? Hello!" There was no point in yelling, because nobody was on the line. By the tweets and cackles I had the distinct impression that the connection was being shunted about in lengthy and mysterious ways. When the hoarse, weak voice came on I felt relieved, then slightly stunned. It was not Lobbe. Which meant that Lobbe might have nothing to do with, might have no idea of, what was going on.

"Are you deWitt?"

"Yes, damn it. Who are you?"

"I need some identification, if you don't mind. Whose jacket are you wearing?"

"Now just one damn minute!"

"Please!" the voice said, with such pitiful overtones that I felt touched.

"I took it off," I said. "It was Milos Ort's."

"Thank you."

"You're welcome. In the meantime, I could use some identification from you."

"Of course. Are you alone?"

"In this room, yes."

"This is Gilliam Ramsey."

"I'll be damned," I said.

The voice laughed slightly; I remembered Ramsey's gentle laugh, which had contrasted so curiously with his leather-sheathed appearance.

"What's this all about, Ramsey?"

"Is Ort still there?"

"No. Meghan threw him out."

He ignored this. It only seemed important to him to know whether Ort was present or not.

"I called to warn you about him," said Ramsey. "I will gladly explain the entire matter to you at some other time, but for the moment I felt it necessary simply to warn you—to instruct you, I would like to say—that this Ort person is potentially, er, dangerous."

"Ramsey," I said. "I've been warned about you too."

"Possibly. However, I do not arrange accidents for other people."

"What was that?"

"Just one moment, please." He groaned and then he sighed. I imagined that he had changed his position.

"Are you in a hospital?" I asked him.

"I'm under care, yes."

"Where are you?"

He ignored that and talked somewhat less hoarsely.

"I have no idea how Ort managed it," said Ramsey, "but circumstantially I am convinced that Ort arranged for the lorry to pile into me. I escaped a fatal conclusion only because I was looking for something like this."

"How so?"

"After I crossed Westminster Bridge into Kingston on the way to the plant we picked up a tail. It was good weather for the job, of course, but the tail was rather a hefty lorry."

"I think I know how Ort arranged it, if any of this isn't pure fantasy."

"No fantasy. He and I have had our differences and my decision to leave the plant alone was entirely engineered by him. He refused to utter a word when I tried to speak to him on the street, so naturally I left. But you were going to tell me how he arranged all this."

"He made a phone call from here before we left for the plant. Meghan overheard the word 'Westminster.'"

"Where the lorry was waiting for us."

"Ort claimed it was the name of the operator who handles his answering service at night."

"That's a patent lie. Meghan has received calls for him and the night man's name is Cushing."

"And how do you know this, Ramsey?"

"Listen, deWitt, I promise I'll tell you more. At the moment I'm not at liberty, except to urge you not to enter into any dealings whatsoever with Ort. Please appreciate that."

"I also appreciate your evasion, Ramsey. What were those differences between you and Ort? And don't say they were over Meghan."

"I won't."

"Then tell me!"

"I'll be in touch, deWitt. Meanwhile, remember my warning."

"I've had you checked, Ramsey!" I was almost yelling, sensing distinctly that he was about to hang up. "I know that you're with Intelligence, Ramsey!"

"Ridiculous."

"*And* moonlighting for that Radford outfit."

He hung up.

My feeling was like the rage of someone about to take a deep breath who finds a hand clapped over his mouth. I could think of only one thing to do for the moment, and that was to establish that Ramsey was at least as much of a liar as Ort. I banged the phone down and fairly stalked into the other room. It was empty. I stalked on and, sure enough, in the little room next to the kitchen....

"What in hell are you doing, Max Garten?" I bent down to look at him.

He lay once again mummified under blankets and under the upside-down cot. Meghan sat on the floor beside him, adding her own witchcraft to the scene. She was holding a sheet of paper over his head so that his one visible eye could look at it. There was a black dot on the page.

"It helps him concentrate," said Meghan.

"That's how this madman got his rhinitic disorder in the first place!"

"I know," said Meghan, whose ever widening spectrum of emotions now included an annoying patience. "He did suggest another method."

"I bet he did. Something he learned in the Shetland Islands?"

"How did you know?"

She seemed on the point of answering when her mouth curved in the slightest of smiles. In my state, that too was completely annoying.

"Unswath his mouth."

"Why?"

"So that the rhinitic oracle can speak!"

She looked at me as if *I* were mad; then she pushed the blankets out of the way. Max had his mouth pursed as if for a kiss, and he whistled gently. I did not bother to ask him what this was about. I was sure it had something to do with Zen breath control.

"Max," I said. "Do you know in your infinite wisdom how I call up your Intelligence?"

"Huh?"

Meghan shook her head and covered him up again. Then she held her hand out to me so that I could help her up.

"I'll call them for you," she said. "The Bureau of Internal Security? Concerning the theft?"

"Yes," I lied.

"Mister Crevassette's work sometimes involved us with the Bureau." We walked back to the bedroom.

"Like, with Ramsey?"

"Gilliam? Absurd. He's a draftsman for Radford Engineering."

"Hah!" I said.

Neither she nor I quite knew what that meant. Then Meghan began to dial.

"You'll get the night operator," she said. "He'll route you."

She gave me the phone and left again.

I felt I was being very clever about it. I never asked them if somebody by the name of Gilliam Ramsey worked for them, but instead made the question into a firm assumption. I said that I had to get in touch with him. Matter of urgent security. The ensuing details took long enough to allow for the theft of an atom bomb, the destruction of the parliamentary system of government, and the establishment of friendly relations between the United States and Red China. In the end, however, I did get an answer. There was no Gilliam Ramsey on their payroll.

CHAPTER 11

And if Gilliam Ramsey were with British Intelligence, would they tell me?

That phone call, I felt, had been entirely a matter of nerves and lack of sleep.

On the other hand, Lobbe had got information about Ramsey. But then Lobbe had better sources of information.

I decided that Lobbe had been out of the picture long enough. If he was not going to call me, I was going to call him. Besides, I was precisely in the sort of up-in-the-air mood of irritation for which I find long distance phone calls a distinct relief. It would be the hour past midnight on Long Island. Lobbe, as was his secret wont, would be rowing away on Oyster Bay in his six-foot dinghy. He was a vain man. He did not want anyone to think that he ever exercised for any conceivable reason, and especially for his bulk. The one time I did surprise him at this surreptitious health regimen he explained the whole thing away with quick gibberish about ancestral stirrings from his family's seafaring past.

So I called him; I felt very good about it.

After Lobbe's man Kalopidos answered the phone there was the expected delay while Kalopidos yelled out of one of the rear windows and into the dark waters of the bay.

Kalopidos was not a typical North Shore butler. There was his name, for one thing, and there was his black handlebar mustache, for another. Each of its ends was like a horse's tail. Lobbe had once said that the filtration qualities of that facial decoration were responsible for the golden tones that were heard when Kalopidos sang Greek mountain songs.

Thinking of the news I had to tell Lobbe, I got nervous. He was surely not going to like some of the things he was going to hear. To add to my misgivings, my crazy companions now came into the room.

Max was draped in a blanket and drenched in sweat. Meghan was carrying her mystic paper and the madman's blanket train.

"He's going to take a bath," said Meghan.

"In what?" I said. "Dragon's blood and milk of snakes?"

"Don't be silly," she said and went into the bathroom. Max kept standing there, looking like an Olympian athlete who had died some time ago.

"Do you mind if I stand on my head?" he said.

"Please do. I was going to suggest something like that myself. After a jump out the window."

Then the phone exploded.

"*Vat, vat, vat?*" thundered at me from across the Atlantic.

"Uh, good morning, Mister Lobbe."

"Is that you, *Ezel? Mein Gott*, vy ask. Vat else calls me in the middle of the night and says good morning to the tune of four dollars a minute and tells me to jump out the window! *Carroña!* There better be something else important for what you call!"

In this case his bad English was patently no attempt to disguise his fluency. He was simply excited. He was also breathing extremely hard.

"Kalopidos!" he yelled. "Bring me dry pants! Wait! First the bottle from over there."

I waited a moment.

"Did you fall into the water, sir?"

He now breathed like a hard-working Percheron.

"Water? What water? I just happen to like dry pants, not wet. Thank you, Kalopidos."

I waited until Lobbe sighed.

"*Prosit*," I said.

But he did not like that at all, and except for nerves and lack of sleep and a harassing *Walpurgisnacht* in the air and on the ground I would not have permitted myself the familiarity. He now called me Manford, not Manny.

"What," he said, "did you want to say, besides to tell me I should jump out the window?"

"Progress report, sir."

"Already?" He forgot about his anguish and sounded eager. "I love you, Manny, my *Wunderkind!*"

He would soon go back to Manford again.

"We have a kind of problem here, Mister Lobbe. We...."

"*We?* What's with *we?* I am sitting here in my room—thank you, Kalopidos—just a minute, Manford—" There was bumbling and grumbling while I caught only the remark, "*Gott verdomme*, not so tight!" And then finally, "Now go out there and fish out the *verdomme* dinghy from the treacherous bottom." He next made a sound as if he were swilling the bottle he had mentioned. He wheezed briefly and readdressed himself to me.

"Mennekin?" Those dry pants and that cannon shot of a drink had done wonders. "You are there?"

"Right."

"What's wrong?"

"I don't know yet, sir. I have obtained the plans from the vault, as instructed. I am ready to enter the transfer papers in escrow in a few hours. Then I'll pick up your check at McEvoy's office and take it in person to Bartholomew Crevassette, at which time I'll pick up the supplementary plans."

"I know all that. I myself told you to do so."

I could hear him sniff, and if that was a sign of disdain it was the very wettest.

"Now about the model, sir."

"I need that *instanter instantis*. Without that, the plans take twice as long to translate."

"I'm afraid the model has been stolen."

There was a pause. It was the pause of a man gathering strength. The curse which followed it should have atomized the transoceanic cable, in fact scorched the very bottom of the sea. Even though it was entirely in Dutch—a language which, mercifully, I do not understand—I felt weakened by its impact. Judging by the subsequent pause, he too must have felt debilitated. Then he said, "Manny? Ho there! Are you all right?"

"Uh, I'm here."

"Is the police on the theft?"

"Yes."

"Their security people?"

"I suggested it to the Inspector, but he said industrial theft did not require the intervention of another office."

"But if the model crosses the border! If Mud and Dreck try to move it out of the country...."

"I told him about Mud and Dreck, sir. He says his department will handle it."

"You must find that Ramsey person! You remember I told you about the one that followed me from the plant?"

"Gilliam Ramsey is not a member of British Intelligence."

"*Quatsch*. Who told you?"

"There was, first of all, the night clerk in the information office of the security bureau...."

"And he is going to tell a voice on the telephone with a foreign accent from the colonies of America who the secret spies are? Manford deWitt," he roared, "as soon as you leave away from here and from my guidance do you also take leave of your senses?"

Something was thumping. I looked away and there was Max standing on his head, of course. He was apparently getting tired, because his heels were hitting the wall.

"Secondly," I said to the phone, "Gilliam Ramsey, according to Miss Bushmill, is a draftsman with the Radford outfit."

"Aha! Find the man!"

"I've tried. He won't be found. Instead, he called me on the phone and urged me to avoid a man presumably dangerous to me and our business."

"You know what that sounds like to me?"

"I'm serious, Mister Lobbe. I'm partly calling to ask you whether your sources of information might check the man out." Then I told him what I knew of Milos Ort and of the animosity between him and Ramsey.

Lobbe was in the middle of asking a number of pertinent questions when Max, still upside down, sneezed violently and fell over.

"*Vat, vat, vat?*"

Lobbe too had heard it. At that moment Meghan opened the bathroom door to see what had happened. The sound of water rushing into the tub was now quite loud.

"Manford! Answer me!"

"Er—yes. What was that?"

"What was that was what I asked! I hear boomping, I hear crashing, I hear wild gushing. I put it all together and I ask myself—is there a natural disaster with a waterfall and a boulder splatting down?"

I looked at Max on the floor and searched for answer.

"Where are you, Manny?"

"It's nothing, sir. I'm in Miss Bushmill's bedroom." The quality of Lobbe's pause had changed. I could see him being very, very busy with his imaginings.

"Hm," he said. "The boomp I can understand. Miss Bushmill just took off a shoe. But the waterfall?"

"She did not take off a shoe and it's not a waterfall. Miss Bushmill is merely drawing a bath."

There was that pause again. And then, "Manny, let me tell you something. I once knew a man who got electrocuted while telephoning from a bathtub."

What prevented me from answering was the sight I now saw. Max was stark naked and Meghan was helping him into the tub.

"So don't go in the tub, Manny," Lobbe was saying.

"As a matter of fact, I'm not. Somebody else is."

The rush of water stopped and then there was a different kind of splash. Max sat down in the water and sneezed violently.

"She is, eh?" He seemed to think he had it all figured out. "What kind of woman is she? She has ice water for a bath?"

"As a matter of fact, Miss Bushmill is fully clothed."

"Most ridiculous thing I ever heard, ice water or not."

"I think, Mr. Lobbe, it would take too long to explain the unusual nature...."

At that moment Lobbe sneezed.

"Aha!" I said, full of pure vengeance. "You too?"

"Never mind the idiot talk, Manford deWitt. I don't take baths in cold water."

"Of course. But if I might suggest a few recent things I have learned about the cure of a cold. There is the Zen procedure."

"*Quatsch mit* Zen. I know the good method. Did I even tell you about this old Dutch custom we have...."

"I have heard it called the Shetland Island custom," I said. "But what does a *woman* do when she catches a cold?"

It is a mistake to take Lobbe's non-business pronouncements in too pedantic a way. He does not like that. He reacts with exasperation to the stultifying touch of logic.

"*Klootzig!*" he yelled. He has never made clear what that awful-sounding word means, but he throws it like a stone. "And now that you feel so smart again, how about we get also the customs, the port authorities, the Inland Security, etcetera etcetera on the job of recovering my loss, *hein?*"

"Right."

"And get McEvoy to come with the pressure from our Embassy on the British so they go over that Radford company with a fine comb with sharp teeth."

"Yessir."

"Don't interrupt. And I want those plans delivered direct under the circumstances, in a direct line from there to here via airplane with Max Garten."

"He has a cold in the head."

"He has something in the head, at any rate. And you," he said, as if addressing a lout, "get the supplementaries from that grieving brother and jet them here the same way as soon as Garten returns."

Somewhere in that schedule Garten would need some sleep. I did not mention this because Lobbe was not through.

"As for Ramsey, stand away from him. As for Ort—did you say something about business?"

"He did propose it—to continue as usual."

"Do it. You're *pro tem*. Then hand it over to McEvoy's office."

"There is some indication that Milos Ort has attempted murder tonight. I mentioned the Ramsey accident to you."

"Good. Uh, *c'est-à-dire*, I will check out Ort and you in the meantime treat him like any prospective business contact, *c'est-à-dire*, like a snake in the grass."

"Right."

"Anything else you want?"

"Nothing else at the moment."

"All right," he said. His voice changed. "Then get some sleep, *hein*, mennekin?"

On that he hung up. Hans Lobbe sometimes surprises that way.

CHAPTER 12

Meghan came into the bedroom and took a quilted robe out of her closet.

"I'll change in the kitchen," she said. "Then I'll make some tea. Would you like some?"

I said yes, that would be fine, and when she left I went into the bathroom. It would not do at this point to let Max drown in his sleep.

He looked long, pink, and somewhat swollen around the eyes. But he was awake. Without a word, he lifted one of his incredibly long arms and I pulled him out of the tub, onto his feet.

He marched into the bedroom without having dried himself and, deaf to my exclamations, crawled into Meghan's bed. Then he looked up at me mournfully and closed his eyes.

"It is no substitute for the Shetland maidens," he said, "but it will have to do."

I hated to keep him awake a moment longer but what I had to say was important. "Look, Max, in spite of the deficient medical facilities, do you think, with a few hours' sleep, you'll be in good enough shape to fly to New York in a little while?" I explained Lobbe's request and he thought about it.

"I'll do my best," he said, "though I'd be surer.... Tell you what. Why not call up Bunny and describe the emergency to her?"

"There isn't time enough. Besides, when you get to the States, Lobbe can offer you the Dutch cure."

"Dutch?"

"Do you think a good thing like that could be confined indefinitely to the Shetland Islands?"

He smiled, and by the time I reached the door Max was asleep.

I went into the kitchen, where water was singing on the stove. Meghan, standing in the quilted robe, was watching the kettle. She was humming, as though she liked what she was doing, and when I came in she smiled at me and did not mind the way I looked back at her.

"You look as if you suddenly like me," she said to my surprise.

"I do."

"Is he asleep?"

"Yes. Finally."

"Why don't you lie down too? I'll wake you whenever you have to be up."

I looked at my watch and shook my head. I knew it would be easier simply to stay up.

"I'd rather sit and then start early. But you go to sleep."

She handed me the tray she had prepared.

"I thought I'd stay with you," she said. She opened the door for me and showed me where to put the tea tray. "I've had some experience, you know. I thought perhaps I might help with the transfer business."

We sat down on the Chippendale sofa, which, in contrast to its gentle curves, turned out to be surprisingly hard.

"Nice of you to offer," I said. "But I'd think you've had enough of this business."

She shrugged and poured tea. She did not look helpless, as it had pleased me to imagine, but she looked irretrievably alone. It was rather a sad sight.

"Do you take cream, sugar, Mr. deWitt?"

"Just plain." The fog outside the window was becoming definable. A very weak morning light was rising. I looked back at Meghan. "Would you call me Manny?" I said.

She looked at me briefly and then down at the cups again.

"Yes," she said. "I know you Americans have that kind of quick way with—with first names."

"That's not the reason, Meghan. I thought it might make you feel less alone."

She put the tea pot down much too hard, not because she was angry but because she was simply awkward.

She looked at me, but instead of saying anything bit her lip. I picked up my cup and drank the very dark tea. Then I put the cup down again.

"You can help me," I said. "Tell me about Milos Ort."

She leaned back against the sofa and folded her arms in front of her.

"Why did I live with him?" she asked.

"All right." Though that had not been the point of my question.

"Because I don't like to live alone." She touched her cup but then did not pick it up. "He did not live here, actually; he just came here. And that was all right too. We shared ideas, which is very important to me, and, yes, we shared the bed. Beyond that, Milos was just a person who did business with Mr. Crevassette, who told travel stories, who somehow knew more than one world." She touched her chin and then dropped her hand again. "Do I make sense to you?"

"Yes, Meghan."

She laughed for the first time, though it was not a very wholehearted laugh.

"He did not like Americans very much."

"I know some I don't like myself."

"Ah yes," she said and looked at the window which was turning milky with light. "You made that point once before. Rather brutally, in fact. About lumping people together."

"I think the lumping is far more brutal. When you and Milos talked ideas, didn't you ever talk about that?"

She eyed me. I had no doubt about her intelligence, but that was not the prime attribute for which I might have wanted to be with Meghan. I liked her calm and I liked her straight gaze. Right then there was something else. She clasped her hands and stuck them between her knees. The gesture pushed her breasts together and opened her robe on top. She was quite unconscious of what happened.

"I don't think you and Milos would get along," she said.

Not for long, I thought, and I said to Meghan, "He has acted quite the contrary toward me."

"He wants something."

"Do you know what?"

"Mr. Crevassette is dead and you are taking over. It's nothing more than that."

"That's all right with me."

"But not with me," she said with a snap. She reached into the pocket of her robe and pulled out a packet of cigarettes. When she put one into her mouth the gesture emphasized how upset she was.

"You have a light?"

"Sorry. No."

She dropped the cigarette on the table.

"He started to use me and forgot who I was," she said. "He dined me to ask about Crevassette's production. He wined me because it makes me lazy in the head. He went to bed with me because he knew I enjoyed it. When that happened I didn't."

"Nonetheless, he wouldn't be the only man who'd use that excuse."

This time she really laughed.

"You actually like me, don't you, Manny."

"You seem surprised."

"Well—" She looked at the ceiling as if she were watching a balloon float away. "Take Max, for instance. He asked me to go to bed with him. It was nice of him, but I knew he asked because I'm a woman and one tries to go to bed with a woman when one is Max. He didn't really ask *me*."

"The bounder! And for purely medicinal reasons besides!"

She laughed, but then she got serious again.

"But it's easy to talk," she said.

"It sounds like more than talk."

She looked a little surprised, but then she nodded and made that little half-smile which had irritated me so the first time I had seen it, but which was charming now.

"Yes," she said. "And if Max had asked me a little later, perhaps, when I wasn't so busy seeing to it that the bath was the right temperature, that there would be no draft—"

"Is it Ort's absence which makes you lonely?"

She thought a moment and then shook her head.

"No. But his absence makes me know again that I am lonely, and there's nothing to distract me from that." She shook her head again, rather sharply, so that her rather short hair flew about and then settled down as if freshly brushed. I thought it looked rather exciting, framing her open face in an open way, like the hair of a woman who has just woken up, feeling well. Then she spoiled the effect with a frown and with that even hardness she could put around her mouth. She went to the window and looked at the fog, which had begun to alter with yellow tones again.

"I'm disappointed in him," she said to the fog. "If you want to call that missing something."

"It's more like having missed something along the way," I told her. Then I walked to the window where she was standing. "Perhaps I'm saying this because I don't want the same thing to happen to me."

She sat down on the window sill, facing me.

"He is good at his work," she said. "Mr. Crevassette got along with him and I respected Mr. Crevassette's judgment. I don't think you have to worry, from a business point of view."

"What do you think of that attempt to kill Ramsey?"

She looked away, and I could see her anger in profile. Her jaw line became prominent and her smooth neck suddenly showed the shadow of a vein.

"We talked such beautiful talk, about the welfare of masses of people. But one man, one no-mass man, Gilliam Ramsey, that was nothing. That would hardly make a topic of social import, would it now?"

"I might have taken that as my line, if you hadn't."

"You know," she said, not looking at me, "I don't mind when a man is like an animal in bed. But to commit violence like that—out there in the street—"

"That was not animal, Meghan. That was cold-blooded, long-range plotting. That was part of a scheme of things which had been operating before I came on the scene."

But she did not pick that up. I don't think she knew any more about the matter than I. Instead she thought of the men in it and how she felt about them.

"I don't care to be lied to for the sake of protection, and I don't care to be adored for reasons which have nothing to do with me."

"Was Ramsey your lover, too?"

"No. I know lots of young engineers because of the business. Ramsey was just one of them. That's all."

"Perhaps," I said, "that's not all. He works for one of Crevassette's competitors."

She looked at me as if I were an enemy. I think, once again, she was faced with the possibility that her attraction might not have had anything to do with herself. She talked very low.

"I did use to think that I could tell the difference between business and pleasure."

"Can you?"

She looked at me slowly and then down at her lap. Or perhaps not that far down. She carefully made the V of her robe smaller.

"I have one more question, Meghan. Would you know what the number nine-three-one might stand for?"

She looked up again and pursed her mouth. It became full in a most attractive way.

"Nine-three-one—sounds like a rural phone number—It is! That's Mr. Bartholomew's private number in Cricklade, Wiltshire. He has a country house there."

"Does Ort know the number?"

"Of course not. It's unlisted."

"There are ways of getting unlisted numbers."

"But why would he? Milos doesn't even know Mister Bartholomew."

"The number was on a slip of paper in Ort's jacket."

Her eyes shut very tight and she bit her lip. Then she said, "Oh, damn it, damn it all. What does it matter—" She got up from the window sill and made a gesture as if to bite into her hand.

"It matters that you are upset."

"To you?"

"I'm here with you," I said. "Just hold still. I'll hold you a while."

I put my arms around her and she tucked her head against me.

"Perhaps you think I'm the kind who's quite blasé and never feels shy."

"Is that one of those types?"

She tried very valiantly not to react and we sat down on the couch. But she did seem to feel that she had to say something.

"Perhaps you have not thought of the fact," she said as if giving a recital, "that I might just as easily have been here with Max." It was a nice, defiant speech.

"Listen, your Shyness," I said. "Do you always have to talk everything over?"

She tried to move away but then gave up.

"And yet," I said, "before we go any further, maybe you should look into the ideological requirements."

She moved again and at first I thought she was trying to get away. But all she did was lean back and look at me. Then she undid the belt of her robe.

"Manny," she said. "Do shut up, won't you now?"

CHAPTER 13

I woke up at eight in the morning with no recollection of having gone to sleep. I was on the couch and Meghan, by the sound of it, was in the shower. When Meghan appeared she was wearing a nifty tweed suit, one quite unlike the knobby, lumpy kind associated with strong, old Englishwomen hiking on the moors. It was impeccably pressed. The skirt ended above the knees. The jacket, which ended above the buttocks, would not button in front, partly because of the way Meghan was built, partly because the cut was meant to point this out. She looked fresh and relaxed. She made no fuss when I gave her money, measurements, and instructions to buy me some suitable clothes. Max looked dry and pink and innocent when I passed him on the way to the bathroom. I used the shaving equipment in his overnight bag and then put on Meghan's robe.

Max woke up when I sat down on the bed to call McEvoy on the phone.

"Good morning, fink," he said.

"How do you feel?"

"Betrayed, you bloody transvestite."

"I'm asking about your cold. You'll be flying to New York in a few hours. Can you make it?"

The question had been phrased correctly. It implied its own answer. Max leaped out of bed, took three and a half extended Zen breaths, and then flew to the bathroom.

McEvoy, swamped by the Crevassette business, had been at the London office of Lobbe Industriel since seven in the morning. I outlined the events which had already transpired and we discussed paper procedures to be completed during the rest of the day. The principal pressure for us was, of course, the short option period. Lobbe's suspicion that Radford might be up to some kind of interference maneuver had to be taken in account. The recent behavior of Ramsey, who worked for Radford, made the threat considerably less academic.

"Can't help you there," said McEvoy with the distinct sideways sound of a man who kept an eternal pipe in his mouth. "Far's I know, there's nothing Radford can do, ekshly."

McEvoy was Eton, Harrow, Magdalene College, and Sandhurst. I don't know how he had managed these overlapping school attendances. He always tried to camouflage the background when speaking to me. Only the ekshly had slipped out.

"Do you know Radford personally?" I asked him.

"Used to. But not since working for Mijnheer."

"You think he's accessible? Radford, I mean."

"Try the club. Has sherry there at ten-thirty."

"What club, McEvoy?"

"Oh. It's the Saddlers. Thought you'd know, ekshly."

"Can I get in there?"

"I'll call. I'm a member."

"All right," I said. "See you about noon."

I hung up and watched Max for a while. He had showered and now he was dressed. He took off his jacket, a blazer with buttons whose arrangement identified his military unit, and loosened his tie. Then he began to shave.

"Where are we going at noon?" he said to the mirror.

"Not we. I. You're flying to New York, remember? It's west of England."

"Out of the question," he said.

"Just try it. And no detours to the Shetland Islands. Lobbe wants these plans earlier than immediately."

"And *you*," he said with the knife at his throat, "are staying *here*? I have more than a few doubts about your competence."

"I will avoid instrument flying in sports cars and I will avoid debilitation in pursuits for which my prowess is deficient."

Right then Max cut himself. I left to go to the kitchen. When I came back with a cheese sandwich he was still trying to stanch the flow of blood.

"I will overlook what you said before, Manny."

"Thank you."

"Your ignorance of how to encounter life...."

"You mean disaster."

"... is of course alarming, and I am loath to leave you to your own devices."

"Fine."

"However, during my twelve-hour absence, keep this," and he pulled a revolver out of his trouser pocket.

"My God—" I said.

"Don't be afraid of it. You hold it this way."

I was not afraid of it, but I was impressed with its quality of over-kill. The gun he handed me was a Colt Python .357 Magnum, which is a mighty cannon indeed.

"I don't need it."

"I won't leave."

We argued. I was standing there with the cannon in my hand and that quilted robe draped on me when Meghan came in. She dropped the clothier's box on the floor and looked from me to Max and then back again.

"Dear," she said, "was he trying to attack you?"

Max thought that was very funny and Meghan did too. I did not see the humor of it and took the box and suitcase into the bathroom.

The box contained a mackintosh. Inside the suitcase was a suit of dark wool, no patterns, and of a clean, slim cut; a striped tie, a pair of socks, two shirts and underwear. I dressed and felt much more competent.

Not knowing what to do with the revolver, I stuck it into the pocket of my brand new mackintosh. Garten insisted on driving me because the Saddlers Club, he said, was on the way to the airport, anyway. I arranged with Meghan to meet me at McEvoy's office after I called Ort's local office number, which she had given me. The man who answered said that Mr. Ort had not come yet.

The fog had lifted enough to make me feel safe about the visibility, though I was racked with other worries. For all I knew, Max might not be able to drive when he could actually see. The car, which had no top at all, was awash inside. I sat on a mound made of the folded mackintosh to keep dry.

"When we get to the club I want you and this mackintosh with the ray gun to wait for me."

"*We're* going in."

We argued about that, but I was at a disadvantage. We had left Meghan's street in Soho, a crooked little lane with no buildings taller than three stories and with chimney pots, and now Max was negotiating Piccadilly Circus.

This square has not been safe for man, beast, or machine since its invention, and I found myself passing through it aboard a rocket ship. I held my eyes shut for a very long time, listening to a John Cage symphony of shouts, whistles, squeals, and horns blowing. When I found the courage to open them again, I was on the other side of the Thames, facing Waterloo Station. I watched the tower of Big Ben in the west, then in the east, and then it was not there anymore. The streets got bigger and less crooked, but this only caused Max to increase his speed. I was about to throw myself out onto the pavement when the car came to a screeching halt.

The oblong building had a façade of darkish stone cut into large, embroidered squares. Long, fluted windows broke up the stone geometry. Three tiers of windows suggested a building which was three stories high, except that the height of the windows required that the building be nine ordinary stories. A diminutive plaque at the entrance identified the Saddlers Club.

We went through an entrance hall wallpapered with Carrara marble, across an acre of parquet, and stepped into a Victorian bird-cage elevator. The operator, who looked as if he had been pickled by Darwin himself, eyed me sourly, then seemed to smile at Max after noting the pattern of buttons on his blazer. I thought he snapped to attention as he bore down on the control lever, but this may only have been the click of his bones.

Approximately fifteen minutes later we were let off on the second floor. After walking past a double door designed to shame the gates of Troy we were stopped by a servant in knee breeches and tasseled satin frock, who might have been a majordomo at the Court of St. James. He was taller than Max and twice as wide and when he looked me up and down I was ready to give him my Colt Python Magnum and apologize for somebody else's armed robbery.

I mentioned my name and McEvoy's and got an imperceptible nod. Then he looked at Max, especially his buttons, straightened and smiled.

"My name—" Max started, but he had to go no further.

"Of course, Commander," said the majordomo.

"We want to see Radford," said Max.

"Of course, Commander."

The majordomo led the way, and I was apparently allowed to follow.

Radford was in the smoking room. He was the big, bent man in the tweeds who sat behind a nose which would have done justice to a bull moose.

"Now listen, Commander," I said to Max. "Allow me to handle this."

"Of course, Manny."

He followed me to Radford's leather chair, which sat next to a round table by Duncan Phyfe, which held a goblet by Steuben, which contained a nut-brown wine.

"Mr. Radford?" I said.

He looked up at me from behind his nose.

"Do I know you?" He also sounded like a bull moose. In view of Radford's particular kind of bluntness I felt that subtleties would be a waste of time.

"My name's deWitt. I've been dealing with one of your employees, matter of business, and I'd like your opinion of the man. May we sit down?"

He looked at Max and said, "Don't I know you?"

"This," I said, "is my associate, Commander Garten."

Radford's nose moved and so did some of the face. It was probably a smile.

"Of course, Commander, of course!" Then he looked back at me. "Your name's what?"

I did not answer until we had sat down.

"DeWitt," I said. "And Gilliam Ramsey is the subject of my inquiry."

"Ramsey? Didn't show up today."

"I know. Nasty accident in last night's fog."

"Izzatso." He looked past me. "What are you drinking, Commander?"

"Thank you," I said, "but we're not staying long enough."

Max did not contradict me, and Radford had to pay attention to me again. He might have been unwilling to talk to me, but I managed to fairly glue him to the subject with my next declaration.

"I am in London as a representative of Lobbe Industriel to supervise purchase of the Crevassette enterprise."

His nose swelled or his eyes narrowed; he turned numb with agitation. I find it helpful at a time like this to emphasize my own cool composure.

"I have here identifying authorization, if you care to look—or possibly the Commander's word will be sufficient?"

"Quite as the Honorable Mr. deWitt has outlined the matter," said Max. "I think I will have that whisky now."

"And the reason I have come to seek you out," I went on, "is Mr. Ramsey's endeavor to interest me in a business proposition."

Radford was more or less regaining his self-possession.

"Mr. Debit," he said, "if you know anything about that Lobbe—the Lobbe operations in this country, then you may have been apprised of the fact that my feelings toward that—that—your employer...."

"DeWitt," I said.

"Eh?"

"The name is not Debit. It's deWitt."

"Oh."

"Quite." And having thus tilted his balance again just a little, I took the lead again. "I am not concerned with your personal animosities, Mr. Radford, though I might regret—together with you—their inception or necessity—but I am concerned with your function as the head of a business and the standing—the authorized standing—of one of your minor employees."

It had been a sentence to numb the mind, which had been my intention. Radford, in order to find air under the jungle of verbiage, had to shout.

"What the devil are you saying?"

"What's Ramsey's authorization?"

"For what, dammit?"

I turned toward Max, who was handing me a tumbler of Scotch, his gesture slow and distinctly ceremonious. I took the drink with equal grace.

"Thank you, Commander."

"You are welcome, Counselor."

We saluted each other earnestly and then sipped the ice-less potion. Radford had started to lean forward in his seat as if someone were pressing a foot on his neck.

"Hamilton!" he called. "Get me one of those!"

Aside from someone who was rattling a newspaper in the high room, there seemed to be no one else present. Hamilton, I assumed, would have heard the bellow in the far reaches of the building.

"As for your question," I said to Radford, "Ramsey, for a price, offered to work in my interest."

Radford rubbed one hand across his forehead. He also closed his eyes.

"I've come here every day," he mumbled. "Forty years. Never in all that time have I had a whisky before five in the afternoon. *Something* is going on," and he opened his eyes to stare at me. "What is it, Mr. Schmitt. *What?*"

"DeWitt."

"Oh."

"Quite. However, I don't follow you."

"*You* don't follow *me*—"

Having once more tilted him I now gave him the kicker. "You intend to interfere with Lobbe's purchase of the Crevassette enterprise."

And then he kicked me right back.

"You're damn right!"

I sipped and watched Hamilton—elder brother to the elevator operator—

while he handed Radford his Scotch. I sighed and put my glass down. Radford's response was, of course, one of the things I had come to learn about. Lobbe, it seemed, had guessed right.

"No need to shout," I told Radford. "Your intentions are well-known. And it was apparently in connection with those intentions that Ramsey approached me."

Radford, morning sherry drinker for these forty years, sloshed that Scotch down as if his life depended on it.

"What was not clear to me is whether he was negotiating for you—as it were, blackmailing Lobbe Industriel by threat of interference—or whether he was speaking for himself, hoping to enrich himself through betrayal of your trust. Which is it, Radford?"

"I'll kill that man—"

"Last night, someone almost did."

"Hamilton," he breathed, "don't go away—"

Hamilton took Radford's tumbler and refilled it at the sideboard.

"Ramsey, I take it, is on his own," I angled.

"Of course!"

"And he doesn't even know what you're about."

"How could he? I haven't figured it out myself!"

He ducked his head so that his nose obscured his mouth. I think he felt like biting his tongue. But while his admission could mean that there was no immediate interference planned by him, that by no means left Radford out of the picture as a potential source of trouble. There was still the good chance that he was well-connected with some kind of government agency.

"Well," I said, "there's time, Mr. Radford. These corporate mills grind slowly."

"Hm," he said and eyed me. "Tell you what, uh—"

"DeWitt."

"Yes. While we're about this like gentlemen," he said, "would you mind telling me just what that Ramsey person said to you?"

I waited while Hamilton brought Radford's second Scotch.

"Mr. Radford," I said slowly. I also hoped that my tone would set a new mood of intimacy. "It is unavoidable that an organization might harbor one, even two rotten eggs. Now, yours is a sensitive business, Mr. Radford. Government contracts, secret work, critical inventions—"

I thought he was smelling my drift, which was fine.

"Might it not be wiser in your case to be able to make incontrovertibly sure that a man like Ramsey is really delivered to the block?"

He drank Scotch. The new tilt of his nose concealed his eyes.

"And while speaking as gentlemen," I went on, "might you not give me, and my interests, some favorable consideration for the help I can give you in absolutely nailing down this Ramsey creature whom you have been harboring with mistaken trust?"

I had no idea if or when it would work. Radford was a man given to bluster. I felt he might therefore be precisely the type who would forgo the dubious chance of success in tackling something big like Lobbe for the certain success in blackballing and ruining something small like Ramsey.

Radford put his glass down and blew out a brown cloud of spiritous vapors. When he came on cagey, I thought it might well be the stalling of a businessman who has really made up his mind that the deal is set.

"I'll think about it," he said.

Max leaned forward and smiled his shy victor's grin. "Wouldn't wait too long, Radford," he said. "DeWitt, I happen to know, can be a vicious fighter."

He gave me a bland look to make clear that he was referring to my soulless blackening of Ramsey. Radford, fortunately, grew thoughtful and did not see me flinch. I decided that this was altogether not the time to press further so I got up, gave Radford my card on which I had written McEvoy's office number. Then Max and I left.

"What did you learn, Honorable deWitt?" asked Max.

"I learned that Radford might mull this thing over just long enough to lose his chance for personal interference with Brother Bartholomew Crevassette. It seems he can't afford to have even a Ramsey run over to the opposition."

"Ramsey's a mere draftsman, for heaven's sake."

"In this business a draftsman with a good memory or a good camera can cost his firm a classified contract."

"Admirable," said Max. "You talk as well as I drive."

Which I considered a magnificent left-handed compliment.

CHAPTER 14

Max dropped me in front of a building which looked a great deal like the Saddlers Club, although newer and less ornate. This was Lobbe's London office. Max followed me in with the roll of plans, and after making sure they were given to McEvoy shot off toward Croyden.

I spent most of the rest of the day in McEvoy's office. Meghan, as a close source of knowledge about Crevassette's, was a time-saving help. We drafted papers and made bank arrangements. We had sandwiches and coffee brought in for lunch, and on two occasions I called Ort again. He had left word that he would call back, but he had not shown up himself. Around two in the afternoon a coded cable arrived from Lobbe—or rather from his office in Essen—which was a compendium of information on Ort. It added nothing much new. He was a manufacturer's representative who was hired variously. He had a degree in electronic engineering from the University of Göttingen, he kept a small villa in Cros de Cagnes, and he owned a few hectares of land outside of Kyrenia, Cyprus. His business reputation was good, his contacts were exclusively in Europe (both East and West of the Curtain), and his political leanings were neo-socialistic, whatever that meant. I looked for evidence of violence and there was one note only to that effect: as a student in Göttingen he had fought an illegal duel with the man whose wife he had been sleeping with at the time. Nobody had been badly hurt.

Once during the afternoon McEvoy and I left for a signature-and-submission session with the bureau which supervised sales by nationals to foreign buyers. It was during this absence that the only annoying thing happened; I found out about it when we got back.

McEvoy was flipping through the chits which a girl had spindled for him. They were records of incoming calls during his absence.

"What have we here?" said McEvoy. "I'm surprised, ekshly."

I was initialing a stack of legal-size which I had on my knees and looked at him briefly across the room. He was sitting on his desk.

"Radford called."

"For whom?"

"You, apparently. Want to call him back?"

I put the papers down and went to the desk to look at the chit.

"I'd like to talk to the girl first who took the call."

"Excellent. Get report on tone of voice, mood, that sort thing."

Maybe, I thought. And I thought for a cagey trader Radford was calling awfully soon.

The girl wore steel-rimmed glasses, marcelled hair which was gray, and a dress which defied anatomical regulations. It defied them, unless the woman was actually built like a sack.

"Mr. Radford," she said, "called to ask if a Mr. deWitt was at this office and I said no, not really, because, properly speaking, I explained to the gentleman, Mr. deWitt is only here on a temporary footing, not like regular employed, though a Mr. deWitt...."

"Agnes," said McEvoy. He smiled at her. The smile showed how his teeth were clamped into the stem of his pipe with a great deal of determination. "What did he say then, Agnes?"

"Well, I said...."

"What did *he* say, Agnes?"

"He said, is he or is he not there and if he isn't when will he be back? Very forceful, Mr. Radford. I thought to myself...."

"And what did you say?" I prompted, because McEvoy was looking out of the window.

"I said that you and Mr. McEvoy had left to talk things over with the government gentlemen...."

"Did you ask him to call back?"

"You'd be back at around now, I said to the gentleman, but that he'd better be right on the button, if you know what I mean, because you were straightaway going to drive out to...."

"Agnes," said McEvoy, allowing us to look at his skull's grin again. The pipe was trembling.

"Let her finish," I said. "You said what?"

"Going to drive to Cricklade, I explained to the gentleman, and then he said, Cricklade, he said, isn't that where Bartholomew Crevassette has a place? And I said, the same, sir, and as far as I know the business would probably take long enough to keep you from coming back here before sometime tomorrow, so he should be right on the button, if you know what I mean, if he wants to catch you on the wire. I always like to let the customer feel that I take a personal interest in the inquiries which...."

I don't know whether McEvoy was going to say Agnes again or whether he simply said *Ack*.... But the pipe fell out of his mouth, and Agnes stood there waiting for him to pick it up.

"That's all," I said to her.

She was going to say something else and looked at me. She gave me that one look and whatever she saw in my face, she promptly fled. Then I blew up.

"Since when is it the custom of this office to dispense information in behalf of somebody else without specific instructions?"

McEvoy stopped with the pipe halfway up to his mouth. "Agnes ekshly only handles such calls as...."

"And dispense business information of—let me understate this—a highly sensitive nature?"

"Sorry, deWitt."

"Do you know what she's *done*?"

"Ekshly—"

"That woman as much as told Radford that I'm setting this deal tonight! And that he should hurry up if he still wants to throw a monkey wrench into the works! We've got about nine hours of option time left. Nine hours to get the next set of signatures from Crevassette on something like two dozen documents! And that's nine hours for Radford to shine up to his dead buddy's brother! *Klootzig!*" I added, hoping it meant something even worse than the sound of it.

Then I got ready to leave. I told McEvoy to sweet-talk Brother

Bartholomew preparatory to my arrival. I had a shot of McEvoy's Napoleon brandy, and then I left with Meghan, who decided, after one look at me, not to say a word.

Nine hours. The trip up the Thames toward the lovely Cotswold Hills would at most take us three hours. Of all the imagined difficulties to be expected, it never occurred to me that we might not make it in time.

CHAPTER 15

Meghan had a little Anglia whose proportions, after Max's rocket ship, were limousine-like. I did not suggest I drive it because my lack of experience with left-sided traffic would have slowed us down unnecessarily. And I knew what happens to my driving when I am in a particular mood. Meghan drove through the heavy traffic and looked at me now and then. I still was not talking. After a while, she talked.

"And now, to your left once again, the river Thames. So far its brackish waters were supervised by the Port of London Authority. You noted why? I think you did. The lower Thames is tidal and teems with oceangoing ships. You agree? Yes, I can tell you do. But now the river becomes fresh, non-tidal, because this is the upper Thames. Nice? You're right. Very. The Thames Conservancy Board takes over now and soon come little villages, meandering brooks, meadows, in short—you're right, of course—the countryside."

She kept that up for a good while, perhaps as much to amuse herself as to prod me into a civilized reaction, and when the towers of Oxford showed beyond a rise I unslouched myself, sat up, leaned over, and gave her a kiss.

"A lovely tour," I said. "But what with all that hard work and driving, don't you think it's time we stopped at an inn?'

"Why, are you hungry already?"

"No."

In a moment she smiled and kept looking straight ahead.

"Go on with you now," she said as if she were a country girl. In a while she pointed out that the traditional country inn with eating place below and sleeping chambers above was not to be expected just because the place said Inn. However, she explained, she would make an effort, by and by, to find one and to point it out to me.

It was a pleasant trip now. The land began to roll. Fences and hedges defined the rise and fall of pastures. Small villages looked calm in the distance and then slow with an evening mood when we passed through them. The sky over the hills ahead of us now seemed to waft and move with color.

Then the light fell very gradually toward the night. Meghan started to sing. She sang in Gaelic, which was now the most beautiful language I had ever heard.

"You know what that meant?" she asked.

"Yes."

"What then?"

"I look at you and I know what it means. It's how you feel right now, Meghan."

"Yes," she said. "Beautiful."

A short while later we had a flat tire and even that did not have the customary depressing effect. A cow watched me with indulgence from across a fence, Meghan stood by and held a flashlight on my labors, and the moist evening air smelled like a meadow breathing. I had never before changed a tire with such equanimity. I put the tire in the trunk—or the tyre in the boot—I washed my hands in the green ditchwater by the side of the road, and I wondered why I did not lead the sort of life, in this sort of place, where a chore is simply a chore, not an annoyance.

"Manny," said Meghan. "When you're done with this business, what will you do?"

I shook my hands to dry them and then looked at her.

"A little while ago, I still knew. I would have said rush around to the next job for Lobbe. But right now I don't know anymore, Meghan."

"I don't either."

It was a happy feeling. She walked over to me and lifted her face for me.

We climbed the fence and walked into a round dip in the meadow. The cow watched with a slow gaze of patience....

Later, in the full dark, we drove along the very young Thames, which was born up ahead of us in a meadow of the Cotswold Hills. Before going on to Cricklade and from there to Bartholomew Crevassette's house in the country we stopped at an inn. It was the real kind.

"Now she shows it to me," I said to Meghan.

"I promised."

So we walked into the low room with long, wooden tables and benches which had the rubbed patina of use. But only so that I could use the telephone. I rang Bartholomew's number to announce that we were almost there. But there was no answer.

"McEvoy's office told him you were coming?" asked Meghan.

"Of course."

"When?"

"In the evening."

"That means not until after nine. And right now, Bartholomew must be out to dinner."

I hung up the beeping phone and hoped there was nothing else behind the silence at the other end. In any event, Radford would not be able to reach Brother Barth either. We thought of food and sat down at a table.

There was roast duck with herbs, but we did not have time to wait till it was prepared. There was rabbit stew, but we were not courageous enough for its mysteries. We ordered fried sausage (pork and lamb with cayenne and sage and laurel), boiled potatoes with parsley and new butter, and a salad made fresh and sourish with a lot of watercress. Meghan drank claret while we waited, and I drank beer. It was good. I don't remember what we said to each other. Two men near the stove were playing checkers, but they might just as well not have been there at all.

When the kitchen door opened and let out the spicy smell of our frying sausages I pushed the beer away, ready to eat. But it was not the heavy woman who had served us. A small boy came toward me and handed me an envelope. He said something, but his dialect got between us.

"He says the man came to the kitchen door," said Meghan. "He said to give this to you."

The two men by the stove had not moved. The little boy ran off again.

"All right," I said. "It's for me. What else. Lobbe wants to know why we waste time eating. Radford wants to tell me there's no point in going on. Max sends word he has successfully landed in Afghanistan."

"Nevertheless," said Meghan. "You should open it." I opened it and read the pencil scribbles on the note.

> Excuse the haste, deWitt. I had waited here to intercept you on the road, to speak to you before you saw Crevassette. But I picked up a tail and must shake it. Please meet me as indicated on the map. It's on your way. Urgent. Please.

The note was signed, *Gilliam Ramsey*.

"Do you happen to know his handwriting?" and I handed the slip to Meghan.

She read it and then she nodded. At that ill-timed moment the food came.

We ate more out of a sense of obligation than because of appetite. Meghan did not want to eat at all.

"Eat," I said. "I'm damned if I'm going to rush to accept an unexplained invitation while I'm supposed to be hungry."

We ate.

"Anyway," I said, "that leaves out Lobbe and Garten. But not Radford."

One of the two men at the checkerboard by the stove sat up and looked straight at his companion. "Hah!" he said. Then he bent over as before and they sat motionless as before.

"You mean Radford sent Gilliam?" asked Meghan.

"Hard to believe. Unless Radford is much more sly than I took him for."

"He's not really," said Meghan. "He always struck me and old Crevassette as highly predictable; straight-laced, even."

"And if I don't watch out I'm going to believe my own yarn about Ramsey trying to sell out his employer."

The heavy woman came from the kitchen and lit the stove. It had been laid and started burning well right from the start. Wiltshire in April gets nippy after dark.

"What would Radford want from you, Manny?"

"He resents Lobbe because of dealings in the past. Or maybe he wants the Gadget."

Meghan shook her head.

"He knew we were building it. He never asked more than a few preliminary questions. He has no use for it as an electronic manufacturer, and besides, he could not afford to buy it."

She sat up and pushed her plate away. "And all that is assuming that Mr. Crevassette wanted to sell it, or its plans. He never did. He is dead now and his brother is selling it."

A slight whispering had started on the outside of the windows. The black panes began to shimmer with a very fine rain. Gilliam Ramsey was out there, waiting for us. He wanted something from me and I wanted something from him. I wanted to know who he was, what he was after, and why all this mysterious interest had started at precisely the point when Lobbe had made his sudden and well-guarded move to buy Crevassette's business.

"We can sit here and speculate till we're blue in the face," I said to Meghan and mostly to myself.

She gave me the half-smile which I would never get used to, but which was now a pleasure to me.

"I'm ready to go too," she said.

A similar thought must have occurred near the stove where the two silent men sat bent over their checkerboard. The one who had said "Hah" before got up, smacked both his hands down on the board, and stuffed all the checker pieces he could grab up with one scoop into his pocket. He also said "Hah!" again. Then he stalked to the bar and stared silently at the wall opposite. His companion stayed by the stove and never uttered a word.

I paid our bill and then Meghan and I went outside. A fine mist of rain was drifting down, making the air heavy with the country smells of leaf and loam. We ducked into Meghan's car and I looked at the map Ramsey had drawn on the note.

"We go to Latton," I said, "taking the first lane to the right after leaving here."

"Wonder why," said Meghan. "We can reach Latton with this highway."

"Shenanigans. Maybe he'll surprise us before Latton. Let's stay on the highway."

We did not take the lane and the marked fork in the road as Ramsey had drawn it. The rendezvous point was clearly indicated, and it would be difficult to miss it. Latton, which we reached without mishap, was a small village on the banks of the river Churn. It had a massive church of obvious Norman origin. Ramsey, according to the map, would be waiting for us on the north side of the building.

We rolled down a main street of compelling, medieval charm, and entered the uneven square almost immediately. It was a small openness in the black air and the wispy rain. A few street lamps at odd intervals seemed to spread more shadow than light.

The church stood to one side of the square, its heavy Norman tower disappearing into vagueness above the wet sheen from the lamps.

"Roll down this street a way, Meghan, and then park away from the first lamp."

"Then we'll walk back?"

"Not we. Just I."

Meghan stopped the car and pulled the brake. She left the motor running.

"Manny, I can't believe any of this," she said. "What's it about?"

"I'm here to ask that very thing."

"But I know Gilliam. He's a perfectly sweet, ordinary young man."

"Who chooses to meet me in some desperate way near a deserted country church because somebody scared him."

"I don't want to stay here alone, Manny."

"You're right. Leave the motor running and come out."

Then I walked her away from the car. I took her to a gate that led into a yard, a dark arch between two buildings, with a view of the square.

"You stay here. You'll see me walk across that way, mostly in the light, and then you'll see me stop just where the shadow from the church starts. You must be able to see me all the time, Meghan. If I disappear in the dark, it'll be against my will. You'll be my back-up man."

"Your what?"

"Here. You know how to fire this thing?"

When I put the Colt Python into her hand she shrank from it as if the thing might bite her.

"I'm afraid of it."

"You should be, and hopefully, so is everybody else. Now look. You'll only use it like a firecracker. If I yell, or if I disappear into the shadow, just point it up, squeeze that grip with your whole hand, and squeeze the trigger with this finger."

"That's all?"

"All. It makes a hell of a racket and it has a kick. So hold onto it."

Then I bent over her and kissed her on the cheek. It was cool and wet like a freshly washed apple. It was Meghan in the rain with an ugly gun in her hand and the sooner she did not have to hold it any more the better I would like it. I could have taken the gun myself, and used it more efficiently. But that would have left Meghan alone in the dark with nothing. I walked into the square.

Since in a quite literal sense I did not know where I was going, it seemed an awfully long walk across the wet square. I walked slowly, I don't know whether in apprehension or just plain fear. So far the square had been empty and the closed fronts of the little stores had looked blank. Now all this was changing. The whisper of the rain began to sound a great deal like human voices and the shadows seemed alive with motion. The somebody who had been following Ramsey might have followed him here. Or might have followed me. Or Ramsey, in the dark ahead, might be waiting for a better view to shoot me.

This last possibility was utter nonsense. Whatever Ramsey had to gain from me he would most certainly not gain while I was dead. But I thought about it....

An empty village square with a view from the church toward several access roads was not a bad choice from Ramsey's point of view. How good it would be from my point of view remained to be seen. I did not know enough about anything so far to make an intelligent judgment. Armed with full knowledge of my ignorance, I stopped where I had said I would stop. I faced the north wall of the church, a massive sight of dark gloom. The nearest lamp of the square cut a diagonal shadow from one corner of the church toward but not reaching me. I was visible, but Ramsey was not.

"Are you there?" I said to the stone.

"Yes." It was Ramsey's voice.

"Where are you?"

"You did not follow the map," he said without answering me.

"Are you going to be pettish about it?"

"As a matter of survival, yes. I suggested the route so that I could watch your approach from here, together with anyone else's who might be following you. This way, I did not see you until you entered the square."

"You do take all this most seriously."

"I suggest you do, too. Can you see anyone else from where you stand?"

I looked around and saw no one, not even Meghan. I told him so.

"And I can't see you either," I added.

"Please step closer, deWitt."

"Sorry."

"I see," he said in a moment. "Can't blame you." Then I could hear him sigh. "Very well," he said. "I suppose we can talk in your car."

"Meghan is with me."

"I saw."

Then he stepped out of the shadow. He wore a raincoat with a turned-up collar and his hair, like mine, was thoroughly wet.

"Let's hurry," he said. "I'm not at my best in the open." Observing the awkward stiffness of his gait, I thought he looked neither comfortable nor competent.

"Damn ribs," he muttered.

I fell into step with him.

"Why are we here, Ramsey?"

"You are about to close a deal with Crevassette. Before you do, I want you to know what you're buying." He stopped very suddenly, apparently causing himself some pain. "Did you hear that?"

I was not sure I had heard anything. I had been listening to Ramsey and the way he never quite answered a question.

"That was Meghan, I suppose." I turned toward the gate and called to her. "Meghan? Come out, honey!" She did not come out.

"Meghan!"

Ramsey grabbed for my sleeve.

"This way, deWitt. Out of the light!"

But I did not listen to Ramsey or look at him. I tore my arm loose and ran straight for the black gate and into it. Meghan was gone.

"DeWitt!" Ramsey was calling. "Let me handle this! You get down!"

I briefly turned his way and could see him, busted ribs and all, coming back out of the shadows he had gained and trying to move very fast, and then he made a funny step on the wet cobbles, a bizarre dance motion with head flung back and hands clawing up.

Actually, I must have heard the sound first. It went *rapp*, like a hand slapping down on an empty, wooden box.

He, they, or it were still at the other end of the dark passage. My God, I thought, Meghan has gone out of her mind, and where did she get that silencer to fit on the heavy gun, because that Colt cutting loose in a vaulted passage between two houses would have bellowed like thunder....

I heard footsteps scurrying off in the dark, which triggered all manner of haste and sudden energy into me. I ran after the sound, feeling safe in the darkness. It did not once occur to me that the shot might have been meant for me.

I ran into a yard full of barnyard odors and then toward a low stone fence where I saw the movement. Just when I was ready to jump I fell flat on my face.

CHAPTER 16

It had been neither mud nor rock but quite human, and with that discovery I got smartly rapped over the head. Next, she bit me.

"Meghan—cut that out! Let go—that gun!"

She now had the plump muzzle poked very accurately tween my fifth and sixth rib. I put my hand on the gun, being very delicate about it. Her hand was still clamped on the butt and her index finger was curled on the trigger. If she cut loose now, at least I would never know about it. She suddenly let go, almost dropping the gun.

I caught it before it fell into the mud. I got up and before I held my hand out for Meghan I smelled the gun very fast. It smelled of oil and nothing else. It was a cold gun which had not been fired. Meanwhile, Meghan got up by herself.

"Did they get Gilliam?" she said.

"Come on, let's look." We ran back down the passage. "How many?"

"Two. They came from behind, down here, and seemed just as surprised as I."

"They dragged you back here?"

"And after the other one shot they dropped me by the fence."

"You should have screamed, goddamnit."

"I bit his hand very hard but he didn't let go."

And then we stopped where the nearest street joined the square, where the lamp at the corner had made of Ramsey a solid, clear target. And now he was dead.

There was a hole in his chest, put there by an expert. Ramsey's face was wet and looked drowned. The rain and the blood on his front made a stain like cheap fabric running. The blood which had burst out of his mouth was almost all washed away.

I started to shake. Only moments earlier I had presumed to match my naïve bravado against two professionals who had moved well in the dark. Ramsey had appreciated their quality. Now even I knew why.

"We're cutting out of here," I said. "Come on."

I could feel Meghan go numb.

"But—" she said a few times.

"No buts. I want you to drive. Now!"

I dragged her to the car and put her behind the wheel. While I rounded the hood to get in on my side she crashed the starter badly, having overlooked the fact that the motor was still running. The awful sound made her come to a little.

"Sorry," she said.

"Fine. Now the clutch and then the gears."

She got angry. She said she did not like to be treated like an idiot and she resented being pushed around. This cleared her head further.

"You know how to get to Crevassette's house from here?"

"Of course I know how to get to Crevassette's house from here, particularly in view of the fact that it's a mere four miles away."

She made the car jump into gear and drove off. She kept on talking gibberish a little while longer.

I took the gun out again and broke the cylinder open. I felt around to make sure there was no mud interfering with the action. I also checked the bullets. There were five. I snapped the cylinder back so that the hammer came to rest on the empty hole. Maybe it was the sound which reminded Meghan that we had left a dead man in the village square in the rain.

"Manny, we can't just leave him like that."

"The hell we can't."

"But—I *knew* him, Manny!"

"I did, too, and I know he's got nothing to say to me anymore."

"What did he say?"

"Somebody made sure he couldn't say it. Drive, girl."

"Are you trying to make me angry again?"

"Right."

For a while she refused to communicate anything but silence. But then, "We should call the police, Manny."

"I will."

"I could turn back and we could...."

"No Crevassette is next. I'm here to close a deal and that comes first."

The lights of Cricklade were showing up ahead when Meghan slowed to look for the lane which led to Crevassette's house. We soon found it, and, as if to invite our eyes, the moon slid out slowly and gave us something beautiful. We entered what must surely have been one of the loveliest pastoral scenes anyone would care to remember. Old trees spread their large crowns over the lane, a hedge climbed and dipped over the hillocks which rolled away from the road. We passed a pond with a mill house at one end, a sight with the true fairy-tale quality of everything that is impossibly lovely.

It was a shame to spoil it by watching for two professional killers. Once I asked Meghan to stop the car and to cut the motor. Then she turned off the lights and I stood outside, listening for the odd break in the quiet. The moon slid away and then there was just the sibilance of the thin rain which drifted down again.

"Manny, come back in, please."

"Don't worry."

"But I *do*."

"They got their mark and they left. If they had wanted us we wouldn't be here."

As a matter of fact, it suddenly struck me, they had handled the matter almost as if they wanted to be sure I would make it to Crevassette's without interference.

When I leaned one way a little more I could see the yellow light.

"It's his house," said Meghan.

I got back into the car and we drove.

"What's he like? Any special advice?"

Meghan shrugged.

"I don't know him too well. He's a little phony."

"Lobbe suggested I should love him for his greed."

"His brother wasn't greedy in any sense."

"How much is Brother Barth involved with the running of the business?"

"Not at all. The brothers would discuss things, but there was no active working together."

"What's this one live on?"

"He lives on his brother."

After one more bend came the house. It was a cottage with dark half-beams in white stucco and the one-story structure seemed to be sinking under the great hump of the thatched roof. There was a light from a wired lantern which hung over a massive Dutch door. There was also light from several windows. It was a most friendly sight.

We went to the door and I pulled a bell wire. There was no sound. I had the unreasonable suspicion that the house was empty.

"It flashes a light," said Meghan. "He tinkers with things like that."

"While his brother invents."

"He is dead, Manny."

"Of course," I said, feeling fairly absentminded about it.

The door made an oiled swoosh and there was Bartholomew. I let go of the Python and took my hand out of my pocket.

Bartholomew Crevassette was a short, roundish man with a face whose color and sheen made me think of butter. He smiled as if he had known us all his life. His small bony beak of a nose supported round, steel-rimmed glasses. Behind these his eyes were so light that the black pupils seemed like little black beads swimming in milk.

"My dear, dear Meghan," he said and took both her hands. "But my child, you must have fallen in the mud. Come in, come in, and you too,

Mr. deWitt. You are Mr. deWitt? Of course you are *the* Mr. deWitt."

This went on from the door, down a short, red tiled hall, to a lovingly overstuffed room with a coal fire in the grate. There was a round table in the middle of the room, prepared for our arrival. On it lay a pair of reading glasses, an ink well, two pens, a copy of Spyros Crevassette's will, a carafe of yellow wine, and two cut-glass goblets. He had not expected Meghan.

"And you too are full of mud, Mr. deWitt," said Bartholomew. "But first we must let dear Meghan clean up."

Crevassette's accent was French with some slight contamination. Any of the Balkan languages could have done that.

"While you're showing Miss Bushmill the way, may I use your phone?"

He insisted that I must by all means consider his phone my phone and showed me where it was.

"The operator answers when you pick it up," he said and left with Meghan.

It was a sleek, plastic model with a luminous dial, not at all in keeping with the fussy comfort of the cottage room.

I made it short. I got my party after learning that the constable (who was the Latton police) could be found, on a night such as this, in the Rampant Lion. I told him that there was a dead man lying in his square. Then I hung up.

There was a pack of Players lying next to the phone and I took one of the cigarettes out of nervousness. The peaceful night rain outside was deceptive, the quiet room was deceptive, my own self-control was deceptive. I stuck the cigarette in my mouth, but I did not have a match. The sound which went click made me jump.

"Who is dead?"

Bartholomew was back. He stood close behind me, holding out his lit pocket lighter. I sucked smoke until it was much too hot. Then I sat down on the deep window sill.

"A man I hardly knew. Have you got something stronger than that wine, Mr. Crevassette?"

"Why, of course, dear Mr. deWitt." He bustled to a low cabinet and got out a bottle and tumbler. "I know well," he said with a lot of unction, "that death destroys more than the one who has died." Then he poured.

"Yes," I said. "Sorry about your brother."

"You were saying who this dead person was."

I hadn't been saying, but gave him a little more. "Some young engineer whom I was going to meet on the way here."

I took a good pull from the tumbler while Bartholomew stood by, wishing me well with his milky eyes behind the glasses.

"A friend of yours," he prompted.

"No. He was a friend of Milos Ort. You know him."

"Ort?"

"Yes. Milos Ort."

"I don't think I know him."

Here, then, was another liar. I finished the Scotch, then Meghan came back. Her moist hair shone the way only black hair can glisten, and her face looked quiet and tired. I put the tumbler down and said that I'd wash up now, if I might, and then we should by all means get down to business. The old-fashioned room and the buttery friendliness of the host only rankled me. I really felt only the threat of lies and deceptions. When I went to the bathroom I took my mackintosh along. It had mud on it too. It also had the Python in the pocket.

I washed up and brushed at the dry mud on my pants. I gave the Mackintosh a wipe or two and checked the Python again. It was not necessary and it made little sense, but I was nervous. When I got back to the sitting room Bartholomew was on the phone.

Meghan, in the window seat, was sipping a glass of wine. She looked up to smile at me, as if asking whether I was all right. I almost shook my head. I nodded and went to pour Scotch.

"Yes," said Barth Crevassette to the phone. "I am sorry too. I did not know the young man, but I am sorry."

I looked at Meghan with such suddenness that I think it must have startled her. I went over and sat down next to her on the window seat.

"Is he talking about Ramsey?" I whispered.

She nodded, holding her lip in her teeth.

"But that son of a bitch let on that he didn't know who it was!"

I felt so agitated by the invisible presence of somebody else's scheme that only the simplest and most childish action occurred to me: to tear the phone out of the wall and beat Brother Barth over the head with it. Meghan, sensing my feeling, put her hand on mine.

"Please, Manny. He asked me about the dead man when you were gone and I told him it was Ramsey. I saw no harm."

There was no harm. There was only Morbid Manford inventing paranoid plots while ignoring the simple explanation....

"No," Bartholomew was saying on the phone. "I'm sorry you did not reach me earlier but I was out. And at the moment I am busy. Would you care to meet tomorrow?"

"Whom did he call up?" I asked Meghan.

"He didn't. Radford called him."

CHAPTER 17

I do not claim that I function best in an emergency, but when the corner is tight or the rope is at its end, I do not have any taste for the millions of little aids which some people muster to distract them from disaster.

I put the tumbler down and squashed the cigarette out. I took my hand out of Meghan's and got up. Bartholomew's cozy room could have been made out of marshmallow or steel wool, I could not have cared less. All I thought about was that Radford was on the phone and I was supposed to close a million-dollar deal with a man who was now getting poison poured into his ear.

"May I have that phone, please," I said to Crevassette.

He did not blink an eye.

"Here he is," he said to the phone, and then he gave me the instrument with that fattish smile of his. The grimace made his bony nose even sharper. "Actually, Mr. deWitt," he said to me, "Mr. Radford was calling you."

"Calling me?" But then I took the phone so I could find out what went on from the bull moose's mouth itself.

"DeWitt here," I said. "What is it, Radford?"

"So!" he said. "I see the situation is changed."

"From what, Radford?"

"I learned where to reach you from some female at the McEvoy office."

"I know about that."

"Regular fount, that woman. Anyway, I was trying to learn from you where I might find Ramsey. After all, before you and I could make our little deal—the one we discussed at the club, you remember?"

"I remember."

"Before that, in fairness, I wanted a word or two with Ramsey himself."

"Damn white of you, Radford."

"Er, yes." Then his tone of voice changed from merely rough to nasty. "But all that's over the dam at this point, isn't it, deWitt?"

"Because Ramsey's dead."

"And now that he's dead there's no deal to make for you and me, is there, deWitt?"

"Get to the point, Radford."

"I will!" he roared. "There's nothing to keep me from ruining your little Lobbe deal now, is there, deWitt?"

"Except," I said, "your own stupidity," and then I hung up.

It had been pure bravura. I had nothing to say to Radford at that point but for all I knew, the Crevassette business transfer and the Gadget acquisition were already down the drain. Radford had gotten to Bartholomew Crevassette first and the two of them, it seemed, were going to meet tomorrow. That would be after my option had run out.

If Bartholomew said, "Let's sign," I'd be dreaming. If Barth said, "I won't sign," that would be that.

"Last year," he was saying to Meghan, "I tried forget-me-nots, but I think the soil was too wet."

I turned around before he drifted off altogether into small talk and garden lore. He looked up and smiled at me.

"Mr. deWitt," he said, "shall we get down to it and close the deal?"

It took two hours, but that was only because of the mass of signatures, annotations, and explanations which had to be rendered. Meghan acted as witness. When the papers were fully executed and ready for final processing, Bartholomew Crevassette reached into his pocket and gave me a capsule the size of a sleeping pill.

"It's on microfilm," he said. "The drawings, patent numbers, detail sections for insertion with the plans which you already have, plus duplicates of operating instructions which were also contained with the other plans. Would you like to view it?"

I did not care to view it but I viewed it with the aid of a projector in his study. That took another hour. The plans did not make much sense to me and I hardly looked at them, but it took time to copy section and patent numbers and to compare them with the respective entries in the papers we had signed. It was mechanical work, and it left my mind free to think of something else.

Ort and Bartholomew knew each other but Bartholomew had denied it. Ort and Ramsey were on opposite sides of the fence, and Ramsey had been against the deal. And while engaged in an effort to keep me from consummating it, Ramsey had been killed.

I knew the battle lines now. Bartholomew and Ort for the deal, Ramsey and Radford against.

I need not have worried about succeeding with Bartholomew, though his stringent option had misled me completely. It had not meant that he was going to be hard to handle. It had simply meant that he was greedy for money.

But I had my deal, the price including the death of a man. That too was finished.

And I had a curious, slack sense of incompletion....

CHAPTER 18

I am not authorized to state the amount of the check which I gave to Bartholomew Crevassette, but in addition to that amount I gave him a folder of negotiable bonds on one of Lobbe's French subsidiaries. Together the amounts constituted the full purchase price for Special Developments Company, Ltd., including all its assets, unsold products, and inventions, both patented and not. The latter included specifically the Gadget and all its special parts. I noted that Bartholomew put the bonds into a drawer without checking the due dates. Then, after a moment's thought, he asked me to deposit the check for him in his London bank. It occurred to me that a greedy man would not act this way.

At midnight Meghan and I accepted Crevassette's hospitality and went to bed in separate rooms.

I lay in an icy bed, staring at the fussy wallpaper, the slanting ceiling, and the sky through the deep-set window. The rain had stopped. The overcast had become wispy and the moon, though filmed over, showed a cold eye. I felt tired. But it was not the good tiredness after having won. I had fulfilled my assignment, but in a very real sense the success was not mine. I felt somehow lonely and left out. The old saw that success makes you so is pure rot, as far as I am concerned. The success which leaves a man lonely is no success at all.

I got up and went to the window. Since I do not wear anything when I go to bed, I now put on the long nightgown which Bartholomew had furnished, because it was cold in the room. I opened the window and looked out on the park-like moonscape. Everything was silver and black. In the distance two yellow headlights moved without sound.

"You couldn't sleep either, Manny."

I turned and saw Meghan two windows away.

"Perhaps," I said, "it's the cold. Are you cold?"

"Yes."

"Cold and can't sleep. There is a custom I know which works in both cases."

"I was going to mention it," said Meghan, and then we both disappeared from the windows.

We sat close in Meghan's bed while she smoked. We did not feel a lovemaking mood as much as a desire to get warm. Meghan wore the same kind of nightgown as I and the tableau we made was distinctly unromantic.

"Have you thought what you'll do, now that Crevassette is gone, Meghan?"

I could feel her shrug.

"Perhaps I'll stay with my father for a while."

The alternative had not occurred to me. I had assumed that she was supporting him with her work in London. "What'll you do for money?"

"He has an income of sorts. Royalties from something he invented."

"Ramsey told me that he was retired."

"I never understood it," she said and put her cigarette out. "Crevassette and my father had words. They used to get along. But some short time after the trade-fair incident—do you know about that?"

"Ramsey told me."

"Well, after that they had words. I always thought that might have had something to do with it."

"They became enemies?"

"No. They just parted."

"What was that invention of his?" I asked her.

"I don't know. Some little doodad for computers. As a matter of fact," she said as if remembering something, "it developed out of his work on the analyzer you bought."

"He must have been good," I said. "Makes it hard to understand why he quit."

"My father is altogether hard to understand," said Meghan. She slid down and lay on her back. "And the thought of him there in Rineanna is depressing to me."

"Then we must change the subject," I said.

"Yes. I notice your feet are now warm."

"As a matter of fact," I said, "the climate has changed in a way to make flannel night shirts unnecessary."

"You really think so. I can tell."

"Oh yes. Let me help you with that thing, why don't you?"

We slept so well that we did not wake up until nine in the morning.

But immediately the feeling of failure or, rather, of success without achievement returned like a nagging toothache. Bartholomew was as friendly and solicitous as the evening before, but his smile and his talk did not improve my patience. I longed to be off and, despite Meghan's obvious disappointment, declined his offer of toast and tea.

But then the beautiful Wiltshire landscape took us over again. The sky was calm and bland, leaving all prominence of detail and change to the pastoral scenery. We smelled the fresh spring air and we looked at the fresh spring green while Meghan drove slowly. It was precisely this leisurely pace which drew my attention to the other car. It followed apace.

I am convinced, even today, that I would not have paid any attention to the black Humber behind us, if I had not had that maddening feeling of incompleteness. As it was, an entire series of irritating events first developed out of it.

Meghan speeded up when we drove through Latton. A small boy was dribbling a ball by the corner lamp where Ramsey had been lying on the ground. After Latton Meghan did not slow down again but went even faster. I said nothing. I reached over once and gave her hand a squeeze, but we did not talk. I looked back and saw that the black Humber had fallen behind. I felt rather foolish now.

"Shall we stop at the same inn?" Meghan asked.

I liked the idea. I was hungry and I felt it would be a nice thing to try the inn once more, this time without interruptions to spoil the appetite.

The low-ceilinged room looked a little different now. The shadowed daylight in the paneled room made for a much cozier and sheltered effect than the bare light bulbs of the night before. The sanded floor boards must have been scrubbed in the meantime. I could smell the slight pungence of the old-fashioned soft soap which comes in a can. The two checker-players were near one of the windows. In the daytime, it seemed, they played the ancient game of skittles. The wooden ball—pear-shaped actually—hung from a string and went plop when it hit the short pins, which sat on the board like good little soldiers.

Meghan had tea and muffins with honey and I ordered scrambled eggs, plump sausages, and a light cheddar. The cheese came on the same board as the yeasty bread.

We ate with concentration, without looking up. It was perhaps for this reason that the sounds of the room were more prominent to me, and when the plops of the skittle game ceased for a moment I heard the expensive hum of the car outside.

The black Humber pulled up and I watched the two men who came out of it through the leaded window.

They looked fitting enough passengers. A Humber is an expensive car and Wiltshire is also gentlemen's country. Both men wore puttees and hunting coats made of tweed and with very large pockets. Their elbows had leather patches and there was a big patch at the right shoulder of the taller man's jacket where a gun stock would fit. Only he carried a gun. He had a bristly mustache and came in first. The other man, who was short and chunky, might well have been his retainer. He opened the door for the one with the gun and pulled his cloth cap off his head at the same time. That was when I noticed the bandage on his right hand.

They sat down at the other end of our table and both ordered ale. The man with the mustache put his gun under the bench.

"Any luck?" I asked him.

"Not yet," he said. "Rabbits seem scarce this year."

He had an engaging smile and a strong British accent, the kind that comes with a higher education. His friend had not said a word.

I pushed my plate away, got up, and went to the bar where the heavy woman was drawing ale. I paid her. Meghan, who was not done with her tea, watched me. I took my mackintosh from the rack and my briefcase from the bench. Meghan asked no questions but got up from the table. We went outside. She did not say anything until she was behind the wheel.

"What happened?"

"Those two hunters," I said, "were not after rabbits."

"Are they out of season?"

"No season on rabbits."

I waited till Meghan had made the swing onto the highway.

"That was no varmint gun under the bench," I said. "That was a Weatherby Magnum. It can kill a full-grown elk at a thousand yards."

Meghan straightened out on the highway.

"Drive fast," I told her.

She did not say anything right away, but I could tell her mood by the tilt of her head and the cast of her mouth. She either thought me a fool or she was worried about my imagination.

"I have heard," she said with a certain amount of restraint, "that a man will go out and shoot small game for practice and the gun might be of any size."

I did not answer right away.

"Did you tell me," I said in a while, "that one of the men covered your mouth and you bit him in the hand?"

She gave me a quick look.

"Which hand?" I asked her.

"His right hand."

"His right hand." I leaned toward her. "Did you see it today?"

Meghan chewed her lip and looked straight ahead.

"My God," she said very low. "What do they want?"

"We're going to try and find out. Take the first lane, any lane, that leaves the highway and cuts into the country."

She looked up at the rear-view mirror and saw the Humber. They could not have finished their ales in leisure.

When Meghan cut off to the left the two hunters could not have failed to see it, but the big car barreled right by our Anglia while we were still in view on the country lane. I thought they had done this quite well.

Our lane wound and forked a few times, following two walls of thick hedges. Every time the road split we would take the side of the fork which tended to the east and in the same direction as the highway. Then the hedges stopped and we followed a stone fence. We could see farther. We saw a copse ahead, we drove through it, and when we came out there was dip and a good view of fields.

The Humber was pulled off to one side of the road, parked with the nose pointing in our direction. The man with the gun stood in a field with his back to the road. He looked for all the world like a man waiting for game. The smaller man was next to him but he was watching the road.

"Meghan, stop the car."

"But they are hunting! All they are doing...."

"Stop! We're within range already!"

She flinched. I had not meant to sound that sharp, but it made her stop quite abruptly.

"Scoot over my way. I'm driving."

"For Godsake, Manny, you don't think they'll shoot through the window?"

I took a deep breath and rubbed my hands over my face. Then I said, "Meghan, I don't know what they'll do. I don't know, and as long as Ramsey is dead from a rifle shot, for the length of time it takes to pass them I'm damn well going to play it like life and death. The way Ramsey tried to."

I got behind the wheel and started up. I skimmed gears at first, but that was not bad for me shifting left-handed. Better still, the window was on my right, the Humber was on my right, and the Python was in my lap.

The man with the gun walked slowly into the field, away from the road. I would have thought nothing of this if the other man had not turned and started to walk toward the road and the car. There was nothing wrong with the movement. What possessed me when I saw the small man approaching is hard to describe, and the only thing I can think of does not sound especially sensible, though it made sense to me at the time. I was sick and tired of being followed, of feeling threatened, of knowing so little and of suspecting so much. I gunned the car down the incline and when I was close to the Humber I hit the brakes. The Anglia stopped right next to the black car.

"Stay put," I told Meghan and, then jumped out on my side.

Even then the encounter in the lane could have turned into nothing more than some talk back and forth, about having lost our way and where might the highway be, about didn't we see you just now at the inn—but the man did the wrong thing. He did not stop and just look, as a man might who has not sized up a situation and waits for it to develop would do, but instead he stopped, turned around, and walked rapidly back into the field to the other man.

I watched from behind the hood of the Humber, and even though the Weatherby throwing a .300 cartridge might well drill through all the metal in the distance between us, the shot would have been problematic. But then he did a curious thing.

"Move your car!" he shouted. "For heaven's sake, man, move your car!"

He had seen the stake truck before I had known it was coming. It was a tall vintage model which came cautiously over the rise and then bore down on me.

Meghan had apparently heard the shout, too. I was going to tell her to stay right where she was, but she had moved behind the wheel and was already pulling past the Humber and out of the road. I quickly looked back at the field. The two hunters were gone.

This impression was really a result of surprise because in a moment I did see them, belly down on the ground, caps showing, and the long nose of the rifle. In the distance the truck slowed. As soon as that happened the two hunters, in an incomprehensible effort to improve their position, jumped up and raced for the road. They came directly for the Humber, running hard. The odd surprise of the situation was that the taller of the two was now hefting a gun too. It was a heavy automatic, not the sort of gun I would expect to be carried by a man who hunts rabbits in the field. At this point I'd decided I'd had it. I drew the Python on them and yelled, "Hold it right there!"

They did not stop, but they were startled. And the man with the automatic made an almost reflexive turn toward me. I squeezed and the Python roared like a dragon.

I had never fired Max's cannon before, and as soon as I felt the kick in my palm I knew that the shot had gone high. But it did the job. Both hunters stopped in their tracks. Meanwhile, the vintage truck came bounding by with a frightful racket of old iron. The driver might not have believed what he'd seen, but he was apparently not taking any chances. Maybe there were three men with guns about to shoot up the countryside.

"Drop them!" I yelled at the field.

They hesitated just too long. I overcorrected and fired a slug into the sod about two yards in front of their feet. It made a spectacular spray of wet dirt.

If they thought nothing of my marksmanship they nevertheless showed a professional regard for the big-caliber roar I had produced. First the Weatherby dropped and then the automatic. It occurred to me then that I might be playing it wrong.

"Pick them up again. By the barrel. Butt end my way!"

I could tell that the small man was reacting to the situation much more emotionally than his companion. Instead of stooping down to pick up his automatic, he kneeled as if preparing for a snap shot from low down near the ground. I did not want him to pull such a dumb play.

"Hold it!"

He held.

"You with the potato nose. Yeah. You. Throw your cap up in the air."

He shrugged and then he threw his cap up, not too high and with a show of negligence, but that was fine with me.

My gun arm steady on the Humber's hood, I blasted the cap back no more than two or three feet over his head. He and his companion were impressed.

"You can get up now." I said. "And when you pick up the hardware, bend down from stiff legs, slowly, and according to my previous instructions."

I let them walk as far as the ditch between the field and the lane.

"Toss them over."

They did. The small man was swearing heavily and the man with the mustache was trying to find his voice.

"I would like to say..." he started.

"Don't. Instead, I want to know why you're after me."

"That I cannot say." He was regaining his dignity and his upper-class accent became considerably snotty. "Because, sir," he went on, "we are not after you."

I had no desire to begin a long and probably fruitless interrogation. I had no desire, now that I had their weapons, to start shooting again. I was wondering when the police would come barreling up from the nearest village.

"Meghan. Turn the car around, honey."

While she went through the maneuver, I pocketed my cannon, picked up the rifle and examined it. The chamber held high-powered longs, a very accurate, long-range ammunition. The automatic was a 9mm Smith and Wesson. I hefted it, then jacked the slide open. It contained low-velocity bullets. Whoever had loaded it was not interested in range, but in the sort of accuracy gained by reducing the kick of the stubby gun.

"Sir," said the upper-class mustache. "May I suggest a proof of our good intentions?"

"You can try." I put the automatic in my other pocket. The rifle was aimed directly at him.

"We are perfectly willing to be weaponless," he said. "We will go with you while you carry all the armament."

It was the most ridiculous suggestion I had ever heard, except for one thing. They might have had no intention of killing me, but only been ordered not to let me out of their sight.

Meghan had finished turning around the car and pulled up behind me. In the distance I could hear the hysterical yammer of a police car coming.

I did not bother to answer the suggestion. I stepped in front of the Humber and blasted the radiator at pointblank range. Besides the expected gush and hiss there was also an instant splatter of oil under the car. The bullet had cracked the block. I got into the Anglia and Meghan drove off very fast.

CHAPTER 19

I clanked into Lobbe of London heavy with artillery. There was no noticeable eyebrow raising in the outer offices, because that would not have been polite. But McEvoy behind his chambered desk took the pipe out of his mouth.

"I suppose," he said politely, "that there is ekshly some sort of explanation for this." He looked at the Colt Python Magnum, the Smith and Wesson automatic, and the Weatherby Magnum, all of which I had laid out on his desk.

"Not from me," I said. "I wasn't given any."

McEvoy was too intelligent to ask further questions, and I continued:

"I would like the rifle and the pistol boxed and delivered anonymously to the Yard, together with a note."

"Very well." He put the pipe back in his mouth. "And the note?"

"Plain white paper, two typed sentences: Apropos Ramsey murder in Latton. Owners of the guns in vicinity of Chadington."

"I'll have that done," said McEvoy.

"One proviso. Let us not have your girl Agnes involved in any of this."

"Er, quite. What about this other pistol here?"

"That belongs to our Mr. Garten."

"Ah yes," said McEvoy. "*That* Mr. Garten."

McEvoy got up and tugged at his jacket as if about to make a presentation.

"Mr. Garten," he said, "has arrived. He has terrorized my typing pool and I would not venture to guess just what he is doing now, or where he is doing it."

"Did he have any message from Lobbe?"

"He did not see Lobbe. He delivered the plans to a representative at the airport, accepted a receipt, added petrol to his aeroplane, I would imagine, and flew back across the Atlantic to us."

"I am glad to hear it," I said. "I am glad he landed in New York and in London respectively. McEvoy, how would you like to make the hop to New York with Garten? You've got a conference with Lobbe's U.S. contract lawyers tomorrow, and by going with Garten you can take the supplementary plans along and deliver them even tonight." I took the microfilm capsule out of my pocket and laid it on the table.

McEvoy showed his teeth. But in the case of a man with a pipe in his mouth, it is not always easy to tell whether he is smiling at you or whether he is getting ready to bite.

"If you don't mind, deWitt, I'll take a commercial plane. I have heard some rather incredible things about the Commander's flying."

"Rumors," I said.

"I would still prefer an airline pilot. Garten, as you may know, learned his flight style while perfecting the dog fight."

I left it at that, particularly after McEvoy told me that he had made a standby reservation for the afternoon, expecting that I would show up in time with the additional plans which Lobbe required. I went in search of Max.

There were eighteen offices in the building. Max was in none of them. Meghan, who was waiting in the reception area, had not seen him leave. She looked tired in the large room, as if the heavy decor oppressed her. I suggested she go home and get some rest. After I promised to call her she gave me a kiss and left.

I found Max shortly afterward, with the aid of a maidenly scream.

The screamer turned out to be the sack-like Agnes, who sat all alone in the deserted typing room. Her gaze was transfixed, glued on one of several tall, cathedral-type windows. Beyond those windows ran a narrow, ornamental balcony. In the frame of one of these windows I could see a pair of upside-down shoes which encased two large feet on top of two very long legs. The window sill cut off whatever followed.

I went to the balcony door and stepped outside.

"Max?"

He immediately collapsed himself and came erect like a spring knife.

"My dear deWitt," he said and held out his hand. "I am so glad to see you well."

"Thanks. Are you?"

We shook hands. Max yawned.

"How was your flight? Did you take a copilot?"

"Of course. Totally reliable fellow. Woke me up every time I fell asleep."

"You mean to tell me you flew both ways yourself?"

"Couldn't trust the fellow," said Max. "Commercially trained. All he knew about was safety."

"He sounds like a bore," I said.

"For example, one thousand miles out we encountered a storm. Do you know that young man suggested in all seriousness that we detour toward Greenland?"

"You didn't, of course."

"Don't blame him. He lacked experience. I took her up to forty thousand feet and progressed in the clearest, calmest weather you might wish to encounter."

"I guess that taught him a lesson."

"Curiously, no. He insisted that a plane with a thirty-thousand-foot ceiling must not be flown above thirty thousand."

I suggested that Max go to the hotel and get two day's worth of sleep. We were walking down to the street where I hoped to find a place to lunch. I offered no comment while Max explained, in detail, why he did not need sleep (something about his control over the metabolic rate), how he would feel remiss in his duty (something about his protective instinct and my accident-proneness), and that his affection for me was altogether such that he hated to think of me alone amongst strangers in the wild streets of London.

"I no longer carry anything of possible value to anyone," I told him. "And I am no longer in the position to affect changes in the Lobbe-Crevassette transaction, even under torture."

"But I have an instinct for this sort of thing."

"For disaster."

"And an abiding faith in the occurrence of the unexpected."

"With you around, yes."

"You don't know who your enemies are."

"With the deal closed, there are no enemies."

"Hah!" he said like the checker player of the night before. He also put his hand into the pocket where he had replaced his Colt Python.

I thought his theatrics quite ridiculous until I saw them too.

If the two men in the field had played the parts of hunters, these two were playing the part of intentional nondescripts. They were sparely built and of equal height, with no pipes, no mustaches, no funny hats, no ominous limps—nothing to distinguish them. They wore raincoats and kept their hands in their pockets. They wore black hats and had humorless mouths. The only reason I noticed them in the lobby was that they were coming straight at me.

"Mr. deWitt?"

"Yes?"

"My name is Tythe." He did not introduce his friend. "If it is convenient, we would like to have a word with you at our office," and then he brought out his leather ID case. He held it open long enough for me to look at his picture, fingerprint, number, and the name of his government bureau.

"Am I under arrest?"

"Of course not, Mr. deWitt."

"In that case, goodbye."

"However," said Tythe, without really moving his mouth, "it can be arranged."

"On what grounds?"

"Leaving the scene of a murder."

Max snapped his head around at me and looked totally accusing.

"I leave you for fourteen hours—" he said.

"All right," I said to Tythe. "We'll go with you."

Max liked that but Tythe did not.

"We would like to see you alone."

"Not a chance," said Max.

Tythe gave him a look of official disclaimer, but then his silent partner spoke.

"That's Commander Garten, I believe. Am I correct, sir?" He held out his hand and introduced himself as Simpson.

Max and Simpson shook hands and then Max and Tythe shook hands. In the car Max and Simpson discussed exploits that they had in common, both having erred into neutral Spain during the war and both having made good their escape into Gibraltar via the Bay of Algeciras. Simpson had done so in a hold of not-so-fresh fish. Max had done it by crossing to Gibraltar in a commandeered Spanish patrol boat.

Tythe drove and did not talk to me. Then Max and Tythe discussed exploits that they had in common, both having crashed in Germany and both having made good escapes into Allied-held France. Tythe had let himself be carried in a *Lastwagen* filled with strictly organic fertilizer. Max had driven his damaged Spitfire down a highway at great speed, a feat made plausible by the fact that he had sheared off his wings while negotiating the first railroad underpass. I felt left out.

I did not become important again until we shot through the gates of Scotland Yard and stopped by one of the lesser buildings.

The room we used was on the second floor. There was only a number on the door and there were only some chairs, a table, and an old leather couch in the room. The view from the window was dismal: a stone wall.

We sat down variously while a girl in thick glasses set up a stenographic machine. She plugged it in and made it hum while I cast about for one redeeming feature in the scene. The girl was not one of them. She looked bored with her chore and angry with everyone in the room. Even Max's innocent smile did not affect her. The one possibly redeeming feature in all this was that I might find out what it was about.

"We found Ramsey," said Tythe without any transition, "pursuant to an anonymous phone call to the Latton constabulary. Was that you?"

"Yes."

"What did Ramsey say to you?"

I got off my chair and went over to the couch. I hoped it would be more comfortable. I sat down, causing a dry wind to hiss out of the cushions.

"What Ramsey said to me is neither here nor there," I said to Tythe. "I have been talked to, threatened, aimed at, and puzzled. As a matter of fact, I am still puzzled. And I've had enough of it."

The girl at the steno machine gave me a malignant look. Tythe, it seemed, had not even heard me.

"Ramsey," he said, "saw you for a purpose. I want to know...."

"To hell with that. I want to know how you knew that Ramsey was waiting to see me."

Simpson and Tythe looked at each other, but Max was the one who then got things rolling.

"Might as well tell him," he said. "Or he'll answer all your questions at considerable length without saying anything. He's rather good at that."

"The Commander," I said, "is a friend of mine. It does not always show to the untrained mind, but he is."

"We respect his judgment," said Tythe. "Now, about your meeting with Ramsey. How much did he discuss with you concerning your visit to Bartholomew Crevassette?"

"Oh, that! He first left me a note, describing the proper approach to the entire matter to which you are alluding when you refer to Crevassette. The indications, though guarded in tone, made a relatively clear point—relative to clarity, that is—of the manner in which a confrontation, without inviting or dragging in, as it were, irrelevant or even undesirable consequences, could be effected."

Tythe said, "Oh." The girl with the steno machine flashed her lenses at me. Simpson, of the three, seemed the most naïve.

"I didn't get it. He told you what?"

"He told me to take the first lane to the right instead of continuing on the highway."

"I told you," said Max, and he looked up at the ceiling.

"Once more," I said to Tythe. "How did you know that I was with Ramsey when he got shot?"

Tythe shrugged. Like Max, he started to look at the ceiling.

"Ramsey was one of our agents. With your arrival his assignment included you. We knew that he was going to meet you. It was part of his job and the best he could do at the time."

"Did you know that he might get shot for his pains?"

"Some interference was expected." Tythe looked down at his shoes. "Though nothing this severe."

"Am I to understand," I said, "that your spy was on a job?"

"Spy is a romantic misnomer in this case," said Simpson. "Our division deals with inland industrial espionage."

"Am I to understand," I started again, "that your man was on a case, a routine case even, and murder was not on the agenda?"

"Yes," said Tythe. "We were as surprised as you."

"I doubt that, Mister Tythe. Why wasn't I apprised of your activities upon my arrival?"

"We had to check you out. Confidence comes dear in this work, Mr. deWitt."

"I notice. Then what is it about the Gadget that's worth all this conning and sneaking around?"

"Gadget?"

"The analyzer."

"Oh," said Tythe. "Nothing. Nothing at all."

I looked at Max for some relief from the dead spell of astonishment. But he seemed to be asleep.

"We have checked you out," Tythe was saying. "We might as well tell you the circumstances of your arrival and involvement."

"If you want to get any place, please do."

"So it seems. Our concern is with Crevassette's operation, which goes under the name of Special Developments Company, Limited."

"And you just bought it, rather suddenly," Simpson said.

"Spyros Crevassette," Tythe went on, "died at an inopportune moment, for our purposes. We were ready to close in. Arrest, exposure, roundup."

"What was he?" I said. "A thief, a photograph, a cow?"

"Old Spyros," Tythe said, "aside from his legitimate function, with which you are familiar, ran his company as a clearing house for industrial espionage."

"*What?*"

"He bought and sold and traded secrets, Mr. deWitt."

"Your own country," Simpson added, "was a customer. In addition to every European and Asian nation of any importance."

I got up and sat down again. I understood about Ramsey, but not much else.

"Ramsey's job with Radford was a cover?"

"Yes. Radford himself, I might add, was unaware of this."

So much for that speculation. Radford and his beef about Lobbe—that was a personal matter, not a plot.

"And does a certain Milos Ort figure in all this?"

"Very much so. It would have been his function to influence you in such a way as to continue the illicit function of the company you have just bought."

"And the two guys who shot Ramsey...."

"Two?" Tythe and Simpson said it at the same time.

"You didn't know? Then I have a suggestion. Look for two men in the vicinity of Chadington, possibly in jail. They own a black Humber with a bullet hole in its vitals. One is chunky and short, the other has a ginger mustache and the look and manners of what we in the colonies would call a member of the Establishment. I personally relieved them of two guns, one of which may be the murder weapon." And then I told them were the guns might be found.

Simpson left the room immediately in order to make use of the first piece of helpful information I had given them. Tythe, however, was not through.

"Is it customary in your country, Mr. deWitt, or is it possibly a personal habit of yours, to simply disappear from the scene of illegal activity?"

"It's a good habit, Mr. Tythe, as long as there's no agency of the law around. For that matter, how else could I have managed to convey the word to you people?"

This exchange did not increase our happiness with each other, but it did put proceedings on a more efficient, impersonal basis. I learned that the two hunters fit the description of a team known to the British authorities. The two had variously hired out as bodyguards, gunmen, and enforcers. They might easily have been hired by Ort, though their function in regard to me was by no means clear. There had been no apparent attempt to kill me. But the men had clearly intended not to let me out of their sight.

"To protect me from the likes of you," I suggested to Tythe.

Tythe did not think much of that theory. He also said he thought the gunmen were no longer interested in me.

"Are you forgetting Ort?" I asked him. "He might contact me again."

"Unlikely," said Tythe. "He has been deported."

The rest of the four hours I spent with Tythe were concerned with giving him information: How the Crevassette operation would be reorganized, how Lobbe intended to use it, and who the people might be who could be expected to operate the company under Lobbe's jurisdiction.

The girl with the steno machine got the sort of brief sentence exchange which she liked, Max got four hours of sleep, Tythe got his information, and I got the conclusive impression that the Crevassette caper was closed.

CHAPTER 20

Max, invigorated by his rest, dared the laws of gravity and momentum with a meteoric trajectory from the Yard back to Lobbe of London. Except for the switchboard man, everybody had already gone home. I asked him to get Tythe on the phone; his people might by now have found the two hunters and learned why they had been following me.

Tythe's office gave me what they had. They had the two hunters, holding them under suspicion of murder. They had a determination that the Weatherby was the murder weapon and they had a positive nitrate test from the man with the mustache. But they had no idea why Meghan and I had been followed.

I found Max behind McEvoy's desk, trying the drawers. I put my mackintosh on.

"We'll pick up our things at Meghan's," I said, "and move to Claridge's."

"You're not serious, deWitt."

"Oh yes. At any rate, *you* are moving there."

"We might discuss it," he said. "For the nonce, we'd better wait out the home-going traffic. I'll make up the delay when the traffic thins."

I had no doubt about that. Outside the window the fog was settling in again. When I turned back to the desk I saw Max open McEvoy's bottle of Napoleon brandy. The glasses were already on top of the blotter.

"Did I ever tell you of the time—" he started to say, but I waved him off.

"Please don't. I'm anxious enough already. I'm going to call up Meghan."

Her phone was busy.

We had one pony each and then I called again. The phone was still busy. This was reasonable, since we had drunk the pony too fast. We then had another.

"At the time I was telling you about—" Max said.

"You didn't tell me."

"Merely because you interrupted."

I hunted around in a carved cabinet and found the humidor in which McEvoy kept cigars. I offered one to Max and lit us up.

We had a third pony, by and by, and listened to the traffic ranting below in the street. I called Meghan again. This time the phone was not busy. It rang a dozen times or so before I hung up.

"She is out buying groceries for the meal she is going to make us," said Max.

It was nice of him to try and be reassuring, but I was just irritable enough to resent his bland assumption that he was going to Meghan's too.

"And we'll invite Bunny," he went on, "and make it a nice evening at home."

"Listen, lecher," I said. "You've got a room at Claridge's and enough of an expense account to pay for your own supper."

But Max did not worry about that. He knew he first had to go to Meghan's with me.

I phoned Meghan again. The phone rang and rang. When I hung up I said that we had to leave immediately.

When we pulled up in front of Meghan's house it was about as dark and as dim with fog as the first time I had come there with Max. I could see a sheen of light coming from her windows on the third floor.

"Party?" Max said and grinned at me.

This time her door was closed and there was no sound of any sort coming through. I rang the bell.

The silence afterward was just long enough to make me consider breaking the door down; then it opened one moment later.

Meghan did not look well. Her eyes looked the way they had the first time I had seen her, though now the vulnerability was quite real. She also seemed pale. When I bent to give her a hello kiss she surprised me with a hug which felt like a clutching for support.

"I phoned a few times."

"I was on the wire," she said, letting go. "Then I had to drive to the airport."

The room with the yellow light spreading from the hanging lamp looked as inviting as ever. Meghan stopped in the middle of it and turned to look at me.

"My father came unexpectedly, Manny."

"Oh? How nice."

"Yes," she said without much feeling in the word. "I'm sorry, though. I can't see you tonight."

"That's all right," I said. "But something is wrong, Meghan."

Max had wandered to the kitchen and was now standing in the door.

"Nothing serious," he said. "It's just that the old boy is boffed."

"You mean drunk?"

"Quite," said Meghan.

Max had made his remark with his characteristic lack of malice but Meghan did not take it well. Or perhaps it was the entire situation that made her frown and look away. I took her arm and led her to the couch.

"Sit down, honey," said. "It's probably not the first time, is it?"

"No."

"Then what else is it?"

"The horrible way he is doing it. The way he feels—hunted."

"By whom?"

She took a breath, clamped a hand over her mouth, and looked as if she were suppressing a scream. But she only shook her head violently and let the air out slowly. "I don't know," she said with a hoarse touch in her voice. "I don't know if he's making sense."

Max had closed the door to the kitchen and come over to us.

"Perhaps you're rushing it, sweets. In his state it's no time to be with a woman in the house, and it's no time for a daughter to spend with her old man. Why don't you let us handle it, eh, Meghan?"

My uncanny assistant had once again taken over. Meghan sighed with what seemed relief.

"As a matter of fact," said Max "in order to reduce his intake on the one hand and to avoid the sin of solitary drinking on the other, I'll just up and join him, seems to me."

His prescription required no answer and Max went off to the kitchen.

"Manny," said Meghan. "Go in there and try to find out what's happened to him."

"I will. How about you lying down?"

"I'm too nervous."

"Then go shopping. Get us something for the kitchen and when you come back we'll cook up a storm. How's that?"

She liked that and smiled. It was nice to feel that not only Max could make a contribution. Then I told her of a few things I would enjoy seeing on the table and gave her a ten-pound note.

"At a time like this it is important that you spend like a madwoman."

"No. I can't take that."

"Dr. deWitt's curative, distractionary, preoccupational nostrum. In the vernacular, nothing but money. And don't come back without having spent it."

Aside from a good meal, I wanted her to spend more time than it would take to pick up a few cans of corned beef and a bag of apples.

"I should introduce you to Father."

"I am sure Max will do that. Goodbye, love."

I took her to the door, hung her coat over her shoulders, and kissed her into the hall. She smiled again, and seemed to be thinking about the shopping chore already.

The dinette, aside from the eternal cot, also contained a wooden table and chairs now. Max, true to his word, was smiling at me across a water glass full of whisky. Mr. Bushmill was more or less present too.

Meghan's looks, it was clear from the outset, must have come from her mother's side. Bushmill, a bent and wispy man, reminded me somehow of a camel. He had the pushed-down nose and the wide mouth which is characteristic of grass-eating animals. Only his eyes were Meghan's. But the pain and anguish in them obscured the resemblance. They showed even through the glaze of his drunkenness.

"And here," said Max with a sweep of his free hand, "is the very person I have just described to you—that resourceful, accident-prone young American, Manny deWitt."

"Mater dolorosa—" said Bushmill while looking slightly past me.

"He's Catholic," explained Max.

Bushmill shook hands with me or, rather, I shook his hand, and then he looked all over the table for his drink.

"Speaking of resourceful," I said, "I'm going to make some coffee."

"I just put it on," said Max.

I went to the kitchen for a glass and then I sat down at the table. Max brought the bottle up from the floor and poured me a few fingers. Next, he also produced Bushmill's glass, which was still slightly filled.

"Treat it like medicine, Mr. Bushmill," he said. "Just one swift but ever so tiny sip."

"Mater dolorosa—" he said again. I wondered whether he spoke any English.

"You don't seem to be used to this," I said to him.

We looked at each other and I think he saw me. However, Bushmill handled his inebriation in a way which is all too rare. He did not talk. Perhaps he could not talk.

"Do you visit your daughter often?" I asked. It was cunningly phrased so as to require only a nod or a shake of the head.

He shook his head.

"Special occasions?"

He neither shook his head nor nodded. His mouth worked as if he were experimenting with an entirely novel set of muscles.

"I'm afraid—" he said.

It left me blinking, but it had actually sounded like the end of his sentence. Bushmill sighed and closed his eyes.

"I don't think he can talk," I said to Max.

"It was not apparent before. I was doing the talking."

"Mr. Bushmill," I said, "would you like to tell us why you are afraid?"

Vigorous nod.

"Please do. Meghan is worried."

Vigorous facial gymnastics, and that was all.

"You need help," I said.

"I think," said Max, "I have just the cure."

"I think the Shetland treatment is contra-indicated, Doctor."

Max ignored that, poured down most of his drink, and then bade Bushmill to get out of his chair. This was accomplished with help fore and aft. And then Max twined his arms around Bushmill's neck, taking a stance close behind the old man, and did something swift and vigorous, something like instant strangulation.

Bushmill's neck cracked horribly, his eyes crossed, and then he turned with alacrity and punched one small fist into Max's nose.

"Mater dolorosa, ye unspeakable scum of a strangler!" yelled Bushmill.

Max straightened up against the wall behind him and sneezed once.

"It worked," I said. Then I went and got two cups of coffee and brought them back to the table. As for myself, I intended to finish what I had started. I had hardly touched my glass.

"The point is," I told Bushmill, "we can help you." I told him a little more about myself, so that he would know why I was here and who I was.

"Ah," said Bushmill. "And did you know old Crevassette?"

"No. I came on the scene only after his death. You knew he was dead?"

"Yes. I just read it yesterday."

Then he fell silent again. He could talk, and he did so with an intriguing burr, but now he looked haunted.

"Did you know Crevassette well?" I asked him.

"Well? Night and day we spent together. For a while." I waited because he was obviously thinking about it. "We worked close," he said.

"Before he fired you."

"Fired me?" For a moment he fairly bristled like a bantam and then, just as swiftly, he collapsed again. "Yes," he said. "After that—that foolishness in Halle."

But he clearly did not seem to think that it had been such foolishness, or else he would not have looked so withdrawn at his own mention of his arrest in East Germany. Then it seemed to me that he tried to cover up by changing the subject.

"Wonder whatever happened to that machine," he said to his coffee cup.

"Which one, Mr. Bushmill?"

"Which one?" and he looked up at me. He was by no means sober, but he grasped at thoughts, one at a time, quite well enough. "That tricky analyzer of his. That big one."

"Oh?"

"That marvel could handle reagent grade, pharmaceutical grade, and all the way down to the fine points of spectrographic grade analysis. Spyros and I spent a great deal of time on it."

I looked at Max and then back at Bushmill.

"My company," I said, "just bought the Gadget."

Bushmill looked at me with his first sober look.

"You don't say. Does it work?"

I thought the question surprising and told Bushmill so, but his answer was an ambush of technical jargon. And then he drifted right back to the annoyance of that time. "Don't know how he finally solved it," he muttered. "It wasn't solved at the time when Crevassette insulted me by taking me off that job. Angry man, he. After that awful Halle affair, that frightful time there, with Orlov."

"Who?"

"Orlov. The man who questioned me in the cell."

"Come on, Bushmill," said Max. "I can tell you worse."

"Drive with him sometime," I explained.

"But look at it, Bushmill. Now it's over."

Bushmill put his coffee cup down and picked up Max's glass of whisky instead.

"Yesterday, in the village of Rineanna where I live, I saw Orlov on the street."

CHAPTER 21

Bushmill finished Max's glass with one violent toss and then took refuge in his drunk dullness again.

"Another neck cracking?" I asked Max.

"Too dangerous."

Instead we gave Bushmill another helping of whisky and then carried him to bed. Meghan returned shortly after.

We helped her unpack great bundles of groceries and then watched her from the table while she prepared the food. I reminded myself gratefully that the London assignment was really over, that there was time for the bottle which Bushmill had brought, and that there was time to watch Meghan in the kitchen.

She was glad that we had found out what had troubled her father and that it had only been Orlov. She had heard about the man from her father. At least Orlov was real, she explained, and nothing like the ominous blathering she had gotten from the old man when he had arrived. The Orlov experience in Halle had most certainly not been pleasant, but it had not been political, there had been nothing worse than questioning without sleep, and besides, the authorities had apologized about it being a mixup later.

"What did they ask him, Meghan?"

"Technical things. Set the table, Max, would you?" Then she finished answering me. "They thought he had been spying."

"On what?"

"Electronics, I suppose. That's all they asked about. Then they let him go."

"Through Crevassette's intervention."

"Yes."

"And now Orlov is back."

Max finished setting the table and Meghan laid out serving dishes with fresh-smelling cucumber slices, dark brown sprats, black bread, and tiny North Sea shrimp in shimmery aspic.

"Is he back?" she said. Then she put the appetizers down. "Over the years," she said, "I'm afraid Father has seen Orlov several times. Take any man with a belly, thick eyebrows, and black hair parted down the middle, and Father is apt to remember Orlov. Now let's eat. But not so fast. The sauce for the lobsters will take me at least half an hour."

Three hours later we were done at the table. Bushmill slept. The arrangement for the night was to let the good man be, and to let Max indulge in his sense of adventure. He and his Python spent the night on the cot. There was some talk about having Bunny come over so as to guarantee that Max did not fall asleep. However, he was asleep when Meghan and I left. We went to my room at Claridge's together. There, she and I mostly slept too.

Five days later Max accompanied a now sober but still afraid Mr. Bushmill on a walk to the British Museum. On this walk, in a lovely garden on the east side of the Museum, Mr. Bushmill spotted Mr. Orlov on a bench in the shade of the massive Museum wall.

The account is Max's. He, Max, approached the putative Orlov forthwith, chopped him hard behind the left ear, and was then vastly surprised to see Orlov rise from the bench instead of falling off it like a sack of potatoes. Orlov then delivered three expert blows at three crucial body centers, and was in turn surprised when Max did not die on the spot. Immediately the police arrived. I know this much for sure, because I had to fetch Max at the station.

Mr. Orlov, it seemed, was one Mr. Trentheim, a metallurgist with an address in Birmingham. I did not have the pleasure of meeting him. He had left without preferring charges.

Seven days later I was looking forward to the eighth because the seventh day was the last of my working days at the London office. Meghan and I were going to take a swift fling at Paris. But I anticipate....

I had time during the preceding days to make a few inquiries concerning past unresolved problems. The two hunters had been arraigned for the murder of Ramsey. Ort had landed in Kyrenia, Cyprus. No trace of the stolen model had been found. And Radford had been heard to say at the Saddlers Club that he was about to spring a secret trap.

A few hours before I was to leave I passed Agnes in the corridor and I even smiled at her.

"It's for you," she said.

Agnes, after a number of days during which she and I had infrequent encounters, had turned monosyllabic on me. "What is it, dear Agnes?"

"It's him."

She pronounced it *Him*.

"You mean, I have Received The Call?"

"On the direct line," she said. "Our Mr. Lobbe wants you."

I had not spoken to Him since my one call from Meghan's bedroom, and Lobbe had been routinely informed of my progress by the McEvoy office. What we knew here, Lobbe knew there. Clearly, he was not calling for information. Perhaps an offer of a three weeks' vacation?

I took the call in the conference room in back of McEvoy's inner office. The long table smiled at me, the dour paneling smiled at me, the instrument winked at me.

"DeWitt here, Mr. Lobbe. How's the Gadget?"

"*Verschrikkelijk!!*"

"What was that, please?"

"The *verdomme* Gadget, Manford deWitt, does not work!"

I gave him an expensive, transAtlantic silence. He did not interrupt. Perhaps he thought I was thinking. I looked out of one of the tall windows and wondered why the sun did not shine.

"Well, *vat, vat?* You hanged me up?"

"I didn't mean to. I mean, I'm here."

"So talk, Manford. You sent the plans you got from the sealed safe?"

"Absolutely."

"And the capsule from the hands of the *carroña* brother?"

"Right."

"And what I got here is what you got there?"

"I'm sure."

"And the model?"

"Not found yet."

"*Schweinerei*," he said.

"That might be. Mr. Lobbe?"

"I'm here. Say something good."

"Perhaps, having thrown the thing together in no more than two weeks...."

"It is not thrown together, deWitt. I am telling you of the completed parts only, and in the test runs they don't work!"

"Mr. Lobbe, having no knowledge of the Gadget and no training in the discipline which created it, I can only suggest that we find an expert."

"So," said Lobbe. The scorn was freezing the wires. "You got experts I don't have on my pay?"

"Bartholomew Crevassette should be able to make a contribution. I could get in touch with him."

"The *carroña* expert who makes doorbells that blinkle? Thank you, Mr. deWitt. Next please."

I was beginning to dislike this conversation in the extreme. I pushed the phone over and sat down on the table.

"All right," I said. "Next, Bushmill."

"Hah? You now have promoted the health-fiend secretary of the icy baths from the bedroom to the laboratory? Such nepotism. *Pfui!*"

I had just about had it then.

"I will tell Mr. Bushmill that you do not need his help and that his co-invention of the analyzer does not rate very highly with you when it comes to reading blueprints and connecting wires."

This time he made the silence. I did not interrupt because I wanted him to think my delivery over and also my tone of voice.

It also gave me a chance to think and to note where the exaggerations began and what my fantasy led to. It led to a commitment on Bushmill's services, a little man who might well have been a lab technician with Crevassette, fully qualified to read blueprints and to connect wires, perhaps, and nothing more.

"Mennekin," said Lobbe. "Forgive me. And hire the Bushman *instanter instantis*."

CHAPTER 22

When I saw Bushmill at Meghan's place he was drinking again. He was not clobbering himself the way he had done when he had first appeared, but was merely imbibing enough to maintain a certain intoxication level. He was never so drunk that he forgot his troubles and he was never with it enough to do anything about them. He sat in the kitchen and suffered the ghost of Orlov. Max was at the airport, making dangerous refinements on Lobbe's plane, and Meghan had left a note saying that she was doing some last-minute shopping. I had time alone with Bushmill, though by the way he looked at me I was not sure that he, in turn, was with me.

"How you holding out?" I said and sat down with him. The late light from the kitchen window was gray, and Bushmill's face reflected the color well.

"You despise me," he said with his soft burr.

His eyes were runny and his mouth was slack, but instead of creating revulsion his sad posture and those pitiful eyes brought out the protector in me. Pity is the cheapest emotion but I, nevertheless, felt it and perhaps something more.

"Would you like some help, Mr. Bushmill?"

He held still, looking at me, as if I really meant that I was going to take something away from him. When I smiled he relaxed a little.

"Call me Camden, why don't you," he said.

The request was a little unusual for an Old World gentleman of his age, but I said that was fine with me.

"Perhaps if you'll tell me what you haven't told me about Orlov, I can help you."

"There's the rub," he said and looked out of the window. "There's more, Manny, but I don't know what it is."

There was more talk, one drink's worth, but I got the genuine feeling that Bushmill's fright of Orlov was truly based on something which Bushmill did not quite comprehend.

"I've got to get away," he said. "I can't sit here and wait for that man while I'm sure he knows where I am."

"If Orlov is here, Camden, it's reasonable to assume that he knows you're staying with your daughter. Then how dangerous does that make the man? He hasn't harmed you."

"I'm not reasonable," he said, sounding sober enough. Unsuccessful in the logic department, I then switched to the commercial.

"I have a suggestion, Camden, something which would help me and it would help you. That is, if you think you know enough about the analyzer to work on it."

If he felt insulted he did not show it. All he really showed was an alert face and a look of curiosity.

"Well now," he said, "I suppose it's all right, now that Spyros is dead."

"What's that?"

"I'd sworn I'd never go near the thing again. The way Spyros and I had a falling out—about what, you ask? About little things which I cannot even remember—the way that happened between him and me, Manny, only one thing makes sense, don't you see. He didna want me around anymore. He thought I wasn't good enough for the work on the machine. I was insulted."

"Were you good enough?"

"Yes," he said with simplicity.

"Then you might be able to figure out why the damn thing won't work."

"Eh? Won't work?"

There were some unknowns which Bushmill could not bear. But there were others, apparently, which could still pique the scientist in him.

I took him to Meghan's bedroom and set up a call from there to McEvoy's office, and from there, via the direct line, to Lobbe's inner sanctum in New York. Bushmill talked only briefly, but the change from a quiet mouse to a purposeful thinker was something to behold. He asked for a set of the prints and he asked to speak to the engineer who was handling the assembly. Lobbe had said yes to both, he told me. The plans would not arrive until the next day, but the call from Nimburg, Indiana, where Lobbe had a manufacturing laboratory which was doing the assembly, came through one hour later. The talk with the chief engineer took another hour. There is no point in my trying to describe it. I did not understand a word.

When Bushmill hung up and got off the bed he would not talk for a long time. Even when Meghan came back all he did was pace around and around the bed and stare out of the window. Meghan and I had some coffee royal.

"You want to take him to America?"

I nodded my head.

"Then why send the prints?"

"Because he asked for them. He told Lobbe he wants to look them over both here at the plant, to make comparisons with other records, and on the plane. Remember, he doesn't know the complete assembly."

"Did he talk about the mythical Orlov again?"

"Barely. And not at all after latching on to the new obsession, his interrupted work."

She nodded and looked away.

"I was so looking forward to Paris. I've bought all these things," she said.

"You're free to come along with us."

"That, Mr. deWitt, is by far the most tepid invitation I have yet received!" She sizzled with anger.

When old Bushmill came out of the bedroom I was still trying to make up for my underplay of passion. The first words he uttered were the best words he could have uttered.

"Meghan," he said when he came into the kitchen. "I'm off to America and I want you to come along."

Meghan looked at me and suppressed a smile. "If you want me to, Father."

"I want you to, lass," said Bushmill.

"Then I'll come, Father." She looked at me very sternly, biting her lip.

"In that case," I said, "you might call Max at the hangar, Meghan. Ask him to get the jet-propelled coffin ready so we can leave—when, Camden?"

"Tomorrow night. I care to look things over at the plant."

When Meghan went to the bedroom I asked her father about his conversation with the engineer in Nimburg, Indiana.

"They have tested several of the critical modules," he said. "By the plans, you see, they've got a branch circuit rate of no more than one hundred amps. But in the tests they have blown out every available fuse in the factory circuits."

"I expect that means something."

"Indeed. We don't know yet what. Why that machine should draw so much current is a puzzlement to us."

"Me too, Mr. Bushmill."

"Camden."

"When it's all connected, Camden, maybe there's enough resistance built into the rest of the circuitry so that the whole Gadget will draw just its expected rate of current."

"It's a layman's thought," he said. He picked up my coffee cup and sipped the coffee royal. I don't think he noticed what it was. "There's the puzzle, at that, of the extra parts."

"Naturally."

He looked at me like a father who is trying to love his idiot son.

"You don't understand. The man on the phone says to me that there's parts on the plans which are not covered by patent. They finally figured that out. It's most complicated."

Even though my official part in the acquisition of the Gadget was over I had become involved enough to feel a kind of proprietary interest in the thing. This was especially true now that I had learned that the Gadget was a dud. It was probably for this reason that I thought about Bushmill's remark very seriously. So far, however, I did not know enough about the way the machine worked to make any use of the guesses and the information which Bushmill had given me.

I did not get a clearer picture of the Gadget until we were airborne at midnight the following day.

We strapped in with a relative sense of safety, due, I think, mainly to the fact that Max was at his controls behind a closed door. As for the manner of flight, I will say only that I was grateful for the cover of darkness that gave me no clue whatsoever as to what was really going on. Meghan and I talked in the dim cabin atmosphere for a while and then she went to sleep. Camden Bushmill, all this time, was going over plans, which were scattered on a swing-out table. I brought him a cup of coffee. His bony head glinted in the intense light of his stork-neck lamp.

"The radioactive element has been altered since I last worked on it."

"Oh? Is that good or bad?"

"It means nothing."

"I'm glad."

"It only means something if the gain in space is of significance."

"Well, well."

"You don't know what I am talking about," he said to me.

I sat down in the swivel chair at the other side of the table and tried to look open as well as intelligent.

"All right," I said. "Tell me how it works."

He sat down, too. He composed himself with a look of patience.

"The analyzer is not new. What is new is the versatility of the Crevassette model."

"I've gathered that much."

"Analyzers like ours are used today in many fields—foods, pharmaceuticals, biochemistry, pulp and paper, cement manufacture. They analyze the steroids in the blood, and they determine the quantitative constituency of fertilizers. They do innumerable other things."

"How?"

He smiled at me. It was a valiant smile.

"Like a chemist. They find chemical groups by the use of reagents. I call that method, which is chromatographic, a process of step-wise labeling."

"You didn't say how."

"Because you are not a chemist. At any rate, this scanning by chromatography is not the technique of Crevassette's analyzer."

"Very well then, I bite."

"This one does not use the labeling method. It is the only machine which has achieved full operational use of a technique in which the substance analyzed is made to give its very own, individual signal."

"More accurate?"

"As accurate, but applicable at greater speed over a much wider range of substances. In this model, that is."

"How?"

"Simple. The stuff to be checked is passed over a radioactive element, a neutron source, and the impingement of the neutrons on the test material produces a differentially typical secondary radiation. You read the radiation pattern, and you know what you have."

I was impressed and showed it by not saying anything. But then I had a question which I hoped Bushmill had not actually answered before.

"All this goes on in a gadget no bigger than four telephone booths?"

"No. You need a computer. Like this." He got up to draw the answer for me on a piece of paper. It was already covered with figures and symbols, but he seemed to feel that it would serve for his simplified explanation.

"Box one. This is a programmed computer. You tell it the problem." He made a wiggly line. "Via microwave link the computer tells it to the analyzer, which is this box here, number two. The analyzer does what it is told and, wiggle-wiggle, sends a microwave answer to the computer, which translates the answer for you."

I thought about what he had said for a while.

"The computer tells the analyzer what to do."

"As I said."

"This command goes over some distance, line of sight, I suppose."

"In this case, yes."

"Within the built-in capacity of the analyzer it will take any signal, from any tape put in the computer, and from any computer, as long as the microwave link is maintained."

"In line of sight, yes."

"Hm."

"Did I miss something?" said Bushmill politely.

"I think we all have," I said to him, since I could not think of anything concrete.

"One question," I added. "Can you make the Gadget work?"

"Of course. I worked up from the designs I knew. They are still buried in here." He tapped the stack of blueprints. "It will work when you leave out the extra parts which, as they found out, are not covered by patent."

I added this to the oatmeal in my head and sat down in my dark seat. Meghan slept on the other side of the aisle, and the sky slept outside my window. I sat and worried about the Gadget, because something was amiss.

Or, something was missing!

Whatever used all that extra power in the machine, that was missing.

Whatever could explain all those extra parts, that was missing.

And whatever that was had really nothing to do with the analyzer!

"Bushmill!"

My yell woke Meghan and it gave Bushmill a start.

"You invented something?" he asked mildly.

I scrambled back to his table, but did not quite know how to begin.

"A radioactive condition is a state of excitation in the substance, isn't it?"

"If you like."

"Can you conceivably feed a signal to the Gadget, which causes it to produce excitation in a sample that is not in the analyzer, but somewhere long-range?"

"Possible, of course. It would need vastly more power."

"*Aha!*"

Bushmill stared at me.

"All those fuses," he mumbled.

He had understood me. Then he added something which I did not quite understand. It came out like a reminiscence.

"That was when he fired me—when he wondered about long-range use—"

"Bushmill," I said, feeling unaccountably anxious. "I've got a worried mind. Can you figure out why?"

"No, Manny." Then he smiled. "In contrast to Spyros, I am just a technician."

"Can you figure out what you would need for long-range use?"

He looked down at himself and I noticed that I had grabbed his lapels. I let go of him.

"What would be needed, Camden?"

"The beaming problem of particles is something extreme. Only Spyros might have handled that...."

And Spyros Crevassette was quite dead.

CHAPTER 23

New York took one day. Lobbe wanted to shunt Bushmill to Nimburg, Indiana, within the hour, but when it came to persistence he had met his match. Bushmill did not want to budge until he had talked out and thought out all the technical worries which his and my questions had produced when we had talked on the plane.

"So that is the long and the short of it," he said to Lobbe. "I am working on a machine that I don't know the function of."

Lobbe sat behind his carved castle of a desk and confused the mood by alternately showing three chins and then one. I could not tell whether he was thinking or whether he was angry. The number of chins had been an indication of that.

"My very dear Mr. Bushmill," said Lobbe, staring resolutely at the ceiling for fear of burning Bushmill down with his eyes. "Since we talked we had a brilliant idea. We left out the extra parts of the Gadget when making the hook-ups and all the fuses held. Each little one of them."

"I figured that out on the plane. But about the other things I was telling you, the things Mr. deWitt brought up—"

Lobbe stopped looking at the ceiling and instead looked at me. I expected at any moment to smell burning flesh. And yet he smiled his Buddha smile.

"Ah yes," he said. "Our own, dear Manny. How he does manage to muddle, meddle, and nettle along. Mennekin," he said with a slight alteration toward the Northern icecap. "Do I make myself clear?"

"Yes, sir."

"And Mr. Bushmill."

"Yes?"

"Would it not serve you well if you could spend some more time discussing these phantasmologistical paramodulations with the very man who has created them?"

"What's that you say?"

"DeWitt's going to Nimburg with you!" The voice was hard now, but Lobbe was controlling himself. "In Nimburg are all the little experts who wait for you with the Gadget and for your genius. Your answers are there. Any questions you need, just talk to our Mr. deWitt. Therefore he is going with you."

Bushmill agreed to that and thought that Lobbe was brilliant. I thought so too. When Bushmill walked out of the inner sanctum Lobbe took me aside with a glance that felt like a longshoreman's hook.

"You give him the nice double-talk conversation, like you are trained, mennekin, and you keep him off the booze. If this man kinks out on me...."

"Conks, I believe."

"Kinks. I was not talking English. If he does, I will have your head. *Garnée avec* leaves of hemlock and deadly nightshade. *Compris?*"

"Quite."

"And to lessen the distraction I have invited the lovely Meghan to stay as my guest."

"She won't."

"Ask. She and Miss Moon have a great deal of shopping to do."

Max flew Bushmill and me to Nimburg.

It was a very small and very inactive town. It had a park with a bandstand and one hotel without a bar. It had lovely maples, ugly neon signs, and the kind of wide, bland streets which were laid out when land was still plentiful. Lobbe's manufacturing lab, which was called Nimburg Machine Company, stood among the farms out of town, though that was within walking distance of the hotel. Bushmill spent all of his time out there. Max spent most of his time in the farm equipment store, from which I expected a harvester to emerge and spin off into the air any minute.

I mostly sat in my room with the flowery wallpaper and smelled the farm smells coming through the window. I remembered the Wiltshire country and how good Meghan and I had felt there. I thought of my plight—employed by a Dutch pirate and doing almost everything he asked because I had no valid thought or direction of my own. I was thus occupied when the fat woman who sat behind the desk came into my room and gave me the card. She had not even knocked.

"He's downstairs," she said.

The visiting card said *Piotr Orlov, Representative*. Penciled on the back was the message: *Also Trentheim from Birmingham. Urgent I see you.*

I flew out of the room, and when I came to the stairs I yelled down for him to come up. A moment later I wondered where Max's Colt might be. And then it was too late.

Orlov wore a heavy dark suit like a peasant's Sunday clothes. The material was made for the ages. The pants were very wide and the lapels had big, pointy wings. I noted the belly, the heavy eyebrows, and the black hair parted in the middle. He was panting up the stairs, and each time he grabbed the banister the whole thing trembled. His low forehead, his high cheekbones, and the short Tartar nose all shone with sweat. He stopped two steps below me and looked up.

"We are alone?"

"No."

"It is to our interest that we don't lie and that we are alone."

I did not know whether his tone conveyed his mood or the quality of his native tongue, but it sounded soft, almost pleading. Even his very long eyes, which might have impressed me as being cunning, had more a look of longing than of calculation.

"Please come in," I said.

Once in the room he immediately sat down on the one upholstered chair. He more or less collapsed into it.

"I lost you in New York," he said. He had started to dab his wet face with a very large, very blue handkerchief. "I was so lucky to pick you up again."

There would have been no point in asking him how he had done this. I watched his labored breathing and the new sweat which started to shine on his face.

"And you ran all the way," I said.

It took him a moment to understand me. Then he smiled, showing artificially even teeth.

"No, Mr. deWitt. I sweat when I am very anxious. I pant when I am afraid."

"You afraid? The Inquisitor of Halle? The Karate Master of Birmingham?"

"Yes," he said. "That one. I am not a super-agent." He offered a half-hearted laugh. "I am not even a real agent."

"For whom?"

He looked at me and so help me if those long, slanted eyes did not look trusting.

"Piotr Orlov, Division of Armaments and Weaponry, Politechnicum Murmansk, specialty high frequency developments. My passport is Russian and what I told you is true. It is also true, between you and myself only, that I have been sent, not because I am a spy, but because I am a scientist."

"Why talk to me, comrade?"

"I am not your comrade," he said primly. "Here is why I talk to you. Bushmill he sees me and he runs. Garten he sees me and he hits."

"If you're not an agent, how come you know karate and interrogation, and shadowing, and picking up a trail?"

He shrugged with surprising charm.

"Perhaps I am not an agent because I do not lie so well. Nevertheless, what I told you is true."

"Why see me?"

"You interrupted. Lobbe sees me and the difficulty would be great. He is really not involved, and to involve those who are at a distance from the business at hand is like pulling on a string where you do not know what hangs at the end. And I do not see your great government because in their greatness they would disbelieve me on principle."

"They do have their rules of thumb."

"But you," he said, "are already in the business and you have an amorphous role. It gives the leeway for, I hope, credulity and flexible action."

"What business, Mr. Orlov?"

"The analyzer."

"You mean it isn't one?"

"It is one. But it is dangerous." Before I could interrupt him he went on. "Has it been assembled?"

"Completely. And it works."

"Of course. What about the extra circuitry and scanning plates?"

"Why should I answer you?"

He sighed heavily, opened his jacket, and then pulled out an enormous revolver. He plunked it on the table next to himself and sighed again.

"Of impossible weight and heat," he said to himself. Then he also opened his vest, for additional ventilation.

"Why should you answer me? Because I need your help. I need to know about the state of the analyzer so that I can appraise just how dangerous it might be."

"Dangerous to whom, Mr. Orlov?"

"To whom—" He stood up and spread his arms. He looked helpless. He started to turn in an awkward dance, his eyes wandering all about. "To whom? The world, Mr. deWitt!"

He was sweating badly again. He collapsed back into the chair. I considered the situation. Orlov was most likely quite mad. Meanwhile it was getting dark outside.

"Maybe you should talk to Bushmill. Maybe he'll understand you better."

"Bushmill! You don't know Bushmill? You don't know he blanks out at the sight of me or under any sort of unusual pressure?"

"Like in Halle?"

"Please, Mr. deWitt, the arrest was false and it embarrassed me. As a fact, I and my agency tried to find out how far progress had been made on that infernal machine! I tried to be clever and never ask directly, but it only confused Bushmill, and it made me very tense. Failure!"

"Why didn't you ask Crevassette, the chief inventor?"

"Him?" Orlov rose from his chair again, then collapsed again. "Why do you suppose he exerted available pressure to get Bushmill back? For fear of talk! Why do you suppose he fired Bushmill at the crucial point? For fear of knowledge! Why do you suppose that his faction tried to guard your progress with the plans so that there would be no interference with delivery?"

"I don't know."

"Precisely!" Hired by that slime—and a Slav yet!—that Milos Ort. And have you considered why Bartholomew Crevassette sold to you with such speed and simple ease?"

"That was rather peculiar for a major transaction."

"Only to expedite removal of the machine from England and its introduction into this country! And you ask why I did not consult with Crevassette himself there in Halle? Hah! *Because he is the enemy!*"

His fervor was infectious. I did not take him entirely seriously, but I was getting concerned. There was a lamp on the table where Orlov had put his gun, and I snapped the light on. We both ignored the gun.

"Orlov," I said quietly. "You talk as if Crevassette were alive."

"He is alive!"

"If you'll make me believe that, I'll believe anything."

Orlov smiled. "It is really very simple. Spyros Crevassette is not only a brilliant inventor, he is a fanatical Stalinist, a dedicated agent of Mainland China. He created a device that could forever poison the air of peaceful coexistence. The only problem was to get it over here where it could be used. It could not simply be shipped over. Then your Mr. Lobbe entered the picture. He wanted another of Crevassette's inventions, the analyzer, which contained many of the same functions as the infernal machine. So it occurred to Spyros Crevassette to build the second machine into the first and let Lobbe bring it to this country.

"Which would explain the extra circuitry," I said aloud.

"Exactly!"

"But not the faked death."

"That developed later. You see, to import a new and complicated machine is not easy here. There are customs, tariffs—in short, examinations. That is when Spyros Crevassette decided he had to die. At this point your Mr. Lobbe was so eager to get the analyzer that he was willing to buy the rest of Crevassette's company just to get it. As you know, negotiations were in progress when the so-called accident happened. Crevassette left instructions for his brother and sole heir to conclude the sale. Which he did. And among the other assets of the company were the analyzer plans or, rather, the plans for the combined analyzer and infernal machine. And so was solved the transportation problem. It was eliminated. Lobbe would get the machine into the United States by simply building it in a factory here!"

CHAPTER 24

I grabbed the phone and dialed the laboratory. Bushmill had to be in on this. I hung onto the phone while the lethargic exchange tried to find the right connection. On the street below a large trailer flatbed crept through the turn by the park. The canvas over the single load was stenciled Nimburg Machine Company. Once through the turn the big rig started shifting up progressively.

"Hello! Hello? Give me Mr. Bushmill, please. This is deWitt calling."

"It's past quitting time," said the girl. "Even for the back lab today."

"Could you find out for me where Mr. Bushmill might be?"

"I know where. He always stops there."

"Where, damn it!?"

"The farm equipment store. He always meets some feller there before going home."

Orlov was sweating again. I myself was unusually tense. At the farm equipment store I got Max on the phone.

"He is doing things to the worm-type posthole digger," Max said, but before he could go into details I cut in on him.

"Get him over here fast. Orlov is here in my room."

"Gad! He's got a gun on you?"

"No. He's friendly."

"I leave you alone for a minute and...."

"Just shut up and get your ass over here! And Bushmill too—" But he had already hung up.

Orlov got out of the chair and stood in front of the window flapping his jacket.

"Better take that gun off the table," I told him. "You know Garten."

He knew Garten, he said, and stuck the big gun out of view.

When Max burst into the room Orlov had just accepted a glass of bourbon from me, which he dropped when he saw the Colt Python Magnum at the ready. Max was on top of Orlov in no time at all. Orlov stepped away, holding his own and also Max's gun in his hands. Max was sitting on the floor, shaking his head.

"Did you know he had a gun?" Max asked me. "And now he has two, Baron Blitz."

I held my hands out for the guns and Orlov gave them to me. I put them in a dresser drawer. Then I got Bushmill to come in from the hall and closed the door behind us. I gave Bushmill a shot of bourbon because he was upset and I gave Orlov two shots of bourbon because he was twice as upset.

"Now tell him what you told me," I said to Orlov.

Orlov did.

"Now you see," he concluded, "that a programmed computer can sit at point Alpha, the completed analyzer responds to the message at point Beta, and from there it beams its excitation at the chosen substance, at point Gamma. The substance changes—"

"Just a minute," said Bushmill. "I grant you, if it is true that Crevassette is alive, he might conceivably have added the beaming component."

"Never mind idle talk," said Orlov. "You completed assembly of the machine?"

"Totally. Including the incomprehensible extras."

"And it is safe at this plant?"

"Safe? Yes, safe. But we are shipping it to Chicago. There isn't enough power available here in Nimburg to make fuller tests."

"The truck we saw—" and Orlov pointed out of the window. "Which route?"

"I don't see..." Bushmill started when Orlov began to shout.

"You have never heard of sympathetic vibrations? You have never heard of the possible use of them to excite with a substance which is emitting its own inert brother which lies somewhere else? Do you know that an atom bomb which is stored but completely safetied cannot be detonated mechanically, or electrically, but that none of those safeties interferes with direct sympathetic impulse excitation—so that this Gadget, from a distance, *can blow up an atom dump?!*"

I don't know how much time elapsed before I thought of calling the chief engineer to ask him which way the flatbed was going. It might have been a few seconds only, but it seemed an awfully long time. The rig was not going to Chicago. It was going to the airport at Lafayette, for air transport from there to Chicago.

I called Lafayette. The chartered transport had been loaded, I found out, and had just taken off. Then, unaccountably, it had changed course. There was no evidence of mishap or malfunction in the air, but simply a smooth change in course. Also, the plane was not answering the tower....

CHAPTER 25

At this point I called the FBI. It was the proper thing to do under the circumstances, and it was also doing it by the book. But then again, it might not be the best of all possible courses.

While we waited in my room we thought back and forth where the Gadget might be logically taken. A SAC base? A bomb dump? A plant of manufacture? Orlov contributed the only feasible method to help find this out. He could devise, he explained, a detection device which would be sensitive to the presence of the microwave contact which a computer would have to maintain with the Gadget. In terms of progress we got no further once the FBI arrived.

They had not heard of the Gadget, they had no conception of its use. They had not seen it leave the plant and they had not seen the plane in Lafayette. They were working with hearsay. But they had Piotr Orlov in the flesh. He was promptly arrested.

He offered a chance to devise a detection device. He pointed out that his function made clear that Russia was as anxious as the United States to disarm the Gadget. But those were words.

"How do we know that?" said the smooth-skinned agent who headed a team of three. He was as featureless and as bland as his training could make him, and the same seemed to be true for his brain. "Maybe you just want to find it so you can push the button yourself."

Orlov groaned.

"Please, this has been a long time in the making. Our agents got wind of a sabotage plot of this sort in Mainland China, four years ago!"

"Our own CIA got the word in Shanghai that the Asian flu was a Red Chinese plot."

"Please," said Orlov. He seemed close to tears. I brought him a shot of bourbon.

"Don't give it to him," said the agent.

I gave it to Orlov, who started talking again.

"A plot, you understand, to discredit the Soviet Union. Your dumps blow up, your watchdog planes explode—who could possibly have the means for such an achievement—besides you, I hasten to say—but the Soviet Union? And then the international repercussions! U.S.-Soviet relations getting worse and worse! Perhaps war, finally. Who gains, without firing a shot? China!"

"I'm not a politician," said the agent.

"I am not either. But I think! I research! I have the assignment to research the possible nature of such a machine. Next, we get wind of Crevassette being engaged on a very special assignment. We trace, we trail, we piece together. We are almost too late!"

The agent got up and made a mouth. I thought he was next going to say something pithy like, "Tell it to the judge." He said, "Get your hat. You're coming along to Lafayette."

"If you're going to be an ass about this," I told him, "at least take him to Washington where they reputedly keep the brains."

He was immune to outer influences and did not even answer me.

"We're taking over," he said ominously. One of his helpers put the cuffs on Orlov. "The rest of you stay here till you're called."

I called the Lobbe operator in New York and gave a progress report to be transmitted to Lobbe. Then Bushmill and Max and I spent a goodly time thinking out all the angles and chances which might be involved in this entirely bizarre and impossible situation. There were too many possibilities of what might happen next. It might all be, for that matter, a conjecture by many madmen getting together.

We got a helping hand the next morning when the Chicago papers came in. There had been a minor explosion in a factory outside a medium-sized Kentucky town. While it was known that the plant assembled atomic weaponry, the explosion—mushroom-crowned—was of minor size and had caused no chain detonations. There was no danger, the paper said.

We took our rented car to Chicago, which was the closest town to Nimburg, Indiana, that Max had been able to land the jet in. We communicated our suspicions concerning that blast to a number of sources by way of Lobbe Industriel. Mijnheer Lobbe himself, we learned, was in Peru. He was being called back to New York.

We spent most of the day in Chicago's main library.

With all that's available in a major U.S. library it is possible to plot a war, to handle an invasion, to learn any trick one might need for anything. Of course, one has to do one's own thinking.

The primary question was: Where would they strike next?

"Oak Ridge," said Max.

Bushmill shook his head.

"It's research and development, and while a fitting noise might be created, the outcome is problematic. I do believe, in view of the expanded reports in the papers, that only one bomb was blown up. It makes sense, in terms of the speculative capacity of the device."

"Next blast then," said Max, "is where the big ones are. Not artillery shells, as it says here."

"Makes no sense," I said. "The big ones, to the extent that their locations are known, are going to be better guarded. What's the range of the Gadget, Bushmill? Make a guess."

He thought, in view of the limitations of available power, that the effective range would not exceed one quarter-mile. I stopped him before he could start explaining why.

"I know one dump," I said, "where no truck, bus, man, or mouse can get closer than a one-mile radius. In addition, I think this: The aim of a very major explosion—assuming that the Gadget can excite a large mass—is to cripple the war potential. The attempt would be totally self-defeating. A large explosion, with fallout and such, would put the nation on an immediate war footing. Which would have indiscriminately devastating effects. Our overkill potential is such that no matter how badly we're hit there's always enough left over to blow up the world several times in a row. But look at this morning's explosion. No alarm. A regrettable accident. No major stir."

"Then it's the little ones they're after," said Max.

"Yes. One little pop? An accident. Then another depot and another little pop. It's beginning to look queer. And another one, in relatively short succession. And now the impression is unavoidable that it's sabotage! Naturally, the appropriate anti-Russian rumors are now being planted. In the end they might even leave the Gadget to be found. It has Russian stenciling on it by now. Imported by Lobbe, who trades with anyone. Built by Crevassette, who is self-protectively dead, on the record. Spin it from there."

We took the maps and noted the dump locations which had been publicly identified. Then we made our diagrams. If the Gadget started out from Kentucky....

Bushmill contributed the approximate weights: Diesel-driven generator, infernal machine, and computer. Max contributed the air-transport information. The weight made air transport en masse highly improbable. Such a plane could not land anywhere near the small-town isolation or the desert isolation of the dumps.

Air mobility was not ruled out. The first strike had been an example. The Gadget itself weighed only six hundred pounds and the other equipment was waiting in place.

But we did make one other elimination.

"Line of sight transmission of the signal," I said, "means that object interference between computer antenna and the Gadget is out."

"The signal wouldn't get through."

"If they are going to keep their equipment dispersed, which would stand to reason, they'd pick flat terrain, is that right, Bushmill?"

"Clearly. Or they could use a fixed antenna in the terrain. Commandeer it, so to speak."

"And attract attention by leaving the clobbered crew or the cut cables behind?"

They would use their own, mobile antenna, mounted above the computer, which would most likely be in a van. They would need a six-to-eight axle rig to move the Gadget plus generator into position. They would need flat terrain.

We picked the town of Feston in Tennessee as the next possible target. It would be too much of a plum to forego. It was within one day's trucking distance from the Kentucky explosion, it was flat, and it had an artillery dump which was largely atomic. It had a trucking route going through where no rig, no matter what size, would attract attention. The conspicuous beaming antenna would undoubtedly be out of sight until nighttime. Bushmill estimated that the time between start of the generators, computer activation, and the Gadget beaming phase need not take more than twenty minutes.

I called Lobbe from the airport and found him in. I gave him the speculations we had developed, for dissemination and use, and hung up on him just when he started yelling. He had probably figured out in a split second what would happen to him if what the Gadget did could not be blamed on somebody tangible other than him.

Max lifted us off six minutes after I had hung up the phone.

CHAPTER 26

We could not land any closer to Feston, Tennessee, than Memphis. Once the ramp was up and the copilot had unlatched the door we found that we were expected. The man had an affable smile, shortcropped hair, and a young indoor face. He was wearing mufti.

"Colonel Benjamin," he said and gave an incomplete salute. "Security." He smiled as if that were the nicest thing ever.

I introduced him around and asked him what it might be he wanted.

"Learned you were coming to Feston through your offices. Nice of you to let us know."

"What? The town?"

"Fact is, we reasoned the same as you. And have covered three other possible locations. What I meant was, nice of you to let us know where to find Mr. Bushmill."

Bushmill quaked.

"You're the only one here who can identify the myth—the mysterious Mr. Crevassette."

"I am not moving an inch," said Bushmill, "without Mr. deWitt and the good Mr. Garten."

"But why not?" The young colonel smiled like a receptionist.

"Or better yet," said Bushmill, "let Orlov make the identification."

"Orlov? Ah yes, Orlov. But he is being deported. Matter of courtesy, you understand."

It was a sweet way of disguising stupidity with politeness. Bushmill looked at the colonel and humphed with disbelief. Then he tried to go back into the plane.

"But why?" said the colonel. "You have our protection."

"Like Orlov," I said.

"He will not go without deWitt," explained Max, "because those two talk to each other. It calms them down."

Colonel Benjamin frowned.

"And I'm along to protect them while they talk," Max added.

It ended up with all of us going together, though Bushmill really did not want to go at all.

"He won't be here," he muttered during most of the drive from Memphis to Feston.

"It's his Gadget, Camden," I explained. "And since he has no inkling whatsoever from anything that has happened in front of Ort, or Brother Barth, or the hunters, that we have unraveled this thing to this point, it's likely he's decided to run the machinery."

In Feston there was no evidence of the machinery. There was a flat-roofed, dusty town, there were truck stops on the highway coming and going, and there were at least four six-axle rigs which I could spot.

"They've all been checked," said the colonel. "Two carried generators, powered. Consigned to New Orleans and Baton Rouge respectively."

"Bona fide?"

"We checked them out."

Partway out of town on the other side we bumped over a railroad crossing.

"Our spur," said the colonel. "It leads to the dump."

The light was failing and I could not make out the ordnance installation, even though the distance from town was no more than three miles and the land was very flat.

Colonel Benjamin did not take us into the compound. A restricted road ran across open country and then came the big wire fence. At the gate stood an Army trailer and, as it turned out, that was the place where we were told to wait.

"What forethought," said Max. "What safety! Right next to the dump that might blow up any time after dark."

"The bigger stuff has been moved," said the colonel. "There was time. And the little stuff isn't heavy enough to lift the slab of concrete that's on top of it."

"If they all blow up at once?" said Max.

His smile was not frightened. His smile was expectant, as if he were thinking of a gorgeous birthday cake. My own reaction was something else again.

"The assumption that the Gadget can only blow up so much mass at one time, one of those shells, for example, is brilliant speculation. But it is no more than speculation. And I damn well don't want to prove you wrong,

Colonel, once I'm in a thousand pieces."

I got the look which regular Army reserves for civilians. And he got the look which I reserve for those who think they are going to take over simply as a matter of course.

"We're getting out of here," I told him, "with or without your peculiar protection. And if you know what's good for whoever is left in that compound, I suggest you arrange to get them out of there too."

"The Army...."

"To hell with the Army. Would you like me to list a few of the more famous Army mistakes?"

There was an MP who watched us from the lit trailer, but he did not come into play. The colonel handled it with a reminiscence of his own, foolhardy civilian days and drove us back to town.

On the way, past the boxcars which sat near the dump on their siding, I looked for a dish antenna. On the way down the dusty road I looked for a dish antenna. On the way into town I checked out every rig and pickup truck that was passing or was parked near a diner. So much for counterspy deWitt.

We put up at the two-story hotel in town in preference to one of the motels because I did not care for the sound of a trailer truck taking off at five o'clock in the morning. It was sound reasoning, and foolish. We did not sleep.

We sat in the deserted foyer, which was made gloomy by one sixty-watt bulb. The bare walls did not help, and the calendar of the year in the early thirties did not help either. It happened to be near the year of my birth, an innocent time, and a carefree time when inventions meant comfort to me, or marvelous toys.

At five in the morning I was done with the feed catalogue. Max, naturally, was asleep. Bushmill was shaking from too many cups of coffee.

"I need a drink," he said.

"Can't buy it."

"Crevassette never worked without a cup of coffee royal by his elbow."

Colonel Benjamin checked with us and said that nothing was stirring outside.

"Half an hour till daylight and their chance is over. Buck up."

I particularly detest that expression, especially when I am as taut as a string. But the well-meaning colonel left at that moment.

"Listen, Bushmill," I said. "Check me out. This plot has been years in the making. They've had time to check out each target area and its comings and goings till they know it by heart. Now they see an emergency move which because of its emergency nature cannot be too well disguised. What's Crevassette going to do?"

"He will not stir. They move the bombs and he will figure that the whole place is under surveillance."

"He pulls out."

"Not Crevassette. He is the sort of man who does not give up because of a mishap. Professional training, I suppose. He stays and checks it out."

In the distance three diesels started up with a clatter.

"No," said Bushmill. "It would not be one of his. He will wait for days before starting the generators."

"Discouraging thought," I said. "Here I'm sitting not knowing what will be while Crevassette sleeps like Max."

"Crevassette? He sleeps possibly two hours out of twenty-four."

I hesitated and then I said, "Doing what?"

"What? What does a man with a restless brain do all his waking hours? He thinks, he sits and stares at the air without seeing. All night long."

Overhead the flimsy ceiling transmitted somebody's pacing.

"Does he pace, Bushmill?"

"I told you he sits. He sits, and sips."

"Garten!"

He jumped up, ready to scramble into his Spitfire. "There are about six diners strung out at the outskirts of town. We're going to have coffee in each one of them."

"*Royal*," said Bushmill. "Not just coffee."

"That'll be Crevassette: Coffee in front of him, hooch bottle in pocket."

"Naïve of you," said Max. "Why would he show?"

"Why not, for an insomniac? He can't have any idea that there might be somebody in Feston, U.S.A., who might recognize Spyros Crevassette, who died in Algeciras, Spain."

We walked out and down the dim street. A tint of cold white was beginning to show on the eastern horizon. Only the neon signs at the end of the street, it seemed, kept the night pulled down over us.

Max stopped. With his hands in his pockets he looked casual.

"Have you considered, counselor," he said, "that while Bushmill might spot Crevassette...."

"Mater dolorosa!" Bushmill said. "He spots me!"

It had been one of those small, insane things to have sat in the lit lobby of the hotel all night. I felt lame with surprise. This accounted for the lame remark I made next.

"So what. If he has spotted Bushmill then he has bolted town one second later."

"I can assure you that such is not my intention."

He stepped out of the shadow of the arcade which ran the length of the store fronts on the block. The other man stepped out the same way, only behind us. I looked at the man in front. Brother Bartholomew without the fat.

Crevassette had the thin nose of his brother and the bony face to go with it. He was thin and old, but with the intense aura of an arc flame at its height.

Max whipped at his pocket, slapped himself tentatively, and then dropped his arms.

"Of all the bloody times," he said as if it were a curse, "and I forgot my gun."

He stood next to me and I could feel the hard iron in his pocket.

When I talked I sounded calm; it was only because a partial weakness prevented my shouting from tension.

"Crevassette won't shoot," I said. "He cannot afford it. He will take us along."

Max shrugged and put his hands in his pockets.

"True," said Crevassette without any emotion. The man behind us nudged each of us with his gun. "Just as far as that innocent camping trailer up ahead."

It sat by the curb, like any such vehicle resting in transit, and like many of them it had an antenna on top. It looked like a television antenna.

"How high does it telescope?" I asked Crevassette.

"Ten feet. No more is needed. How did you guess that the computer is inside?"

"And the Gadget?" I asked him. "Your dual purpose machine?"

"In a pickup truck. It looks like a crate at the moment."

"And the rest?"

"Ingenious, I might say. The generators are on a lorry quite some miles out of town, by the side of the road, you see, with flares placed appropriately. Looks like repairs. On the opposite side, as if stopped for help, is another lorry, which holds the same thing. Reduces the visual evidence of the combined weight, you see. Of course, they have been moved by now, even though they were quite a way beyond the search area of the last several hours."

Crevassette smiled at Bushmill as if at a fool. I thought they might have an exchange, but Crevassette showed his disdain by not saying a word to his former colleague. We walked toward the camping trailer.

"How far from the dump are the trucks?" I asked him.

"Immaterial, largely. The power cable which runs to the—er, Gadget you call it?—is, or was, in a ditch which ran back for one mile. Effective hookup takes no more than three minutes, you see, and then everybody drives away." The sound he made might have been a laugh.

We stopped, and Crevassette opened the door of the fifteen-foot trailer.

It was dark inside. I turned to Bushmill, who looked small and shrunken next to me.

"Are you faint?" I asked him.

"No. I feel—I am stiff with fright—"

"I thought you were weaving because you were faint, Camden," I said, while pushing down on his near foot with my heel.

I thought he would never catch on, but then he finally fainted. He added a surprisingly artistic groan and crumpled to the ground, backward.

The man with the gun behind us jumped back.

"Pick him up," he said to me.

I looked at the lightening sky and shook my head.

"If you'll permit me to take my hands out of my pockets," said Max to Crevassette, "I might oblige by taking Mr. Bushmill's feet."

Crevassette had seen me look at the sky. He undoubtedly also remembered that we were, after all, on the one main street of Feston.

"All right," he said. "Hurry up." He jerked his head at his helper.

When the helper pocketed his gun and took Bushmill by the arms, Max bent down and took his hands out of his pockets. And when he took his hands out of his pockets he was ten times faster than an old man like Crevassette could ever hope to be. The Python tore a screaming hole into Crevassette.

I don't remember the sequence, but I think that was when I kicked the helper in the head. Then I stumbled over Bushmill, or I tried to help Bushmill up, but finally and for certain I was kneeling down next to Crevassette. There was a lot of blood.

"Is he dead?" I asked like an automaton. I could hear three separate sirens spring into life in the distance.

"Upper lung, I think," said Max.

Then I came alive.

"Crevassette!"

I could see his mouth working.

"Crevassette, they stole your model! They stole it, Crevassette!"

"*Sacre*—" he breathed at me.

"Can they work from it and build your machine?"

"*Sacre*," he said again. "Yes—"

"Who, Crevassette? *Who??*"

"*Sacre*—" and then he was dead.

Meghan and I decided to go once more to the Wiltshire country. Of course Meghan had bought entirely too many clothes.

Lobbe had bought a patented Gadget. The rest of the parts, which no one had known about, went to the government. It was a good thought. It would have been a better thought if we could have been sure that no one else had it too....

But as a recompense for the final delivery Mijnheer Lobbe gave me three weeks off. We went back to England.

I, as a recompense, allowed Max to fly us there.

In the lovely Wiltshire country I rarely thought of the model. I determined instead to enjoy the land. After all, I did not know how long it would still be there....

THE END

Crime classics from the master of hard-boiled fiction...

Peter Rabe

The Box / Journey Into Terror $19.95
978-0-9667848-8-6
"Few writers are Rabe's equal in the field of the hardboiled gangster story." –Bill Crider, *Twentieth Century Crime & Mystery Writers*

**Murder Me for Nickels /
Benny Muscles In $19.95**
978-0-9749438-4-8
"When he was rolling, crime fiction just didn't get any better." –Ed Gorman, *Mystery Scene*

**Blood on the Desert /
A House in Naples $19.95**
978-1-933586-00-7
"He had few peers among noir writers of the 50s and 60s; he has few peers today." –Bill Pronzini

**My Lovely Executioner /
Agreement to Kill $19.95**
978-1-933586-11-3
"Rabe can pack more into 10 words than most writers can do with a page."—Keir Graff, *Booklist*

**Anatomy of a Killer /
A Shroud for Jesso $14.95**
978-1-933586-22-9

"*Anatomy of a Killer*...as cold and clean as a knife...a terrific book." –Donald E. Westlake

**The Silent Wall /
The Return of Marvin Palaver $19.95**
978-1-933586-32-8
"A very worthy addition to Rabe's diverse and fascinating corpus."—*Booklist*

**Kill the Boss Good-by /
Mission for Vengeance $19.95**
978-1-933586-42-7
"*Kill the Boss Goodbye* is certainly one of my favorites."– Peter Rabe in an interview with George Tuttle

Dig My Grave Deep / The Out is Death / It's My Funeral $21.95
978-1-933586-65-6
"It's Rabe's feel for the characters, even the minor ones, that lifts this out of the ordinary." –Dan Stumpf, *Mystery*File*

The Cut of the Whip / Bring Me Another Corpse / Time Enough to Die $23.95
978-1-933586-66-3
"These books offer realistic psychology, sharp turns of phrase, and delightfully deadpan humor that make them cry out for rediscovery."—Keir Graff, *Booklist*

In trade paperback from:

**Stark House Press
1315 H Street, Eureka, CA 95501**
griffinskye3@sbcglobal.net
www.StarkHousePress.com

Available from your local bookstore, or order direct with a check or via our website.